In Cold Blood

JANE BETTANY

ONE PLACE. MANY STORIES

HQ
An imprint of HarperCollins*Publishers* Ltd
1 London Bridge Street
London SE1 9GF

1

This edition published in Great Britain by
HQ, an imprint of HarperCollins*Publishers* Ltd 2020

ISBN: 9780008412746

MIX
Paper from
responsible sources
FSC
www.fsc.org   FSC™ C007454

This book is produced from independently certified FSC™ paper
to ensure responsible forest management.

For more information visit: www.harpercollins.co.uk/green

Printed and bound by CPI Group (UK) Ltd,
Croydon, CR0 4YY

For Howard, with love

Chapter 1

The pantry was musty and airless and smelt faintly of curry powder and something that Amy couldn't identify. It was a tiny space, crammed with out-of-date food, a battered collection of saucepans, and containers filled with dried fruit and breakfast cereals. She emptied the shelves doggedly, thrusting everything into a heavy-duty bin bag.

Reaching into the corner of the highest shelf, she retrieved the last items: a jar of pickled onions and some homemade blackberry jam. Strictly speaking, she should throw the contents away and wash out the jars for recycling – but sod that. She had better things to do with her time. Instead, being careful not to break the glass, Amy placed the jars in the bag and tied it with a double knot ready to take to the bin.

It was as she turned to switch off the light that she noticed the marks on the wall. Height marks. Just inside the door.

A child grew up in this house, she thought, as she traced the pencilled scratches with her fingers. *An only child. One set of marks.*

The first measurement appeared in the lower third of the wall, alongside a date – 15th January 1965. The marks crept higher with each passing year. The last was dated 15th January 1977 and recorded a height of 5' 6'.

Perhaps the 15th of January was the child's birthday, Amy thought. *There must have been an annual ritual to record his or her height on the pantry wall.*

She wondered why the marks had stopped in 1977. At 5' 6', a teenage girl would be fully grown. A boy might have gone on to gain a few more inches.

The measurements were a part of the history of the house that would soon be gone forever. When the new kitchen was installed, the pantry would be removed and replaced with tall, sliding larder cupboards. She and Paul had chosen a range of expensive, glossy units that would provide the kind of high-quality finish they hoped would sell the house.

Planning permission had been granted for a huge extension that would more than double the size of the existing kitchen. Amy's vision was for a light-filled, open-plan living space with shiny work surfaces, top-of-the-range appliances, and a vast dining area. There would be skylights and bi-fold doors opening onto the rear garden. Once completed, the bright, airy room would be the redeeming feature of the otherwise unremarkable 1960s house they had bought at auction eight weeks earlier.

Grabbing the bin bag, Amy took one last look at the height marks before switching off the light and closing the pantry door. It was cold, so she flicked the kettle on to make a hot drink. Paul had been outside for most of the day, digging out the foundations for the extension. He would be ready for another brew.

As she waited for the water to boil, the back door opened and Paul came in, shivering. He was pale. Unsmiling.

'What's up?' Amy said. 'Has something happened?'

'You could say that. I've only gone and found a fucking body.'

Amy tutted. 'Yeah, right. Very funny, bro.' Paul had been a wind-up merchant all his life. It was a trait he should have grown out of by now.

'Seriously. I'm not kidding, Ames.'

2

'Course you're not. What is it? A cat? Dog? Someone's long-dead hamster?'

'It's an animal, all right. Of the human variety.'

Dread tugged at Amy's stomach muscles. 'You'd better be joking,' she said.

'Come and take a look for yourself if you don't believe me.'

She followed him outside. They skirted the partially excavated foundation trench and stood next to what would eventually be the far corner of the extension.

'Down there.' Paul pointed at something protruding from the soil.

Leaning in closer, Amy realised it was the upper part of a human skull; the forehead and eye sockets jutted out from the damp layer of earth at the bottom of the metre-deep trench. If it had been buried a few inches lower, Paul would never have known it was there.

'Shit!' She blew air through her cheeks. 'This is awful.'

'You can say that again. It's going to delay everything. There's no chance of getting the extension finished before the new year now.'

Amy wrapped her arms across her body and glared at her brother.

'Paul! Are you for real? A body, *somebody*, has been lying here for God knows how long and all you're bothered about is the extension?'

'Come on, sis, don't give me a hard time. Our inheritance is tied up in this house. We need to get the work finished, sell up and move on to the next project. That' – he pointed into the trench – 'is a bloody disaster. The delay it'll cause is bad enough, but if word gets out, it's going to knock thousands off the property value. No one will be interested in buying this place, with or without a swanky kitchen. Who wants to live in a house where someone's been murdered?'

Paul's usual flippancy had vanished, replaced by a demeanour that was uncharacteristically sombre, almost hostile. He was obviously worried.

'Do you think that's what happened here then?' Amy said. 'Murder?'

'Of course it is. Use your nous. The body didn't bury itself, did it?'

'It could have been here for hundreds of years,' she said. 'A body buried during the civil war or something.'

'Civil war?' He scowled, shaking his head dismissively. 'What are you on about, Amy? This isn't an ancient battlefield.'

'OK. So maybe it *was* buried a lot more recently. Either way, the local paper's going to have a field day.'

Paul trailed the fingertips of his right hand along his jawline and studied the trench thoughtfully. 'Only if they find out about it,' he said.

'What do you mean?' She narrowed her eyes, staring at her brother in disbelief. 'Of course they'll find out.'

'Not if we don't report it.'

'What?' she said, incredulous. 'No way!'

'Think about it. If I hadn't dug such a deep trench, or the body had been buried a few inches further down, we'd have been none the wiser.'

Amy lifted her hands and locked her fingers across the top of her head. 'You're not seriously suggesting we keep quiet about this?'

'Why not? If I pour the concrete foundations now, this little problem will stay buried forever. No one will know but us.'

He leaned back and let the muscles in his shoulders relax. Just talking about a solution seemed to have calmed him. Paul's proposal offered a quick fix, an easy way out – but Amy was horrified by the idea.

She spun away from the trench, groaning with exasperation. 'Firstly,' she said, 'this is not a "little problem". Whoever it is lying down there was once a living, breathing human being. Don't you

4

think they deserve some kind of justice, or a proper burial at least? And secondly, what if the person responsible for this is still around? They know what's hidden here. If they get away with it, what's to say they won't do it again somewhere else?'

'Bloody hell, sis.' Paul rubbed the back of his neck and kicked irritably at a clump of soil with his work boot. 'Why do you always have to be such a goody-two-shoes?'

Amy peered down at the skull – into the empty eye sockets from which someone had once looked out at the face of their killer. *Every house has its own secret history*, she thought, remembering the height marks scratched into the pantry wall. *Some things are best left hidden, but this definitely isn't one of them.*

She pulled out her phone and dialled 101.

Chapter 2

Detective Inspector Isabel Blood gripped the steering wheel of her car and drove through the streets of Bainbridge as fast as the speed limit would allow. She was heading to the secondary school where her youngest daughter was a pupil. At Isabel's age, attending a parents' evening should have been a thing of the past, but life had ricocheted off in an unexpected direction when Ellie was born.

It was damp and starting to get dark by the time she pulled into the school car park. She'd promised to meet Nathan outside the main entrance at five o'clock and she was already five minutes late.

There was no sign of him as she ran towards the school. He must have gone inside already. Pushing through the revolving glass door, Isabel dashed down the central corridor towards Ellie's form room. Nathan was waiting outside.

'I didn't think you were going to make it,' he said.

'Sorry. Something came up. You know what it's like.'

'You should have taken the afternoon off. They owe you enough hours.'

Isabel pressed her shoulder against a wooden locker and smiled. 'It's not always possible, as well you know.'

A door opened behind them and Ellie's form teacher, Miss Powell, beckoned them into the classroom.

They sat down and listened as the teacher began to deliver her verdict on how their fourteen-year-old daughter was doing in her lessons.

'Ellie is highly intelligent, self-assured, eloquent ...'

Nathan was unable to contain a grin.

'However ...'

Nathan's smile evaporated.

'Although Ellie is extremely capable, I'm concerned about her recent behaviour. She used to be a model pupil, but she's been acting very negatively since the beginning of term. She's become argumentative and she wastes a lot of time messing around with her friends.' The teacher paused to let her words sink in. There was a note of frustration in her voice as she continued. 'She's studying for her GCSEs now and she really needs to take her schoolwork more seriously, otherwise she'll fall behind. So far this term, she's handed homework in late on five separate occasions and she's not engaging in class like she used to. More worryingly, she's been turning up late for school in the mornings.'

'Late?' Isabel leaned forward, a sense of unease rippling somewhere beneath her ribs. This didn't sound like Ellie. Not at all. She'd always been a good kid.

'She's been catching the school bus, hasn't she?' said Nathan. 'Perhaps it's been running late, or she missed it.'

Miss Powell was unswayed by his line of defence. 'There have been no problems reported with the school buses. Besides, when I spoke to Ellie, she told me she'd been walking to school. That's fine, of course, if it's what she wants to do, but the school is a long way from where you live. If she's going to walk, she needs to set off earlier and get here on time.'

Isabel looked at Nathan, who appeared to be as baffled as she was.

'We had no idea she was walking to school,' Isabel said. 'We'll ask her about it.'

'Perhaps you could also find out why she's stopped coming to the after-school book club,' Miss Powell added.

Inexplicably, it was this final revelation that shocked Isabel the most. Ellie's love of books was legendary. The possibility that her love affair with literature might be over prematurely saddened Isabel inordinately.

'She still does plenty of reading at home,' Nathan said.

Miss Powell smiled. 'That's reassuring to hear, but I'm worried that Ellie is losing interest in her work here, at school. I'm disappointed. She could do so much better.'

'We'll talk to her … find out what's wrong. Won't we, Nathan?'

Although Nathan nodded supportively, Isabel knew that she would be the one who would have to deliver the reprimand. As far as her husband was concerned, their youngest child could do no wrong – and nothing the teacher said would change his opinion.

Having delivered the negative elements of Ellie's report, Miss Powell allowed herself a tight smile. 'There is one subject in which Ellie has been excelling …'

Nathan nudged Isabel and winked.

'Her art tutor is very impressed with the work she's been producing.' The teacher picked up the written report and read from it. 'He says … *Ellie is creative and talented and has a natural gift.*'

'She gets that from me,' said Nathan.

Isabel gave him a sideways glance and focused her attention back on the teacher.

Miss Powell put down the report and leaned back. 'There's an exhibition of artwork in the main hall,' she told them. 'Please take a look on your way out. Several of Ellie's pieces are on show.'

Isabel had switched her phone to silent, but she felt it vibrate in her pocket. Pulling it out, she glanced down at the screen. It was her colleague Dan Fairfax, her sergeant. He knew where she was. He wouldn't be ringing unless it was important.

'I'm so sorry.' Isabel stood up. 'Technically I'm still on duty, so I need to take this.'

She answered the call on her way out of the classroom. 'This had better be important, Dan.'

'It is, boss. I wouldn't disturb you otherwise. We've had word that a body's been found. I thought you'd want to know.'

Nathan had followed her out into the corridor clutching a printed copy of Ellie's report.

'Hang on, Dan. I need to have a quick word with Nathan.' Isabel turned to her husband. 'There's a body. I have to go.'

'Can you spare a couple of minutes to look at Ellie's artwork on your way out?'

'I'd rather not rush it,' she said, shame clawing at her conscience.

Nathan sighed, disappointed. Over the years, he had reluctantly accepted that sometimes her job had to take priority over family commitments. It was a regrettable reality they'd both come to terms with, but that didn't stop Isabel feeling guilty. Occasionally, being a good copper meant being a bad parent, or a rubbish wife. Mostly, Isabel loved her job, but there were times when she hated the way it screwed with her life.

'It's better if I come back another time and have a proper look,' she said, suppressing a flush of self-reproach. 'Sorry, Nathan. I'm needed urgently.'

She planted a swift kiss on his cheek before hurrying back along the main corridor towards the exit, the phone clasped to her ear.

'I'm on my way, Dan. Tell me where I need to be and I'll meet you there.'

'The property's on Ecclesdale Drive. Number 23,' Dan said. 'It's on that big, sprawling estate on the eastern side of town. Head for Winster Street and then turn left—'

9

'It's OK.' She cut him off. 'I know where it is.'

Isabel didn't need directions. She knew it well.

***

Ecclesdale Drive sliced through the centre of a housing estate that had sprung up in the early 1960s and had grown every decade since. The outlying fields that Isabel remembered from childhood had burgeoned into a confusing network of streets and cul-de-sacs, each one crammed with showy red-brick properties.

The houses in the original part of the estate were plainer, but built on bigger plots, with long gardens filled with well-established trees and shrubs. Isabel turned onto Winster Street, driving past the recreation ground she'd visited frequently as a child. The old slide was still there, as well as a vast climbing frame and a new set of swings. The flat wooden roundabout the local kids had called the 'teapot lid' had been removed on safety grounds in the 1970s, as had the conical swing that had been shaped like a witch's hat. Isabel smiled as she recalled the wild, spinning rides she had taken on that pivoted swing.

She took the second left into Ecclesdale Drive. The street was long and crescent-shaped, curving down towards an infant school and the newsagent's shop at the end. It was years since Isabel had been here. Ecclesdale Drive held lots of memories, but not all of them were good.

She pulled up behind two police vehicles that were parked halfway along the road. Her hand trembled as she switched off the engine, her fingers quivering involuntarily like the blue-and-white police tape that was fluttering around the outer cordon of the crime scene. Battling a growing wave of unease, Isabel took a deep breath and got out of the car.

Chapter 3

She stood for a moment and looked up at number 23. It was one of a long row of identical detached properties of boring 1960s architecture. Like a child's drawing of a house, its pointed eaves faced the road and a chimney protruded from the left-hand side of the roof. The front of the house had originally consisted of three windows and a door, but at some stage over the last couple of decades, someone had added a small porch extension.

Isabel went to the boot of her car and retrieved a pair of blue latex gloves and overshoes. Suitably protected, she walked to the edge of the temporary barrier where a uniformed officer was standing.

'Evening ma'am,' he said as she showed him her warrant card. 'It's round the back. DS Fairfax is here already.'

She stepped onto the front path and ducked under the inner cordon before unlatching the side gate at the end of the driveway. At the back of the house, she passed a pale-faced young couple who were gazing out from the dining-room window. DS Daniel Fairfax was standing in the garden with his arms folded, next to a set of lights that were illuminating an area of ground directly behind the property's brick-built garage.

Isabel pulled up the zip of her coat to fend off a chill that was wrapping itself around her neck. 'OK, Danny boy,' she said. 'What have we got?'

'Human remains,' he said. 'The new owners came across them when they were digging out foundations for a kitchen extension.'

Her chest tightened. 'Human remains? I thought you said there was a body.'

'That's what the duty officer told me initially,' he said. 'When I got here, I realised the body had been in the ground for quite a while.'

Isabel forced herself to breathe slowly to fend off a rush of nausea. 'When you say "a while", how long do you mean?'

'I don't know yet, boss. You'll have to ask Raveen.'

Raveen Talwar was kneeling a few feet away at the edge of a half-dug trench. Isabel was glad it was Raveen. He was consistently polite and helpful, and one of the best crime scene investigators she had worked with. He dealt efficiently and graciously with questions, but he could be brash if he thought someone was trying to step on his overshoed toes. Whenever he worked a crime scene, he had a grating habit of crunching mints, the hard-boiled variety. He devoured them nonstop, even through the longest of examinations.

Despite his penchant for mints, there was something agreeable and reassuring about having Raveen around. Everyone liked him. His popularity was such that, when his wife had recently given birth to a boy, the CID team had taken the unusual step of clubbing together for a baby gift.

Isabel stumbled towards him on legs that wobbled, as though they were made of elastic. 'What can you tell me, Raveen?' she said.

He looked up. 'Are you OK? You look pale.'

'I'm fine,' she replied. 'Just tell me what you know.'

'Nothing certain at this stage, I'm afraid,' he said. 'Any soft tissue is long gone, but these definitely aren't bones of antiquity. If you're going to force me to guess – which I know you are – I'd say the body has been here for at least twenty years, but it could have been in the ground much longer.'

'How much longer?' Her heart was pounding and she was aware that her voice was cracking treacherously.

'It's too early to say. The skeleton is only partially exposed. I'll be able to tell you more when it's been fully uncovered and removed. Don't push me into making a rash assessment. I need to have a proper look.'

Isabel tried hard to hide her exasperation. 'Come on, Raveen. Don't be coy. You must be able to tell me something.' She shifted impatiently. 'I won't hold it against you if you get it wrong, but I need to know. Please. How long? It's important.'

Raveen stood up and narrowed his eyes. 'I'd estimate the body has been here somewhere between twenty and forty years, give or take a few years.'

Isabel's stomach reeled. Hiding her shaking hands in the pockets of her coat, she walked along the edge of the muddy trench and looked down – but instead of seeing human bones, her vision blurred and a creeping black mist began to close in, threatening to shut her down.

'We've also found a partial dental plate,' Raveen said. 'It might help us to establish a more accurate timeframe.'

His voice was coming to her as if from a distance, his words muffled and distorted. Lurching away from the trench, Isabel went over to the rear wall of the garage and leaned against it. Blood rushed in her ears and she took a series of deep breaths to clear her head.

Dan was observing her closely, his brown eyes watchful. 'You all right, boss? I didn't have you down as someone who would get queasy over a bunch of bones. I'd have thought you'd seen way worse than this.' A half-smile pulled at the corners of his mouth as he took in her obvious discomfort.

'If you don't mind, Dan, I'm going to stand down and let you take over for now, while I put in a call to the Super.'

'OK …' His forehead creased into a frown. 'Was it something I said? I was only joking about the bones, you know.'

Isabel chose to ignore his wisecrack. 'Will you be all right picking up the questioning?' she asked.

Dan nodded confidently, but his expression wavered as he clocked the serious expression on her face.

'Is there a problem?' said Raveen.

'Possibly,' Isabel said. She was clenching her fingers so tightly, her nails were digging into her palms. 'You see, I grew up in this house. Forty-one years ago, I lived here with my parents.'

Chapter 4

Isabel walked away from the crime scene with a torrent of questions sloshing around in her head. One in particular was vying for attention. Could it be him? Was it possible?

She reached the side gate on legs that felt so watery and weak she wasn't sure they would take her the short distance back to the car. She paused to look back at Dan, fending off a stab of guilt for abandoning him. Left in charge, he seemed tense and uncertain. Raveen stood next to him, deep in thought.

'Before I go,' Isabel said, 'can you tell me whether the body is male or female?'

Raveen nodded. 'Based on what I can see of the skull, I'd say male.'

'Are you sure?'

'The slope of the forehead, the prominence of the supraorbital ridges and the shape of the eye sockets are all consistent with a male skull. So, yes, I'm pretty certain. I'll be able to confirm it when I've had an opportunity to examine the rest of the bones.'

'Can you tell how old he was?'

'Definitely an adult, but age, as yet, is undetermined.'

'OK. Thanks.' She paused to regain control and, pointing to

Dan, said, 'Don't forget. Make sure everything is recorded correctly. Log all decisions, actions and information.'

With clumsy fingers, she fumbled with the latch on the gate. It was stiff and clunked loudly when it eventually lifted. As she returned to her Toyota and climbed into the driver's seat, a pair of curtains twitched at the downstairs window of the house next door. Some things never changed.

The car's interior was warm and stifling. Isabel leaned her head on the steering wheel, closed her eyes and took a deep, shuddering breath. *I have to know*, she thought. *I need to find out one way or another.*

Reaching for her phone, she scrolled through the contacts stored alphabetically, stopping at the name of the only person who could answer the question that was burning a hole in her brain.

Her finger hovered over the name on the screen. All she had to do was ask one question. The answer she received would either put her mind at rest or plunge her into a deep pit of despair – but anything was better than not knowing.

Before she had a chance to make the call, her phone began to ring. The incoming caller was Detective Superintendent Valerie Tibbet.

'DI Blood? What's the situation?'

Isabel closed her eyes. 'We have a body. The site's been cordoned off and we're treating it as a crime scene … but there's a complication.'

'What kind of complication?'

'The house where the victim was found,' Isabel said. 'I used to live there. A long time ago.'

'Right. Well, you'll need to disclose your connection to the address during any future prosecution case, but there's no reason why you can't carry on as SIO.'

'The problem is, the timeframe's unclear,' she said. 'Forensics estimate the body's been there for between twenty and forty years, possibly even longer.'

16

'I see. And does that coincide with your time in the house?'

'Potentially. My mother sold up in 1978.'

'Do you have any reason to believe the body was buried while your family lived at the address?'

This was it. The moment of truth: the point at which she should tell the Super everything. Except there wasn't much to tell, was there? Just an old story with an unknown ending. Best to say nothing – at least for now.

'No, of course not. I'm trying to do everything by the book, that's all. There's no escaping the fact that the address is linked to me and I don't want to jeopardise the enquiry. It's best that I stand down pending confirmation of the timescales. In the meantime, Dan's in charge at the scene.'

'Fair enough,' said Val. 'That seems sensible, given the circumstances. When we've got a better idea of the timeframe and any overlap with your family's occupancy of the house has been ruled out, you can re-join the investigation. In the meantime, I'll find someone to take over as SIO. For now I'll have to trust DS Fairfax to make the initial enquiries.'

'I have every faith in Dan,' Isabel said. 'He's very capable.'

'Has he been involved in this kind of investigation before?'

Isabel sighed. 'Not that I know of, but this will be good experience for him. He needs to start taking on more responsibility.'

'Is that a problem with him? Is he shirking?'

Isabel rubbed her forehead. 'No, Val. That's not what I meant. Dan's a good detective, but he needs to believe in himself. This case will help boost his confidence.'

'OK, if you're sure. I'll give him a call and have a word. I'll ask him to keep me updated for now and I'll get back in touch with you as soon as I hear anything.'

Isabel ended the call, started the car and drove home through the rush-hour traffic.

Chapter 5

A month ago, when Dan had joined DI Blood's team, everyone had warned him that she was a stickler for procedures, so her swift retreat based on a decades-old connection to the house came as no great surprise. What did puzzle him was her physical response to the crime scene. Dan was aware she'd worked some pretty gory cases in the past, so he was fairly certain she wasn't squeamish – but her face had definitely looked pale, unnaturally so. What was that all about? She'd done her best to hide it, but something was bothering her. He felt sure of it.

It was all a bit weird. He could understand his boss's desire to do the right thing, but he was also pissed off that she hadn't given him a few more pointers before buggering off. As it was, she'd dropped him right in it. He hadn't been involved in an investigation involving human skeletal remains before and now, here he was, seemingly in charge of the scene.

Left to his own devices, Dan decided to begin his enquiries by talking to the owners of the house. Leaving Raveen and his team to their forensic examination, he went round to the front of the house and rapped on the door.

A woman of about thirty answered. Her dark brown hair, pale skin and wide cheekbones gave her face an exotic look.

'I'm DS Dan Fairfax.' He flipped open his ID wallet. 'I need to ask you a few questions, if that's all right?'

The woman nodded. 'Yes, of course. I'm Amy Whitworth. Come in.'

She led him into the kitchen, where a man was perched on a stool at an old-fashioned breakfast bar, his hands wrapped around a mug of steaming coffee.

'This is my brother, Paul.'

'Your brother? Right. Sorry, I assumed you were … you know … a couple.'

Amy smiled. 'No. We're brother and sister. Twins actually.'

Other than the colour of their hair and eyes, Dan could detect little resemblance between the siblings, although the comparison was somewhat hindered by the enormous hipster beard that dominated the lower half of Paul Whitworth's face.

'But you're joint owners of the house?'

'Yes.' Amy nodded. 'Our father died last year and left us some money. This is our first foray into property development, isn't it, Paul?'

'It could well be our last if the whole thing goes tits up.' Paul Whitworth seemed tetchy and disillusioned.

'You'll have to excuse my brother, Detective. Finding a skeleton in the back garden has come as a shock.'

'That's understandable,' Dan said. He pulled a notebook from his pocket. 'Can I ask how long you've owned the house?'

'We bought it at auction and got the keys eight weeks ago,' Paul told him.

'And yet you've only recently started work on the extension? I thought property developers liked to turn things around quickly. Get the work done, sell the house and make some fast money.'

'That's the general idea,' Paul said, 'but we had to wait for planning permission to come through.'

'What can you tell me about the previous owner?'

'We never met her,' Amy replied. 'We were told she was an

elderly widow who'd gone to live in a residential home. Her son auctioned off the house to get a quick sale.'

'Do you recall her name?'

Paul shrugged. 'Can't say that I do. Our solicitor will have all the details.'

'I think it was Repton,' Amy said. 'Rhoda Repton.'

Dan made a note of the name. 'And have you any idea how long she'd lived here?'

'No. Sorry. You could check with the neighbours though. They might be able to tell you.'

'Someone's doing that right now.' Dan smiled. 'Tell me, when you got the keys, had the house been cleared? Was it completely empty?'

Paul and Amy exchanged smiles.

'As it happens, we had to get rid of a lot of furniture and other stuff that had been left behind,' Paul said. 'It was a right load of old tat – even the charity shops didn't want it. We took everything down to the tip in my van.'

'Was there anything unusual or out of place? Anything that seemed odd? Something hidden away?'

'Not that we noticed,' Paul said. 'It was the sort of stuff you'd expect to find … a few clothes had been left in one of the wardrobes, and there were some old magazines and newspapers … a crappy framed picture. An old rug. Nothing much else.'

'I finished clearing the pantry this afternoon,' Amy said. 'There was all sorts of junk in there. Tins of food, cereals, jars, old pans and utensils. I put everything in the dustbin at the side of the house.'

'But nothing out of the ordinary?' Dan wasn't sure what he had hoped to hear. The discovery of a decades-old blood-stained knife perhaps, or a bottle labelled 'poison' hidden away behind a can of mushy peas.

'I think the family took away anything of value and left the rubbish for us to dispose of,' Paul said.

'You didn't come across any letters or bills?' said Dan, knowing he was grasping at straws. 'No correspondence of any kind?'

'There was an old bureau in the hallway,' Paul replied, 'but it was empty.'

'OK. Well if you think of anything, let me know.' Dan handed them a card with his telephone number on it. 'I'll get someone to come in and take a statement from you in a few minutes.'

'Do you know how long those guys are going to be out there?' Paul nodded towards the forensics team whose white scene suits stood out, ghost-like, in the dark garden.

'The remains you found have been confirmed as human,' Dan said. 'The body was buried recently enough to warrant a forensic and police investigation, so we'll need to do a thorough search of the site. It'll be a while yet. Several days, I would imagine, but we'll let you know as soon as they've finished. In the meantime, I'm afraid your back garden is off limits.'

***

As Dan let himself out of the front door of the house, he ran into the uniformed officer who'd been tasked with speaking to nearby residents.

'Any joy with the neighbours? Learn anything interesting?'

'Not so far,' the officer replied. 'The family at number 21 only moved in three months ago, so they didn't know the previous owner. I wasn't able to get an answer at number 25. I'm going to try across the road next.'

'OK, keep me informed. Someone must be able to tell us something useful.'

As he watched the officer weave around the parked vehicles and cross the road, Dan pulled out his phone and rang the office. He needed some background information and if there was one person he could rely on to pull everything together quickly, it was DC Zoe Piper.

21

'Zoe,' he said when his colleague answered, 'I need you to run some checks for me.'

'No problem.' She sounded remarkably perky for someone who was working the late shift. 'What do you need?'

'Find out who's owned or lived at 23 Ecclesdale Drive over the last forty-five years. Can you also check whether the address is linked to any reported incidents ... domestic violence, mispers ... or whether there's any criminal activity associated with anyone who's lived there. Let me know as soon as you find anything.'

'Consider it done,' Zoe said.

As he ended the call and strolled back to the rear of the house, Dan marvelled at the way Zoe always managed to sound so upbeat. He suspected her positive attitude was driven by ambition and a desire to make the right impression, but maybe that was unfair. Perhaps she just had a naturally optimistic view on life and work.

He noticed a light go on in the kitchen at number 25, and the silhouette of a person began to move around inside. It was obvious someone was at home, so why hadn't they answered the door when the uniform had knocked?

A yawning Raveen ambled over and stood next to him.

'You look knackered,' Dan said.

'The baby's keeping us awake,' Raveen replied. 'I'm hoping he'll start to sleep through soon, but at the moment the little tyke only seems able to manage a few hours at a stretch.'

Dan held up his hands. 'Don't expect any advice from me. I know absolutely nothing about babies, and I hope it stays that way ... for a few years, at least.'

Raveen grinned. 'We'll be taking the skeleton away shortly, but I thought you'd appreciate a quick update. The remains are definitely male, and there are signs of bone spurs around the knees, which suggests he was suffering from osteoarthritis. We've also found a cigarette lighter. I'll clean it up when I get back and let you know if it can tell us anything.'

'In a perfect world it would be inscribed with the victim's name and date of birth.'

Raveen laughed. 'As we both know, there's no such thing as a perfect world. A good thing too, otherwise you and I would be out of a job.'

Dan smirked. 'Keep me posted, Raveen. Zoe's doing some checks back in the office ... hopefully she'll find something that will help with an ID. I'm going to nip next door and have a word with the neighbours. Perhaps they can shed some light on who these bones belong to.'

***

Dan looked up at number 25 and the house peered back at him through dark, grubby windows. Its architecture was identical to the other houses on the street, but its shabbiness made it stand out from the rest. Unlike number 23, it didn't look as if it would be getting a makeover any time soon. The wooden window frames were poorly maintained, with shrivelled putty and peeling paint, and moss was growing in the cracks on the concrete driveway.

His knock on the front door went unanswered, so he wandered around to the back of the house and peered through the kitchen window. A silver-haired woman was standing at an old-fashioned oven, cooking something on an eye-level grill. She jumped when he knocked on the window.

Dan heard the rattle of a security chain sliding into place. The door opened marginally and the woman squinted suspiciously at the warrant card he held in front of her.

'I'm DS Dan Fairfax, I wonder if I could have a word?'

'You'd better come in.' She closed the door again to slide off the chain and then opened it wide, allowing Dan to step into the kitchen.

'I saw the police cars and wondered whether someone would be round to talk to me.'

'A police officer did knock a while back,' Dan said, 'but there was no reply.'

She shrugged. 'I'm a bit deaf. I'm supposed to wear hearing aids, but I can't get on with them. They keep whistling.'

She was grilling kippers. The smoked, fishy smell was unmistakable.

'Were you about to eat? I can come back in half an hour or so if you'd prefer.'

'It's all right.' She turned off the grill and led Dan through to the living room. 'I can always warm them through again when you've gone.'

'Do you live on your own, Mrs ...?'

'Littlewood. Joyce Littlewood.' She sat down in a winged armchair that faced a huge widescreen television. 'My son lives with me, but he's at work. He does shifts over at a distribution centre near Matlock.'

'And have you lived here long?'

'Since the house was built. Me and my late husband moved here in 1963.'

'Wow! That's a long time ago. I imagine you must have got to know everyone who's lived at number 23 over the years.'

'Some better than others,' Joyce Littlewood replied.

Dan could see that she was weighing him up, gauging whether to trust him.

'Rhoda was a nice lady,' Joyce continued. 'Rhoda Repton. She left last year. Went into a care home somewhere near to where her son lives. Wirksworth way, I think.'

'The couple that have bought number 23 are building an extension at the back,' Dan explained. 'They've uncovered some skeletal remains in the garden ... human remains ... which is why the police were called.'

Joyce pursed her lips. 'I thought it must be something like that,' she said. 'I've been looking out of the back bedroom and I spotted the people in white suits. I couldn't see what they were doing, but I knew it had to be serious. I have to say, it's not the sort of thing you expect to see when you look out of your window.'

'They should be finished in a few hours,' Dan told her. 'At least for today.'

Joyce tilted her head inquisitively. 'Is it Celia?'

'Is what Celia?'

'The bones. I always thought something bad must have happened to her.'

'Who's Celia, Mrs Littlewood? And why do you think something might have happened to her?'

Chapter 6

'Celia Aspen,' Joyce Littlewood said. 'She lived next door. Took off one day in 1986 and hasn't been seen since. Her disappearance was reported to the police, so you'll have it all on record. I'm quite willing to tell you what I know about it, but it could take a while, so you'll have to listen while I eat my tea. Hang on two ticks and I'll be back in with a tray. Shall we have a cup of tea as well? Or coffee, if you prefer it.'

Dan knew that a shared cuppa was often the best way to get people talking – the older ones at least. 'I'll have tea please. White, one sugar.'

As Mrs Littlewood pottered in the kitchen, Dan prowled around the living room, examining the collection of framed photographs on the mantelpiece. They showed three children at various stages of their lives – two boys and a girl, all of whom had inherited their mother's beaky nose and wide blue eyes. There was also a more modern studio shot which he guessed was of Mrs Littlewood's grandchildren. The distinctive facial features seemed to have continued down the line to the latest generation.

On the teak coffee table next to her chair was a pair of knitting needles that held a partially completed cable-patterned cricket sweater. Behind the chair was a corner cupboard full of the same type of Royal Crown Derby china that Dan's own gran collected. Imari pattern. A dense dark blue and red design, finished off with gold. Definitely not Dan's thing at all.

When Joyce came back, she was carrying a tray containing a pot of tea, a milk jug, sugar bowl and two china cups. The crockery wasn't as grand as Crown Derby, but posh enough to make Dan feel he should crook his little finger as he drank.

He sat on the sofa and sipped his tea while Joyce scurried back to the kitchen. She returned with a plate of kippers and another piled high with bread and butter.

'It helps the fish bones to go down,' she said, when she saw Dan eyeing up the excessive quantity of bread. 'Now, tell me, young man, what is it you need to know?'

'What year did Celia Aspen move in next door? Can you remember?'

'What?' Joyce cupped her ear. 'Speak up.'

'Can you remember when Celia moved in?'

'Of course I can. I may be old and hard of hearing, but there's nothing wrong with my memory.'

Between mouthfuls, she told Dan what she knew about the history of the house next door.

'Now … the Corringtons. They lived there until 1978 – lovely family – I was sorry to see them go.'

That must have been the DI's family, Dan thought. *Sounds as though they got on well enough with the Littlewoods.*

'A young couple moved in after the Corringtons,' Joyce continued. 'Davidson or Davison … something like that. They seemed nice enough, but I didn't get to know them very well. They'd only been living there a year when she ran off with another bloke. They sold up and got a divorce.

'It must have been the autumn of 1979 when Celia Aspen bought the house. She was all right I suppose, but she did have rather a superiority complex. She was pernickety; always very careful about her appearance … never went anywhere without

27

make-up and a touch of lippy. A bit up herself, if you know what I mean. Quiet and reserved, but a decent enough neighbour … at least in the beginning.'

'Did something happen to change your opinion of her?'

Joyce stirred her tea. 'It's all water under the bridge now, of course. I don't want to speak out of turn …'

Dan waited.

'It was her attitude to my youngest son that I didn't like. Timothy got on well with Celia to start with. In fact, she was patient with him at a time when others weren't so kind. Timothy did odd jobs for her … mowing the lawn and so on, but I put a stop to that after a while.'

'Why was that?'

'Celia had a niece called Julie Desmond. She was a cocky sort. Absolutely full of herself, if you ask me. She was three years older than Timothy, and he was in awe of her. Celia reckoned that Timothy was making a nuisance of himself … accused him of following Julie around and saying things that were inappropriate.'

'And was he?'

'Was he heck as like. Timothy may have been different to other lads his age, but he wasn't stupid. He has autism spectrum disorder, so he can be clumsy … socially, I mean. He talks too much sometimes and goes on about stuff that isn't relevant to the conversation you're having with him – but he's kind and hard-working and a good son. He did like Julie, fancied her even … but he was never a pest.'

'Is that what Celia Aspen accused him of being? A pest?'

'Not in so many words, but it was what she inferred. Timothy stopped going round there after that and things became rather frosty between Celia and me. It was a shame, but no one criticises my son and gets away with it.'

It was obvious that Joyce Littlewood was a devoted mother-hen and Dan had no doubt she would be quick to defend her chicks.

28

She was proving to be a great source of information, but he couldn't help comparing her narrative to the complicated pattern of the pullover she was knitting. He needed to take back control of the conversation … unpick it, otherwise he'd be here all night.

'Mrs Littlewood, can I ask you to backtrack a little? What can you tell me about Celia Aspen?'

She pulled a couple of bones from her kipper and placed them on the side of her plate. 'I can't tell you very much at all. I know that may sound odd when you consider I lived next door to her for over seven years, but she was a very self-contained sort of person. She hardly ever talked about herself and she certainly didn't encourage anyone to ask questions. She had this way of letting you know if she thought you'd overstepped the boundaries. She'd narrow her eyes and glare. It was her way of telling you to back off.'

'Do you know how old she was?'

'Not very old. Late sixties I would say.'

Dan smiled.

'I can see you grinning, young man.' She laughed. 'Late sixties may seem ancient to you, but you'll change your mind when you reach that age yourself.'

'Was Celia married?' Dan asked. 'What was her background?'

'She never married, although I got the impression there had been a romance once … during the war. She was retired, but for years she'd been the Head of Fashion at Bradshaw and Trent.'

Dan arched an eyebrow involuntarily and Joyce laughed before continuing.

'It was a small department store in Derby,' she said. 'It closed down years ago, not long after Celia moved to Bainbridge. She was made redundant and I believe she may have used her severance pay to buy the house next door, but I don't know that for certain. To be perfectly honest, there's not a lot else I can tell you about Celia. She kept herself to herself. She was an odd one really.

29

She was usually polite and could be quite friendly when she wanted to be, but if she did talk to you, it tended to be about neutral subjects … the weather or her garden.'

'Did she have many visitors?'

'No,' Joyce said, the skin on her neck quivering as she shook her head. 'Her niece used to call round about once a fortnight. As far as I know, Julie was her only relative.'

'No friends?' Dan turned to a new page in his notebook and looked at Joyce expectantly. 'A boyfriend maybe?'

Joyce dismissed that idea with a brief flick of her hand. 'I don't think Celia had many friends, male or otherwise. If she did, she wouldn't have invited them round. She wasn't one for having people in her house. Timothy went inside occasionally if there was a job needed doing, but she kept me at the door if I went to see her. Not that I went round there very often.'

She drained her tea cup.

'As far as I can recall, she only ever had one male visitor. I remember it because it was such an unusual occurrence.'

'Do you know who it was?' Dan asked.

'No, haven't a clue. I was out in the back one day, hanging out washing, and I saw them over the fence. Celia was showing him her garden.'

'When was this?'

Joyce tapped the side of her head as if to dislodge a long-forgotten memory. 'It must have been the spring of 1986, about a month before Celia disappeared.'

'And you have no idea who her visitor was?'

She shook her head again. 'We weren't introduced. I did wave and say hello, but I don't think Celia was in the mood for idle chatter. When she saw me she tried to usher the man inside. I could tell she didn't want me talking to him.'

'So you didn't speak to this bloke at all?'

'Hold your horses, I didn't say that.' Joyce grinned. 'I don't appreciate being snubbed, so I ambled over to the fence and

30

spoke to him directly – more to wind Celia up than anything else.'

If Celia Aspen was as reserved as Joyce Littlewood says, having a nosy neighbour must have been a right pain in the jacksy, Dan thought. To him, however, Joyce was a gift. She had a huge store of knowledge tucked away in her head, although it was clear he'd have his work cut out, teasing it out of her.

'What did you say to him, Mrs Littlewood?'

Joyce paused, as though replaying the scene in her head. 'When I heard him chatting to Celia, I thought I detected an American accent, so I asked him if he was from the United States.'

'And was he?'

'No. He said he'd lived in Canada since the late Forties, but he was originally from Nottingham. He'd come over to stay with his sister's family and he'd decided to look Celia up and pay her a visit. Apparently they knew each other when they were young.'

Dan was holding his pencil like a baton, using it to conduct the steady to-and-fro rhythm of the conversation.

'He said that?'

'Yes.' Joyce leaned back. 'That's what he told me.'

'Do you think he might have been Celia's old flame?'

She thought about it for a moment. 'Possibly, but there was no way for me to find out because she whisked him back inside PDQ. It was obvious she didn't want me poking my nose in. Our relationship had already cooled by then, but things got even frostier after that.'

Dan's gut was telling him that the information Joyce Littlewood was divulging was connected in some way to the bones discovered next door. He just wasn't sure how.

'You say that Celia went missing in 1986?'

'That's right. The last time I saw her was in early May, although Timothy saw her a couple of times after that.'

Dan put down his pencil, slowing the pace of their exchange.

'Did Celia tell you she was going away?'

'No, but she and I weren't exactly on friendly terms, so why would she?'

He tried to conjure up a set of circumstances in which Celia Aspen had killed someone, disposed of the victim in her own back garden, and then done a runner – but the whole scenario seemed implausible. Something had happened next door, but what? And why? And how did Celia Aspen's disappearance fit in to the picture?

'Anyway, it looks very much as though Celia didn't go anywhere.' Joyce stared at him expectantly. 'I'm guessing that's who you've found in the back garden?'

'We don't know who it is yet,' Dan said, deciding not to disclose the sex of the unidentified skeleton at this early stage in the investigation. 'Is there any particular reason you think it could be Celia Aspen?'

'Well, it's got to be more than a coincidence, hasn't it? Celia went missing and now you've found a body. It would certainly explain what happened to her. I always found it hard to believe she'd clear off without a backward glance, leaving her house and her precious garden behind. Unless, of course …' Joyce sat up, her eyes gleaming.

'Unless what?'

'She ran away because *she'd* killed someone. Flipping heck! Do you think that's what happened?'

'We don't know, Mrs Littlewood, but we're going to do our best to find out.'

'I'll tell you something for nothing …' She tapped her fingers on the arm of her chair. 'If she is still around, Celia Aspen will be about a hundred by now.'

'In that case, I think it's unlikely she's still alive.' Dan stood up. 'Thank you for your time, Mrs Littlewood. You've been very helpful. I might need to talk to you again at some point, but I'll let you get on with your evening for now.' He handed her a card. 'If you think of anything else that might be relevant to our enquiries, please give me a call on that number.'

His phone began to ring as he left the house. It was Zoe.

'Let me guess,' Dan said. 'You're ringing to tell me about Celia Aspen who moved to 23 Ecclesdale Drive in 1979 and was reported missing in 1986. Am I right?'

'You already know? How did you find out?'

He grinned. 'I'm a detective, Zoe. It's my job.'

Chapter 7

Isabel turned into her driveway at the same time as a pizza delivery bike was pulling away.

She found Nathan in the kitchen, pouring a glass of red wine. 'Blimey,' he said. 'That was quick.'

She shuddered. 'It's a long story. Pour me a glass of wine and I'll tell you about it.'

A pair of French doors led from the kitchen into a garden room at the back of the house. Ellie was in there, stretched out on the sofa in front of the log burner. She was watching television and stuffing her face with a slice of Margherita, seemingly oblivious to the backlash over her school report.

Compared to the maelstrom of worry set in motion by the discovery at Ecclesdale Drive, Isabel's concerns over the school report seemed trivial now – but that didn't mean Ellie should get off scotfree. Her behaviour was probably nothing more than a teenage blip, but it had to be addressed. Steeling herself for confrontation, Isabel straightened her shoulders and wandered into the garden room.

'When your brother and sister were your age, a pizza delivery was considered a treat. From what we've heard from your teacher, that's the last thing you deserve.'

Ellie lifted one shoulder. 'Dad got pizza to cheer me up.'

'Did he now?' Isabel turned to Nathan, who had come up behind her with a large glass of wine in his hand. 'After listening to your teacher this afternoon, I think your dad and I are the ones that need cheering up.'

Frowning, Ellie reached for the TV remote and turned up the volume. 'Miss Powell's a cow,' she said. 'She's hard on everyone.'

Isabel took the remote control from her daughter and switched off the television.

'Listen up, young lady. You need to pull your socks up. You're clever and capable, but from what I've heard today, you're wasting your talent. Turning up late for school and being argumentative with your teachers is not acceptable. Do you understand? We need to have a serious talk about this, but not tonight. For now I suggest you take your pizza upstairs and eat it while you do your homework. As of tomorrow, one of us will be dropping you off at school and I'll be checking with the teachers to make sure you hand your assignments in on time.'

Ellie scowled and, snatching up the pizza box, stormed out of the room. Isabel sank onto the sofa she had vacated.

'I take it this new school run will fall to me?' Nathan said, as they listened to the sound of footsteps thudding up the stairs and across the landing, followed by the slam of a door. 'You're too hard on her, you know. You measure her behaviour by what you did when you were her age. Life's different now. As older parents, we have to accept that.'

Isabel tried not to think of herself as an older parent. Discovering that she was pregnant again at the age of forty-one had hit her like a lightning strike. She'd assumed her child-rearing days were behind her: the prospect of going through it all again had been crushing. Nathan had been a lot more philosophical. He'd likened the arrival of another baby in their lives to a googly; a curve ball. Fate threw one at you sometimes, he said.

Isabel accepted the wine Nathan held out to her. 'Ellie's sudden aversion to school has nothing to do with our age,' she said. 'She's getting lazy, that's what it is. The little madam doesn't know she's born. She lives in a nice house in a good neighbourhood and wants for nothing. She has absolutely no reason to misbehave.'

Isabel thought back to her own life when she was fourteen. It was the year her parents had split up and everything fell apart. She felt a spasm of grief as she remembered her dad standing at the front of the house on Ecclesdale Drive, waving reassuringly as Isabel set off on a three-day school trip. When she returned home, it was to the news that he had left without saying goodbye.

His departure had thrust Isabel's mother into a depression that, for a while at least, rendered her barely able to function as a parent. Left to her own devices, Isabel had clung to the belief that her dad would get in touch once he'd found somewhere new to live. But as the days rolled into months and she heard nothing, the pain of his absence had tightened its grip. His abandonment had left her feeling hollow and bereft. It was as though something vital had been ripped from inside her, leaving an ache that was chronic and incurable. Whenever Isabel thought of that time, a dark curtain of pain wrapped itself around her.

Unable to keep up with the mortgage payments, her mother had been forced to sell the house on Ecclesdale Drive. She and Isabel had moved to a cramped mill cottage in an unfashionable part of town. It was damp and dark, with an overgrown garden that backed onto the railway line.

Isabel swallowed a slug of wine. 'When I was her age I had all sorts of crap to deal with.'

'I know you did.' Nathan sat next to her. 'But Ellie isn't like you. She's growing up in a different century to us. Kids today have different kinds of pressure. All I'm saying is … ease off a little.'

'Actually, you need to ease off on me.' She glanced at him sternly. 'I've had one of the worst afternoons I can remember in a long time.'

Nathan put his arm around her and she leaned into him, comforted by his warmth and strength. Even when she didn't deserve him, Nathan was always there for her, offering a constant supply of love and support.

'That body they found … it was at my old house – the one I lived in with Mum and Dad.' She bit her bottom lip to stop it trembling.

He rubbed her shoulder. 'It's obviously upset you.'

'Of *course* it's upset me.' Isabel shivered. 'I feel as though my earliest memories have been contaminated.'

She closed her eyes to hold back the tears that were threatening to spill over, unwilling to give in to her emotions. 'The body was buried in the back garden and apparently it's been there for yonks. Anywhere between twenty and forty years.'

'Crap!' Nathan sat up as he pieced together the implications of what she'd told him. 'When did you leave?'

'January 1978. Three months after Dad walked out. There's a potential overlap, so I've had to stand down from the case for now.'

'Bloody hell.' He settled back. 'You don't think this has anything to do with your family?'

Isabel kicked off her shoes and pulled her legs onto the sofa. 'I don't know what to think. My mind's all over the place, but I do have a bad feeling. *Really* bad.'

'Jeez.' Nathan reached out and pulled her back into his arms.

'My worst fear is that it could be him.' She swiped away an escaping tear. 'After all, I have no idea what happened, do I?'

Nathan balked. 'Surely not … there's no reason for you to think that.'

She pulled back and looked up at him, doing her best to rein in her emotions. 'I know you mean well, Nathan, but let's be realistic. Dad walked out in 1977 and I haven't seen or heard from him since. I think there's *every* reason to worry.'

Chapter 8

'But you don't have any proof that it's him?' Nathan was studying her face. He sat rigidly, the muscles on his neck strained and stiff.

'The SOCOs found a partial dental plate with the body.' Isabel tipped her head back to hold in her tears. 'Dad had a dental plate.'

'Can they check whether it's his?' Nathan asked. 'What did your boss say?'

'I haven't told her. Not about Dad.'

'Christ, Isabel.' He rubbed a hand across his chin. 'Why the hell not?'

'Because I don't want to. It's none of her damned business.'

'Of course it's her business.' He stood up, thrust his hands into his pockets and began to pace. 'What were you thinking? You need to tell her. It's not like you to go against procedure.'

'I've informed her about my connection to the house,' Isabel said, her voice terse and defensive. 'I offered to stand down immediately ... that's procedure, but I'm not telling Val bleeding Tibbet about my father. Not unless I have to.'

'But you're holding back important information. Won't you get in trouble?'

'Give me a break, Nathan. I'm hardly going rogue. I'm keeping quiet, that's all. If there are questions for me once the investigation is underway, I'll answer them, but I'm not volunteering anything until I have to.'

With his shoulders bent, Nathan continued to pace.

'For God's sake, sit down,' Isabel said. 'You're making me nervous.'

Reluctantly, he lowered himself onto the sofa and stretched his legs.

'I'm relying on the SOCOs to pinpoint when the body was buried,' she explained, more to reassure herself than to pacify Nathan. 'It shouldn't take them long. Hopefully, the timeframe will rule out any connection to my family. This whole thing could be nothing to do with me.'

'Isn't that wishful thinking? If there's any chance the remains could be your father's, you should speak up. It's the right thing to do, Isabel. You know it is.'

There was a part of her that agreed with him, but she wasn't going to admit it. Instead, she swallowed another glug of wine and opted for bravado. 'I've spent most of my career doing the right thing and what good has it done me? Come on, Nathan. Even you've got to admit this is an extraordinary situation. I don't make a habit of breaking the rules … but in this instance I'm willing to bend them if I have to.'

He frowned disapprovingly. 'So why bother to stand down at all? Why not go the whole hog and ditch the rule book completely? You could have carried on with the investigation.'

'Don't think I wasn't tempted,' Isabel said, 'but there are some things you can't get around. Dan's a smart guy. He'll run checks on who's lived at the house. If I *had* kept quiet, he'd have worked it out for himself soon enough.'

She ran a hand across her eyebrows to try and erase a headache. 'Look, I had no choice but to be honest about my connection to the property and stand down, but that doesn't mean I have to tell anyone about Dad.'

'I don't get it.' Nathan screwed up his face and scratched his chin. 'You've carried this around for years … always in the dark about what happened. Don't you want to find out if it's him? Wouldn't it at least bring you some closure?'

'Of *course* I want to know, but if it is Dad's body, who do you think their prime suspect is going to be?'

For a moment Nathan looked puzzled, and then, as realisation dawned, he grimaced. 'Your mother.'

'Exactly,' she replied, determined not to let this become one of those situations where her job took priority. 'Mum and I don't always get along, but if I'm forced to choose between honesty and loyalty, family wins every time. I don't want my parents being investigated unnecessarily. I'd much rather wait and hope the forensics will rule them out.'

Nathan reached for her hand and laced his fingers through hers. 'I understand where you're coming from,' he said, 'but if you keep quiet and the body *is* your dad's, you could be putting your job at risk.'

'I'm aware of that,' she replied, retrieving her hand and using it to reach for her glass of wine. 'It's a risk I'm willing to take.'

'OK.' He nodded, grudgingly accepting her decision. 'I guess you'll just have to sit back and wait and see what happens.'

'Actually …' She smiled weakly. 'I thought I might talk to Mum. See what she says.'

'Make your own enquiries, you mean?'

Isabel snorted. 'I'm not planning an off-piste investigation, if that's what you're insinuating. I just thought I'd call her, tell her a body's been discovered and gauge her reaction.'

Nathan poured what was left of the bottle of wine into his own glass. 'I must admit, your mum is always tight as a clam about your dad. She gets very cagey when you talk about him. I always assumed it was because she was still angry with him for leaving, even after all these years – but maybe there's another reason. A more sinister one.'

Isabel kept her mouth firmly shut and held up a hand to stop him talking. She'd come to the same conclusion herself, but she couldn't bear to listen to someone else giving voice to the same doubts.

Upstairs, Ellie had switched on some music. A hard bass beat reverberated through the ceiling and throbbed in Isabel's temples.

'Why not ask her straight?' Nathan nudged her. 'Tell her about the body and then ask her to explain what happened when your dad left home.'

'There's no way I can be that blunt.' She reached into her pocket to retrieve her phone. 'It would be tantamount to accusing her of murder.'

Nathan acknowledged her point with a tilt of the head. 'I suppose you know better than anyone how to ask the right questions,' he said. 'But your *willingness* to ask them … well, that depends.'

'On what?'

'On whether you're ready to hear the truth.'

Chapter 9

'Issy! What a surprise. It's not like you to ring midweek. Is everything all right?'

Isabel felt a pang of guilt. Barbara Corrington sounded twitchy and tense, clearly alarmed to hear from her at a time other than the usual Sunday afternoon duty call. Since her mother's move to Spain five years ago, Isabel saw her only sporadically. She could and should ring her more often.

'I've had a shock today, Mum.'

'What's wrong? You're not ill, are you? Are the children OK?'

She noticed that her mother's concern didn't extend to Nathan.

'I visited a crime scene in Bainbridge. Someone found a man's body buried in their back garden.'

'That's dreadful,' Barbara replied. 'But why are you telling me about it?'

A few years ago, Barbara would never have used the word *dreadful*. Since becoming a Spanish ex pat, she'd embraced a whole new vocabulary.

'Because …' Isabel hesitated. 'The body was found at our old house on Ecclesdale Drive.'

'What? How ghastly. It used to be such a nice area.'

Aside from the use of the word *ghastly*, her mother's cool, unflustered reaction seemed genuine. Isabel experienced a flicker of hope. Surely if Barbara was hiding something, the news that a body had been uncovered in their old garden would have thrown her into panic. She didn't seem even slightly ruffled.

'Being back there ... it got me thinking about when we lived on the street.'

'That was a long time ago, Isabel. At least forty years.' Barbara's tone was abrasive, verging on dismissive.

'We moved out in 1978,' Isabel reminded her. 'But the body wasn't buried recently, Mum. It's been there for several decades.'

The ramifications of this extra piece of information made no impact on Barbara. 'Well, at least you know the area,' she said, without missing a beat. 'That should help when you do your ... *investigating*.'

Isabel resented the way her mother had managed to add the hint of a sneer to the word investigating, as though it was something illicit or shameful. Then again, such flippancy came as no surprise. Barbara had never come to terms with her daughter being part of the force. She'd regularly tried to persuade Isabel to pursue a more genteel career, something safe and sedate. As far as Barbara was concerned, being a detective was unladylike, undignified and dangerous.

'I'm not involved with the case at the moment,' Isabel said. 'We need to rule out any possible connection or crossover with my time at the house. With *our* time at the house.'

'What on earth do you mean?'

'I've agreed with the detective superintendent that I won't work on the case until it's been confirmed that the body wasn't buried while we lived there – you, me and Dad.'

Her mother had gone quiet. Was it a silence induced by fear? Or outrage that the Corrington family was being associated with a crime? Or was it because the forbidden word had been uttered: *Dad*. The person they didn't speak of.

43

There was something automatic about her mother's reticence whenever her father's name was mentioned. Isabel had always assumed it was an instinctive resistance to the peeling back of old wounds, but now she feared there was more to it. A reluctance to reveal a dark secret, maybe? Or even a guilty conscience.

'Mum? Are you still there? Did you hear what I said?'

'Of course I heard.' Barbara's tone was snappy and defensive. 'That bloody boss of yours has got a nerve. I hope you put her straight.'

'Not exactly. It's not easy to refute something unless you're absolutely certain yourself.'

Barbara laughed – a mirthless, scraping sound. Isabel held the phone away from her ear and rolled her eyes at Nathan, who was watching and listening from the other side of the room.

When the sound of laughter died away, Isabel pressed the phone back to her ear.

'What's so funny?'

'You have to ask?' Barbara replied. 'You can't possibly be giving any credence to the idea that your father or I were involved in … what? Murder?'

'It's difficult to know what to give credence to when you've been kept in the dark for most of your life.' The searing anger that Isabel had suppressed for so long was beginning to erupt, bubbling slowly to the surface like molten lava. 'Dad walked out of our lives and we haven't seen or heard from him since. How do you think that makes me feel, Mum? And why don't we ever talk about what happened?'

Nathan came over and sat next to her on the sofa. Isabel moved the phone to her right ear so that he could listen in.

'Ask her,' he mouthed.

Isabel was struggling to compose a suitable phrase in her head. Why did conversations with her mother always have to be like this? So strained and stilted?

Nathan nodded gently, encouraging her to speak. Her words,

when they eventually emerged from her mouth, were a watered-down version of the question she really wanted to ask.

'Is there something you're keeping from me, Mum?'

She could hear her mother hyperventilating at the other end of the line. Deep, rasping, uncomfortable breaths.

'Why do you always refuse to talk about Dad?' Isabel persisted. 'I need you to tell me.'

When Barbara spoke, her voice was firm and uncompromising. 'Trust me,' she said, 'there are some things you're better off not knowing.'

And then she ended the call.

Having kept her secret for forty-two years, it seemed Barbara Corrington intended holding on to it for a while longer. Furious, Isabel stared at her phone and then threw it across the coffee table where it skidded along the glass top and came to a spinning halt.

'Well?' Nathan said. 'What did she say?'

'Nothing. She hung up on me. Shut me down, like she always does whenever I ask about Dad.'

Isabel felt dizzy with frustration, and disorientated, as though a gaping black hole had opened unexpectedly beneath her feet and she was falling into it. And then she felt Nathan's arms around her, holding her up. Keeping her safe.

Chapter 10

It was after seven o'clock by the time Dan finished talking to Joyce Littlewood. The information she'd provided was useful and could well turn out to be connected to the case, but he'd still made no significant headway on identifying the anonymous bones. Perhaps the forensics team would come up with something. He bloody well hoped so.

The smell of smoked herring lingered in Dan's nostrils as he drove along the A6 towards his flat in Duffield. Aside from a quick sandwich at lunchtime, he hadn't eaten anything all day. He toyed with the idea of calling in at one of the local Indian restaurants for a takeaway, but decided he wasn't hungry enough to justify the expense. Those stinking kippers had taken the edge off his appetite.

If he was honest, there had been something off about the whole day. Admittedly he was still getting to know DI Blood, but her behaviour this afternoon continued to baffle him.

He knew from experience that she could be cranky, but mostly, what he'd learned so far was that she was plain-speaking and straightforward. Even taking into account her connection to the house on Ecclesdale Drive, her reaction had been way off kilter. His boss was hiding something, Dan was sure of it.

He wondered how the DI would have handled things if she'd stuck around long enough to question Joyce Littlewood. Would she have concluded that the disappearance of Celia Aspen in 1986 must be linked in some way to the discovery of the bones?

If that *was* the case, the body had been buried years after DI Blood and her family moved out of the house. Dan wished he could update her, but he'd be in trouble with the Super if he shared information about the enquiry with his boss, now that she was officially off the case.

Detective Superintendent Tibbet had already been in touch, checking up on him. She hadn't said as much over the phone, but he could tell from her clipped tone that she was disappointed at how little there was to report.

After he'd updated her, the Super had instructed him to arrange a meeting for eleven o'clock the following morning. She wanted him to brief the team, including the new SIO in the event that one had been appointed by then.

As he swung the car into his parking space and yanked on the handbrake, a text message pinged onto his phone. It was his ex, Alice. Dan had lived with her in Sunderland for almost a year, but she'd struggled to adjust to life with a policeman. His erratic work hours, mood swings and occasional bouts of hyperactivity had been too much for her to cope with. He'd moved out of their shared flat six months ago and then moved away from the north east completely when he got his promotion. They still kept in touch, and Alice had visited his new flat in Duffield a couple of times. They were what they jokingly referred to as 'friends with benefits'. Neither of them had started a new relationship, so they weren't averse to sleeping together whenever they met – but it was more out of habit than anything else.

He read Alice's message.

I'm free this weekend if you fancy meeting up for a drink? xx

Dan knew how it would go. She would drive down to see him, or he would go up there, back to their old flat. He knew he should

47

put a stop to it. Clinging on to a relationship with Alice, even as friends, wasn't a good idea. It was time they both moved on.

Sorry, I've started investigating a new case. Will probably be working all weekend. Maybe another time. I'll let you know.

He added a couple of kisses, but then deleted them. He didn't want Alice to think he was pining for her.

Chapter 11

When Dan got out of bed at six-thirty the following morning, he was weary and out of sorts. It had rained heavily during the night and, even now, was still drizzly and cold. He made himself a quick breakfast of muesli and a yoghurt that was two days past its use-by-date, and then set off for work. An early start would mean a long day, but at least he would avoid the worst of the rush-hour traffic.

When he got to the office at seven-thirty, he was disconcerted to find DC Piper already at her desk, fingers tapping at the keyboard of her laptop.

'Blimey, Zoe,' he said. 'Have you been here all night?'

'I couldn't sleep.' She stared at her screen and squinted. 'I thought I'd come in early to update you … run through the checks you asked me to do for the briefing.'

Typical Zoe. Organised. Professional. Thoughtful. All the things Dan should be and wasn't.

He smiled. 'Thanks. I appreciate it.'

She stood up, wheeled her chair over to Dan's desk and began to go over the background information he'd asked her to dig out.

'As well as Celia Aspen's missing person's file, I've got the names of the people who've lived at 23 Ecclesdale Drive over the last forty-five years.' She handed over a list of names.

'The next-door neighbour gave me some details yesterday,' Dan said, pulling out his notebook and comparing the names on Zoe's list with those provided by Joyce Littlewood.

'Do you want me to get some intel on them?' Zoe asked.

Dan pushed the list back towards her. 'The first name on that list ... that's the DI's family. Turns out she has a connection to the house. Lived there as a child, apparently.'

'No way! The Corringtons?' Zoe craned her neck sideways to check her recall on the names.

'I know. What are the chances, eh?' At this stage, he thought it was best to play down his boss's link with the house. 'Anyway, until such time as we can determine a more specific timeframe, there's a potential conflict of interest – so the DI's had to stand down from the case.'

Zoe was no fool. She sat up, her eyes bright like a rabbit on alert. 'Do you think the DI's family could be involved?'

Dan put on his best poker face. 'I doubt it,' he said. 'Then again, you know her better than I do. What can you tell me about her family?'

'Not a lot,' Zoe replied. 'I know that her mum lives in Spain, but she never talks about her dad.'

'Does she have brothers or sisters?'

'Not that I'm aware of. She's never mentioned them.' She shifted in her chair, leaning forward to close the space between them. 'Seriously, is the DI's family being investigated?'

'Let's just say they haven't been ruled out.' He hesitated before continuing, reluctant to sound disloyal. 'The thing is ... yesterday, at the crime scene, I got the impression she was keeping something to herself. Not being totally honest, you know? It's probably my imagination. I mean the DI is known for her reliability, isn't she.'

Zoe smiled. 'You make her sound very dull and boring.'

'I don't mean to,' Dan said, 'but *honest* is her middle name, right?'

'I'm not so sure about that.' Zoe joggled her head. 'It's true she has a reputation for playing things straight, but I don't think she's quite the stickler she's tagged as. Don't get me wrong, she wouldn't do anything crooked, but I get the feeling she'd break a few rules if the circumstances justified it.'

'Like protecting her family, you mean?'

Zoe opened her mouth to respond but was halted by the shrill ringing of the telephone. Dan snatched up the receiver, wondering who was calling so early.

'Morning, Dan. I wasn't sure whether you'd be in yet.'

It was Raveen.

'I'm trying to get a head start on the case,' Dan replied. 'To be honest, I had a restless night ... couldn't switch off.'

'I sympathise,' Raveen said. 'I didn't get much kip either, although the reason for my restlessness was a fretful baby. My son finally fell into a deep, blissful sleep when it was time for me to get up. It's all right for him ... he doesn't have to go to work.'

'I'm hoping this phone call means you've got some news on the bones?'

'They're still being examined. The post-mortem results should be back in a day or so, but what I can tell you is the skeleton is that of a male aged between fifty and seventy. Other than that, there's nothing else to report as yet, but I do have something that helps with the timeframe. The forensics team have cleaned up the lighter we found.'

'And does it have that inscription we talked about?'

He heard Raveen give a low chuckle.

'Not exactly,' he replied, 'but surprisingly, it does have some markings. Why don't you come down and I'll show you what we've found?'

***

Dan decided to take Zoe with him. Their first stop was the Coppa Café opposite the police station, which opened punctually at 7.45 a.m. every day, except Sundays. Its front windows were steamed up, and two dripping umbrellas had been propped up by the door. The hunger-inducing aroma of bacon, coffee and fresh bread wafted towards them as they joined the queue. By the time they reached the counter, Dan was tempted to order a breakfast baguette, but he didn't fancy taking it with him into the forensics unit. Instead, he ordered coffees to go: a flat white for himself and an Americano for Zoe.

'Are we taking one for Raveen?' Zoe asked. 'He likes a latte with one sugar.'

'How do you remember these things? Where do you store all this information?'

Zoe gave him an old-fashioned look. 'In my head, in a file called "useful-to-know". You'd be amazed what I keep in that file.'

Clutching their takeaway coffees and sachets of sugar, they stepped back out into the drizzle and dashed around to the rear of the police station, where Forensics was based. The department had a separate entrance, accessed from Devonshire Street, which necessitated a short walk around the block.

They found Raveen in the lab. There were dark circles under his sleep-deprived eyes and he looked ridiculously grateful when Zoe handed him the coffee.

'Cheers,' he said. 'You don't know how much I needed this.'

He retrieved the evidence bag containing the lighter and placed it on a metal workbench. Dan and Zoe moved in to get a closer look.

'It was clogged with dirt when we found it, but when we removed the soil, we realised it was a Zippo – which is good news.'

'It is?' Dan regarded the plain, white-metal lighter sceptically.

'Definitely. Every Zippo tells its own story. The first examples date back to the 1930s. The lighters are designed to be windproof and they come with a lifetime guarantee. More importantly for us, since the 1950s, every Zippo lighter has had a date code stamped on the bottom, as part of the quality control process.'

'Similar to a hallmark?' Zoe asked. 'To show when the lighter was made?'

'Exactly,' said Raveen. 'The code tells us the year of manufacture.'

He held up the evidence bag, tilting the lighter so that they could read the marks on the bottom of its metal casing. Engraved on either side of the words 'Zippo, Bradford PA' were three backward sloping diagonal lines. Backslashes.

'I looked it up and these slashes are the date code for 1984,' Raveen said. 'The lighter was found underneath the body, which means it was either buried before ... which is unlikely ... or at the same time as the body. My guess is that it was in the victim's back pocket when he was buried and, although his clothing hasn't survived, the lighter has.'

'So the body must have been buried sometime after 1984?' said Dan.

Raveen nodded. 'Sometime between 1984 – the date of the lighter – and about 2007.'

'Why 2007?' Zoe asked.

'Buried without a coffin and in ordinary soil, it takes an adult corpse around twelve years to decompose to a skeleton,' Raveen explained. 'So, it could have been buried as recently as twelve years ago, but possibly as long as thirty-five.'

'That's still a wide timeframe,' Dan said, 'but at least it rules out the years DI Blood's family lived at the house.'

'Does that mean she'll be back on the case?' Zoe asked.

'I'd imagine so, but it'll be up to the Super. I'll ring her when I get back to the office.'

'We also found the remains of a metal zip,' said Raveen. 'Probably from a pair of jeans. There was no sign of any shoes, which is surprising because rubber-soled shoes can take around fifty years to decompose.'

'So the victim wasn't wearing shoes, when he was buried?' said Dan.

'He could have been wearing something lightweight,' Zoe suggested. 'Leather sandals maybe? Slippers or flipflops?'

'We do have the dental plate, of course,' said Raveen. 'We could try and trace dental records, but there's no single database, so it would mean contacting local dentists individually.'

'That sounds time-consuming,' said Zoe.

'Quite,' Raveen said, 'and not guaranteed to be successful either. Realistically, the chances of finding a dental match are pretty slim, especially if the bones date back as far as the 1980s. So … we'll need you guys to do your thing if we're going to have any chance of identifying the victim.'

'In that case, we'd better crack on,' Dan said. 'Come on, Zoe. We'll get a refill on the coffees on the way back. Something tells me we're going to need all the caffeine we can get.'

Chapter 12

Isabel drove to work through the morning rush hour, gazing out at the road through heavy eyelids. She'd had very little sleep the previous night. Lying awake, she'd stared at the bedroom ceiling, turning and fidgeting as she'd mulled over the previous day's events, and speculated on what it was her mother wasn't telling her. The questions had multiplied in her head overnight, like fast-growing bacteria in a petri dish.

As she parked her car in the last staff space at the station, her phone rang. It was Detective Superintendent Tibbet. Before she answered the call, Isabel reminded herself to be careful. She was tired and on edge, and that's when mistakes crept in.

'Morning, Isabel,' the Super said. 'Where are you?'

'I'm parking my car,' she said. 'I'll be inside the station in less than a minute. Do you want me to call in to see you on my way up to the office?'

'Actually, I'm in Matlock for a meeting at the moment,' Val said. 'I'll be out for most of the day. DS Fairfax has just called me with an update, so I thought I'd give you a ring.'

'Sure.' Isabel's heart was banging against her ribcage. 'Any news?'

'Apparently Forensics found a Zippo lighter buried with the

body. They've dated it to 1984, which is obviously several years after your family moved out. The bones are those of a male aged between fifty and seventy and he was suffering from osteoarthritis, but there's no obvious cause of death. I'm sure DS Fairfax will fill you in on all the details. I've asked him to arrange a briefing for eleven.'

Isabel leaned into the headrest as a wave of relief crashed through her solar plexus and pulsed out to every one of her nerve endings. The body wasn't her dad's. It had been buried *after* her family moved out of the house. Thank God she was still sitting in her car. Her knees would have buckled if she'd received this news as she was walking across the car park.

'I haven't had a chance to hand the investigation over to anyone else,' Val said. 'And now that we've got confirmation on the timescales, I can't see any operational reason why you shouldn't be the SIO. You're back in charge, Isabel.'

When the call from the Super was over, Isabel placed her left hand on her midriff to steady her breathing. She felt reprieved. Overwhelmingly so. And yet, irrationally, she was also perturbed – frustrated that her dad's whereabouts remained a mystery.

Her focus right now would have to be on getting up to speed on the case and learning everything that Dan and the team had discovered – but that didn't mean she was going to let go of her own burning questions. Serendipitously, this case had brought the Corrington family secret back under the spotlight. She would call her mother again tonight, and this time Isabel wouldn't let the conversation slip away from her.

***

At one minute to eleven Isabel looked around the light and airy CID room. Located on the top floor of Bainbridge police station, it had a long picture window with an impressive view of

Bainbridge Mill and the river. It was a striking vantage point, but one the CID team rarely had time to admire. Over the last few years, they had been struggling to cope with an increasingly heavy caseload – although, thankfully, murders in the town were few and far between.

Two minutes earlier, DC Lucas Killingworth had sidled into the room ready for the briefing. He lived close to the office and, consequently, was able to time his arrival at work to within minutes of his scheduled start time. As usual, he looked as though he'd just rolled out of bed. His red hair needed combing and his white shirt was clean, but un-ironed.

In stark contrast, DC Zoe Piper looked smart, bright and alert, despite having worked the late shift the night before. Isabel couldn't fault Zoe's work ethic, but there was something slightly tiresome about her eagerness. She was like an anxious, over-zealous puppy, constantly striving to please its owner.

The uniformed officers who'd attended the scene yesterday had been invited to the briefing. They sat together along the back wall, chatting among themselves as they waited for the meeting to start.

Dan had pinned a photograph to the whiteboard and a question mark was written next to it. Isabel hoped they'd be able to make some progress with an ID after the team had discussed and reviewed what they'd learned so far.

Someone had cobbled together a tray of hot drinks and a plate of digestive biscuits. Isabel grabbed one of the mugs gratefully. The coffee was cheap and instant, but it provided a much-needed dose of caffeine.

At eleven o'clock, she stood by the whiteboard next to Dan and clapped her hands. 'OK, everyone, let's make a start, shall we? As you know, the skeleton of an unidentified male was found at 23 Ecclesdale Drive yesterday and, as some of you may have heard, it's the house I lived in as a child. Because of my links with the address, DS Fairfax took charge of the scene initially while we established a more accurate timeframe on when the body was buried.'

She turned to Dan.

'A lighter was found with the body,' he explained. 'It was manufactured in 1984, which means the victim has to have been buried sometime after that.'

Isabel smiled brazenly, daring anyone to challenge her. 'My family moved out of the house in 1978. So, I'm pleased to say I've been eliminated from enquiries.'

A murmur of nervous laughter tumbled across the room.

'Although this means I'm back on the case, I'm going to let Dan lead this morning's briefing. Right now, he knows far more about the situation than I do.'

Dan pushed his hands into his pockets. 'So far, we have very little to work with,' he said. 'Our priority will be to identify the victim. Based on the forensics team's estimated timeframe on the bones, we're looking into anyone who occupied the house between 1984 and 2007.'

'That's one hell of a massive window, Sarge,' said DC Killingworth.

'You're right, Lucas, but we're going to have to work with it – at least until we can narrow things down. Forensics are checking for a possible dental match. A partial dental plate was found with the body, so they might strike it lucky, but it's a long shot, and we can't rely on them to do our job.'

He tapped the grainy black-and-white photograph he'd pinned to the board.

'We do have something that is definitely worth prioritising. This photograph was taken from a missing person's file. Celia Aspen moved into 23 Ecclesdale Drive in 1979 and she disappeared in 1986. She was last seen there in May of that year. There's no evidence yet, but it seems likely her disappearance is connected in some way to the body discovered yesterday.'

'What do we know about Celia Aspen?' Isabel asked.

'A neighbour told me she was a quiet, reserved kind of person who valued her privacy. In other words, she kept herself to herself. Apparently a niece came to see her regularly but, other than that, Celia Aspen had few visitors. However, the neighbour does remember seeing a man at the house about a month before she disappeared.'

'Do we know who he was?' said Lucas.

'I'm afraid not. According to the neighbour, he was in his late sixties or early seventies, he lived in Canada, and he was originally from Nottingham. That's all the information we have.'

'What was the name of the neighbour you spoke to?' Isabel asked.

'Mrs Littlewood. Joyce Littlewood.'

Isabel smiled. 'Mrs L? Blimey, is she still around?'

'Yes, I spoke to her last night. She's lived at number 25 since the house was new, so I thought you'd remember her. She must be in her eighties, but she seems razor-sharp and fairly spritely for her age. There certainly doesn't seem to be anything wrong with her memory.'

'When I lived there, she knew everything and everyone on the street. Nothing much got past Joyce Littlewood.'

'That doesn't surprise me in the least,' Dan said wryly. 'I don't think I'd want her as my neighbour, but she was a mine of information once she got talking. She even remembered the name of the niece.'

'Which was?'

'Julie Desmond. She was the person who reported Celia missing in September 1986.'

Zoe jiggled her mouse to wake up her computer screen. 'She also inherited the house ... once her aunt was declared dead, that is. According to the case file, the niece was in Australia when her aunt went missing. She flew out to Sydney on 11th May 1986 and Celia Aspen was last seen on 15th May. Julie was away for three months and, when she came back, she assumed her aunt

59

had gone to visit a friend in Canada. When she hadn't heard from her by September, she checked her aunt's belongings, found her passport, and realised she wasn't in Canada after all. That's when she reported her missing.'

'Who was the last person to see Celia Aspen alive?' Isabel said.

Zoe checked her notes. 'A Timothy Littlewood. Presumably a relation of Joyce Littlewood?'

'Her son,' Isabel and Dan said simultaneously.

'He lives with her,' Dan explained. 'He has ASD and, interestingly, both Timothy and Joyce Littlewood had a few run-ins with Celia Aspen over the years.'

'I knew Tim,' Isabel said. 'He was a few years younger than me, but I do recall some of the kids on the street giving him a tough time. Back then – and we're talking the Seventies, so don't expect political correctness – people used to say that Tim was slow or odd. *Not quite the full shilling.* Horrible, I know, but that's how people were in those days. Cruel and insensitive. As far as I know, Tim hadn't been flagged as being autistic back then, although I'm not sure whether that kind of proper diagnosis would have been available. Even if it was, I don't suppose I would have been told about it.'

Dan wrote Joyce and Timothy Littlewood's names on the board before turning back to face Zoe. 'Is there anything else in the missing person's file that we should talk about? Anything that could connect Celia Aspen's disappearance with the body found yesterday?'

Zoe shook her head. 'Sorry, 'fraid not. The usual enquiries were made when she went missing, and a body did turn up a few months later on Beeley Moor. They ran a check, but the remains weren't Celia Aspen's.'

'What about the people who moved into the house after she'd disappeared?' Isabel said.

'The house stood empty for several years,' Zoe told her. 'It was eventually sold in 1993 to Joseph and Rhoda Repton. He died a couple of years ago and Rhoda Repton is now living in a care home. Two months ago, the house was sold at auction to the current owners, Paul and Amy Whitworth.'

'Anything we should know about the Reptons?' Dan said. 'Any incidents? Reports of domestic violence?'

'Nothing so far.' Zoe looked guilty, as though it was her fault there was nothing to report.

'In that case, it's looking increasingly likely that the body was buried sometime during Celia Aspen's ownership of the house,' said Dan. 'We can't be certain though. It could have been later. We can't rule anything out – so we need to keep looking and exploring every possibility.'

'Not wishing to state the obvious,' Isabel said, 'but to stand any chance of finding our killer, we first need to establish who the victim is. In order to investigate the crime, we have to investigate the victim. If we can identify who the bones belong to, we can begin to work out why they were killed and who our suspects are.'

'Isn't Celia Aspen the most obvious suspect?' said Lucas. 'Seems likely she killed this bloke, buried him in her garden and disappeared to avoid detection.'

'If that is the case, I doubt we'll ever find out why she did it or get a conviction,' Zoe said. 'Celia Aspen was sixty-eight when she was reported missing. I'd rate the likelihood of her still being alive as somewhere between improbable and impossible.'

'Joyce Littlewood said much the same thing,' Dan said. 'She reckoned Celia would be over a hundred if she is still alive.'

Isabel held up her hands. 'Hang on a minute, guys. There are quite a few assumptions being made here. I agree that Celia Aspen's disappearance may be linked to the murder – but let's not automatically assume that she's the perpetrator. What's to say she isn't a second victim?'

Dan looked sceptical. 'The CSIs have carried out an initial

61

search of the whole garden,' he said. 'There are no obvious signs of a second body.'

'Her body could have been disposed of elsewhere,' Isabel remarked. 'Anyway, even if she did kill this bloke, why would she go to the trouble of burying him in her garden and then do a runner? If she *was* guilty, staying put would have been far more sensible. Why draw attention to herself by disappearing.'

Isabel was met with a wall of silence.

'All I'm saying is that we need to keep an open mind about who the possible perpetrator might be. Murder is rarely straightforward and we owe it to the victim to follow every lead, no matter how tenuous it might seem.'

Dan frowned. 'The problem isn't following up the leads, boss. It's finding them in the first place.'

'So, what's the plan, Dan?' Isabel smiled. 'What lines of enquiry do you suggest?'

Dan exhaled anxiously. 'We need to track down Celia Aspen's niece, and I think we need to go back and talk to Joyce Littlewood again.'

'OK.' Isabel pointed at DC Killingworth. 'Lucas, see if you can track down what happened to Julie Desmond. Zoe, carry on with the background check on the Reptons.'

Dan nodded at the uniformed officers. 'We also need to ask around in the neighbourhood,' he said. 'There must be people other than the Littlewoods who remember Celia.'

'Do your best, everyone,' said Isabel. 'This crime may have been committed a long time ago, but we need to show that we're taking it seriously. Bainbridge residents won't be happy about having a possible unsolved murder in the town.'

'According to the Super, the comms team have already been fielding enquiries from the media,' Dan said.

'I'll contact the media officer and agree a statement for the press,' Isabel said. 'We'll make an appeal for anyone with any information to come forward.'

She looked through the window. Outside, the sky was pigeon grey and fat raindrops were trickling down the window. 'Get your raincoat, Dan. You're with me. You and I are going to see Joyce Littlewood.'

Chapter 13

By the time they got to Joyce Littlewood's place the grey clouds had begun to clear and the rain had reverted to a light drizzle. They walked round to the rear of the house and Isabel stood back as Dan rapped his knuckles on the door's frosted pane.

'Careful,' she said, indicating the desiccated putty that was barely holding in the glass. 'That whole panel will fall out if you knock too loudly.'

'She's hard of hearing,' Dan explained. 'Apparently she doesn't wear her hearing aids. Says they whistle.'

'Nathan's eldest sister said the same thing. She abandoned hers before she'd given herself time to get used to them. I've got this theory that there are thousands of unused hearing aids sitting in drawers all over the country. It must be costing the NHS a fortune.'

When Joyce Littlewood opened the door, she peered out at Dan and smiled. 'Oh, it's you again. Got more questions for me have you, duck?'

'Yes, if you don't mind. And I've brought my boss with me today.'

Mrs Littlewood opened the door, took one look at Isabel and beamed.

'You can put that away,' she said, pointing to the warrant card

Isabel was holding up. 'No need to show your ID. I'd know you anywhere. It's young Isabel Corrington, isn't it? You've hardly changed at all.'

Isabel smiled. 'If only that were true. As for young Isabel Corrington ... well, I'm old Isabel Blood these days. DI Blood.'

'I heard you'd joined the police force. Even saw you on telly a few years back doing some sort of press conference. I knew you'd end up doing well for yourself. You always were a clever girl.'

They followed Joyce Littlewood through the kitchen and into the living room, where she invited them to sit on the settee. Its patterned nylon covers clashed with the swirling-rose design on the Axminster carpet.

'Must seem funny for you, Isabel. Working a case at your old house.'

'You could say that,' Isabel replied. 'I know that you and DS Fairfax had a chat yesterday, but I wondered if we could trouble you for some more information.'

'Course you can. As I'm sure you remember, there's not much I don't know about the residents of Ecclesdale Drive. Some people call me nosy, but I like to think of myself as neighbourly. Folks don't look out for each other anymore, not like they did in the Sixties and Seventies. Things were better back then.'

'People tend to spend most of their time at work these days,' Isabel said.

'You're right about that. They don't even stop for a chat. Plenty of time to look at their phones, mind you, but not to pass the time of day with a nosy old bugger like me.'

'We wondered if you'd remembered anything more about Celia Aspen, specifically the weeks prior to her disappearance?' Dan said. 'Or about the man you saw her with in the garden?'

Joyce ignored Dan's questions and fired off one of her own.

'How are your parents, Isabel? Still alive and well, I hope.'

Isabel fidgeted uncomfortably. The last thing she wanted to

do was discuss the wellbeing of her family with Joyce Littlewood.

'Mum's lived in Spain for the last five years.'

'Very nice. Can't beat a bit of sun and Sangria, can you?'

Isabel smiled inwardly at the thought of her mother drinking Sangria.

'What about your dad?' Joyce always had been persistent. It was a characteristic that clearly hadn't diminished with age. 'It was a real shame when he and your mum split up.'

Isabel pulled a 'help-me-out-here' face at Dan, who was quick to pick up on her distress signal.

'Do you know anything about whether Celia Aspen was planning a trip to Canada?' he said. 'Prior to reporting her aunt missing, the niece had assumed she was out there visiting a friend.'

Grudgingly, Joyce turned towards him. 'I don't know anything about that,' she replied. 'That's something you'd have to talk to Julie about. As I told you yesterday, Celia and I weren't on friendly terms. If she did have travel plans, she kept them to herself. It's not the sort of thing she would have shared with me. Mind you, she wasn't in the best of health, I can tell you that. It's hard to imagine she'd want to fly all the way to Canada.'

'What kind of health problems did she have?' said Isabel.

'I don't know any details. As I've already told your colleague, Celia was a private person, certainly not the sort to talk about her ailments. Everyone has a right to their privacy, I suppose. I only know she wasn't well because Julie once let it slip that Celia was on the waiting list for an operation.'

Dan scribbled something in his notebook.

'The man I saw in the garden was Canadian, of course,' Joyce added. 'Well ... not Canadian born, but he said he lived there. Who knows, perhaps Celia intended visiting him.'

'I realise it's a long shot,' Dan said, 'but do you remember if the man in the garden was smoking a cigarette when you saw him?'

'Not a cigarette, but he did have a pipe. He was smoking it

while he was out in the garden. I remember the sweet smell of the tobacco. It was typical of Celia to make him light up outside. She'd have the occasional ciggy herself, but she only ever smoked in the garden. She hated the smell of cigarettes in the house, you see. I'd see her standing on the back yard in all weathers, puffing away. There's no way she would have allowed anyone to light a pipe indoors.'

'I understand that Timothy was the last person to see Celia Aspen before she disappeared,' Isabel said.

'Yes, he went round there to do some work for her. To tell the truth, I wasn't too happy with the arrangement. Julie had asked him for a favour. She had Timothy wrapped around her little finger.'

'What kind of job was he doing? Can you remember? Was it gardening? Something in the house?'

'He wouldn't have gone inside. Not with the way things were. It was a minor outside repair as I recall. Something to do with a trellis. Timothy saw Celia through the window, but he didn't speak to her. You're welcome to come back and talk to him about it, but it all happened a long time ago. I'm not sure how much he'll remember.'

'You said you weren't happy about Timothy going round next door,' Dan said. 'Were you tempted to tell him not to bother?'

'Yes, to be frank, I was – but Timothy was a grown man by then and capable of making his own decisions. I think the job was something that Julie would normally have done, but she was abroad and she asked him to go round and do it instead.'

'Do you know where Julie is now?' Isabel said.

'Not a clue. I haven't seen her for donkey's years. From what I heard she went back out to Australia after her aunty disappeared. I think she'd met some bloke out there.'

'What about Joe and Rhoda Repton,' said Dan. 'Did you get on well with them? What kind of neighbours were they?'

Joyce's face softened. 'The best kind,' she said. 'We were a similar age and we got on like a house on fire. They were so kind to Timothy and lovely with my grandkids.'

'How many grandchildren do you have, Joyce?' Isabel asked.

'Four. My daughter has two boys and my eldest son has a boy and a girl. They're grown up now.'

She reached for one of the framed photographs on the mantelpiece and passed it to Isabel.

'Did the Reptons ever have any problems?' Dan asked. 'Did they argue with each other or with anyone else? Were they ever bothered by any troublesome family members?'

'No.' Joyce shook her head emphatically. 'There was never any hassle with the Reptons. They had one son and he was a nice lad. He worked in London for a while but came back to Derbyshire about ten years ago. Lovely family.'

'OK, well I think that's all for now, Joyce.' Isabel stood up and returned the photograph to its position above the fireplace. 'We may need to come back and speak to Timothy. What time does he get in from work?'

'Depends what shift he's on. He's doing earlies for a couple of weeks, so he'll be home at about two o'clock today and all next week.'

Isabel gave the old woman's arm a gentle squeeze. 'It's been good talking to you again. Glad to see you looking so well.'

'You too, Isabel. You're a real blast from the past. Give my best to your mum next time you speak to her.'

Isabel nodded. 'I'll be sure to let her know I've seen you.'

Chapter 14

'Well, that was a waste of time,' Dan said, as they walked back to the car. 'We're no further forward.'

'We do have one extra piece of information. We know that Celia's visitor smoked a pipe.'

'Do you think he was the owner of the lighter?'

'It's possible. Zippos are made in the USA. Do you think someone living in Canada is more likely to own one than someone in the UK?'

'Not necessarily,' Dan said. 'I owned a Zippo once, and I don't even smoke. Anyway, we found a lighter with the body, but there was no sign of a pipe.'

'Good point,' Isabel said. 'But aren't pipes usually made of wood? Surely it would have rotted away by now?'

'I'm not sure about that. I'd imagine the stem would be made of some kind of plastic or resin. We'd have to check with Raveen.'

Isabel dug around in her coat pocket for her car keys. 'Joyce also said that Celia wasn't in the best of health. That makes her even less likely to be our killer. Do you honestly think she would have been capable of digging a grave and moving a body if she was ill?'

Dan shrugged. 'Perhaps she had help.'

'You could be right. It's something to bear in mind.'

She unlocked the car and they got inside, but instead of starting the engine and driving away, she sat for a moment and stared up at the first floor of number 23, to the window that had once been her bedroom.

She wished she could have remembered the house as a warm, cosy place to live – but when her family had moved in, there had been no central heating or double glazing. The only source of warmth had been a coal fire in the living room, which her mother had insisted on calling 'the lounge'. At night there had been winceyette nighties and brushed cotton sheets, hot water bottles, and woollen blankets topped with a pink feather eiderdown. Isabel would wake on winter mornings to find Jack Frost patterns frozen onto the inside of her bedroom window.

She supposed she had been impervious to the cold in those days because, despite a lack of heating, the house had seemed a safe, loving place in which to grow up. It had been far from perfect, but there had been days, sometimes weeks of happiness. And then her father left and everything had changed.

'Looks like the forensics team have nearly finished,' Dan said, his voice jolting her back to the present. 'The owner will be pleased. He was chomping at the bit to get on with his extension.'

'Champing,' Isabel said.

'Sorry?'

'The original expression was *champing* at the bit. A lot of people say *chomping* these days but, strictly speaking, it isn't correct.'

Dan frowned. 'Right, well, thanks for correcting my grammar, boss. Sorry if my misuse of the English language has offended you.'

Isabel smiled. 'Sorry. I didn't mean to be picky.'

The way Dan lifted an eyebrow suggested that he didn't believe her.

70

'Should we go and see if they're in?' she said. 'The Whitworths, I mean?'

'It's up to you ... although I'm not sure what else they can tell us. It's not as if they're suspects. They've only owned the house for a few weeks.'

'You're right.' She pushed the key into the ignition, but still didn't start the engine. 'Maybe I'm looking for an excuse to have a poke around my old stomping ground.'

'Are you sure you don't mean stamping ground?'

She laughed. 'Touché.'

Dan looked out through the windscreen towards the house. 'Must be weird for you, being back here.'

Isabel cocked her head. 'I wouldn't call it weird,' she said. 'It's more unsettling than anything. This is my childhood home ... for me it has a kind of primordial pull. I've changed, and the house has changed, but when I look at it now, I see things as they were and it makes me feel sad.'

'Memories, eh?'

She gave a shallow sigh. 'Yep. Some happy times. Unhappy ones too. I had my whole life ahead of me when I lived here. Being back makes me grieve for all the people and things I left behind. Once something's truly lost, I'm not sure you can ever get it back.'

'Well, in my opinion, there are some things you're better off without. Onwards and upwards, that's what I always say.'

Isabel forced a smile, trying to quell the inner turmoil that was threatening her equanimity. 'You're probably right.'

'If you don't mind my saying, boss, you seem out of sorts. Are you OK? Is there something you're not telling me?'

She hesitated, wondering how best to respond. 'This case has opened up a can of worms for me, Dan – on a personal level.' She blinked to disguise the sadness in her eyes. 'I know I've been subdued. I can be a right maudlin cow at times, can't I?'

Dan grinned. 'No comment.'

71

She laughed, warming to his sense of humour.

'There are some things I've not told you,' she admitted, 'but they're not connected to the case, so they're not really relevant now.'

'Fair-dos,' Dan said. 'It's up to you, but if you do want to talk, I'm a good listener.'

Isabel drummed her fingers on the steering wheel, trying to decide whether or not to confide in him. She barely knew Dan, but a lack of familiarity often made it easier to open up about things.

'My parents split up in 1977,' she said, making up her mind to share. 'My dad walked out one day and didn't come back. We've never seen or heard from him since.'

Dan grunted sympathetically. Isabel waited, watching his eyebrows shoot up as he realised the implications of what she'd told him.

'Bloody hell!' he said. 'So you must have wondered …?'

'Whether it was my dad buried in that garden?' She inclined her head towards number 23 as she finished his sentence. 'Let's just say that my imagination bombarded me with all sorts of possibilities.'

'I had a gut feeling something wasn't right,' Dan said. 'I'm still getting to know you, but you seem like a pretty tough cookie, and I could tell something had shaken you. I just didn't know what.'

'The whole scenario was a complete fucking nightmare,' Isabel said. 'Everything was spiralling out of control. The thought that it might be him terrified me, and yet … in a way, it would have been the answer to my prayers.'

She paused, mortified by her own words. 'You must think I'm awful saying that, but all my life I've carried this vexing, unanswered question around with me … It's been an agonising puzzle, and there have been times when it's sabotaged my happiness. Obviously if the body *had* been my dad's, it wouldn't have been the outcome I wanted, but I would have welcomed an answer – any answer – no matter how unsavoury.'

'Doesn't your mum know what happened to him?'

Isabel shook her head. 'She's never told me anything. I asked often enough, at least in the beginning, but she's always been tight-lipped on the subject.'

Dan listened silently.

'As a kid, I found it incredibly frustrating,' Isabel continued. 'It was probably the reason I ended up joining the force. I wanted a career that was a complete contrast to my own life ... a job that gave me the authority to investigate, find explanations and solutions. Naïvely, I hoped being with the police might help me locate my dad. Early on in my career, I even made a few covert searches of the police database – that's how desperate I was to find him.'

'Wow, you wouldn't get away with that nowadays.' Dan seemed shocked and mildly disapproving.

'I wouldn't have gotten away with it then if they'd found out.'

'Why didn't you say anything about your dad when you stood down from the case?' Dan asked. 'Seems to me you're not as squeaky clean as people say, DI Blood.'

His audacity made her laugh, which dissolved any tension between them. 'I would have said something eventually, if it had been necessary. But surely you can understand my reluctance? This was a big deal for me. I was on the verge of accusing my mother of ...' She glanced at him, wondering if she'd already said too much.

'Accusing her of what?'

'It doesn't matter.' She pinched the bridge of her nose. 'The things that were running through my head don't bear thinking about. As it turns out, there was no need for me to worry, was there? The body was buried years after Dad left home.'

'True.' Dan nodded. 'I'm guessing that news must have come

73

as a huge relief, but it does kind of leave things in the air. You still don't know what happened to your dad, do you?'

He was right. Despite the emotional rollercoaster she'd been riding for the last twenty-four hours, Isabel remained firmly in the dark, and it rankled.

Determined to pursue and unscramble the riddle of what had happened to her father, she doubled her resolve to ring her mother again later that evening.

***

When they got back to the station, Dan was called out almost immediately to investigate reports of an armed robbery at a petrol station on the outskirts of Bainbridge. Isabel retreated behind her glass-partitioned office to update the case log and catch up on emails and paperwork.

At three o'clock, Zoe stuck her head round the door to ask if she wanted a cup of tea.

'Thanks, I'd love one. Nice and strong, eh? Make sure you squeeze the teabag.'

Zoe was munching on a bar of chocolate when she placed the steaming mug on Isabel's desk. 'There you go,' she said. 'How did the interview with Joyce Littlewood go?'

'OK.' She sipped the scalding tea tentatively. 'She told us that Celia Aspen's visitor smoked a pipe, so it's possible he was the owner of the lighter. We're still grasping at straws though. What about you? You were going to double check on the Reptons. Find anything?'

'Nothing at all,' Zoe said. 'No criminal records ... absolutely nothing on the PNC or any of the other databases. They weren't on our radar at all, although I did find an online obituary for Joe Repton. He sounds like a model citizen. He was a member of the local allotment society, he enjoyed watching cricket, and Rhoda was described as his devoted wife – hardly the kind of couple that would kill someone and bury the body in the back garden.'

'Crimes aren't always committed by bad people, Zoe. Even the nice ones can do terrible things if circumstances drive them to it.'

Zoe lowered her eyes. 'I've traced Rhoda's son,' she said. 'Do you want me to talk to him?'

'Give him a call and then pay him a visit if you feel you need to. What about Lucas? Has he located Julie Desmond yet?'

Zoe pushed the last piece of chocolate into her mouth and licked her fingers. 'I don't know,' she said. 'Shall I send him in?'

'Do that,' Isabel said. 'And thanks for the tea, Zoe.'

***

Lucas gave her door a cursory knock before sloping into the office and flopping onto the chair on the other side of her desk.

'You wanted to see me, boss?'

Lucas was a nice lad and good at his job. His manners, on the other hand, left a lot to be desired. Isabel felt sure he didn't mean to be rude. To Lucas, it came naturally.

'How are you getting on with tracking down Celia Aspen's niece?' she asked.

'I've got an address for her in Melbourne. Turns out she's actually Celia's great-niece. Julie's paternal grandmother must have been Celia's sister. I got the address from Julie's mother, Mary Summers. She lives in Matlock. She was also questioned at the time of Celia Aspen's disappearance, so we might want to talk to her again at some point.'

'I'm sure we will. For now, we'll start with Julie Desmond. Email the contact details to me and I'll get in touch with her.'

***

Isabel left the office just before five o'clock, but instead of heading straight home, she decided to drive to Ellie's school to see the art exhibition. She was feeling increasingly guiltridden about not staying to see it after the parents' evening, especially as art seemed to be the one subject her daughter was taking seriously.

From an early age, Ellie had loved to express her creativity through a variety of artistic media, and Isabel was determined to do everything possible to encourage her talent. Viewing the exhibition at the school seemed an obvious way to do that.

There was something weird about walking into the unnatural silence of an empty school. It was like lifting the lid of a piano and discovering the keys were missing. The main entrance was deserted and the reception area shuttered, but Isabel knew where to find the main hall. Forty years ago, she'd been a pupil here herself – she was familiar with the building's puzzling architectural layout.

Her shoes squeaked on the polished floor as she approached the hall. Pulling back one of the double doors, she stepped into a space illuminated by a set of brash lights. A huge showcase of student artwork had been pinned to large boards positioned along the walls. Each piece had the artist's name printed above it, together with their age and the title of the piece. Three other people were wandering around, admiring the exhibition.

It was easy to spot Ellie's work among the displays. Her style was distinctive and detailed and used bright, bold blocks of colour. Isabel went straight over to the first of her daughter's paintings, which was called *Distance*. It showed Bainbridge's main shopping street from above, as though viewed from a drone. Next to it was a pop art style cartoon. Ellie had drawn herself alongside a male figure Isabel didn't recognise. A speech bubble coming from the man's mouth said *Why, Ellie, this painting is a masterpiece. Soon you'll have all of Bainbridge clamouring for your work.*

'It's a play on Roy Lichtenstein's *Masterpiece*,' said a voice.

When Isabel turned, she found herself staring at the man from the cartoon.

'That's you … in the picture.' She laughed.

'Yes, I'm David Allerton, Ellie Blood's art teacher.'

'And I'm her mother.' Isabel shook his hand.

'Your daughter really is very gifted. I hope she'll continue with her art through to A level and beyond.'

'I hope so too,' said Isabel. 'My husband's an illustrator and I think Ellie must have inherited his artistic gene. She certainly doesn't get it from me.'

David Allerton smiled good-naturedly.

'We came to see Ellie's form tutor yesterday,' she said, wondering if he might be able to offer an insight into Ellie's recent behaviour. 'My daughter seems to have acquired a bad rap with the teachers. Your report was the only one that said anything positive about her.'

The art teacher looked disappointed and a little embarrassed. 'The trouble with Ellie is, she's easily influenced,' he said. 'A couple of her mates have been displaying very negative behaviour this term, and I think some of that has rubbed off on her. The good news is she's started to be more selective about her friends over the last couple of weeks. She's been hanging out with a new girl … Lily Nashwood. Have you met her?'

'No, not yet.' Isabel speculated on whether Nathan knew about this burgeoning friendship. 'Is she a good kid?'

'I'd say so,' David Allerton replied. 'She and Ellie seem to have a lot in common. I'd try to encourage the friendship if I were you.'

'Thanks,' Isabel said. 'I will.'

Chapter 15

When she arrived home, Isabel was greeted by the spicy aroma of chicken curry, prepared by Nathan using one of his secret recipes. It was comfort food at its best: hot, filling and delicious.

She had rung him earlier to let him know about the new timeframe on the bones, and she knew this culinary offering was his way of helping her to de-stress.

'Thanks for cooking.' She stood behind him in the kitchen, wrapped her arms around his waist and rested her head in the space between his shoulder blades.

'I had a sudden craving for curry,' he said. 'It's been a while since I made one.'

'Ellie'll be pleased. It's her favourite. Where is she?'

Nathan stirred the pot and tilted his head at the ceiling.

'Upstairs. Doing her homework.'

Isabel raised her eyebrow in surprise.

'I know. I almost don't want to shout her down for dinner.'

Isabel picked up a damp dishcloth and used it to wipe away a blob of tomato puree that had crash-landed on the worktop.

'I called in at the school on my way home,' she said. 'To see the art exhibition.'

'What did you think to Ellie's work?'

'Brilliant,' she said. 'Really good. They were the best pieces on show.'

Pride played with the edges of Nathan's lips. 'I agree,' he said. 'Then again, I suppose we're biased.'

'That's true.' Isabel rinsed the dishcloth and folded it into a neat square. 'Did you know she's been hanging out with someone called Lily?'

'Yes, she's new to the area apparently, started at the school at the beginning of term. She's been here a couple of times after school. Seems nice enough.'

'You've met her? When was this?'

'Earlier last week,' Nathan said. 'She called round while you were at work. She didn't stay for long.'

'Right.' Isabel tried to sound nonchalant, but inwardly she was chastising herself. Here she was again, playing catch-up. She wished she could be more like Nathan, tuned in to what Ellie was doing. He was so much better at the whole parenting thing. Always had been.

'Dinner's ready to serve up,' he said, giving the pot one last stir before turning off the heat. 'I'll give her a shout.'

'It's OK,' Isabel said. 'I'll go up and get her.'

***

She found Ellie sprawled across her duvet with her earphones in. Sure enough, she was writing in a notebook and there was a history textbook open on the pillow.

'Ey up, love. How's it going?'

'OK,' she said, removing one earphone. 'Checking up on me, are you?'

'As a matter of fact, I came to tell you that I went to see the school art exhibition on my way home. I was massively impressed with your pieces. I'm very proud of you, but you know that already, right?'

79

Ellie grinned and frowned at the same time.

'I spoke to your art teacher while I was there. He was full of praise for your work. He thinks you're really gifted.'

Ellie accepted the compliment self-effacingly, but the quick smile she flashed suggested it had pleased her.

'I hear you have a new friend ... Lily.'

'Yeah.' Ellie sat up. 'I like her. She's nice. She's asked if I want to go to her house after school tomorrow. They've asked me to stay for dinner.'

If I hadn't mentioned Lily, would Ellie even have bothered telling me about this? Isabel wondered.

'That's nice of her, although perhaps we should speak to her parents before you go over to her house. Where does she live?'

'Does it matter?'

'We need to know where you are, Ellie.'

'Everything's cool, Mum. Dad knows where Lily lives. He's met her already.'

'I know. He told me. Does he know you've been invited to her house tomorrow?'

Ellie picked up her phone and began to scroll through something on the screen. 'I was going to tell him tonight. Lily's going to ask her mum to send Dad a text, to let him know it's OK for me to go.'

Unaccountably, Isabel felt left out. Snubbed.

'Talking of dinner,' she said, pushing aside her hurt feelings, 'the other thing I came to tell you is that Dad's ready to serve up, but I can ask him to hold off for a while, if you want to finish your essay.'

Ellie slapped her notebook shut, pulled out the other earphone and leaped off the bed.

'No, you're all right. He's done a chicken curry and I'm starving.'

As she watched her daughter tear down the stairs to the kitchen, Isabel realised she hadn't seen her in such an upbeat mood for ages. Such unbridled cheerfulness pleased Isabel. Perhaps this new friend was exactly what Ellie needed.

***

A text buzzed on Isabel's phone as Nathan was serving second helpings. Glancing down, she saw it was from her mother, and decided to ignore it until after they'd finished eating. After all, she was the first to complain if Ellie used her mobile at the table.

She left the text unopened until after she and Nathan had done the pots. They rarely used the dishwasher, preferring instead to stand side-by-side and talk as they washed and dried. It was 'their time': a chance to catch up on their respective days.

'Mother's sent me a message,' Isabel said quietly, after they'd finished discussing the sense of relief she'd felt when she'd found out the body wasn't her father's.

'Did she say any more about your dad?'

'I don't know, I haven't read it yet.' She tossed the tea towel over her shoulder after drying the last piece of cutlery. 'I didn't want to spoil our meal together. I'll go and read it now, see what she has to say for herself, then I'll ring her. She owes me some answers.'

Isabel put the plates and glasses away and then went to sit in the garden room. Outside, cold autumnal rain was tapping on the windows and, after lighting the wood burner, she settled back into the closest armchair to get warm. Pulling out her phone, she opened the text message from her mother.

It's time I told you the truth. I need to see you, face-to-face. The things I have to say are too important to discuss over the phone. I've booked myself on a flight to East Midlands tomorrow. I land at 14.40. Please pick me up at the airport. xx

'Shit!' Isabel sat up and ran a hand through her hair.

Nathan came in, carrying a cafetière and two mugs.

'Mum's coming over,' she said, shock resonating in her voice. 'Tomorrow.'

'Hell's teeth.' He stopped mid-stride and jerked back his head. '*Tomorrow?* Did you know she was planning this?' He plonked the cafetière and mugs on the coffee table and dropped heavily onto the sofa.

'No. She didn't say anything about it when I spoke to her last night. She just refused to answer my questions and then hung up on me.'

Isabel felt conflicted. On the face of it, she was annoyed that her mother was imposing herself on them at short notice, but deep down she felt a sense of relief. The needy, insecure part of her soul yearned for answers that only her mother could provide.

'Call me naïve,' Isabel said, 'but I thought she'd check with me first before booking a flight.'

'It's typical of old Babs. Act first and think later.'

'She'd be livid if she heard you calling her old Babs.'

Nathan laughed. 'Good job she's not here then, isn't it?'

'Well, make the most of it, because she'll be here soon enough – and she'll need picking up from the airport. Her flight lands at 2.40 p.m.'

'And you're telling me this because ...?'

'I'll be at work,' Isabel said. 'I've got visits scheduled for tomorrow.'

'Contrary to popular belief, I also have a job.' Nathan sat up and pushed the plunger into the cafetière with a tad too much force. 'Just because I work from home doesn't mean I can break off whenever it suits me. I do have deadlines to meet.'

'I'm sorry. I know you do. Ordinarily, I'd text her back and tell her to cancel the flight, but this situation is anything but ordinary. It seems she's finally willing to talk to me, but the only way she'll do that is face-to-face. Part of me is dreading her coming over, but another part can't wait for her to arrive so that I can find out about Dad.'

'OK.' Nathan sighed and began to pour the coffee. 'I'll pick her up, but make sure you finish work on time tomorrow.'

'I will. I promise. I'll even get a takeaway on the way home. It'll save you having to cook.'

'No, don't do that,' Nathan replied. 'I'd prefer to be in the kitchen, out of the way. You need to have some time alone with your mother. You've got a lot to talk about.'

Chapter 16

The next morning Isabel pulled on her warmest running gear and let herself out of the house. She ran down the street and veered onto the lane that led to the fields above the town. The dawn had pushed aside a wet blanket of overnight rain, exposing a new day in all its brittle beauty. The sun was appearing shyly in a glowing sky, and delicate wisps of cloud trailed high above the copse at the top of the hill, drifting like white feathers. Somewhere in the distance, a dog barked. Isabel had the hillside to herself, which was exactly how she liked it.

She usually went for a run every couple of days, using the time productively by sifting through whatever was worrying her. With each step, she sorted things in her mind, categorising them as either significant or insignificant. As she pushed on up through the fields, she threw off the unimportant things, crushing them underfoot like dry, autumn leaves.

By the time she reached the top of the hill Isabel was pulling in deep, noisy breaths, but she felt refreshed and energised. For the first time in two days, her head was clear and she felt ready to face the day ahead.

***

She got to the office a few minutes before eight. By starting early, she hoped to be able to finish on time. Her mother's imminent arrival would rule out any possibility of turning up late for dinner this evening.

DS Fairfax ambled into the office at eight-thirty. 'Morning, boss,' he said. 'We got a good result on the armed robbery yesterday. Footage on the CCTV ties it in with a similar incident last week over in Derby. We're bringing the suspects in for questioning later today.'

'Great. Are you OK to do the interview?'

'Yep.' Dan gave her a thumbs-up. 'I'll get Lucas to sit in with me.'

'Did I tell you he managed to get an address for me yesterday for Julie Desmond? She's living in Melbourne. I think we should go and speak to her face-to-face. Is that OK with you?'

'Melbourne?' Dan looked surprised. 'Sure. Not a problem.'

'I've already given her a call,' Isabel said. 'We're going today.'

Dan shuffled his feet. 'What about the interviews this afternoon?'

'No worries, as the Australians say. You'll be back in plenty of time.'

When a puzzled frown creased Dan's brow, Isabel decided it was time to put him out of his misery.

'You didn't think I meant Melbourne, Australia, did you?' She released the pent-up laughter she'd been holding on to. 'Julie Desmond moved back to the UK about twenty years ago. She's living in Melbourne, Derbyshire. It's a small market town in the south of the county.'

Dan smiled. 'You had me going there for a minute, boss.'

'Sorry, Dan. I couldn't resist. Let's wait for the traffic to ease off and then we'll get going. We're expected at ten-thirty.'

***

Isabel had arranged to visit Julie Desmond at her place of work, which was a hair and beauty salon on Melbourne high street. The exterior woodwork of the building was painted a de rigueur shade of gunmetal-grey, and the name of the salon – *Jules* – was etched in a minimalist typeface on a silver sign above the door. A metallic-blue BMW with a personalised number plate was parked directly in front of the entrance.

Isabel and Dan went inside and waited at a walnut-veneered reception desk, where a price list for a range of expensive hair and beauty treatments was prominently displayed.

A young woman approached them, wearing a name badge that identified her as 'Daisy'. Her highly stylised eyebrows were too dark for her fair complexion; they clung to her forehead like a pair of hungry leeches.

'I'm DI Blood and this is DS Fairfax. We're here to see Julie Desmond.'

'She's expecting you.' Daisy fluttered her eyelash extensions at Dan and pointed towards the rear of the building. 'You'll find her down there, in the office at the back.'

The salon was long and narrow with mirrored walls, cream leather chairs and a tall, glass shelf unit displaying a range of luxury hair products. Crossing the tiled floor, Isabel and Dan walked past a row of treatment rooms to a door marked 'Office'. As it was ajar, Isabel felt no compulsion to knock. Instead, she poked her head into the room and smiled.

'Julie Desmond? I'm DI Blood and this is my colleague DS Fairfax. We spoke on the phone.'

'Yes. Of course. Please, come in and sit down.'

She and Julie were about the same age, but that's where any similarity ended. Isabel's own hairstyle was a flyaway fringed bob, whereas Julie sported a short, neat, precision cut. Its brown base colour was highlighted with flashes of chestnut, chocolate, caramel and blonde. The finished effect reminded Isabel of the wings of a house sparrow.

Julie was tall and thick-set but elegantly dressed in casual clothes – a long, white linen blouse over a pair of black designer jeans. A chunky pendant dangled from her neck.

'You have a nice place here,' said Isabel. 'Very swish.'

'Thanks. I have six salons actually. Soon to be seven. This is my favourite though – probably because it was my first.'

'How long have you been in business?' Isabel asked, as she and Dan sat down.

'This salon opened in 1999. The others followed one-by-one over a period of about six years.'

'That's quite an empire. You must have a good head for business.'

'I like to think so.' Julie placed her elbows on her desk and steepled her fingers. 'However, I don't suppose it's my business acumen you came here to talk about.'

Isabel held up her hands. 'You got me there. We're here in connection with the discovery of human remains at 23 Ecclesdale Drive in Bainbridge. We understand the property used to belong to a relative of yours. Celia Aspen.'

Beneath her subtle spray tan, Julie blanched.

'Is it Aunt Celia?'

'We've yet to formally identify the body,' Isabel said, 'but we don't believe the remains are those of your aunt.'

'Great-aunt. Celia was my great-aunt.' Julie stood up and went over to the water dispenser in the corner of the office. 'Whereabouts was the body found?'

'In the back garden of the property,' Dan told her.

'I don't understand. If it isn't Aunt Celia, then who the hell is it?'

'We were hoping you might be able to shed some light on that,' Isabel said. 'We know you reported your aunt missing, and we've also learned that she was visited by someone from Canada not long before she disappeared. Do you know who that was?'

Julie's hand was trembling as she placed a cup of water on the desk and sat back down. 'It was someone called Jim. An old friend from before the war, I think. Aunt Celia didn't say much about him, other than he'd invited her to visit him in Canada.'

'And do you know if she was planning to make that trip?'

'I think she was seriously considering it. So much so that when I came back from my own trip to Australia and found that Celia wasn't at home, I assumed that's where she'd gone.'

'Surely your aunt wouldn't have gone off without telling you?' said Dan.

Julie gave them a wry smile. 'Telling me would have required a long-distance phone call, and Aunt Celia would have considered that an extravagance. She regarded the telephone as something to be abrupt on, to avoid racking up a big bill. She used her phone very frugally.'

'According to the missing person's file, you were away in Australia for three months,' Isabel said. 'I gather you and Celia spoke on the phone while you were away?'

'Yes, that's right. I rang her a couple of times at the beginning of my trip to check she was OK, but we didn't talk for long. From her snippy tone of voice, I got the impression she wasn't too fussed whether she heard from me or not – but let's give her the benefit of the doubt. It's possible she kept our conversation to a minimum to keep down the cost, even though it was me who was paying for the calls. Force of habit, I guess. Either way, I didn't bother ringing her after the first week or so.'

'But she could have written to you to tell you she was going away,' Dan said. 'Or left you a note to explain where she'd gone.'

'Well, yes, and at the time it hacked me off that she hadn't bothered. Then, when I found her passport and realised she hadn't gone to Canada after all, I felt awful. Looking back, I appreciate she may not have been in a position to leave a note or give me a call.'

'Did you try to get in touch with her Canadian friend?' Isabel asked. 'This Jim?'

Julie took a sip of water and cleared her throat. 'No. I couldn't find a phone number or address for him. Besides, there didn't seem any point. I'd found Aunt Celia's passport, so it was obvious she hadn't left the country.'

'Was there anywhere else she might have gone to?' asked Dan.

Julie nodded. 'There was a hotel in Torquay she visited from time to time, usually out of season. She'd jump on a train on the spur of the moment, turn up there, and stay for a week or two.'

'And did you or the police check with the hotel?' Dan said.

'That wasn't possible because I didn't know exactly where it was that she stayed. Aunt Celia never told me the name of the hotel, I never asked and it wasn't in her address book. The police did post an appeal in the local Torbay papers, but no one came forward with any information.'

'Can you think of anywhere else your aunt may have gone?' Isabel asked.

'No, and believe me, I racked my brains at the time. If I'd had any inkling of where she was, I would have told the police or tried to find her myself.'

Isabel scratched her forehead. 'I'll be frank with you, Julie. I'm surprised at how you're describing your relationship with your aunt. Am I right in thinking the two of you weren't close?'

Julie smiled. 'That wasn't really an option with Aunt Celia. She kept people at a distance. As far as I know, she'd never been close to anyone.'

'What about your grandmother?' Isabel asked. 'She and Celia were sisters. Weren't they close?'

Julie laughed disdainfully. 'You're kidding, aren't you? We didn't even know Granny *had* a sister until after she died. Aunt Celia saw the death notice in the paper and turned up at the funeral out of the blue. Mum and I couldn't believe it when she introduced herself.'

'Your grandmother didn't talk about Celia?' Isabel was surprised.

'Never. We knew Granny had a brother who was killed in the war, but she never told us anything about her sister. When I asked Celia about it, she told me they'd had a big falling out. The sisters hadn't spoken for years.'

'And yet Celia chose to go to your grandmother's funeral?' Isabel said. 'Didn't you find that strange?'

'Not especially. Celia was old-fashioned like that. She'd have felt compelled to go to the funeral out of a sense of duty.'

'Even though the sisters didn't get on?' said Dan.

'I suppose Celia wanted to pay her respects … although, given the state of their relationship, perhaps "respects" isn't quite the right word. It was more a chance to say goodbye. As it happened, going to the funeral worked out well for my aunt.'

Dan looked at her through narrowed eyes. 'In what way?'

'She and I kept in touch after that and, when she eventually moved to Bainbridge, I used to visit her quite often.'

'So you saw her regularly, but you weren't close?' said Isabel.

'That about sums it up,' Julie replied, tapping her fingers on the desktop. 'I'd be lying if I said Aunt Celia and I had a warm, loving relationship – but there was definitely a bond of sorts between us. My dad died when I was twelve and, with my grandmother gone, I was the only blood relative Celia had left. They do say blood's thicker than water, don't they?'

Dan raised an eyebrow. 'It worked out well for you too, didn't it? I understand you inherited your aunt's house.'

Julie lifted her chin. 'Eventually, once she was declared dead.'

Isabel stood up and zipped her jacket. 'One last question … did your aunt ever talk about her early life? Or about any relationships or friendships she may have had?'

Julie flapped a hand dismissively. 'I told you, Aunt Celia kept people at a distance. She seemed incapable of letting anyone in, and she hardly ever talked about the past. When I first met her, she was working in a department store in Derby and I do know that she loved that job. She was devastated when she was made redundant. It's one of the few times she let her guard down.'

'She didn't take voluntary redundancy then?' said Isabel.

'Oh, no … she would never have done that, even though she was coming up to retirement age anyway. The shop was losing money and the owners decided to make cutbacks. Aunt Celia had no choice but to take a severance deal. I think they tried to modernise the business and turn its fortunes around, but it didn't work out. The store closed down anyway a few years later.'

'Do you know if your aunt kept in touch with any of her old colleagues?' Dan asked.

Julie wrinkled her nose. 'She was head of her department. I think she viewed the people she worked with as her staff, rather than as friends.'

'Well, thank you for talking to us.' Isabel moved towards the door. 'We'll leave you to get on with your work.'

'Can I ask something before you go?'

Isabel nodded.

'If the body you've found isn't that of my aunt, why are you asking all these questions about her?'

'Because we believe the body could have been buried while she lived at the house and, if that's the case, her disappearance may well be linked to the death of the victim.'

'I see.' Julie chewed her bottom lip. 'In that case, it seems I knew even less about Aunt Celia than I thought.'

Chapter 17

Amy Whitworth was in the larger of the two front bedrooms at the house on Ecclesdale Drive. The back garden was being guarded by a policeman, who'd told Paul it would be at least twenty-four hours before they'd be allowed back in there. They had full access to the front garden and the inside of the house, but the rear garden was still completely out of bounds.

With work on the extension on hold, Paul had taken the opportunity to go off to meet a mate for a game of pool, leaving Amy alone in the house.

She'd taken two weeks' annual leave and was determined to achieve *something* during her time off. Her plan for today was to strip the wallpaper in the back bedroom and rub down the woodwork. First though, she would take up the hideous rose-pink carpet that looked as though it had been down for decades.

Peeling back one corner, Amy prised the rough nylon carpet away from the spiked gripper rods. Age and wear and tear had reduced the original in-built foam underlay to a grey, rubbery dust.

The good news was that there were floorboards under the carpet. Perhaps she could sand them down, varnish them and turn them into a 'character' feature. In her experience, bare wooden floors were cold and impractical but, for some reason, house buyers loved them.

Amy tugged at the carpet, trying her best to roll it width-wise down the room. It was a cumbersome task – one that would have been a whole lot easier if Paul had stuck around to help. Standing on the exposed floorboards, she pushed the carpet from the centre. It began to move, rolling reluctantly towards the opposite wall.

The job was almost finished when she hit a snag. The section of carpet in the far corner was proving difficult to manoeuvre. When Amy bent down and examined it, she discovered it had been tacked to the floorboards. Grabbing the frayed edges, she yanked the carpet, releasing it raggedly from the fierce grip of the rusting tacks.

The removal of the carpet had revealed something lying beneath: an A5 manila envelope. Amy picked it up and turned it over. It was plain and ordinary-looking. There was nothing written on the front. No name. No address. Intrigued, she lifted the end flap and tipped the contents onto the palm of her left hand.

The envelope contained two items: a photograph and a ring. The latter was rose gold and featured a row of three round, brilliant-cut diamonds. Instinctively, Amy slipped it onto her ring finger, but it was too big, so she moved it to her middle finger instead.

Next, she picked up the photograph and studied it carefully. A man and a woman stared back at her from the creased black-and-white image.

Amy always found it hard to guess the ages of people in old photographs, but even she could see this couple were young – in their late teens or early twenties. The photo was one of the old-fashioned 'walking' pictures that had been so popular in the first half of the twentieth century. The man and woman strolled hand-in-hand along a windswept seafront location. They were similar in height and were both slightly built. The man was ordinary-looking, but the woman was dazzlingly beautiful. Happiness radiated from her serene, smiling face.

Amy turned the photo over. *Photo by Walkie Snaps* was printed vertically below the words 'Post Card'. Nothing else. No names. No date.

She held up her hand to examine the ring. The weather outside was dreary, so the amount of daylight seeping into the room was minimal – but still the diamonds sparkled. As Amy moved her finger, the refracting stones twinkled with an impressive display of rainbow colours.

The ring could be worth a couple of hundred quid, and Amy knew that if she rang Paul and told him about it, he'd suggest they sell it. Finders, keepers and all that.

But what if the contents of the envelope were connected to the body in the garden? They could be important evidence.

Still wearing the ring, Amy picked up the envelope and the photograph and went downstairs to the kitchen, where her mobile was charging. From her pocket, she pulled out the card the good-looking detective had given her. She picked up the phone and dialled his number.

Chapter 18

'Did you know this is the longest stone bridge in England?' Isabel said, as they drove back towards Derby along the medieval Swarkestone Bridge that crossed the River Trent. 'It's supposed to be haunted by Bonnie Prince Charlie's troops. Some people reckon they've heard ghostly shouts here and the sound of horses' hooves.'

'Who's Bonnie Prince Charlie?'

Isabel laughed. 'The Young Pretender,' she said. 'He tried to reclaim the British throne for the Stuarts. Swarkestone Bridge is as far as he and his army got on their march to London. When they found out there was no support for them in the south, they turned back to Derby and retreated to Scotland. Didn't you learn about the Jacobite rebellion at school, Dan?'

'If I did, I don't remember. History's not really my thing.'

Isabel was about to ask what Dan's *thing* was, when his phone began to ring. Listening to his side of the conversation, she deduced that he was talking to Amy Whitworth.

'Oh aye, definitely,' she heard him say. 'You did right to ring me. I'll arrange for someone to pick them up within the next hour or so.'

'That was interesting,' Dan said, when the call was over. 'Amy Whitworth has found an envelope containing a ring and a photograph. It was hidden under an old bedroom carpet.'

'Do you think it might help with the case?'

'Let's hope so. Apparently it's an old black-and-white shot of a young couple. Who knows, it might be Celia Aspen and the mysterious Canadian bloke in their younger days. I'll get someone to go over there and collect it.'

'Why don't we call in on our way back to the office?' Isabel suggested. 'We should be back in Bainbridge in half an hour, providing the traffic isn't too slow through Derby.'

'That's fine with me,' Dan said. 'Plus, it'll give you a chance to have a gleg at your old house.'

Isabel stifled a wily smile. 'So it will,' she said.

***

'I see the scene hasn't been handed back yet,' Dan remarked, as Isabel parked the car on Ecclesdale Drive.

'When I spoke to the Super yesterday she was fretting about whether there could be another body somewhere in the garden,' Isabel said. 'The SOCOs haven't found any obvious signs, but I thought it was best to play it safe.'

'Do you fancy having another look around the back before we go and talk to Amy Whitworth?' Dan said.

Isabel nodded. 'I didn't get a chance to check things out properly when I came the other day. It'd be useful to see it again.'

After a quick chat with the uniformed officer on guard at the gate, they went through to the back of the house and stood on the patio.

It was strange being back on such familiar territory. Isabel realised that the lofty silver birch tree in the garden must be the sapling her mother had put in for the plant-a-tree-in-73 campaign. Forty-six years later, it was tall and elegantly mature, giving the property an established, suburban look it had never managed to achieve while her family had lived there.

'I don't understand why no one saw anything,' said Dan, pointing to the row of properties that backed on to the rear gardens on Ecclesdale Drive, the upper rear windows of which had a good view of the burial site. 'The body was about a metre down. It must have taken a good few hours for someone to dig a hole that deep.'

'When I lived here, the garden backed on to open fields,' Isabel told him. 'The houses you see now are on the newest part of the estate. I think they were built in the Nineties – probably well after the body was buried.'

'What about the neighbours on either side? Surely they would have spotted something.'

Isabel walked over to the trench where the bones had been found and signalled to Dan to join her.

'Look around you,' she said. 'We're directly behind the garage, which blocks out the Littlewoods' view of this corner of the garden. The house on the other side is set further back from the road. I've been inside it and, trust me, you can't see into this section of the garden from there – not without a periscope.'

'Even so, whoever dug the hole was taking a big risk.'

'Perhaps they did it at night, under cover of darkness.'

Dan sighed. 'Yeah, maybe. But that's the trouble with this case, boss. There are too many maybes and no certainties. We don't even know who the victim is.'

'Patience, Dan,' Isabel said. 'We're bound to find something if we ask the right questions. Think positively. This photo might be the key we need to unlock the case.'

Dan looked unconvinced. 'If only life were that simple,' he said.

***

They went back to the front of the house and rang the bell. Amy Whitworth came to the door wearing a pair of grey jogging bottoms and a Levi's T-shirt. She seemed surprised to see them.

'Oh, it's you!' She ran her fingers through her hair and smiled at Dan. 'When you said someone would come round, I thought you were sending someone else.'

'We were in the area,' Dan said. 'This is DI Blood.'

'Is it all right if we come in?' Isabel asked.

'Of course.' Amy pulled back the door to let them inside.

As Isabel crossed the threshold, she braced herself for something momentous. A sense of déjà vu perhaps, or of coming home. A wave of nostalgia at the very least. Instead, she felt nothing.

The hallway was smaller than she remembered, but being back inside it didn't trigger a sudden slideshow of memories. There were no flashbacks. It was simply a hallway in a house that she used to call home.

Amy Whitworth led them into the kitchen, which was very different to how it had looked in 1978. At some point since then it had been fitted out with dark oak units, including a breakfast bar that sliced the room in two. An envelope, a photograph and a ring sat on its marble-effect worktop.

'I don't know if they're anything to do with … you know, what Paul found in the garden, but I thought you should see them.'

Dan placed the items into plastic evidence bags, examining both sides of the photograph before passing it to Isabel. She looked at it closely. The picture was obviously from another time. It was black and white and yellowed with age.

She scrutinised the two young people, mentally comparing the woman to the snapshot of Celia Aspen that Dan had pinned to the whiteboard back in the office. There was no obvious resemblance, but Isabel was aware that time could play tricks on a person's face, morphing them into someone different. Unrecognisable.

The girl in *this* photo was in the bloom of youth, extraordinarily pretty, with fair, wavy hair. Even though the image wasn't in colour, Isabel could tell she was wearing lipstick – most likely red. The young man next to her had dark hair, a roundish face and a nervous smile.

Next, Isabel picked up the bag containing the ring. It was small, but lovely. Three diamonds winked at her through the evidence bag, but there was no inscription.

Amy pointed to the snapshot. 'I took a module on the history of photography at uni,' she said. 'Those are known as walking photos. They were taken by professional photographers who plied their trade in British seaside towns.'

'Interesting.' Dan smiled and peered at the photo. 'It certainly looks as if it was taken a long time ago. You said you found the envelope under a carpet?'

'Yes, in one of the front bedrooms. I'll show you, if you like.'

As Isabel followed Dan and Amy up the stairs, she felt the shadows of time shifting around her and experienced a momentary slippage into the past – but the sensation was a fleeting one. By the time she entered the double bedroom at the front of the house, she was firmly back in the present.

'It was in this corner,' Amy told them. 'Someone had tacked the carpet down, so I'm pretty sure the envelope was hidden deliberately.'

There was nothing to see, except a rolled-up carpet and bare floorboards. The room was empty, as it had been the last time Isabel had seen it, on the day she and her mother had moved out.

This had been her parents' bedroom. She walked over to the window and looked out. The familiar view had matured into something different. Better. The trees were bigger and the houses had bedded in, as though they had always been there.

'You didn't find anything else?' Dan asked.

'No. Only the envelope.'

'OK. Well, if you do come across anything, even something seemingly insignificant, please give me a call.'

'There is something I haven't told you about,' Amy said. 'It's easier if I show you.'

Isabel trailed behind Amy and Dan as they went downstairs and back into the kitchen.

'I noticed these just before Paul found the body.' Amy opened the pantry door and switched on the light. 'It's probably nothing, but I'll let you decide.'

Unexpected tears welled in Isabel's eyes as Dan peered behind the door. She knew precisely what he would see.

'Boss?' Dan's voice cut into her thoughts. 'Do you want to take a look?'

Against all expectations, the house had dragged her back in time, injecting her with a shot of nostalgia and a mawkish sense of loss.

Moving towards the pantry, Isabel stared at the height marks scratched behind the door. She peered at the one furthest down. 15th January 1965. Strange to think she had ever been that young or that small. Reaching out, she touched the last mark, the one from 1977. She never had grown any taller than five foot six.

Every one of those marks had been made by her dad. His job meant he worked away for long stretches, but he always made sure he was home for Isabel's birthday. He'd been a stickler for routines and on every one of those days, after breakfast in the kitchen, he would insist on measuring her. Isabel had enjoyed the feel of the ruler on her head and the scratching sound the pencil made as her growth was recorded on the wall. She'd once asked if she could be measured more often, but her dad told her it was better to do it once a year.

'The change is more noticeable that way, Issy,' he'd said, pulling a silly, wide-eyed face. 'More dramatic.'

On her last birthday in the house, Isabel had asked her mum to mark her height on the pantry wall. It was January 1978, three months after her dad had left, and they were already packing, ready to move out.

Her mum had been reluctant to measure her. She said there was no point, but Isabel had insisted. She'd wanted to leave one last record of her presence in the house.

When her mother had placed the ruler on her head, she told Isabel that she wasn't any taller. She didn't record her height because she was still five foot six. Isabel had finished growing.

It was astonishing that the marks had survived all these years and not been painted over. They were a tangible reminder of her old life: the life that lay buried beneath a thick layer of silence.

Through secrecy and taciturnity, Barbara Corrington had done everything she could to erase the past, but the past had never gone away completely. Like the height marks in this house, it was still there, waiting to be rediscovered. Anticipating her mother's imminent arrival, Isabel felt excitement rise up inside her like bubbles in a glass of sparkling wine. In just a few hours, she would finally know the truth.

Pulling her thoughts back to the case, Isabel turned to Amy Whitworth, who was nibbling a cuticle. The presence of the height marks in the pantry was clearly troubling her.

'Do you think they could be something to do with … the bones?' Amy asked.

'No,' Isabel said firmly. 'I can say categorically that they aren't.'

Amy gave a sigh of relief and smiled. 'That's all right then. Only we'll be knocking out the pantry when we refit the kitchen. The marks will be gone for good then.'

Another remnant of the past that will disappear forever, Isabel thought. *Something rediscovered that would soon be lost again.*

Chapter 19

'Before we go back to the station, why don't we pop next door and let Joyce Littlewood have a look at the photo?' Isabel suggested, as she and Dan made their way back up the drive. 'She might be able to tell us whether the woman in the photograph is Celia.'

Joyce Littlewood slapped her hands together when she opened her door. 'Isabel! I don't set eyes on you for over forty years and then I see you twice in as many days.'

'I'm sorry to bother you again so soon, but we need your help.'

They went into the kitchen, where Dan handed the bagged photograph to Joyce.

'We'd like you to take a look at this,' he said. 'Could it be the man you saw in Celia Aspen's garden?'

Joyce squinted at the photo and then opened a kitchen drawer to retrieve a pair of reading glasses. Perching them on the end of her nose, she inspected the image more carefully before shaking her head.

'No, I don't think it's him.'

Dan sighed. 'Are you sure? Take another look.'

'Don't sigh at me, young man. I'm not a hundred per cent sure, but you're asking me to compare the man in this photo with someone I saw briefly over thirty years ago. The chap I saw back then must have been seventy if he was a day. The lad in this photo is still wet behind the ears. Is it any wonder I'm uncertain?'

'Don't worry, Joyce,' Isabel said. 'It was a long shot, but we thought it was worth checking with you. What about the woman. Do you think that might be Celia Aspen?'

'No, definitely not.' Joyce handed the photo back to Dan. 'That I am sure of. The girl in that photograph is very pretty – a real stunner. Celia Aspen was a plain sort of woman. Even with youth on her side, she could never have been that beautiful.'

'So you're absolutely certain it isn't Celia Aspen,' Dan asked.

'That's what I said, isn't it?' Joyce pressed her lips together. 'The man may or may not be the same person I saw in Celia's garden in 1986, but the woman is *definitely* not Celia.'

To avoid irritating Mrs L any further, Isabel decided that she and Dan should make a swift exit.

Heading out through the front gate, they passed a short, wiry man coming in the opposite direction. With a jolt, Isabel realised it was Timothy Littlewood, changed beyond all recognition from the freckle-faced boy she remembered.

'It's Timothy, isn't it?' she said.

He stopped and looked back at her, and a wide smile of recognition swept across the lower half of his face. 'I know you,' he said. 'You used to live next door. A long time ago.'

'Yes, I did. I lived here with my mum and dad.'

'Isabel,' said Timothy. 'Your name's Isabel.'

'That's right. Well remembered. And this is my colleague, Dan.'

'We're detectives,' Dan said. 'We've been talking to your mum.'

'Detectives?' Timothy began to flap his hands. 'Mum's done nothing wrong. She's a good person.'

'It's OK, Timothy. We know she is.' Isabel smiled to reassure him. 'She's been helping us, that's all. Telling us some things we needed to know.'

His hands stopped flapping. 'She knows a lot of stuff, my mum does. She always says that nothing much gets past her.'

'You can help as well, if you want to.' Dan held out the photograph, nodding for him to take it. 'Have a look and see if you recognise either of these people.'

Avoiding eye contact with Dan, Timothy took the bagged photograph between his thumb and index finger. His mouth puckered as he examined the faces of the man and woman in the picture.

'Does it look like anyone you know?' Dan asked. 'Or anyone you used to know?'

Isabel silenced him with a glare. She didn't want Dan planting ideas in Timothy's head.

Timothy brought the photograph closer to his face. 'It looks like Celia,' he said. 'She used to live next door ...'

'Celia Aspen?' said Dan. 'Are you sure? Your mum said it wasn't her. How certain are you?'

Isabel was annoyed with Dan, disappointed. He'd rushed in too quickly and now Timothy was shaking his head and thrusting the photo back at him.

'No. Sorry,' Timothy said. 'It's not. Sorry.'

'It's all right,' said Isabel. 'If you think the woman is Celia, it's OK to say so. You won't be in trouble.'

'No.' Timothy shook his head forcefully and pointed to the photo Dan held in his hand. 'She's not Celia.'

Isabel sighed. 'Well, thanks for taking a look anyway, Timothy. We'll let you get into the house. It was nice seeing you again.'

'Yes. I'm going to go inside now and have my tea. Goodbye.' Timothy lowered his head and hurried down the driveway.

'I thought you'd been specially trained on interviewing vulnerable adults, Dan,' said Isabel.

'I have. You know I have.' He looked offended. 'I did the training last year.'

'Well, you handled that badly.' Isabel grimaced. 'You should

104

have taken a more gentle approach. He was adamant it was Celia until you told him his mother didn't agree.'

'I thought he was trying to please you … tell you what he thought you wanted to hear.'

'But why would he mention Celia?'

'Perhaps his mum told him we'd been asking about her.'

'Maybe,' Isabel said. 'But what if Timothy was telling the truth, and Joyce was lying when she said the woman wasn't Celia?'

'Why would she do that?'

Isabel looked back at the Littlewood house. 'Why indeed.'

Chapter 20

As soon as they returned to the station, Dan went off to interview the suspects in the armed robbery case and Isabel hurried over the road to get some lunch before the café closed up for the day.

She bought a tuna sandwich and carried it back to the office to eat at her desk. Lucas had gone to the interview suite with Dan, and Zoe was writing up a report on a violent assault that had taken place a few days earlier. Isabel trawled through a pile of paperwork and tried to forget about her mother flying in from Malaga. Whenever she thought about the conversation they would have later, she felt sick with apprehension. Although she was desperate for news of her father, she dreaded what her mother might say. Sometimes the truth could be unpalatable.

At ten past three she received a text from Nathan.

The eagle has landed. Heading back to Bainbridge now. Don't be late home. xx

Isabel rested her head in her hands and tried to scrub out the scenarios that had been playing around in her imagination. Over the years she'd considered a raft of reasons that might explain why her dad had disappeared from their lives. Now, for the first time, she was finally on the verge of getting an answer to the question that had plagued her consciousness for more than four decades.

In the early Eighties, when Isabel joined the police force, she'd had to provide her parents' names so that background checks could be carried out as part of the vetting process. On the form, in the address section next to her father's name, she'd had no choice but to write 'not known'. With or without an address, she'd been convinced the police would be able to trace her father if he had a criminal record. When she'd received her formal job offer, she'd assumed they'd drawn a blank, or found nothing serious enough to prevent her joining the force.

It was early on in her career and overcome by curiosity that she had risked her job by making furtive, unauthorised use of police databases to try and track down her father. Each and every one of those searches had proved fruitless. Donald Corrington had no criminal record, she'd found no vehicles registered in his name, and he wasn't on the electoral roll. Reluctantly, she'd had to accept the logical conclusion – that he was dead.

Now, finally, after decades of speculation, she was close to learning the truth. Whatever the secret was that her mother had been clinging to for the last forty-two years, it must be pretty massive if she was only willing to talk about it face-to-face.

A heavy feeling settled in Isabel's stomach, as though she'd swallowed a rock. Filled with a suffocating weight of dread and unable to concentrate, she switched off her computer, pulled on her coat and went out into the main office.

'Zoe, I'm going to finish for today,' she said. 'My mum's over from Spain.'

'Righto, boss. Are you in tomorrow?'

'Yes, I'll be here, bright and early. We can review progress on the Ecclesdale Drive case first thing.'

'Do you want me to let Dan and Lucas know?'

'Yes, do that. Tell them to be here for a meeting at nine.'

'OK. See you tomorrow. Have a good evening with your mum.'

'Thanks,' she said. 'I'll do my very best.'

***

Isabel arrived home ahead of Nathan and her mother. She lit the log burner and a couple of vanilla-scented candles, put the kettle on and was in the process of switching on more downstairs lights to make the house seem cheerful and welcoming, when she heard the car pull up outside.

Her mother came into the kitchen carrying a small leather holdall. She was huddled inside a long, black woollen coat and had an emerald green scarf wrapped around her neck. Barbara had grown used to the Spanish climate and invariably felt the cold whenever she visited the UK, especially in the autumn and winter months.

'Hello, Issy, love.' She opened her arms, but Isabel wasn't in the mood for displays of affection. She leaned in and planted a kiss on her mother's cheek and gave her a loose, cautious hug – near enough to breathe in her expensive perfume, but not close enough to be drawn into a tight embrace.

'How was your flight?'

'Full of holidaymakers, but mercifully short. How are you, darling?'

'I'm OK,' Isabel said. 'I'll feel better when we've talked ... once you've answered all the questions that are banging around in my head.'

Bloody hell, her mother was barely through the door and already she'd jumped straight into her interrogation. Isabel felt a flush of shame, but quickly brushed it aside. Now wasn't the time to put her mother's feelings before her own, she'd been doing that for the last forty years. It was time to harden her heart and push on to get the closure she needed.

'I've been worried about you,' Barbara said. 'Ever since our telephone conversation the other night.'

'You could have talked to me over the phone, Mum. It's great to see you, but you really didn't need to fly over here. We could have Skyped.'

'No, darling. Trust me. This is something I have to do in person.'

Nathan appeared in the doorway.

'You finished early.' He moved over and kissed the top of Isabel's head.

'I couldn't concentrate at work, so I thought I'd better come home.'

Nathan turned to his mother-in-law. 'I've taken your suitcase upstairs, Barbara. You're in the usual room.'

'Thank you, Nathan. And thanks for picking me up from the airport.'

'My pleasure.' He turned back to wink at Isabel. 'I'm going to start prepping dinner, so why don't you ladies make yourselves scarce? I know you've got lots to chat about.'

'Let's go and sit in the garden room, Mum. I've lit the log burner. Go on in and I'll follow in a minute with a pot of tea. Ellie's made a new friend and she's been invited round to her house straight after school. She won't be back until seven-thirty, so there's plenty of time for us to sit and talk.'

***

The garden room was at the back of the house, right next to Nathan's work studio.

Isabel rarely ventured into her husband's workspace. It was a masculine, monochrome room. White walls. Black furniture.

In stark contrast, the garden room was an explosion of colour. The polished floorboards were covered by two large cotton rugs in shades of turquoise, terracotta and gold. During the day, light poured in through wide, floor-to-ceiling doors onto a diverse collection of furniture that Nathan had picked up at auction. He had chosen to mix antiques with classic contemporary pieces and, despite the eclectic clash of styles and colours, Isabel found the room comforting and calming. The exotic house plants and cacti that filled every spare corner were her passion and joy. Tending to them and watering them had become her favourite way to unwind after a difficult day at work.

She and her mother had settled at either end of the long sofa that stretched across the middle of the room. Barbara sat stiffly upright, her fists clenched in her lap.

'Where do you want me to start?' she asked, as she reached out to warm her hands on the mug of tea Isabel had poured for her.

'Tell me what happened when Dad left. Where did he go to? Don't hold anything back. I want to know everything.'

'It's difficult, talking about this.' Barbara had the good grace to look embarrassed. 'And before I start, I want to apologise for keeping you in the dark all these years. I did it because I made a promise, but I realise now that I should have talked to you when you were old enough to know the truth. The thing is, when you've carried a secret around for so long, it becomes easier to keep quiet than to speak out. The more time that goes by, the harder it becomes to break the silence.'

Isabel nodded. 'I'm sure that's true,' she said. 'But have you any idea what it's been like for me ... not knowing? And can you imagine what went through my mind when I heard a body had been found at our old house? I thought it was him, Mum. I honestly believed I was witnessing the exhumation of my own father.'

Barbara stared at her, open-mouthed. 'How could you even think that?'

'It's easy to think all kind of things when you've never been given any answers. When you've spent your whole life not knowing.'

110

'So what exactly *were* you thinking, Isabel? That I killed your father?' Her mother stared at her wide-eyed, making no effort to disguise her shock.

'It did cross my mind.'

Barbara tutted fiercely before sipping her tea through pinched lips. 'Quite frankly, I'm hurt and offended that you could think me capable of doing such a terrible thing.'

'And it hurt me to have to consider such a scenario, Mum, but in the absence of the truth, I didn't know what to believe. I know *now* that the body isn't Dad's, but only because of forensic evidence that turned up yesterday.'

'I could have told you it wasn't him.'

'Then why in God's name didn't you?' Isabel could feel frustration building in her chest. She was finding it hard to keep her voice on an even keel, but she knew her mother well enough to understand that losing her temper wouldn't get her anywhere.

'You didn't ask,' Barbara said.

Isabel gave a low wail. 'You didn't give me a chance, Mother. You ended the call, remember?'

'You should have rung me back. I would have told you straight that it wasn't your father.' She seemed so definite. Convincing.

'You sound very sure about that.'

There was an ominous pause before Barbara answered.

'I am,' she said. 'You see, your dad is alive, Isabel. He's alive and well and living in France.'

Chapter 21

'What do you mean, he's alive?' Isabel felt as though she was floating, weightless. 'You know where Dad is? You've known all this time?'

'Now, Issy, don't fly off the handle. Please keep calm.'

'Don't tell me to keep calm!' Her words hissed with fury, her earlier resolve to maintain her composure quickly dissipating. 'How *could* you? What gave you the right to deny me that information?'

'I can explain.'

'No, you can't, Mother. There's nothing you can say to explain this away. I'll never forgive you for lying to me all these years.'

Isabel thought about the times she had longed to see her father, remembering situations when she'd needed his advice or wished he'd been there … to give her away when she got married, and be around when she'd had her children. Every one of those absences had felt like a punch in the gut. And then there were the days when she told herself she was better off without him – that he was a bastard for walking out of her life and a scumbag for not keeping in touch – but that didn't stop her from missing him.

Life without her dad had felt incomplete and painful at times, but it was a pain she'd borne valiantly because deep down she'd believed he must be dead. Why else would he stay away? In private, she had found her own way to mourn and it had hurt – but not as much as she was hurting now. Knowing he was alive meant accepting that he had left her willingly. For some reason, her father had *chosen* to break all ties with her, and that was the deepest wound of all.

'I didn't lie to you, Isabel. I'll admit I kept things from you, but only because your father asked me to.' Barbara sighed. 'You know, there was a reason he chose to leave while you were away on your school trip. It was so that he didn't have to say goodbye. That was the only way he could bring himself to leave you.'

Isabel was too angry to look her mother in the eye. Instead, she found herself staring at the stewed dregs of tea at the bottom of her mug. 'In that case, why didn't you keep me at home?' she said. 'You could have saved your marriage.'

'That wasn't an option … there was no marriage to save. We weren't simply two people who were splitting up, Issy. The situation was far more complicated than that.'

'In what way?' She was gripping the handle of the mug so tightly her fingers had begun to stiffen. 'Why didn't Dad stay in contact with me?'

'He had his reasons. At first, he and I kept in touch from time to time, but it was all very awkward. I think he would have contacted you eventually, when you were older, but then you joined the police force. He didn't want to reappear in your life and mess things up for you.'

Salty tears trickled down Isabel's cheeks as she thought of all the lost years. How could he have chosen to stay away? *Why* would he? Why hadn't he loved her enough to stay in touch?

'Oh, Isabel, please don't cry. I'm so sorry. I wanted to tell you, truly I did, but your father wouldn't let me. As I say … it's complicated. That's why I didn't want to have this conversation over the phone. I needed to be with you when I told you. You're bound to have lots of questions.'

Slowly, Isabel lifted her head. She stared at her mother's worried face, short spikes of grey hair framing features that were still classically elegant.

'Come on then, tell me. Why is Dad in France, and why doesn't he want to be part of my life?' She felt the burn of acid reflux. 'It's time to tell the truth, Mum. You've been dishonest for long enough.'

'It's not me that's been dishonest. I never wanted to hide anything, but your dad swore me to secrecy. He went off to another life that you couldn't be a part of.'

Anger and indignation were tearing through Isabel's body like fire. 'I feel so betrayed,' she said. 'By him and by you.'

Barbara looked wretched. 'I know you do. I understand that, and I will tell you everything. That's why I'm here.'

'Then get on with it.' Overwhelmed by a sense of urgency, Isabel's voice had begun to rise. 'For pity's sake, tell me!'

'I intend to, but first can you pour me something stronger than a cup of tea? Trust me, this conversation will be easier over a glass of brandy.'

'Trust you?' Isabel snapped. 'I don't think I'll ever trust you again.'

Her mother tensed. 'Don't say that. I know you're upset, but this isn't my fault. It's your selfish, sodding father who's caused all this hurt.'

Isabel pressed her sternum with the heel of her hand. Acidic fury was burning somewhere beneath her ribcage and her head felt as though it was going to explode.

'You know how much I've missed Dad over the years, and yet all this time you've known where he is. You've excluded me, haven't you?' she said. 'From some big ugly secret that only you and he were privy to. Well, let me tell you something, whatever

114

that secret is … however devastating it may be … nothing will ever shock me more than finding out I've been lied to all these years.'

'I wouldn't be too sure of that,' Barbara said, affronted. 'Now, pour me a glass of brandy and I'll tell you everything.'

Chapter 22

'Well?' Nathan said. 'How's it going?'

He was at the kitchen sink peeling potatoes. Isabel squeezed past him, reaching into a corner cupboard to retrieve the bottle of brandy they kept for emergencies. She poured two generous measures and then shook the bottle at him.

'Want one?'

'No, I'm all right thanks.' He frowned. 'Things must be bad if you're hitting the brandy.'

'It's supposed to be good for shock, isn't it?'

'Shock? What kind of shock?'

'Dad's alive,' she said. 'Apparently he's living in France. Mum's known all along. She said he went off to another life and made her promise not to tell me where he was. He even kept in touch with her for a while.'

'What?' Nathan threw the potato peeler into the washing-up bowl. 'Why would he do that?'

'I have no idea. I don't understand any of it. After buggering off, why bother keeping in contact with Mum at all?'

Nathan shrugged. 'Maybe he wanted to know how to get hold of you if he needed to.'

'Well, he obviously hasn't needed to, has he?' Isabel scowled.

'Forty-two years have rolled by and he hasn't contacted me once.'

'When you lose touch with someone, it can be tricky reaching out to them again: the longer you leave it, the harder it becomes.'

'Are you trying to defend him, Nathan?'

'No. Honestly. I'm not.' He held up his hands. 'What else has she said?'

'Very little, so far. She reckons she needs one of these before she can tell me the rest.' Isabel held up the brandy glasses. 'I'm going back in to hear the rest of it.'

As she returned to the garden room, Isabel thought about her mother's forty-two-year silence. Without that, this whole mind-bending cover-up would never have worked. Barbara may not have set out to be deliberately conniving or cruel, but there was no denying she had been part of a carefully planned conspiracy to keep Isabel in the dark.

When her dad had left, her mum refused to answer any questions and, eventually, Isabel had given up asking them. As a result, her relationship with her mother had gradually deteriorated into something strained and disingenuous. As time trickled by, communication between the two of them had grown increasingly difficult. The words they did exchange tended to be trivial or cautious and, consequently, the important issues – the questions that truly mattered – had been pushed aside.

A suppressed desire for answers was the main reason Isabel had joined the police. She saw it as a way of creating order out of disorder. The law had provided structure in her life and given her the power to ask questions and search for the truth. And now, finally, she was about to uncover the one truth that had always eluded her.

Her mother looked washed-out and nervous. Isabel handed her one of the glasses of brandy.

'Thanks,' Barbara said. 'I'm so sorry about all this, Isabel. Truly I am. I should have told you he was still alive. I owed you that much at least.'

'It's hard to accept your apology until I know why Dad left.' Isabel sat down. 'But I realise that by not telling me where he was, you were keeping the promise you made to him. Who knows, perhaps that was the right thing to do at the time – I won't know for sure until you explain the circumstances. But I'm fifty-six now, Mother – a mature, responsible woman. I've been ready to deal with the truth for decades. You should have found the right time to tell me.'

'Have you considered that *this* might be the right time?' Barbara said.

'Whether it is or not, I'm certainly not going to let you put it off any longer. So, come on. Tell me. Why did Dad leave in 1977?'

Chapter 23

'I was only nineteen when I got married,' Barbara began. 'Your dad was twenty-four.'

'I know that, Mum. You got married because you were pregnant with me. Tell me something I haven't already heard.'

Barbara closed her eyes. 'Please, Isabel. This is difficult for me. You have to let me tell it in my own way.'

'Well, for pity's sake, get on with it.'

Barbara snapped open her eyes and glared for a moment before continuing. 'Whenever he visited the Bainbridge factory, your father would invite me to go for a drink with him. That's all it was to start with: a few drinks or a meal if he was in town. Looking back, I think he was lonely. Away from home. On his own. It didn't mean anything.'

'But then you fell in love with him.'

'Yes.' Barbara smiled wistfully. 'Head over heels, although there was nothing remotely romantic about our relationship in the beginning. Like I said, we were just friends. It was purely platonic. Your dad was the perfect gentleman. It was me who wanted more. He was funny and charming, clever and handsome, and the fact that he was half-French made him positively exotic! I'd never met anyone quite like him. I was inexperienced and naïve but also very determined. I set my sights on him. I seduced him. I only have myself to blame.'

Isabel let out a long sigh. 'I think you're being too hard on yourself, Mum. It takes two to tango. I'm sure Dad didn't take much persuading.'

Barbara shrugged. 'Maybe not, but I knew he wasn't looking for commitment. It came as a huge shock when I found out I was expecting – although for me, it was a pleasant surprise. I loved Donald so much … knowing that I was having his baby made me very, very happy.'

'What about Dad? How did he take the news?'

'A lot less enthusiastically. The prospect of impending fatherhood seemed to terrify him. At first I thought he was worried about money … how we'd manage financially. He was travelling all over Europe, trying to establish himself as a salesman. It wasn't an easy job, although I think he enjoyed the lifestyle. He certainly wasn't ready to settle down in one place – and he sure as hell wasn't keen on getting hitched.'

'And yet he did. Marry you.'

'Yes.' Barbara nodded. 'Although he didn't really have much choice. In those days, if you got a girl pregnant, you stuck by her … did the right thing and made an honest woman of her. At least, you did if you were a decent bloke.'

'Which Dad was.'

'I think that was always his intention.' Barbara smiled sardonically. 'He promised to marry me providing it was a quiet registry office ceremony. I was OK with that. We certainly didn't have the money for a lavish wedding.'

She drained the last of her brandy and leaned forward to place the empty glass on the coffee table.

'To begin with, we rented a little house on the edge of town. I had a few pieces of furniture that my mother had left me and I did my best to make a home for us all. Right from the off, it was clear that my love for your dad was far more intense than his feelings for me, but I accepted that. He cared for me, in his own way. It was only when you were born that I realised how fragile our marriage was.'

'Fragile? In what way?'

'I wanted him to get a different job ... something that didn't involve travelling for weeks or months on end. It was hard for me, coping with a new baby on my own when he was away. Which he was. A lot.'

'But you knew what his job entailed when you married him.'

'That's what *he* said. He told me I was being unreasonable, expecting him to change career. He said he liked his job and had no intention of switching to anything else.'

'And you weren't happy about that.'

'No, I wasn't, but I had no choice other than to accept his decision. I took consolation from the fact that, when he was home and we were together, things were great ... at least, I thought they were.'

'How did he take to fatherhood?'

'Like a duck to water. From the minute you were born, his love for you was immense. You bound us together. We moved into the house on Ecclesdale Drive on our first wedding anniversary. We were by no means a conventional family unit and we didn't spend as much time together as I would have liked, but we were happy in our own way.'

'Obviously not happy enough,' Isabel said matter-of-factly. 'What changed? What made him want to leave?'

Her mother lowered her head and fell silent long enough for Isabel to think she had clammed up again. Eventually, Barbara looked up from beneath her carefully eye-shadowed lids. 'The thing that took him from us had always been there, hidden away,' she said, shuffling forward to get closer to the fire. 'What changed was that he decided to stop pretending. He'd reached a point where he was forced to make a choice. After years of deception, he finally told me the truth.'

Isabel pulled her legs onto the sofa and hugged her knees. 'Which was?'

Barbara took a deep breath and rubbed her neck, as if to smooth the passage of the words that were forming in her throat.

'Your father was a bigamist. He was married to someone else.'

A viscous silence poured into the room, bringing with it a temporary stillness, as though the world had stopped spinning momentarily. Isabel's breath froze in her lungs. She rocked forward to unblock it. Exhaled. Inhaled. Exhaled.

'He married someone else?' She breathed again. In. Out. In. Out. 'While he was still married to you?'

Barbara laughed bitterly. 'I'm afraid it was much worse than that. You see, when he married me, your father already had a wife in France. It was *our* marriage that was bigamous. It turns out he hadn't made an honest woman of me after all.'

Chapter 24

Isabel sat bolt upright, her body rigid.

'What the hell was he thinking? How could he do that to you?'

'Quite easily, it seems.'

Isabel was gripped – in the worst possible sense – by her mother's story. Torn between wanting to hear everything versus a need to block out the unwelcome truth, she put her head in her hands and wondered how best to deal with such an agonising dichotomy.

And that's when her phone began to ring.

***

Of course it was work. Her sodding job again. Why did her colleagues always have to ring her at the most inopportune moments? Weren't they capable of making any decisions on their own?

Casting an apologetic glance in Barbara's direction and holding up an index finger to indicate she would only be a minute, Isabel stood up and wandered into the hallway, answering the phone as she walked.

'This really isn't a convenient time, Dan,' she said. 'In fact, you couldn't have picked a worse moment.'

'Apologies, boss,' he said, sounding embarrassed. 'Do you want me to ring back later?'

Feeling cold and shaky, Isabel rested a hand on the bottom of the stair rail, grateful for the support it provided.

'If it's important, you'd better tell me now,' she said. 'I assume it's about the case?'

'No, actually it's something else.'

Isabel repressed an urge to scream. She was in no mood for intrigue, but she knew Dan well enough to know he wouldn't be calling without a bloody good reason.

'Come on then, spit it out,' she said, 'and make it quick.'

'I've just been given a heads-up that the local authority desig-nated officer for Bainbridge High School has been in touch,' he said. 'The headteacher's received a complaint from a pupil who's saying a teacher touched her inappropriately.'

Isabel straightened her shoulders. 'That's the school Ellie goes to.'

'I know. That's why I rang. I thought I'd better keep you in the loop.'

'Does the LADO want to get the police involved?' Isabel asked.

'Not yet, at least not in any formal capacity. Right now, we're liaising with the LADO on the most appropriate course of action, but initially the school would prefer to deal with the complaint in accordance with their routine practices and policies.'

'They'll be worried about unwanted publicity,' Isabel said.

'If the complaint is substantiated, it won't be good for the school's reputation, that's for sure. As we speak, the school's safeguarding officer is gathering information confidentially, checking for evidence and they're planning to take statements from witnesses. As a precautionary measure the teacher has been moved to other duties while the school investigates the allegation.'

'How old's the girl who reported him?'

'Fourteen.'

Isabel winced. 'Strewth. What's the teacher's name?'

'David Allerton. He teaches art.'

'Shit!' Isabel flopped down onto the bottom of the stairs. 'Ellie's in his class. I met him yesterday at the school art exhibition. I have to say, he didn't look like the sort to abuse underage girls, but you never can tell.'

'According to the headteacher, he's denied any wrongdoing. He's saying the complaint is malicious and maintains the pupil has a problem with him. Her name's Skye Hawton and, apparently, she does have certain issues with discipline.'

'Skye Hawton? Are you sure?'

'Yes, why? Do you know her?'

'Ellie and Skye have been friends since nursery school – although, come to think of it, Ellie hardly ever mentions her these days. I may be wrong, but I get the impression there's been a falling out.'

Isabel glanced towards the garden room, conscious that her mother was in there, waiting, eager to finish her story and unburden herself.

'When did the alleged incident take place?' she asked. 'And what does Skye say happened?'

'I only know the basics,' Dan replied. 'Allegedly it happened in class this morning. Sounds like all the students were sitting at individual easels painting a still life.'

'So he touched her in front of everyone else?'

'According to Skye, he did it surreptitiously. She reckons Mr Allerton was moving around the room, standing behind each of the students, looking at their work. He's supposed to have leaned in close and held her hand, on the pretext of showing her how to make brush strokes.'

'Well, if he did, he's a bloody fool. Anyone working in a school knows that they have to maintain personal and professional boundaries and respect every pupil's personal space and privacy.

If David Allerton held her hand, it was a stupid thing to do, and definitely inappropriate.'

'There's more,' Dan said.

Isabel groaned. Could this week get any worse?

'Go on,' she said. 'Tell me.'

'While he was showing her how to use the paint brush, Skye says he was making a few strokes of his own. She says he touched her left breast.'

Isabel ran a hand through her hair. 'With these kind of incidents, the child's welfare has to be the paramount consideration,' she said. 'The child should be listened to patiently and carefully and their concerns taken seriously. The trouble is, to all intents and purposes, the member of staff is viewed as guilty until proven innocent. If Skye Hawton's claim can be substantiated, then the PPU should get him in fast. However, if – for whatever reason – this *is* a malicious allegation, Skye Hawton is playing with fire and she's being intentionally vindictive. I'm not sure why she'd lie, but if she is, she's in danger of wrecking an innocent person's career and personal life.'

'Either way, it's not our problem, boss. If the school decides to bring in the police, it'll be the PPU that has to deal with it.'

'Well, they are properly trained to deal with those kinds of situations,' Isabel said. 'And I suppose we've got more than enough on our plate as it is.'

Right now, her own plate was pretty full too, in danger of spilling over problematically. And, when she went back in to talk to her mother, she had a hunch things were about to get a whole lot worse.

Chapter 25

Isabel felt sick and nervous as she returned to the garden room and reclaimed her seat on the sofa. On top of feeling anxious about what their mother–daughter tête-à-tête would reveal next, the conversation with Dan had unsettled her. Would the problem at the school impact on Ellie? Should she talk to her, or bide her time and wait and see how things developed?

Concluding that it. was best to grit her teeth and deal with each problem as it evolved, she decided to press on with her conversation with Barbara. After a brief apology for the inter- ruption, she picked things up where they'd left off. 'I'm struggling to get my head around the fact that Dad was a bigamist,' she said. 'Didn't you have any inkling? Weren't you suspicious?'

'Of course not!' Her mother's face creased into a scowl. 'Do you seriously think I would have married him if I'd known? What do you take me for?'

Isabel reached forward and grasped her mother's hand. 'I'm sorry. I'm not suggesting you were complicit in his deception. I'm just staggered that he managed to pull the wool over your eyes for so long. How could he live with himself, knowing that he was deceiving two women?'

A shadow flickered across Barbara's face. 'I think he coped by

127

keeping things distinctly separate,' she said. 'Compartmentalised. He had two discrete lives ... and when I say discrete, I mean in the sense that they were individual and disconnected. I suppose he also had to be very discreet ... careful about what he said and did, so as not to trip himself up. He never made a mistake. Not once. It helped that his two wives were living in different countries. There was no danger of us bumping into each other. We didn't even speak the same language, for God's sake. She was French. I was English. Your father gave a piece of himself to each of us and I'm pretty sure I got the smallest portion.'

'So all those times he was away, supposedly working ...'

'It's true that his job did entail a lot of travelling – but, yes, a lot of the time he was with her.'

'Didn't you suspect that something might be going on?'

Barbara retrieved her hand from Isabel's grip. 'There were times when I thought he might be seeing another woman. I remember one time in particular. He was away for almost three months and only rang me once a week. Looking back now, I realise that sounds rather weird, but at the time it was perfectly normal ... well, not exactly normal, but acceptable. Phone calls were expensive and we didn't have a lot of spare cash. It was only later that I realised why money had always been tight. Your father was running two homes, supporting two families.'

Isabel had been leaning towards the fire, trying to absorb warmth into bones that felt as though they had turned to marble. Her head shot up as her mother's words sank in.

'Two families? Are you saying that Dad had other children?'

Barbara nodded. 'That's exactly what I'm saying. When he first met me, he had a wife and a six-month-old son.'

'Shit!' Isabel stood up.

'It appears that his wife, Jeanne, had some kind of breakdown a few months after the birth,' Barbara explained. 'It was probably postnatal depression. The baby blues, as it was called back then. Apparently Jeanne was struggling to cope and, with Donald working away so often, she took the baby and went to stay with her parents.'

'So, technically, they were separated when you and Dad met?'

Barbara gave a moue of disdain, brushing aside any such misconception. 'Geographically perhaps, but they were still very much together. Jeanne was Catholic. Her marriage may have been going through a rough patch, but as far as she was concerned, it was for keeps. Your dad said divorce wasn't an option and, in fairness, I don't think he ever had any intention of leaving her. He loved Jeanne, and he loved his son.'

'What is he called?' Isabel asked, unexpectedly curious about her sibling. 'The son ... what's his name?'

'I don't know. I didn't ask. All I know is that your half-brother is about eighteen months older than you.'

Isabel dropped back onto the sofa, trying to absorb the salvo of information that had been fired at her. She'd often wondered why her mother had never filed for divorce. She hadn't considered that it might be because there was no marriage to dissolve.

'Our wedding should never have taken place,' Barbara said. 'It was totally illegal. Presumably, your father only agreed to it in order to legitimise your birth. That kind of thing was important at the time – nowadays, of course, it doesn't matter a jot.'

'If that was how he justified his decision to break the law, it's pathetic,' Isabel said. 'It's a feeble excuse, even by 1960s standards.'

'I prefer to believe he was trying to do the right thing,' said Barbara. 'Your father was incredibly unhappy when we first met. He enjoyed my company and we went out a few times. It was all very innocent. I don't think he had any intention of betraying his wife or of being unfaithful. I made that happen.'

Isabel gaped at Barbara, astonished. 'Don't try and shoulder the blame, Mum. You didn't know he was married. He deceived you. Lied to you. You weren't to know.'

'With hindsight, I realise I should have questioned him more thoroughly, but everything happened so quickly. One minute I found out I was pregnant, the next we were married.'

'So when did you discover the truth?'

'That weekend in 1977, when you went off on your school trip. He sat me down and confessed. Told me everything.' A tear ran down her cheek and she wiped it away with the back of her hand. 'Apparently it took Jeanne a while to get better after her breakdown but, eventually, she and the baby moved back into the family home. Jeanne and Donald agreed that she shouldn't have any more children, in case she got the baby blues again.'

'And meanwhile, Dad had acquired another wife and child in England,' Isabel said. 'All those long work trips must have been a convenient cover for his double life.'

'He wouldn't have been able to pull it off without them. And you're right, that's exactly what it was. A double life. A life that may well have continued indefinitely, if Jeanne hadn't ...'

She paused as the clock in the corner chimed the hour.

'If Jeanne hadn't what, Mum?'

'Become pregnant again. In the summer of 1977 your dad began to stay away a lot more than usual. The weather was sweltering that year – not as amazing as 1976, but still rather glorious.'

'I remember,' said Isabel. 'We'd hoped to take a trip to the coast, but Dad was away for the whole of the six-week holiday.'

Barbara sighed. 'He told me he had a new project to set up over in France, but the reality was that Jeanne had found out she was having another baby and had gone to pieces. She was afraid that history would repeat itself. She was very, very down. Depressed. Throughout the summer, your dad stayed close to home ... his French home ... to support Jeanne. He eventually told me all of this in October of that year, right after his revelation about our charade of a marriage. He'd reached the point where he was forced to choose, and he chose Jeanne over me. Donald said I was a strong person and he knew I'd be able to cope with whatever life threw at me.'

'What an utterly selfish bastard he was,' Isabel said. A shudder moved up her spine. 'Although, in a way he was right. You did cope, didn't you?'

'After a fashion, but it was touch and go for a while.' Barbara pressed her lips together to stop them from trembling. 'It cut me up that your dad seemed to think Jeanne was the only one who was vulnerable. He said he had his son to think about, and the new baby. He begged me to understand. He said he couldn't carry on with his duplicitous life. He'd decided to give up the sales job and get an office-based position in France. He felt it was the only way he could give Jeanne the support she needed.'

'And he expected you to go along with that?'

'Yes, without question. He asked me to forgive him and begged me not to report him to the police. He said he'd go to jail if they found out. I think the prospect of a prison sentence terrified him. He'd read a newspaper article about a man who got six months for bigamy.'

'Why didn't you report him? Bigamy *is* a crime. Surely you must have been angry? Didn't you want some kind of revenge?'

'What good would it have done?' Barbara said, rubbing the side of her temple. 'If I'd gone to the police, the case would have ended up in the papers. Everyone would have known what a fool I'd been and you would have been teased or bullied at school. I kept quiet to protect you and to protect myself. It was bad enough having to tell everyone that Donald had left me. If I'd told them the truth, I'm not sure I could have withstood the humiliation.'

Compassion and infuriation flared in Isabel in equal measure. 'But you had nothing to be ashamed of, Mum. *You* were the innocent party.'

'So were you, and so were Jeanne and her children. Donald hadn't told her about us, and he didn't intend to. He wanted to end things with me and walk away, back to his life in France. His real life.'

'And so you let him go?'

131

'Yes.' Sinking her head into her hands, Barbara allowed her tears to flow. 'I thought it was best to minimise the damage. Don't get me wrong, part of me was sorely tempted to expose him and the whole sordid mess he'd created. I had the power to hurt him. One word to the police and your father's world … his *worlds* … would have fallen apart. But I couldn't do it, Isabel. My heart was broken, but I couldn't bring myself to inflict the same kind of pain on anyone else.'

'I'm not sure I could have been so magnanimous,' Isabel said, marvelling at her mother's altruism.

'I did what I thought was best for all of us, including your dad. Despite everything, I still loved him – and, sometimes, when you love someone, the only thing you can do is let them go. I know that sounds cheesy, but it's true.'

As she listened, Isabel rocked back and forth, her heart pounding as she thought about what her mother must have gone through.

'I know your father was to blame for what happened, but I try not to harbour bitter thoughts towards him.' Barbara wrapped her arms around herself as if to hold back another wave of emotion. 'When I got pregnant, I dragged him into a marriage that he never asked for and didn't want. It was inevitable that everything would come out eventually. The lies were always there, bubbling beneath the surface of our lives.'

Isabel had been hungry for the truth, but now that she had it, she was finding it impossible to digest. The man her mother was describing was wildly at odds with the father she remembered.

'You and Dad always seemed so happy. That's why I could never get my head around why he left.'

'I thought we were happy too,' Barbara said, 'but appearances can be deceptive. Things aren't always what they seem.'

Isabel felt an ache beneath her ribcage. 'Why didn't you tell me?' she said. 'You should have explained. *Dad* should have explained. He should at least have had the guts to say goodbye to me.'

'I don't think he could face you, Issy. He loved you so much. That's one thing I am certain of. He couldn't bring himself to tell you the truth. He felt he'd betrayed you.'

'He had.'

Barbara got up and stood in front of the fire. 'It's easy now, armed with the sensibilities of a mature woman, for you to look back and wonder why we didn't tell you – but you were only fourteen when your dad left. It was 1977, for God's sake. It may have been the era of anarchic punk rockers, but the people *I* knew were strait-laced conformists. A bigamy case would have created a huge scandal back then. I'm not sure I could have lived with that.'

'I still wish you'd told me. Not knowing where Dad was tore me up. I thought he was dead, Mum.'

Barbara sat next to her on the sofa. 'In a way, he was. Dead to us anyway. Your father couldn't see us anymore, for the reasons I've explained. He went to live with his other family. He put them first ... but it must have torn him apart, having to choose between his children. I can't begin to imagine what that must have been like for him. My heart would have broken if I'd been forced to give you up.' She ran her hands along her upper arms and rubbed away a shiver.

A lump had formed in Isabel's throat and she found herself unable to speak. This evening, her mother had revealed glimpses of inner strength, but that hard, steely core was swaddled in layers of compassion and understanding. Her father's actions must have cut Barbara to the quick. She had suffered, and yet she could still sympathise with him and see things from his perspective. That said a lot.

'I've finally told you the truth,' Barbara said. 'I can see that it's hurt you, even after all these years. How much worse would it have been if I'd told you at the time?'

133

'What about the baby that Jeanne was expecting?' Isabel said. 'Do you know if it was a boy or a girl?'

'I don't know, and I never asked. Your father did write to me for a while from his work address and, occasionally, he'd transfer money into my bank account, but that all stopped as soon as you were eighteen and started work. I intended telling you the truth at that point, but when you decided to join the police force ...'

'You thought it was best to say nothing.'

Barbara offered up a feeble shrug. 'I didn't want to cause trouble for you.'

'Do you still know how to contact him?'

Barbara nodded. 'Your father made contact again in the late Nineties, when he retired from his job. He wrote to me via a solicitor to let me know and the solicitor told me that if I needed to, I could get in touch with Donald through him, but that I should only do so in case of an emergency. I was told I'd be informed if Donald passed away. I haven't received that message yet, which is why I know your dad is still alive.'

'But he doesn't know I'm married, or that he has three grandchildren?'

'No, love. He doesn't.'

'What if I want to get in touch with him?'

'I'm sure the solicitor would forward on a message from you,' Barbara said. 'I've brought the law firm's details with me. If you want to try and contact your father, I won't object. It's up to you.'

Isabel rubbed her hands across her eyes. She was stunned and perplexed, grappling ineptly with the implications of what her mother had told her. 'I'm not sure what to do,' she said. 'There's a part of me that's desperate to see him again to lay the ghosts of the past to rest, but I'm also very, very angry. I can't understand how he could do that to you.'

'You're bound to be upset.'

'It's more than upsetting, Mum. I feel traumatised ... shaken to the core.' She shivered. 'I need to think carefully about what happens next.'

Barbara squeezed her hand. 'You're shocked.'

Isabel paused to analyse her state of mind, realising that the complicated nature of her emotions could not be summed up in one word. What she felt was a fluctuating sweet and sour combination: disbelief and anger; numbness and pain; pity, sadness, and grief.

'I'm surprised, more than shocked,' she said. 'And sad – for you and for me. And for Dad too. I wish he'd kept in touch with me.'

'I think he was afraid to,' Barbara said, her eyes bright with tears. 'He would have been worried about what you'd think of him and how he'd feel if he saw you again. You're living proof of his double life. Perhaps he preferred not to be reminded of something that he's ashamed of.'

Isabel wondered whether she and her father could have any kind of future together. Things would never be the same between them, but they might be able to find a way back to each other. He was eightyone now. There weren't many years left to forge a new relationship with the parent she thought she had lost.

'Can I give you a hug now?' Barbara asked.

Nodding, Isabel allowed herself to be enveloped in her mother's arms. As she breathed in Barbara's perfume, she felt the heavy weight of wondering slip away. She knew the truth now; there were no secrets burrowing their way between them.

And there was something her mother had said that had rattled an idea in her mind that might unravel another puzzle. Tomorrow, when she got to work, she would be pursuing a new line of enquiry.

***

Lily's mum had promised to drop Ellie off at seven-thirty. A few minutes before the allotted time, Isabel loitered by the window. When a pair of approaching headlights turned into the driveway, she darted to the front door and was waiting outside by the time the car pulled up.

As Ellie clambered out of the back seat, Isabel introduced herself and had a brief chat with Lily and her mum. When the car pulled away, Ellie headed towards the house, her backpack swinging from her arm.

'Is Gran here?'

'Yes.' Isabel caught hold of the backpack to slow Ellie down. 'I know you're looking forward to seeing her, but before we go in ... how was school today?'

Ellie turned. 'It was OK.'

'Just OK?'

'It was school, Mum. What do you want me to say?' She shrugged with one shoulder, elegantly dismissive.

'What lessons did you have?'

'English.' Ellie thought for a moment. 'Art, French, and Biology.'

'And you had a good day? Nothing to report? Nothing out of the ordinary?'

Ellie narrowed her eyes, fine-tuning her antennae. 'Is this you checking up on me?' she said. 'Are you going to be doing this every day?'

Isabel held up her hands. 'I'm just making conversation,' she said. 'You would tell me though, wouldn't you? If something was wrong?'

'What's with all the questions?' Ellie had reached the front door. 'You're acting weird, Mum. Gran's here and I've not seen her for ages. Can I go in now?'

Without waiting for permission, she hurried into the house. Isabel followed, telling herself that if anything untoward had happened at school that day, Ellie would have said. There was nothing to worry about. Was there?

Chapter 26

At nine o'clock the following morning Isabel was standing in front of the whiteboard in the CID room. Dan had added Julie Desmond's name and pinned the black-and-white snapshot next to the photo of Celia Aspen. It was a start, but a tentative one. Nothing could detract from the irritating question mark that still taunted them, serving as a nagging reminder that, until they could put a name to the victim, they were in no position to connect any dots or identify suspects.

Isabel wasn't the kind of person to ignore her gut instincts, no matter how unlikely they seemed, and the conversation she'd had with her mother the previous evening had prompted her to apply some lateral thinking to the Ecclesdale Drive case. What was it her mother had said? *Appearances can be deceptive. Things aren't always what they seem.* Her dad had kept up appearances and fooled everyone about his true identity. What if Celia had been keeping up appearances too? Was the reason she'd been so closed-off and solitary because she was hiding a secret … one she'd held on to for most of her life in order to survive?

As Isabel considered that possibility, an idea had formed in her head. It was only a theory – and a speculative one at that. It would need backing up with proof, and that would take work – but something told her it was a hypothesis worth pursuing.

Dan, Lucas and Zoe were at their desks. Lucas hadn't been due in until noon, but he'd come in early for the meeting. He stretched his arms above his head and tried, unsuccessfully, to suppress a yawn.

Isabel frowned. 'I hope I'm not keeping you awake, Lucas.'

'Nah, you're all right, boss. I was up late watching a film, that's all. I'll be OK when I've had a cup of coffee.'

'If that's a hint for me to make one, you can get lost,' Zoe said.

'But your coffee tastes so much better than mine,' Lucas said, his voice wheedling.

'Forget the coffee,' Isabel said. 'I want to talk about who our victim might be in the Ecclesdale Drive case. I've had an off-the-wall idea. It may seem unlikely, but I'm going to run it past you anyway.'

Dan sat on the edge of his desk. 'Go on then, boss. Don't keep us in suspense.'

'Celia Aspen.' She pointed to the photo on the board. 'I think the body is Celia Aspen's.'

Dan gave a short huff of laughter. 'How can it be?'

'I'll admit this is only a theory, but bear with me. Celia Aspen disappeared in 1986 while she was living at the property. If we'd known that from the off, it's fair to say we'd have expected any bones discovered at the house to be hers. Am I right?'

'Yep, except the skeleton is that of a man. Raveen was very clear on that.'

'What if …' Isabel took a deep breath, wondering whether she was meandering into an illthoughtout side track. 'What if Celia Aspen was born male, but was living as a woman?'

Lucas sat up and tapped a pen against his teeth. 'Are you serious, boss? Isn't that a bit unlikely?'

'Statistically, perhaps. I don't know what percentage of the population is transgender – probably less than one per cent. In

138

1986, when Celia Aspen disappeared, that figure may well have been considerably less. But that's not to say it's not possible.'

Despite her confident tone of voice, Isabel was beginning to doubt the wisdom of what she was suggesting. Could a person really live as a transgender woman without someone knowing?

'Believe me, I've thought the idea through – and it fits,' she said, as much to reassure herself than to convince her team.

'OK,' said Dan. 'Let's assume you're right and Celia Aspen was transgender. Are you suggesting this was a hate crime?'

Isabel tilted her head. 'I'm not saying that, although we can't rule it out. But if the bones we found are Celia Aspen's, it puts a whole new perspective on this case.'

'How do we find out for certain?' Lucas asked.

Dan clicked his fingers. 'We could compare DNA from the skeleton to a sample from Julie Desmond. The two of them were related.'

'That's one option.' Isabel scratched her forehead. 'Trouble is, DNA testing can take weeks. Besides, I'm not sure how easy it would be to get DNA from the bones – we'll have to talk to Raveen.'

Zoe smiled. 'We could just compare Celia Aspen's dental records with the skeleton.' She held up the missing person's file. 'Remember I told you a body was found on Beeley Moor? Celia Aspen's dental records were used to eliminate her as the victim. We should still have them on file.'

Isabel punched the air. 'That is music to my ears, Zoe. Dig out the information and get it down to Forensics. Ask them to get an answer for us ASAP.'

This was a chance to put her theory to the test. Were they getting closer to finding out the truth, or was she sending her team off on a wild goose chase?

Chapter 27

Raveen rang half an hour after Zoe had sent him the dental records. 'I'm at the mortuary with the pathologist,' he said. 'In our opinion, it's a match.'

'How sure are you?' Isabel asked.

'Ordinarily, I'd say only eighty-five per cent … but the dental plate we found is the clincher. It matches with the four missing front teeth on Celia Aspen's upper jaw, so I'm fairly confident. We'll need to get everything checked by a forensic orthodontist though, just to be absolutely certain.'

'But you think it's her?'

'Yes, and it's not only the dental records that check out. Celia Aspen's medical records were on file too. She'd visited her GP and he'd referred her to a specialist to discuss osteo-arthritis in her knees. That corresponds with the bone spurs we found.'

'The neighbour told us that Celia wasn't in the best of health and that she was waiting for an operation. I wonder if that was knee replacement surgery?'

'It wouldn't surprise me in the least,' Raveen replied. 'And if your theory's right and Celia Aspen was transgender, the one person she would have confided in would have been her doctor.

If the GP was young enough, he or she might still be practising. It could be worth checking.'

'We will. Thanks, Raveen. Let me know as soon as you've heard from the forensic orthodontist.'

Isabel ended the call and looked out through the glass partition that separated her office from the open-plan CID room. Dan was at his desk, staring into space. She hoped he was mulling over the case, and not daydreaming about something else, but you never could tell. As the newest member of her team, she hadn't had the chance to get to know him properly and he was hard to read.

She got up and went into the main office.

'Raveen and the pathologist think the dental records are a match. They're getting them double-checked with a forensic orthodontist, but they seemed pretty sure.'

'You're right about your theory fitting with what we've learned so far.' Dan was animated and eager. 'I've been thinking about what Joyce Littlewood told us about Celia smoking her cigarettes outside in all weathers. A windproof Zippo would have been a good choice in those circumstances, don't you think? That lighter didn't belong to some guy from Canada. It was Celia's.'

'It looks that way,' Isabel said. 'But I can't help but wonder about this man from Canada … who he might have been and whether or not he's significant. Do you think his visit could have triggered the chain of events that led to Celia Aspen's death?'

'It's possible. Especially if he knew her before she transitioned. He could be our main suspect.'

'Then again, playing devil's advocate, he might have no connection to the case whatsoever.'

Dan slotted his fingers together and twisted his hands from side to side. 'If he *did* murder Celia, I'd say our chances of apprehending him are zero. From the description Joyce Littlewood gave us, he was quite elderly, even in 1986. He's not likely to still be around thirty odd years later.'

141

Isabel wandered over to the whiteboard and pointed to the print-out of the black-and-white photograph of the unknown couple.

'What was it that Timothy Littlewood said when he looked at this photo?' she said.

Dan rubbed a hand over his mouth. 'He said "it looks like Celia", but when you asked him to confirm whether she was the woman in the photo, he changed his mind. He told us categorically that it wasn't.'

'Maybe he didn't change his mind.' Isabel tapped the photo. 'He said: *it looks like Celia*. What if Timothy was being literal? Perhaps he'd spotted a likeness between Celia and the *man* in the photo? What if this is Celia before she transitioned?'

Dan pushed himself out of his chair, pulled the image from the board and scrutinised it. 'It could be. Joyce Littlewood was adamant the woman wasn't Celia, but maybe the man is.'

'What if, before she transitioned, Celia was engaged to be married? The woman in the photo could be the fiancée?'

Dan grabbed his phone and took a digital shot of the black-and-white photo. With his index finger and thumb, he enlarged the image, zooming in on the woman's left hand. 'She does seem to be wearing a ring, but the image is grainy. It's impossible to tell whether it's the diamond ring Amy Whitworth found.'

Isabel stuck the photo back onto the board. 'We're speculating now and, in my experience, that can be even more misleading than making assumptions. We should really wait until we've heard back from the forensic orthodontist.'

'But if you're right? If the bones are definitely Celia Aspen's?' said Lucas. He and Zoe had been silently absorbing Dan and Isabel's exchange.

'Then we'll need to start again, at the beginning.' Isabel looked at her team expectantly. 'Let's run through a plan of action. What will we need to establish?'

'We'll have to determine whether or not Celia Aspen was

murdered,' Zoe said, lifting the ring-pull on a can of Diet Coke. 'It seems likely, given the circumstances. Even if she died from natural causes, there's nothing natural about what someone did with the body, post-mortem.'

'We also need to ask why,' Lucas said, keen to not let Zoe outshine him. 'And who? Who would have a reason to kill her?'

'Motive, means and opportunity,' Dan said.

Isabel nodded. 'Motivation for murder is usually money, love, revenge or reputation. The killer will either have had something to gain, or be protecting something they don't want to lose. In the majority of murder cases, there's often a clear suspect – normally someone known to the victim. Ordinarily, Julie Desmond would be the focus of our investigation, but with her ruled out we're going to have to turn our attentions elsewhere.'

'We'll obviously do everything we can to solve the case, boss, but I think we need to prepare ourselves for the likelihood that the perpetrator is no longer alive.'

'You could well be right, Dan, but we do need to try and solve this. We should have the results of the dental comparison by this time tomorrow. In the meantime, let's get some intel on the Aspen family tree. We need to check for a record of Celia Aspen's birth. Julie Desmond said she didn't know anything about her aunt until she turned up at her grandmother's funeral.'

'She also said the grandmother had a brother who was killed in the war,' Dan remarked. 'If we find out the brother's name, we might be able to check his military record.'

'Good call, Dan.' Isabel smiled. 'At the risk of speculating again, I'm not convinced the brother was a casualty of war. I'm more inclined to think he survived and, at some point, transitioned and became Celia Aspen.'

Chapter 28

Isabel looked out of Detective Superintendent Valerie Tibbet's first-floor office window towards the seven-storey mill building that dominated the town. Despite a pummelling from the previous day's strong winds, Bainbridge looked almost pictur-esque. The sky was pale and delicate, washed out by the rain, and shiny autumn sunlight gilded the faces of the stone cottages on the other side of the hill.

Isabel had finished bringing the Super up to speed on her theory regarding Celia Aspen and, as always, she'd found their onetoone meeting awkward and discomfiting. Val was her boss, but it felt strange having to report to her.

Fifteen years ago, Val Tibbet had been a detective constable, and a member of Isabel's team. From the moment she'd arrived, Val had made no attempt to hide her hard-nosed ambition. She was on a fast-track to promotion and she wasn't going to let anyone or anything hold her back. Isabel, who'd worked her way steadily up the ranks to detective inspector, was used to the whirlwind arrival and departure of graduate whiz-kids desperate for promotion. She hadn't had time to get to know Val or warm to her. In all honesty, she hadn't tried very hard – mainly because she hadn't expected her to stick around for long.

While Isabel had been on maternity leave following Ellie's birth, Val had transferred to a Nottinghamshire force, taking up the post of detective sergeant in a major crime unit. Isabel hadn't thought about Val much after that – until three years ago, when she'd reappeared in Bainbridge as the newly appointed detective superintendent.

The appointment had taken Isabel by surprise and made her re-evaluate her own situation. Ten years earlier, she would have jumped at the chance of promotion, but the right opportunity had never arisen back then. With hindsight, her circumstances a decade ago had hardly been conducive to taking on a more senior role, not with Ellie still being so young. By the time the detective superintendent vacancy had come up at Bainbridge, Isabel found she no longer possessed the necessary ambition and energy to apply, and she decided to pass up the opportunity for promotion. She'd reached the point where all she wanted to do was retire. Another seven years should do it. Ellie would have graduated by then, assuming she chose to go to university in the first place. In the meantime, Isabel intended to do the job she'd been doing for years. She enjoyed being a DI, and she was good at it. She had plenty of experience and training and she'd been accredited by the College of Policing as an SIO. For the most part, she liked her job – despite the long hours. Even so, she had to admit she'd felt aggrieved when she found out she would be reporting to someone who had once been a subordinate.

Val Tibbet linked her fingers and placed them on her desk. There was a look of scepticism around her eyes, but at least she hadn't rejected Isabel's theory out of hand.

'When can we expect the report from the orthodontist?'

Isabel dragged herself away from the window and sat down in the squeaky black leather chair that visitors were obliged to sit in. The placing of the low-level seating was strategic, of that she was certain. It was Val's way of achieving a psychological advantage. The situation reminded Isabel of the Seventies sitcom she'd sometimes watched with her dad: *The Fall and Rise of Reginald Perrin*. She smiled as the chair's leather creaked flatulently. *This must have been how Reggie felt when he sat in CJ's office*, she thought.

'Sometime tomorrow,' she replied. 'And once the ID's been confirmed—'

'If.' Val interrupted. '*If* the ID is confirmed. There's still a chance you might be wrong.'

You'd like that, thought Isabel.

'Forensics were certain it was a match,' Isabel told her. 'Confirmation from the orthodontist is pretty much a formality.'

'OK, well let me know as soon as you hear anything. If the bones are Celia Aspen's, are you going to start with the niece? You said she'd inherited the house?'

'That's right, but Julie Desmond was in Australia when her aunt went missing. She does have a strong motive, but she has an even stronger alibi.'

'So what are your lines of enquiry?'

'We'll talk to Joyce Littlewood again, and her son. We'll also have a word with Julie Desmond's mother ... and, if we can establish who the visitor from Canada was, we'll follow up on that as well – although the gentleman in question is likely to be deceased.'

'I know you have a personal connection to the house, Isabel. I hope that won't encourage you to give this case too high a priority.'

Isabel leaned forward as elegantly as the positioning of the leather chair would allow. 'I'll treat this case as I would any other. I'm an old hand at prioritising, and I also know how to delegate, as I'm sure you remember. I realise the bones have been there for more than thirty years, Val, but that doesn't mean we shouldn't do everything we can to track down the perpetrator. Word soon gets around in a small town like Bainbridge. Murders are infrequent. Local residents will be jittery and they'll expect us to solve this case quickly, regardless of how long ago the crime was committed.'

Val Tibbet looked down at her desk, stern-faced. 'You're right about word getting around. I've had the comms team on to me again. It seems the news has spread beyond the local rag. The national papers have picked up on the story and we're being pestered for an update. Get onto it as soon as you can and make sure you liaise with comms the minute we get confirmation on the bones. You may want to issue another press appeal to encourage people to come forward.'

***

Isabel felt herself uncoil as she walked back to the CID room. It was a relief to return to the relative comfort of her own office and the support of her team. They weren't perfect, but she knew she could rely on them.

Dan had gone off to Derby in connection with the armed robbery, but Zoe was at her computer, studying the screen while simultaneously making notes and munching on a biscuit. A shower of crumbs fell onto her keyboard as she devoured the last piece.

Lucas looked up from his desk. 'Boss! I've got the intel on the Aspen family.'

Isabel stood behind him and looked over his shoulder. 'Hit me with it, Lucas.'

'Julie Desmond's father was Anthony Desmond, and *his* mother was Elizabeth Desmond, née Aspen. She was born in 1923 and she had one sibling: an older brother. His name was Cecil and he was born in Nottingham on 5th June 1918.'

'No sister?'

'No, but get this …' Lucas reached for his notes. 'The medical records on Celia Aspen's missing persons file confirm she was born on 5th June 1918.'

He closed his notebook, tossed it onto his desk, and smirked.

'No need to look quite so smug, Lucas,' said Zoe, who had swivelled her chair around to listen in on what he had to say. 'Theoretically, Celia could be Cecil's twin.'

'No chance,' he replied. 'If she is, why wasn't her birth recorded?'

'Mistakes do happen,' Isabel said. 'An error could have been made when the birth was registered, but it does seem unlikely. It's more probable that Cecil and Celia are one and the same.'

Zoe spun back to her desk. 'I'm in the process of checking out Second World War records for anyone with the surname Aspen. It'll be a lot easier now that we've got a first name.'

She tapped her keyboard, entering Cecil Aspen's details into the search terms of the website open on her screen.

'Here he is,' she said, when she'd scanned the results. 'According to his military record, Cecil Aspen was shipped out to the Far East. On 1st March 1942 he was captured by the Japanese and held as a prisoner of war at the ... Fukuoka camp.'

Lucas smirked as Zoe stumbled over the pronunciation.

'He was released on 2nd September 1945.' Zoe smiled at them. 'He survived the war.'

Isabel rubbed her knuckles together, pleased that the fog surrounding this investigation was beginning to clear. This was what police work was like sometimes. Boring routine enquiries, checking and re-checking the facts ... often achieving very little. This time, though, they appeared to be on the right track, at least in terms of the identification.

Tomorrow was Friday. Once they received the expected confirmation from the forensic orthodontist, their investigation could begin in earnest. Where it would lead them was anyone's guess.

Chapter 29

As she retrieved her homemade lasagne from the oven, Isabel chided herself for not letting Nathan prepare dinner. The dish she'd rustled up when she got in from work had looked divine until she put it into the oven. Her mistake had been going upstairs and spending too long on her own appearance. Like a snake shedding its skin, she'd peeled off her long-sleeved T-shirt and stepped out of the black trousers she habitually wore for work. After she'd washed and applied a light layer of make-up, she'd decided to 'make an effort' by slipping on a soft, green jersey dress. A pair of sparkling silver earrings had completed her transformation from DI Isabel Blood to Issy Blood – wife, mother and daughter.

By the time she had returned to the kitchen, the lasagne was overcooked. The top was singed and the edges were bubbling fiercely. The heat of the red-hot dish radiated through her oven gloves as she placed it on the worktop to cool down. It would burn everyone's mouths if she served it as it was.

Retrieving a bowl of colourful mixed salad from the fridge, she made her way into the dining room. Her mother, Nathan, Ellie and Kate were already seated at the round mahogany table that was reserved for family gatherings and Christmas. The rest of the time they ate their meals in the kitchen or from trays in front of the TV.

Her eldest daughter, Kate, looked relaxed and happy to be with her grandmother. The two women were sitting next to each other, laughing softly.

Kate was the only one of her children to have fair hair, although her eyes were the same colour as her siblings – dark and rich as raisins. She had eagerly accepted the invitation to dinner, prompting Isabel to wonder – not for the first time – whether her daughter was lonely.

Kate was a teacher at a primary school in Matlock and lived alone in Wirksworth in a tiny terraced cottage built of Derbyshire stone. Isabel wasn't sure whether her tall, willowy and utterly beautiful daughter would ever settle down. Over the years she had dallied with a string of boyfriends, but had never had what could be described as a serious relationship. Isabel suspected that no one would ever match Kate's exacting criteria. She was looking for someone who was intelligent, creative and sensitive, with a love of art, film and books – and she didn't seem willing to compromise. Isabel worried that she'd still be looking a decade from now.

'The lasagne's too hot,' she said, placing the salad in the centre of the table. 'I'll let it cool off for a few minutes before I bring it in.'

Kate and Ellie exchanged knowing looks.

'Have you burned it, Mum?' Ellie said.

'No.' Isabel held up her hands. 'Honestly. Cross my heart. It's not burned. Just … well done.'

Having warned the girls that there was something important she wanted to talk to them about, she was surprised and pleased to find them so ebullient. They were clearly enjoying their grandmother's company.

It would have been nice to have included Bailey in the evening's discussions, but her son was away – 'off travelling' with his girlfriend, Sophie. The pair had met at university and had been inseparable ever since. After completing their degrees, they'd both taken an ESOL qualification and, after five years of living and teaching together in the UK, had decided to go off for a while and see the world.

They were currently in New Zealand, having worked their way there via East Asia and Australia. They were planning to come back in the new year after stopping off in the Caribbean.

When Isabel returned to the kitchen, the lasagne had stopped bubbling, so she carried it into the dining room and served up. Thankfully, it tasted better than it looked and their conversation over the meal was as light and frivolous as the white wine Barbara had selected at the local off-licence.

'So, what is it you want to talk to us about?' Kate asked, over coffee and a dessert of shop-bought tarte au citron.

'Your grandfather,' Isabel said.

Kate tilted her head questioningly. 'Do you mean Dad's dad, or yours?'

'Mine.'

'I didn't think you knew anything about your dad,' Ellie said. 'How come you've suddenly got things to tell us about him?'

Nathan cut himself a second slice of lemon tart and leaned back in his chair. Isabel had shared with him every detail of what Barbara had told her. They'd talked into the early hours and agreed it was best to tell the children the truth. Nathan wanted to be there when Isabel broke the news, but she'd made it clear that she wanted to be the one who spoke to them. She was pretty sure her mother would chip in too, but that was fair enough – it was her story after all.

Kate and Ellie listened, open-mouthed as Isabel talked about their grandparents' bigamous marriage. Surprisingly, Barbara maintained a subdued silence throughout the conversation. She looked nervous and uncertain. Very un-Barbara-like.

'So we have a criminal for a grandparent?' Ellie said.

Isabel flinched. 'Well, yes, that's one way of putting it. How do you feel about the situation?'

'I think it's kind of cool,' Ellie said. 'Are you going to track him down? Are we going to meet him?'

'I'm not sure, love. Let's take things one step at a time, eh? He might not want to see us.'

'I think he will,' said Barbara. 'I'm sure he'd love to meet his grandchildren.'

'You're not going to arrest him, are you, Mum?'

Isabel laughed. 'It's very tempting – but no, Ellie. I'm not going to arrest him.'

'What do you think, Kate?' Nathan asked. 'You're very quiet.'

'I'm a bit taken aback.' She pushed away the plate containing her half-eaten pudding. 'Unlike Ellie, I don't think there's anything remotely cool about what he did. The way he treated you both was appalling.'

She turned to face her grandmother. 'What surprises me most is why you haven't said anything before now, Gran.'

Isabel felt uncharacteristically protective of her mother, whose eyes were filling with unshed tears.

'Mum and I have already talked about that,' she said. 'It was hard for her, keeping it a secret, but she made a promise to Dad that she wouldn't tell anyone. He'd have been in a lot of trouble if she had. Your gran kept her word. That was very brave and selfless, given the circumstances.'

Barbara looked at Isabel and tried to smile, but her lips were trembling too much and her mouth refused to cooperate.

***

Later, when Kate had driven home and Ellie had gone to bed, Isabel sat with her mother and Nathan in front of a roaring fire in the living room. They were watching a tense, much anticipated TV drama that, ordinarily, would have had them enthralled – but the events of the last couple of days had left them feeling tired and unable to concentrate.

Nathan yawned. 'If you don't mind, I think I'll turn in.' He stood up and stretched. 'I've got a commission I need to finish, so I'm going to have to get up early tomorrow.'

Left alone, Isabel and her mother watched television in silence. 'I don't think I'll be late myself,' Isabel said eventually. 'I've not slept very well this week.'

'It's hardly surprising,' Barbara said ruefully. 'It's been a hell of week.'

When the TV drama had come to a cliffhanging conclusion, Isabel reached for the remote and switched off. A hush descended on the room, broken only by the spitting and crackling of the fire.

Barbara split the silence with a sigh. 'Thanks for sticking up for me earlier,' she said. 'If you hadn't said what you did, I got the feeling Kate might have had a go at me … about keeping you in the dark.'

'Don't worry, she'll come round when she's had a few days to process everything. We gave the girls a lot to think about and, overall, I thought they seemed remarkably laid back about the situation. I hope Bailey will be similarly unfazed by the news. We're due to Skype with him at the weekend. We can tell him then.'

'It's much easier for the children than it is for you. I don't suppose they feel as though they've missed out, because they never got to know your father to begin with. They're more accepting because they aren't emotionally invested like you are.'

Barbara was more astute than Isabel had given her credit for. Isabel had been trying hard to hide her inner turmoil. She was still reeling from the news that her father was alive, and wrestling with the reasons he had gone away all those years ago. Even Nathan had failed to notice how fraught she was – but, clearly, her mother had picked up on it.

Over the last few days, Isabel's emotions had been pulled and

153

stretched until they were taut and brittle and ready to snap. She was tense and overwrought; wondering whether to get in touch with her father – scared by the idea, and excited by it too. They were connected. Biologically. Genetically. And yet he was a stranger to her now. Someone she hadn't seen for over forty years.

'I've been mulling over whether to contact Dad,' she said. 'But I'm nervous about it. What if we've left it too late?'

'He's your father. Surely it's never going to be too late.'

The fire had begun to burn down. The ticking, shifting sounds it made were soothing.

'What about you, Mum? How are you holding up?'

'I'm feeling wrung out, to be honest. I thought I'd laid all those ghosts to rest, but talking to you has stirred up memories I'm not sure I want to recall.'

'Try to remember the good times,' Isabel suggested. 'There must have been a few.'

Barbara smiled, lost on a sea of recollections. 'It was far from a perfect marriage, but we did have our moments. But remembering those times only makes it harder.'

'I can't begin to imagine how you must have felt when Dad told you what he'd done.'

Barbara frowned, her thoughts taking her somewhere sad. 'It almost destroyed me. All those times I thought we were happy were nothing more than an illusion. A big fat lie.'

'Not all of it, Mum. I remember how safe and cherished and happy I was as a child. I felt loved. You can't fake that.'

'I'm glad.' Barbara managed a tearful smile. 'It's good to know we got at least one thing right.'

Isabel stood up and turned off one of the table lamps. 'None of us can change the past, Mum. I'm sure Dad loved you. I *know* he loved me. I'm only sorry that he chose to leave us behind, without a backward glance. I'm not sure I can come to terms with that.'

***

Although she longed to go upstairs and climb straight into bed, Isabel decided to run a bath. She poured lavender oil into the water and grabbed the novel she was reading from her bedside table. Nathan was still awake, but he'd switched the light off on his side of the bed.

'I won't be long,' she whispered. 'I'm going to take a quick bath. It might help me sleep.'

Sliding her body into the warm, lavender-scented water, she closed her eyes and tried to drain away the emotional detritus that was floating around in her head, but it refused to budge. She found it impossible to relax. All the things she had learned since Monday were spinning around in her head.

Trying to direct her mind in a different direction, she picked up her book. She read a chapter and was starting another when, without warning, she began to cry. Dropping the book by the side of the bath, she slid further into the water and wept silently. Wretched tears ran down her face and into the bath water, taking with them some of her pent-up anxieties.

She stayed in the bath, crying, wishing and wondering, until the water began to grow cold.

Chapter 30

'We've had confirmation from the forensic orthodontist,' said Raveen, when he rang at nine-forty on Friday morning. 'You have your positive ID. The bones belonged to Celia Aspen.'

It was the news she'd been expecting, but Isabel nevertheless felt a sense of relief.

'Thanks, Raveen,' she said. 'Any news yet on the cause of death?'

'That's going to be tricky, given how long the body has been underground. The pathologist wants to call on the services of a forensic anthropologist, so it might be a few days before you get the full report. What I can tell you is that the skull showed no signs of head injury and there were no marks or wounds on any of the other bones. Cause of death could have been strangulation or poisoning or suffocation. Unfortunately, whatever caused Celia Aspen's death may have happened too long ago to show any trace.'

After the call ended, Isabel picked up the original missing person's file, which was sitting on her desk. As she walked into the main office, she gave Zoe and Dan a thumbs-up.

'It's been confirmed. The body was Celia Aspen's.'

'So what now?' asked Dan.

'Let's start by paying Julie Desmond another visit. We'll also need to talk to Timothy Littlewood again, and we may as well talk to Joyce Littlewood at the same time. Can you arrange for us to go and see them sometime today please, Dan?'

He nodded.

'Before you make those calls, let's go through everything we know from the misper file.' She placed it on Zoe's desk. 'We need to re-examine and reconsider the facts in light of what we know now. Is Lucas due in?'

'No,' Dan replied. 'Not until midday. Do you want me to give him a call? Get him to come in early?'

Isabel thought of the overtime budget. 'No, it's OK. We can update him later. Zoe, you're more familiar with the missing person's report than I am. Talk us through it.'

Zoe pulled the file towards her and leaned forward. 'Julie Desmond reported Celia Aspen missing on Thursday 4th September 1986. She'd last seen her aunt on 8th May of that year, which was a few days before Julie flew out to Australia for a three-month holiday. When Julie got back in August, she went round to see her aunt, but she wasn't there.'

'But Julie had a key to the house?' Isabel said.

'No, but she knew where Celia hid her spare key. Julie didn't enter the house on that first visit, but when she went back three days later and her aunt still wasn't there, she let herself in. She said the fridge was empty and there was nothing to suggest anything was wrong, other than the fact that the lawn hadn't been mowed. She assumed Celia had gone away – possibly to Canada to visit a friend. Julie called round to the house several times over the next few weeks, but there was still no sign of her aunt and, by early September, she was beginning to get worried. She decided to go back inside the house to see if she could locate her aunt's passport. She found it in a drawer in her dressing table. As soon as she saw it, Julie realised Celia couldn't have gone abroad and that's when she reported her missing.'

Dan frowned. 'So, Celia had been missing for almost four months before it was reported. That's a long time. Didn't anyone else wonder where she was?'

'Well, from what we've heard, Celia was a loner,' Zoe said. 'If you haven't got any friends, I guess there's no one to miss you if you're not around.'

'What about her doctor?' Isabel said. 'She was waiting to see a specialist about an operation, wasn't she? Didn't the hospital try and get in touch?'

'If they did, I'd imagine it would have been by letter. Don't forget, this was 1986. Did they even have emails back then? I wouldn't know, I wasn't born until 1989.'

'All right,' said Isabel, feeling her age. 'Don't rub it in.'

Zoe blushed furiously and, ducking her head, went back to studying the file. 'A detective did speak to someone at Celia's GP surgery, but her doctor hadn't tried to contact her. The same detective made a note for someone to get in touch with the specialist at the hospital, but it doesn't look as if anyone followed up on that. There were no letters from the hospital found among Celia Aspen's unopened post.'

'There were long waiting lists for non-urgent operations back then,' Isabel said. 'Even longer than there are now. If Celia needed a knee replacement, it's possible she may have had to wait months, even years.'

'Do you want me to get back in touch with the surgery?'

'Please, Zoe. Find out whether Celia's doctor is still practising or, if not, how we can make contact if he or she has retired. Can you also check whether any of the officers who worked on the case are still around?'

'Were you on the force back then, boss?' Dan asked.

'Yes, in 1986 I was a uniformed officer, but I didn't work on this case. I don't remember hearing anything about it – and it's not something I would have forgotten, given the fact that Celia Aspen was living at my old house.' She sat down at Lucas's vacant desk. 'Based on what you've seen in the missing person's file, what's your view on how the investigation was conducted, Zoe?'

'Honestly? I think it was iffy at best.' Zoe tapped the file. 'I don't like saying this, but the investigation didn't seem to go beyond the routine. Even though Celia Aspen was sixty-eight years old when she was reported missing, she wasn't deemed to be high risk.'

'Why not?' asked Dan.

'She wasn't considered vulnerable. She had no history of depression and, aside from her arthritis, she was considered to be in excellent health. When Julie Desmond reported Celia missing, she admitted that her aunt did sometimes go away for unplanned holidays.'

Dan scowled. 'Yeah, a few days in Devon. Not for four months.'

Zoe flipped through the file. 'All relevant enquiries were made. Details were logged and circulated nationally through the system and to the usual partners, which of course included the local hospitals. A call for information was also launched in the Brixham area, which was Celia's holiday destination of choice. Her house was searched, but that didn't throw up anything helpful.'

'There obviously wasn't a thorough search of the garden,' Isabel said.

'There was a preliminary visual check and the garage and garden shed were checked during the open door search, but that's all. The garden wasn't excavated or searched further because there was no reason to suggest that Celia Aspen had been murdered.'

'Did she own a car?' Dan asked.

'No.'

'Were there any diaries or documents found that could shed light on what Celia had been doing in the period before her murder?' he said. 'Was there a computer?'

'No computer and no diary,' said Zoe. 'A few letters, but mostly unpaid utility bills.'

'Julie Desmond had access to the house,' Dan said. 'She could have gotten rid of things before the search was made.'

'Why would she do that?' Isabel asked. 'It's not as though she had any reason to muddy the investigative waters. She wasn't even around when her aunt was killed.'

'She could have been covering up for someone ... protecting them,' Zoe suggested. 'Her mother or Timothy Littlewood for instance.'

Isabel wasn't convinced. 'Having met Julie Desmond, I don't see her as the sort of person who would want to cover up for anyone. If she'd had any inkling that her aunt had been the victim of foul play, it would have been in her interest to bring that to our attention. After all, she was the sole beneficiary of her aunt's will, wasn't she?'

'Yes, but she might not have known that,' Zoe replied. 'As it turned out, it was several years before she got her inheritance.'

'What about phones?' Isabel asked. 'Mobile phones would have been expensive and brick-sized back then, used primarily by yuppies. Given her aversion to running up large telephone bills, I doubt Celia Aspen would have owned a mobile, but what about her landline? Was there a check on incoming or outgoing calls?'

Zoe pulled a sheet of paper from the file.

'We have a list of calls between March and August 1986,' she said. 'There were very few outgoing calls during that period. The last one was made on 15th April to a Bainbridge number that turned out to be a local taxi company. There were some incoming calls, including two that were identified as being from the niece in Australia. The first of those calls lasted two minutes and thirty-eight seconds. The second was even shorter at one minute fifty-six seconds.'

'Was the call to the taxi company followed up?'

'Yes. Apparently Celia rang to book a cab to an address in

Bramcote. She travelled there on 17th April. The taxi picked her up at ten o'clock and waited for her at the other end. They brought her back home at twelve noon.'

'Bramcote? That's near Nottingham, isn't it?' Isabel said.

'Yes. About five miles west of.'

Dan drummed his thighs impatiently. 'So, come on, Zoe, where exactly in Bramcote did the taxi take her to?'

'The crematorium,' she replied. 'Celia Aspen attended a funeral.'

'Did she now?' said Isabel. 'Was that followed up during the initial investigation?'

Zoe scanned the file. 'Doesn't look like it.'

'Why the hell not? What were they playing at?'

'They might not have had the resources,' Dan said. 'Like Zoe says, Celia Aspen wasn't considered high risk. In most cases, missing people usually turn out to have gone off somewhere of their own free will. They eventually get in touch or turn up again as if nothing has happened. It's rare for a missing person to have come to any harm.'

'Well, Celia Aspen certainly came to harm – and we have a collection of bones to prove it.'

'Hindsight's a wonderful thing,' said Dan, 'but you know as well as I do what happens if a missing person's enquiry doesn't come up with something straight away.'

Feeling vexed, Isabel stood up and rubbed at the stiffness in her neck. 'You're right. These things do have a habit of getting filed away if there's no body and all enquiries have drawn a blank. The funeral angle should have been followed up though, and it's definitely worth pursuing now. Give the crematorium a call, Zoe, and ask them to check their records to find out whose funeral took place just before noon on the morning of 17th April 1986. I'm thinking there could be a connection to our guy from Canada. Didn't he tell Joyce Littlewood that he was originally from Nottingham?'

'He did, yeah,' said Dan. 'His visit to Celia could have been to tell her about the funeral. The timing's right. Joyce Littlewood said she saw the man at Celia's house about a month before she disappeared.'

'See what you can find out, Zoe. Dan, try to set up those appointments for this afternoon. We need to let Julie Desmond know that it's her aunt's body we've found before she hears it on the news.'

Chapter 31

'But you told me you didn't think the body was Aunt Celia's.'

Their second meeting with Julie Desmond was taking place in the Ashbourne branch of *Jules*. The salon was located in an arcade leading off the marketplace. It featured the same grey-painted exterior and polished silver signage as the Melbourne salon. Isabel and Dan had waited at an identical walnut-veneered reception desk before being directed past more cream-coloured leather chairs to Julie Desmond's office. In this building, it was on the third floor, tucked under the eaves.

'Initially, we were certain that the remains weren't hers,' Isabel said. 'Since then, further evidence has come to light and we've established a positive ID through your aunt's dental records.'

Julie pursed pink-glossed lips, managing to look both puzzled and annoyed.

'I still don't understand. What evidence?'

Isabel and Dan were sitting side-by-side on a grey velvet couch in the corner of the office. Julie sat opposite them on its matching pair.

'There are distinct differences between the male and female skeleton,' Isabel said. 'The bones we found were those of an adult male – hence the confusion.'

'Male? How could they be? You're confusing me even more now. One minute you're telling me the body is my aunt's … the next you're saying the remains are those of a man. I don't understand.'

Julie's confusion appeared to be genuine. She seemed unaware that her aunt had been transgender.

'What I'm saying, and let me be absolutely clear, is that the bones are your aunt's and the skeleton is that of a male adult.'

Julie opened her mouth.

'It is our belief that your aunt was transgender,' said Dan. 'She was born male, but was living as a woman.'

'What? No way! I would have known. *I would have known.*'

'Clearly you didn't,' Isabel said, glancing at Dan to gauge his reading of Julie's reaction. Was her stunned expression genuine, or was it a carefully prepared act?

Julie stood up and began to pace. 'What is this far-fetched theory based on? What evidence do you have?'

'Please, Julie, sit down.' Isabel pointed to the empty couch and waited until Julie had lowered herself into it. 'It isn't a theory. Your aunt's dental records were on her case file. They've been checked against the remains found earlier this week, and they match. We believe your aunt was born Cecil Aspen, and he transitioned sometime in the late 1940s or early 1950s. The uncle you were told had been killed in the war did, in fact, survive.'

'When you say transitioned, do you mean he went the whole hog and had the operation?'

Isabel was always astonished at how little the average person knew about what it meant to be transgender. People made judgements and assumptions based on limited knowledge and incorrect information.

Admittedly, her own awareness had been gleaned as a result of attending training courses and dealing with victims of hate crime. If she hadn't joined the force, she may well have been equally uninformed.

'There's no way for us to tell from the remains whether or not your aunt had undergone confirmation surgery,' she said. 'She may have done, but given the period in which we think she transitioned, that may have necessitated going abroad for the operation. Whether she did or not is irrelevant. Many transgender people choose not to opt for confirmation surgery. It's not all about physical appearance. Being transgender is about how people feel within themselves. With or without the surgery, your aunt had chosen to live her life as a woman.'

'Do you think your grandmother knew?' Dan asked.

'My grandmother?' Julie let out an exaggerated sigh. 'How the hell would I know?'

'You said she never told you she had a sister, and that her brother had been killed in the war. You also mentioned that Celia had fallen out with her sister. Do you think the cause of that rift could have been because your uncle decided to start living as a woman?'

Julie raised her eyebrows and pushed a strand of hair behind her right ear. 'It's possible. My grandmother was very uptight. She was all about appearances ... constantly worried about what people might think. If what you're saying is true, I can guarantee it would have totally freaked her out. I'm pretty sure she would have refused to have anything to do with a sibling who was transgender.'

'As I say, the dental records show that the remains found at Ecclesdale Drive are those of your aunt, but we'd also like to run a familial DNA match, to make certain,' said Isabel. 'Would you be willing to give a DNA swab for comparison purposes?'

'Is that absolutely necessary?'

'It's purely voluntary, of course, but it would give us conclusive proof on the identification.'

'OK.' Julie nodded her assent. 'If it helps with the investigation.'

'Thank you.'

'Tell me, Inspector, do you have any proof that my aunt was murdered?'

165

'We're still working on that,' Isabel replied. 'It seems likely, although it's also possible that she was killed accidentally and someone then disposed of her body. Either way, a crime has been committed.'

'Can you think of anyone ... anyone at all, who may have wanted to harm your aunt?' Dan asked.

Julie tapped a finger against her lower lip. 'There was someone she used to go to the theatre with from time to time. I wouldn't exactly call him a friend, but I believe they used to attend Derby Playhouse together. With certain plays the theatre used to offer discounts on a second ticket. Aunt Celia met this man at one of the performances and they decided to keep in touch so they could buy their tickets together and get the discount. I told you my aunt was thrifty.' She smiled at the memory.

'Can you remember his name?' Dan asked.

'Malcolm ... now ... what was his surname?' She paused to dredge her memory banks. 'Hudson! That was it, Malcolm Hudson. The same as Rock Hudson. That's how I used to remember.'

'You didn't mention him the last time we spoke to you,' said Isabel.

'I've only just thought about it.'

'And do you think this man could have had something to do with your aunt's death?'

Julie held up her hands. 'I'm not saying that – but, with hindsight, I do think Malcolm Hudson may have had feelings for my aunt. I poo-pooed it at the time because he was years younger than her and she never did anything to encourage him, but ... knowing what we know now ... what if he found out she was transgender?'

'And what?' said Dan. 'Killed her?'

Julie winced. 'When you put it like that, it does sound improbable. I just thought ... you know, a lonely single man who makes a connection with an older woman and then finds out she isn't really a woman after all. I don't suppose he'd have been too happy about it.'

'So you *are* suggesting he murdered her?' Isabel said.

Julie batted a hand, as if to dissociate herself from the insinuation. 'I don't suppose it's very likely, but you never know. It's up to you to find out whether he was involved or not, assuming he's still alive.'

'Do you know where he lived?' Dan said.

'Not precisely, but I do know it was somewhere on the same housing estate as Aunt Celia. She was thrilled when she made contact with him. Not only did she get a discounted ticket, she also got a free lift to the theatre.'

Dan made a note of the information. 'Thanks. That's useful. We'll see if we can track him down.'

'One more thing,' said Isabel. 'We've learned that your aunt attended a funeral about a month before her disappearance. Do you know whose service it was?'

'No, sorry.' Julie shook her head. 'I've no idea. I wasn't even aware she'd been to a funeral.'

***

After they'd taken a buccal swab for DNA testing, Isabel and Dan walked back to the marketplace, where they'd parked the car.

'Do you think she already knew about her aunt being transgender?'

'No, Dan, I don't. She seemed genuinely surprised and confused. Either that, or she's a good actor.'

'I wasn't convinced,' Dan said. 'She didn't seem as shocked as I would have expected. On the contrary, I thought she took it in her stride.'

'Are you saying you would have acted differently?'

'I reckon so. It's one thing spending time with someone who is openly transgender – but if someone kept that from me and

167

I wasn't made aware of it until afterwards, I might feel as if I'd been hoodwinked.'

'Why? They'd still be the same person? What difference would it make?'

'I don't know. I can't explain it. Wouldn't you feel the same?'

'I'd imagine I'd feel a whole gamut of emotion,' said Isabel. 'I'd be surprised, and sad that the person hadn't felt able to tell me the truth. Then again, there's no reason why someone should feel obliged to tell everyone they meet that they're transgender. They have a right to be accepted for who they are, without having to explain themselves.'

'That's true. It can't be easy for people who choose to transition.'

'I'm not sure that choice comes into it, Dan. I seriously don't think anyone would choose to complicate their life in that way unless they felt compelled to. I think transitioning is something they feel they *have* to do. Escaping the *unchosen*, if you like.'

Their journey back to Bainbridge was taking them along a winding road that cut through the Ecclesbourne Valley. Isabel had forgotten how beautiful the scenery was around here, even in October. Green hills rolled away gently on either side, softened by small clusters of woodland and woven through with sparkling streams that trailed like silver ribbons along the bottom of the valley. Leaves were beginning to show their autumn colours. Flashes of gold and yellow and fiery reds glowed in the afternoon sunshine.

Isabel steered the car over a narrow bridge that nestled beneath the dappled shade of a tunnel of trees. Emerging into pale sunlight, the sky widened. They drove on, past a field dotted with Friesian cows and her mood lifted, as it always did whenever she passed through this part of the county.

'It must have been hard for Celia Aspen back then,' Dan said.

'I'm sure you're right. Things would have been difficult for her, especially if she transitioned as early as the 1940s or 1950s.

I imagine she would have faced a lot of hostility. She'd have had to be extremely circumspect.'

'Or willing to make a fresh start,' said Dan. 'In a place where she didn't have to explain herself.'

'I would imagine her move to Derby would have given her that. Then she came to Bainbridge. No one would have known her there.'

'What if someone found out the truth? Do you think that's what got her killed?'

'I don't know, Dan. I hope not, but it's possible. Sometimes the truth can be a dangerous thing.'

***

Their original plan to call in on the Littlewoods on their way back from Ashbourne had been thwarted. It seemed that Joyce Littlewood had gone to stay with her daughter for a long weekend and, although Timothy was at home, Isabel didn't want to talk to him without his mother being present.

Dan had arranged to visit them on Monday afternoon instead. He'd also lined up an appointment on Monday morning with Mary Summers, Julie Desmond's mother. Isabel wasn't sure what Mary would be able to tell them, but she'd been questioned as part of the original missing person's investigation and was one of the few people on their list who had known Celia Aspen.

They got back to the office to find Lucas sitting at his desk sporting a new haircut.

'Who are you, and what have you done with the real DC Killingworth?' Isabel said.

Lucas grinned.

'I think he looks very smart,' said Zoe.

'Why, thank you, DC Piper.' Lucas bowed his head. 'Make the most of it, this is my bi-annual haircut. My appearance will be back to normal before you know it.'

'Let's hope you're not like Samson,' said Isabel.

'Samson?' Lucas thrust out his bottom lip questioningly.

'He was a character from the Bible. The story goes that when Delilah cut off his hair, he lost all his strength.'

Lucas wrinkled his nose. 'Mmm. Well, I'm not that strong anyway, boss.'

'I was thinking about your intellectual strength, Lucas. That's something I rely on. Wouldn't want you to lose it.'

His face lit up. Whenever Lucas received praise, he glowed. If he was rebuked, he adopted an expression like a slapped backside. Isabel found the transparency of his reactions endearing.

'As a matter of fact, I need you to put your investigative skills to good use right now,' she said. 'See if you can track down a Malcolm Hudson. According to Julie Desmond, he and Celia used to go to the theatre together. He lived somewhere near Ecclesdale Drive and he was years younger than Celia. How much younger, I have no idea.'

'But young enough that he might still be alive?' Lucas said.

'It's worth checking, don't you think? Make it a priority.'

'I'm afraid I drew a blank with Celia Aspen's doctor,' Zoe said. 'Her GP was a Dr Richards. He retired in 1996 and died five years later. There's nothing on Celia Aspen's medical records to suggest that she confided in the GP about being transgender. I guess we'll never know now.'

'Bugger,' Isabel said. 'Thanks anyway, Zoe. It was worth checking.'

***

Lucas knocked on her office door twenty minutes later.

'Malcolm Hudson lived on Highfield Avenue until two years ago,' he said.

Isabel knew Highfield Avenue. It ran off the other side of Winster Street and was part of the original housing estate.

'And is he still alive?'

'He is,' Lucas said. 'He's eighty-six now and a resident at White Laurels, an old people's home a couple of miles from Bainbridge. It's out on the Wirksworth Road.'

'Have you spoken to anyone at the home? Is Malcolm Hudson compos mentis?'

'Yes and yes. They said it would be OK for you to go and talk to him this afternoon, if you want to.'

Isabel looked at her watch. It was already four o'clock, but she sensed this was a visit she shouldn't put off.

Shrugging on her coat, she stepped out into the main office.

'Zoe, have you heard back from Bramcote Crematorium yet?'

'Not yet,' she replied. 'They've said they'll have an answer for me by Monday.'

'They better had. In the meantime, if you're free, I'd like you to come along with me to visit an old buddy of Celia Aspen's.'

Chapter 32

Bringing Zoe along was an inspired decision. Malcolm Hudson's eyes lit up when he saw her.

'You remind me of my niece,' he said. 'You have the same beautiful blue eyes.'

Zoe blushed, which had the effect of charming Malcolm Hudson even further.

'We've come to talk to you about an old friend of yours,' Isabel said. 'Is there somewhere more private that we could talk?'

She looked around the White Laurels day room. Several residents were dozing in a row of winged armchairs lined up to face a widescreen television that was attached to the wall. A couple of elderly ladies were playing cards at a table in the corner, and a solitary gentleman was completing a jigsaw puzzle alongside them.

'I can take you back to my room,' Malcolm Hudson said, winking suggestively at Zoe.

The old man wasn't at all what Isabel had expected. She'd imagined someone quiet and introspective – a shy loner who preferred his own company above that of others. She certainly hadn't anticipated an outrageous old flirt. Perhaps his comments were designed to be amusing and charming, or maybe he was simply an old lech. Isabel decided to reserve judgement until she'd spoken to him further.

Despite walking with a stick, Malcolm Hudson moved along the corridor remarkably swiftly. His en-suite room held a single bed, a double wardrobe, a dressing table, and a desk – on which stood a collection of framed photographs. In pride of place on his bedside table was a large colour photograph of a Jack Russell terrier. Next to that, a small bookshelf was crammed with paperback crime thrillers and biographies.

'What a gorgeous little dog.' Zoe picked up the framed photograph and admired it.

'That's Jasper,' he told them. 'He was a wonderful little chap. Lived until he was sixteen. He died three years ago, just before I moved in here.'

'You must miss him,' Zoe said, as she returned the photo to the bedside table.

'Terribly. There's a lady that brings one of those PAT dogs into White Laurels once a week, but it's not the same.'

'PAT dog?' said Isabel, puzzled.

'Pets-as-therapy dog,' Zoe said.

'That's right.' Malcolm nodded. 'It gives residents a chance to pet a dog, give it a bit of fuss … that kind of thing. It's supposed to be good for your stress levels – or so we've been told. Not everyone is interested, of course. The cat people tend to steer clear.'

Malcolm Hudson sat down in the one armchair in the room. Zoe sat next to him in an upright visitor's chair. Isabel remained standing, preferring not to have to sit on the bed.

'I wonder if you can tell us about a woman you used to know back in the Eighties,' she said. 'Celia Aspen.'

'Celia Aspen.' He nodded slowly. 'That's a name I haven't heard for a while. We used to go to the theatre together, me and Celia. She was a nice lady – very reserved – but highly intelligent, with a very dry sense of humour. She was good company.'

173

'As you know, Celia disappeared back in 1986. We understand a detective questioned you at the time.'

'Questioned me? You make it sound as though I was a suspect.'

'Sorry.' Isabel steepled her fingers. 'I meant that a detective talked to you as part of the missing person's investigation.'

'Well, if you know that, then you must also know what I said at the time. I would imagine the police keep a record of these things on file?'

'We do.' Isabel smiled. 'And as Celia was never traced, that file has remained open.'

'And I take it something has happened that's caused you to re-examine the case?' He looked at Isabel over the top of his glasses. 'Or are you simply reviewing it as a cold case?'

Isabel glanced pointedly at the paperbacks on the bookshelf. 'You seem very interested in police procedures,' she said.

'I read crime novels and I watch a lot of police dramas on television. There's not a lot else to do in here except watch TV and read, unless you like playing cards or board games.'

'Who's your favourite detective?' Zoe asked.

'Oh, definitely Vera,' he replied immediately. 'Without a doubt. I love that hat she wears. My sister used to have one just like it, God rest her soul.'

'Vera's my favourite too,' Zoe told him.

'Actually ...' Malcolm Hudson grinned wolfishly. 'I think you might be my favourite detective now. You've elbowed Vera into second place.'

Zoe's laughter rang with a veritable tinkle. *My God*, Isabel thought, *Zoe is turning on the charm.* She sat on the bed and decided to leave the questioning to her DC.

'It would help if you could tell us about your friendship with Celia,' Zoe said.

'Happy to, my dear, but I'd like your boss to answer my question first.'

'What question is that, Mr Hudson?'

'Are you reviewing this as a cold case, or is there some kind of new development you've not told me about?'

Despite his age, Malcolm Hudson was remarkably astute.

'I'm sorry to report that we've recently found Celia Aspen's remains,' Isabel told him. 'We're treating her death as a murder enquiry.'

Malcolm lowered his head, silently contemplating what Isabel had told him.

'Poor Celia,' he said. 'Although I have to say, I'm not surprised by what you've told me. I always knew something awful must have happened – she would never simply have run off. It's distressing to think about her coming to such a sad end. Celia was a gentle soul and, while I'll admit she wasn't one of the warmest people in the world, she never did anyone any harm. At least, not that I know of. She certainly didn't deserve to be murdered.'

'I don't think anyone does, Mr Hudson,' Isabel remarked.

'Tell us about your friendship with Celia,' Zoe said.

He sat up and puffed out his chest. 'We bumped into each other at the theatre one evening. We didn't exactly know one another – not then – but I recognised her. I'd seen her in the local shop, so I knew we lived in the same area.'

'You lived in Highfield Avenue?'

Malcolm Hudson nodded. 'Celia and I got talking about how the ticket discounting arrangements penalised single people,' he continued. 'We decided to join forces to beat the system. We began to buy our tickets together, which meant that we got a ten per cent discount. As Celia didn't drive, I was also able to offer her a lift to and from the theatre. To be frank, I'd hoped she might chip in with some petrol money, but she never did. I didn't mind though. It was nice to have some company. We were both single and we both loved the theatre, so our friendship seemed logical.'

'And is that all it was?' Isabel asked, playing bad cop to Zoe's angelic cop. 'Was your relationship purely platonic, or were you and Celia romantically involved?'

'Oh heavens, no!' Malcolm Hudson sniggered. 'That was never on the cards. She was years older than me. To put it bluntly, Detective, I wasn't attracted to Celia. She wasn't my type.'

Isabel wondered what his type was.

'When was the last time you saw Celia?' said Zoe.

'Now, let me see ... that would have been sometime in April 1986. Round about the middle of the month, I believe. As I'm sure you will have gleaned from your file, Celia and I fell out on that occasion.'

'But you didn't consider it to be a serious falling out?' asked Isabel.

'I think she was pretty hacked off with me, but it was a quarrel that would have mended in time. Sadly, it turned out to be the last time I saw her. We never did get a chance to heal the rift.'

'Your argument was triggered by your refusal to give her a lift,' Zoe said. 'Is that right?'

'Yes, that's correct. I was still working in those days and Celia wanted me to take a day off to drive her to a funeral. I was an accountant and April was always a busy time. Tax year end and all that. I told her I couldn't do it. That I had to work.'

'What was her reaction?' Isabel asked.

'She wasn't best pleased ... told me to forget it, that she'd get a taxi instead. Then she stormed off.'

'Our enquiries show that she did, in fact, book a taxi.'

'She wouldn't have been happy about that,' said Malcolm. 'A taxi would have cost a small fortune. Whoever's funeral it was, it must have been someone pretty special to warrant Celia getting her purse out.'

'She didn't tell you who it was who'd died?' Isabel said.

'No. If I'd agreed to take her, no doubt I would have found out – but as soon as I told her I couldn't give her a lift, she clammed up.'

'So she didn't say anything at all?' said Zoe, gently encouraging him to open up. 'About whose funeral it was?'

'Only that it was someone she knew from before the war. Someone she'd cared about.'

'Male?' said Isabel. 'Female?'

'She didn't say. What she did say was that life always found a way to surprise you. That you could never truly leave things behind. She seemed quite down and rather shaken by it. If you must know, I felt a bit of a heel, having to turn down her request. But I wasn't running a taxi service.'

'What about her niece, Julie?' said Zoe. 'Couldn't she have asked her for a lift?'

'Hardly.' Malcolm Hudson rolled his eyes. 'For starters, Julie didn't have a car. I believe she could drive, but she was going away ... off to New Zealand or Australia or somewhere. From what Celia told me, Julie had sold her car to raise money for the trip.'

He folded his arms. 'Besides, even if she'd had a car, I doubt Celia would have asked Julie for a lift. I got the impression she hadn't told her about the funeral.'

Isabel stood up. 'Thank you for your time, Mr Hudson. You've been very helpful.'

'Time is all I have to give these days,' he said. 'Quite how much of it I have left is anyone's guess.' He laughed softly and, as Zoe got up, he squeezed her hand.

'It was nice meeting you, my dear. Come back and see me any time.'

***

'We didn't ask him whether he knew that Celia was transgender,' Zoe said, as they walked back down the corridor.

Isabel signed them out of the visitors' book and they stepped out into an October evening that was chilly and dark. It was also raining again.

'I didn't think it was necessary at this stage,' she said. 'We may

177

have to go back and question Mr Hudson again. If we do, we can ask him then.'

They began to walk to the back of the building, where they had left the car.

'You did a good job in there,' Isabel said. 'You built a rapport with Mr Hudson and, as a result, he gave us some useful information. Well done, Zoe.'

'Thanks.'

'Are you doing anything this weekend?' Isabel asked when they reached the car. She wasn't usually interested in the social lives of her colleagues, but there was something about Zoe that bothered her.

'Nothing special,' Zoe replied, her face downcast and her voice subdued. 'I might drive over to Leicester to visit my parents. I haven't decided yet.'

This girl is too focused on her job, Isabel thought. *Unhealthily so.*

Perhaps it was raging ambition that compelled Zoe to clock up far more work hours than she needed to, but Isabel worried there was something more troubling at play. There was an indefinable vulnerability about Zoe: the solitary aura of someone longing for companionship. Isabel hoped she was wrong, but she suspected Zoe was lonely.

She studied the DC's sad expression, her long blonde hair and her jacket, which was a little too tight. 'How old are you, Zoe?' she asked.

Zoe hesitated before answering, as though it were a trick question. 'Twenty-nine.'

'Exactly,' said Isabel. 'You're young. You're single. Call some friends. Go out somewhere. Enjoy life. Before you know it, the time will come when you're as old as Malcolm Hudson. Try not to have any regrets.'

***

178

The visit to the residential home had pricked Isabel's conscience, stirring tender pangs of nostalgia. Observing the frailness of the elderly people in its care, she was aware that most of them were only a few years older than her father. It had been an alarming realisation; a reminder that he would not be around forever. Guilt and longing and curiosity were infusing her with a growing sense of urgency. It was time for her to take action. A first, tentative step.

That evening, when everyone else had gone to bed, Isabel opened up her laptop and wrote an email to her father's solicitor. Even though the message was a short one, it took half an hour to compose.

I am writing to you in connection with my father, Donald Corrington, who is your client and, I believe, currently residing somewhere in France.

My mother, Barbara Corrington, has recently explained the circumstances surrounding my father's departure from Bainbridge in 1977. She has passed on your email address so that you can put me in touch with him.

Can you please arrange to forward a message to my father? Please let him know that, having heard the details of what he did, I am able to forgive him. Can you also tell him that I am well (as is my mother). I hope he is also in good health.

You have my permission to pass on my email address in case my father wishes to get back in touch with me.

She re-read the message and then read it again. She counted the words. There were 131, but none of them accurately described how she was really feeling or said what was truly in her heart.

She read the message one last time and then pressed send before she had time to change her mind.

Chapter 33

The following day had been dubbed Super Saturday by the media, but Isabel couldn't muster any interest in listening to the scheduled parliamentary debate aimed at resolving the Brexit crisis. Frankly, she was tired of the whole bloody thing.

Instead, she decided to do something nice for her mother. When Isabel was young and her father was away, she and Barbara had often gone for picnics in Bainbridge Park. On the way, they would call in at the local bakery to buy filled rolls and a couple of the enormous chocolatecovered, creamfilled choux buns known locally as 'elephants' feet'. They would sit together on their favourite park bench and eat their rolls in companionable silence. Then they would move on to the highlight of their picnic lunch. With a flourish, Barbara would open up the cardboard cake box and offer an 'elephant's foot' to Isabel.

'Go on,' she'd say, 'get your laughing tackle around that.'

There was no way her mother would say something like that these days, not now she'd gone all posh, but maybe they could still recreate one of those long-ago picnics. The weather wasn't ideal, but at least the rain was holding off.

Isabel had gone to the bakery first thing to buy the rolls and cream cakes, which she had packed carefully in a carrier bag.

Now, she and Barbara were in the park, wandering past the bandstand towards their special bench.

As they walked, Isabel considered telling Barbara about the email she'd sent the previous evening but, on reflection, decided against it. There was no guarantee that her father would reply, and even if he did, she still wasn't sure whether she wanted to see him.

Aside from a couple of dog walkers, the park was deserted. Their bench was empty, waiting for them. Barbara smiled as they sat down.

'We always used to sit here,' she said. 'Do you think this is still the same bench?'

Isabel was pleased she'd remembered. 'It's probably been replaced a few times over the years,' she said. 'Same position though. I always think you get the best view of the park from here.'

She pulled the filled rolls from the carrier bag – cheese and tomato for Barbara and tuna mayonnaise for herself. They ate their lunch slowly and in silence.

'I used to love coming here,' Isabel said eventually. 'Just you and me. I never understood why we stopped coming ... after Dad left.'

Barbara brushed crumbs from the front of her coat. 'We stopped doing a lot of things, Issy. It was silly of us. We should have carried on, but back then it took all of my strength just to get through each day.'

'I was probably getting a bit too old for picnics anyway,' Isabel said.

Barbara smiled. 'Trust me, you're never too old for a picnic.'

Across on the lake, a duck crash-landed. Isabel reached into the carrier bag and withdrew the cake box. Opening it up, she offered it to her mother.

'There you are,' she said. 'Get your laughing tackle around that.'

Barbara began to laugh, and the sound set Isabel off. Together they descended into a fit of giggles. Even the duck began to quack, joining in with their hilarity.

***

When they walked out of the park, Barbara slipped her hand through Isabel's arm.

'Can I ask you to do something for me?' she said.

'What's that, Mum?'

'On the way back, can we drive past our old house. It's years since I've been there, and I'd like to take another look.'

'Of course,' Isabel was surprised. 'It's not like you to want to see the old place again. You always used to avoid the area.'

Barbara squeezed her arm. 'I know, but this picnic and all this talk about your father and our old life has made me nostalgic. It's time for me to face up to what happened and close the door on it for good. I've made a start by telling you the truth. Going to see the house seems like the next logical step.'

As they drove into Ecclesdale Drive, Barbara fell silent.

'Is it how you remember it?' Isabel asked, as she stopped the car in front of number 23.

'It all looks so familiar, and yet different ... it's strange. Coming back feels like stepping into another person's life, as if the memories aren't quite my own. When I think of the things that happened here, it's as though they happened to someone else ... an old friend that I've lost touch with.'

'Forty years have gone by. You're a different person now, Mum.'

'I loved that house,' Barbara said. 'It broke my heart to have to leave, but there was no way I could have afforded the mortgage on my own. Moving was the only option. I know our new home wasn't ideal, but at least it wasn't a constant reminder of our old life.'

'I hated the new house,' Isabel said. 'Nothing was the same after we left Ecclesdale Drive.'

'Everything changed when your dad left. *We* changed, Issy. We'd always been so close, but after he left you were cold and distant ... I felt that you blamed me.'

This was proving hard for them to talk about. Despite Barbara baring her soul and telling the truth, there remained an element of restraint in their exchanges, and Isabel sensed it would be a while before their conversations became easy and freeflowing. Old habits died hard.

'In the absence of any information about where Dad was, I suppose I did blame you,' Isabel said, blinking back tears. 'I was angry that he'd gone, but even more furious that you wouldn't tell me why. I'm sorry, Mum. If I'd known the truth, I would have been more supportive.'

'For months you were convinced he'd come back,' Barbara said. 'Even after we'd moved to the new house.'

'And all the time you knew we'd never see him again. You'd been abandoned. That must have been devastating ... and there I was, acting like a selfish teenager.'

'You *were* a teenager. You didn't need to act.'

Isabel smiled. 'Yes, but was I selfish?'

'Aren't all teenagers?'

Isabel thought of Ellie and laughed. 'Back then, I thought the world revolved around me. I should have had more consideration for what you were going through. You must have felt broken. It's a wonder you managed to hold things together.'

'I almost didn't. There were days when all I did was cry. You'd go off to school and I'd crawl back into bed and weep.'

'I should have been there for you,' Isabel said, regretfully. 'I'm sorry, Mum.'

***

They had all been invited to Kate's house for an early dinner. Inevitably, the girls had more questions about their grandfather, but the conversation soon moved on to other topics. Isabel was amazed at how quickly her children had absorbed and accepted the family scandal. Since when had they developed a shockproof shell?

'It all happened a long time ago, Mum,' Kate said, when Isabel asked how she was feeling about the situation.

Easy for her to say. For Isabel, the pain would always be there: a festering gash that recent events had ripped open. Perhaps it was time to tend the wound and let it heal properly once and for all.

The best way to do that would be to meet her father. Talk to him. Shout at him. See him at least one more time. It was the best way – the only way – to heal the rift. But even if he agreed to meet her, Isabel wasn't sure she was ready to face him. Perhaps they had left it too late.

***

As they drove home from Kate's, Isabel found herself thinking about Celia Aspen. If her mother hadn't been visiting, she would have worked over the weekend, pressing on with the investigation and expecting her team to do the same.

Barbara hadn't given any clue as to how long she intended staying with them, and Isabel didn't like to ask in case it sounded as though she was trying to get rid of her – she saw too little of her mother as it was. The children loved their grandmother and it was nice to see them together – but it really wasn't a good time, work wise. Then again, there never was a good time. If she let it, work would consume every spare minute Isabel had.

If she thought she could get away with it, she'd go in for a few hours tomorrow, but she knew it wouldn't go down well with

Nathan. Besides, a few hours had a habit of turning into a whole day.

There were still so many unanswered questions, that was the thing. Isabel hoped that when those answers were unearthed, they would lead directly to the killer.

There was no getting away from it, this case was an enigma; one that had lain unsolved for thirty-three years. She supposed a couple more days wouldn't make any difference in the greater scheme of things.

Chapter 34

With the questions surrounding Celia Aspen's death pushed reluctantly to the back of her mind, Isabel began to relax.

After returning from Kate's, the family gathered round the TV in the living room, arguing over whether to watch *Strictly* or a rerun of *Dad's Army*. Ellie won the argument.

As her daughter changed channels, Isabel heard the signature tune for the local news which, on Saturday evenings, was given a truncated slot just before *Strictly*. She listened as the newsreader summarised the latest political manoeuvres in the Brexit crisis before moving on to a report about a royal visit to a local factory. The news ended with the item that had been Isabel's lead story all week.

Human remains have been found in a garden in Bainbridge, the newsreader announced. The report continued over footage taken outside the house. *The skeletonised body was discovered on Ecclesdale Drive on Monday, and police have now confirmed the remains are those of Celia Aspen, who lived at the house until 1986, when she was reported missing.* The identity photo from the missing person's file flashed onto the TV. *Anyone with any information that might help the police with their enquiries is urged to come forward by contacting Bainbridge CID at the number shown on the screen.* A telephone number popped up and then the presenter moved on to a summary of the local weather forecast.

'That was our old house,' said Barbara, who had sat, transfixed, throughout the short report. 'Did you know it was going to be on TV?'

'Yes,' Isabel said. 'We issued a press release and the TV station got in touch for more information, but I didn't know when they'd be airing the piece.'

Isabel wondered whether they should have publicised the photograph that Amy Whitworth had handed over to them. Someone might have recognised the couple and come forward, but she'd held the photo back because Val Tibbet had made it clear she thought it was too early for such an appeal. For now, it would be up to her team to uncover that information for themselves, without the help of the great British public.

Roll on Monday, Isabel thought, as the da-da-da-da of the *Strictly* theme song bounced from the screen.

Chapter 35

Isabel and Dan were expected at Mary Summers' flat at eleven o'clock on Monday morning. Their journey to Matlock took them down to Cromford and along the A6. It was a crisp, clear day. Sunny, but cold. As they entered Matlock Bath, Isabel reflected on how empty the town looked at this time of year.

Weaving alongside the River Derwent, the main street was set beneath a wooded hillside dotted with grand villas, built in the town's heyday as a spa resort. Grey limestone crags towered above the river on the other side of the gorge.

At weekends between September and the end of October, bustling crowds flocked to see the Matlock Bath illuminations, but on this nippy Monday morning the place was almost deserted. Most of the ice-cream parlours, amusement arcades and fish-and-chip shops were closed up, although several cafés were open. Local demand for good coffee never abated, no matter what the time of year.

The pavements were much busier in Matlock itself, the town centre occupied by shoppers in hooded coats. They hurried along, heads down, trying to keep warm as they dashed from shop to shop. Isabel navigated through the town, out onto the Chesterfield Road. Mary Summers' flat was located on the left-hand side as they began to climb the hill.

'What's our line of questioning going to be?' Dan asked, as she reversed the car into the only vacant spot in the visitor parking area.

'Let's start by asking her about her relationship with Celia Aspen and see where that leads.'

The woman who answered their knock was in her seventies, slender and petite with white hair shaped into a short bob that sat on her head like a helmet.

'Come in,' she said, when Isabel and Dan had introduced themselves and produced their warrant cards.

Her ground-floor flat was compact and cosy, if a little cluttered. A brindle cat was asleep on the windowsill, catching the warming rays of the morning sun. Isabel and Dan were invited to sit on armchairs draped with colourful, cat-hair-infested throws and cushions.

'As we mentioned on the phone, we'd like to talk to you about Celia Aspen,' Isabel said. 'I'm sure your daughter's already been in touch to let you know that we've found her aunt's body.'

Mary lowered herself into a tub chair tucked between an ornament-festooned wall unit and a faux Adam-style fireplace.

'No, I didn't know, and I'm sorry to hear about it. Julie hasn't been in touch. She and I aren't in contact all that often. She comes round to see me occasionally if she's over in her Matlock salon, but she never stays long.'

'That's a shame. Do you have any other children?'

'No, Julie's an only one. My second husband and I were never blessed.' She placed the flat of her hand across her chest. 'Tell me, where was Celia found?'

'Buried in the garden of her home in Bainbridge,' Isabel said. 'We're treating this as a murder investigation.'

Mary winced with distaste.

'Can you tell us about your relationship with Celia Aspen,' Dan said. 'We understand you first met at your ex mother-in-law's funeral?'

'Yes, that's right. It would have been in early 1978, or thereabouts. Julie's dad had died a few years earlier, and I'd just started seeing my second husband. Julie and I were surprised when Celia introduced herself after the funeral service. We didn't know anything about her.'

'Were either you or Julie concerned about her turning up out of the blue like that?' Isabel said. 'Were you worried she might be there to make a claim on your mother-in-law's estate.'

'Not at all.' Mary laughed. 'My mother-in-law may have had delusions of grandeur, but she lived in a council house and was as poor as a church mouse. There was nothing for me or Julie to inherit, if that's what you were wondering.'

'So what did you think of Celia Aspen?' Dan asked. 'Did you get on all right with her?'

'We didn't *not* get on,' she replied. 'At least not at first. Initially, it was all very neutral and we didn't see a lot of each other. Julie kept in touch with Celia after the funeral, but I only met her a few more times. She didn't seem like an easy person to get to know.'

'I understand Celia was living and working in Derby when you first encountered her,' said Isabel.

'Yes, that's right. She was made redundant about six months later. She moved to Bainbridge the following year. I went to her new house once with Julie, but I wasn't made to feel particularly welcome.'

Isabel furrowed her brow. 'Why was that?'

'I was only related to Celia by marriage. My first husband, Anthony, was her nephew. Celia and Julie got on all right because they were blood relations, but I think Celia saw me as an outsider, especially after I married my second husband.'

'When did you get married again?' Isabel asked.

'The week before Christmas 1979 – although Robert, my second husband, had moved in with me six months before that.'

'And is that when things changed between you and Celia?'

Mary folded her arms. 'No, that happened later. She and I fell out for good in 1983. I may as well tell you about it because, if I don't, I'm sure my daughter will.

'My first husband died suddenly when Julie was twelve. His death was a terrible shock. He was never ill, so it was all very unexpected. Julie and I were devastated … obviously. Thankfully he worked for a company that provided me with a widow's pension, and there was insurance which paid off the mortgage. Financially, at least, we were OK.'

She paused for a moment and then took a deep breath before continuing.

'I didn't think I'd find happiness again, and then I met Robert. He made me laugh, paid me compliments. He stood up for me. I fell for him in a big way – but even before we got married, I realised he was a gambler.'

'How did your daughter feel about that?' Isabel said.

'Julie never liked him. She didn't even try to pretend. She left school when she was sixteen and got a job at a hosiery factory as a typist, but even then she had dreams of travelling the world. In 1982, when she was nineteen, my daughter moved into a flat with a friend of hers that she knew from school. To be frank, her leaving was a relief. Robert and Julie were always bickering, and it used to create a horrible atmosphere in the house.'

'So, after Julie left, did you and your second husband live happily ever after?' Isabel said.

Mary looked dejected. 'No, I'm afraid we didn't. What I hadn't realised was that Robert had forged my signature and re-mortgaged the house to pay off some of the debts he'd run up with a dodgy bookie. To be frank, I wouldn't have minded if that had been the end of his gambling addiction but, of course, it wasn't. He refused to get help – he would never admit that he had a problem. He was delusional. He thought one big win would set us up for life. He kept placing bets, spending money we didn't have, and the mortgage I knew nothing about wasn't being paid.'

'Surely there were letters … final demands and warnings,' said Isabel.

'I'm sure there were, but Robert always got to the letterbox first, you see. He was sneaky like that. Good at hiding things … covering them up.' Her fingers plucked nervously at the collar of her blouse. 'The first I knew of what he'd done was when he told me the bailiffs were coming to repossess the house.'

'That must have been a terrible blow for you,' said Dan. 'Did you report him to the police?'

Mary shook her head. 'I couldn't do that. In spite of everything, I still loved him.'

Isabel thought of her own mother's reluctance to report the man she loved to the police. How was it that love made some women so tolerant? Isabel felt sure she would never be willing to sacrifice her own peace of mind and happiness in order to protect some bad boy. Then again, she was lucky. She had married Nathan.

'Julie was incensed when she found out,' Mary continued. 'We stopped speaking for a while. Once the house had been repossessed, I was homeless and so the council gave me this flat.'

'What about your husband,' Dan said. 'What happened to him?'

'He buggered off. Left me in the lurch without one word of apology. I heard he'd moved to Chesterfield … probably found some other mug to take advantage of.'

Isabel was surprised at the level of stoicism Mary was able to maintain as she recounted her ordeal. Despite the appalling way she'd been treated, Mary's voice was steady, if a little bitter.

'How did all this affect your relationship with your daughter?' Isabel asked.

'Nothing was ever the same between us after that. It was months before Julie came here to see me. She was furious with Robert, but even more angry with me. She said I was an idiot for letting myself be taken in by him. She was right, I know, but if I had my time again, I'd still have married him.'

'Celia Aspen fell out with you as well, I take it?' Dan asked.

Mary nodded. 'She wasn't the sort of woman to forgive the kind of mistake I'd made. I think she despised me. As far as she was concerned, my reckless choice of husband had cost Julie her inheritance. I did appeal to Celia for help ... she could have put things right if she'd wanted.'

Dan paused in his notetaking. 'How do you mean?'

'I went to see her as soon as I learned what Robert had done. The bailiffs were due to come to the house the next day and Celia was the only person I knew who might be able to lend me some money. I asked her for a loan so that I could pay the arrears and fend off the bailiffs. She refused. She could have rescued the situation, but she said she wasn't willing to throw good money after bad.'

'And that made you angry?'

'Of course it did. I found her lack of sympathy hard to forgive. We didn't stay in touch after that, although I did bump into her once in Bainbridge. I'd gone back to visit a friend and I saw Celia in the bus station.'

'Did you talk to her on that occasion?' said Dan.

'No. She blanked me.'

'I believe you were questioned when Celia went missing,' Isabel said.

Mary nodded again. 'Yes, but there was nothing I could tell them. I'd had nothing to do with Celia for ages. I didn't know anything about her disappearance.'

'Did Celia ever talk to you about her life before the war?' Isabel asked. 'Did she ever mention anyone from her past?'

'Not that I recall. She was pretty much a closed book. I've no idea what her story was.'

'Did you know she was transgender?' said Dan.

Mary twisted her neck and looked at him as though he was speaking a foreign language. 'Transgender? Celia? What do you mean?'

'I mean that although she was living as a woman, Celia Aspen was born a man.'

'A transvestite, you mean?'

'That term is outdated and totally inappropriate in this instance,' Isabel said. 'The terms transvestite and transgender aren't interchangeable. Being transgender isn't the same thing at all. It's not about dressing as a member of the opposite sex, it's about living every aspect of your life as the gender you feel you belong to.'

Mary curled her top lip and looked Isabel squarely in the eye. 'I'm afraid I'm not up-to-date with all the latest thinking. To be quite frank, I don't understand people like that. Most of them do it for attention, if you ask me.'

'Well, we weren't …' said Isabel. 'Asking you. The question we did ask was whether you were aware that Celia was transgender. I take it from your response that you weren't.'

'No. I most certainly was not, although now that you've told me, it does make sense. No wonder Celia was so closed up – probably didn't want anyone finding out.'

'Is it any wonder that Celia was such a private person?' Isabel said, keeping calm by carefully regulating her tone of voice. 'There are a lot of disapproving people who might have taken pleasure in making life difficult for her. Based on your reaction, you may well have been one of them.'

Mary gave a defiant shrug. 'Do you think Julie knew?' she asked.

'She reckons not,' Dan replied.

'I bet she was gobsmacked when you told her.' She snorted spitefully. 'Fancy finding out your great-aunt is actually your great-uncle.'

Isabel stood up brusquely and Dan followed suit. 'We don't have any more questions at this stage, Mrs Summers, but it's possible we may want to talk to you again. We'll be in touch if we do.'

***

194

'Well, I found her thoroughly nasty and small-minded,' said Isabel, as they got back into the car.

'Is she a suspect?'

'I think she has to be. Mary lost her house because Celia refused to give her a loan. That's got to be a motive, surely. She admitted it made her angry.'

'Angry enough to kill?'

'I don't know, Dan. Maybe. Maybe not. We need to keep asking questions. Our luck's got to change sooner or later.'

Chapter 36

'Ey up, Zoe. What are you up to?'

DC Piper was beavering away at her keyboard. Tap. Tap. Tap. She was relentless, stopping only to make notes or eat a crisp from the open packet on her desk. She and Isabel were alone in the CID room. Dan had gone to talk to Joyce and Timothy Littlewood, and Isabel had opted to send Lucas with him, rather than go along herself.

'I was mulling something over, boss,' Zoe said. 'Contemplating whether we should be appealing for information about who this couple might be?' She held up the black-and-white walking photograph. 'The woman's very striking ... very distinctive. Someone might know who she is.'

Isabel was sceptical. 'It was taken a hell of a long time ago. Do you think anyone would remember her?'

'Someone might recognise one or other of them from a family album. It's worth a try, isn't it?'

'I agree,' Isabel said, 'but I don't think the Super does. She didn't want it included in the last press release. I think we should wait until we've heard back from the crematorium. Once we know whose funeral Celia attended, we can track down the family members. Let's show the photo to them first, eh? If they recognise it, there'll be no need for a wider appeal.'

'Shall I chase him up? The chap from the crematorium?'

'Yes, do that. He's had long enough to look through the archives.'

Ten minutes later, Zoe had an answer.

'According to their records, there was only one service between 10.45 a.m. and noon on 17th April 1986. The person cremated was a woman. Her name was Violet Mundy and she died on 11th April aged sixty-six.'

'Any information on the relatives?'

'The next of kin was Violet's son, Eric. I've found an Eric Mundy, aged seventy-seven, currently living at address in West Bridgford, Nottingham.'

'Sounds like he could be our man,' said Isabel. 'Get in touch with him and find out. If he is Violet's Mundy's son, Dan and I will go over in the morning and talk to him.'

'There's something else, boss. Malcolm Hudson called me. He's remembered something he thought we might be interested in.'

Isabel smiled. 'I hope it is something interesting and not just an excuse to ring you up for a chat, Zoe.'

She grinned. 'I must admit, it was hard getting rid of him once he started talking. I think he must be lonely.'

'What is it the old guy's remembered?'

'He said that Celia used to moan about the lad next door – by which I assume he meant Timothy Littlewood. Apparently, Celia used to complain that Timothy would go into her garden uninvited and start working, even though she hadn't asked him to. Malcolm thinks she was worried she'd have to pay him, even though the lad said he didn't want any cash. He said he was doing it because he liked digging and that Celia needed to get her vegetable patch ready for planting.'

'Is that so?' Isabel rubbed her knuckles together. 'What's the betting it was the same patch of ground that she was buried in?'

'I'll ring Lucas and tell him what Malcolm Hudson said, shall

I?' Zoe said. 'He can ask Timothy about it when he and Dan get to the Littlewoods.'

'I'm still having a hard time thinking of Timothy as a suspect,' said Isabel. 'He was always such a gentle lad.'

'What about Joyce Littlewood?' Zoe said. 'She may be old and frail now, but in 1986 she would have been … what?' She did some mental arithmetic. 'Late forties?'

'She is extremely protective of Timothy, and her relationship with Celia Aspen wasn't the best,' Isabel admitted. 'But I can't imagine her being capable of murder either – not the Joyce I knew anyway. Having said that, I was just a kid back then, and I can't let past friendships affect my judgement. Have to keep an open mind.'

'It's hard, isn't it? Trying to solve a murder that happened so long ago? I'm beginning to wonder if we'll ever find out who killed Celia Aspen, let alone why.'

'It might seem that way right now, but stick with it Zoe. This is a complex case. It's knotty. It won't be easy to unravel, but do what you've been trained to do and follow your instincts. Let's keep going … work on finding some answers. We owe it to Celia.'

Chapter 37

Dan was chuffed that the DI had decided to let him take the lead on questioning the Littlewoods. DI Blood's presence at the last couple of meetings with Joyce Littlewood had been useful, but the case was becoming increasingly complicated. He was in a much better position to handle things neutrally, unencumbered by the sway of old loyalties and childhood memories.

Joyce Littlewood seemed confused when she answered the door.

'Hello, Mrs Littlewood. You seem surprised to see us.'

She stepped aside and beckoned them in.

'You did tell me you were coming,' she said. 'I thought Isabel would be with you, that's all.'

'The DI isn't with me today. I've brought DC Killingworth along instead.'

'Yes, lad. I can see that.'

She led them into the living room, where Timothy Littlewood was sitting watching *Countdown*.

'You'll have to switch that off, Timothy,' Joyce said. 'The detective has some more questions for us.'

Timothy muted the TV, but didn't switch it off. 'Questions?' he said, as he continued to stare at the screen. 'What about?'

'I'd like you to tell me about the last time you saw Celia Aspen, Timothy,' Dan said gently. 'Take your time. I know it's a long time ago, but we need to go through it again.'

'It's all right,' said Timothy. 'I've got a good memory.'

Lucas smiled. 'I wish all witnesses were like you.'

'I hope that's all my son is,' said Joyce. 'A witness. I hope you're not treating him as a suspect.'

'Right now, we're simply trying to establish the facts,' Dan replied. 'Celia Aspen disappeared a long time ago, and we need to take a fresh look at what happened back then. Timothy was a key witness.'

Lucas referred to his notes. 'According to the statement you gave at the time, you last saw Celia Aspen on 15th May 1986. Can you tell us what you remember about that day, Timothy?'

Joyce took the remote control from her son and turned off the TV. Timothy stared down at his knees and picked up a ball-point pen, which he proceeded to click on and off as he answered Lucas's question. 'I went round next door to repair the trellis near the front window,' he said. 'It had come loose and it was blowing about in the wind. Julie said that Celia was worried about her roses. Celia loved her roses, didn't she, Mum?'

He glanced at his mother, who smiled at him reassuringly.

'She certainly did. She used to have a lovely pink double rose growing up that trellis.'

'That's right.' Timothy nodded. 'It was about to bloom. Julie said that Celia was concerned the loose trellis would damage the rose. I think she was worried it would knock the flower buds off. She asked me to go round and fix it back on to the wall.'

'Who asked you to go round?' asked Dan. 'Celia or Julie?'

'Julie. Celia didn't talk to me and Mum that much. We'd fallen out.'

'And yet Julie still expected you to help out her aunt by fixing the trellis?'

'I had to climb a stepladder to mend it,' Timothy said. 'Celia

200

had poorly knees, so she wouldn't have been able to get onto the ladder. I think Julie would have done it for her, but she'd gone to Australia by then. She didn't have time to sort it out before she left.'

'So when did Julie ask you to do the work?'

Timothy had retrieved the remote control from his mother. He was staring at it, running a finger over the raised, numbered buttons.

'She sent me a note,' he said. 'It was in an envelope addressed to me and there was a five-pound note inside.'

'And what did the note say?' Dan asked.

'I can't remember.'

'I still have the letter somewhere,' Joyce said.

'You do?'

'Only because the whole thing annoyed me at the time,' she replied. 'I rang Celia to have it out with her, but all I got was her snooty message on the answering machine. I decided to have words with her about it the next time I saw her, so I shoved the envelope behind the clock in the kitchen. That's where it stayed, along with a load of other junk mail. I didn't see Celia again. Months later, when she was declared missing, I dug the letter out and put it somewhere safe in case the police needed to see it.'

'We don't have a copy of the note in the missing person's file,' Lucas said.

'That's because no one asked for it,' said Joyce.

Lucas rolled his eyes. 'And you didn't think to volunteer it?'

Joyce sniffed contemptuously. 'I didn't think it was important.'

'Can you show us the note please, Mrs Littlewood?' Dan said. The old woman's shenanigans were beginning to try his patience.

She shuffled over to the corner of the room to a small Welsh dresser. After scrabbling through the jumbled contents of both of its drawers, she pulled out a tatty envelope and handed it to Dan.

It was addressed to Timothy and had been posted second class.

Dan scrutinised the postmark. The date stamp was faded but still legible. It read 12th May 1986.

'Can you remember when you received the envelope?'

'The letter was waiting for me when I came home from work,' Timothy said. 'I'd just started a job at the supermarket. I went round to fix the trellis the next day.'

There was a sheet of lined notepaper inside the envelope. Not surprisingly, the five-pound note had long since disappeared. Dan pulled out the letter and unfolded it.

Dear Timothy,

Can you please fix the trellis at the front of aunty's house because it's come loose and she's worried that her favourite rose will be dashed down (you know how she fusses about her flowers).

By the time you get this letter, I will be in Australia. I would have fixed the trellis myself, but I didn't have time before I left (I had so many things to sort out!).

Enclosed is five pounds for your trouble. Aunty Celia is expecting you, so she won't tell you off if she sees you at her house. Don't bother knocking though. There's no point in bothering her, and try not to make too much noise – you know how grumpy she can be!! Just give her a quick wave when you've finished and know that I will be eternally grateful.

I'll send you a postcard from Oz when I get settled.

Thank you. You're a star.

Love from,

Julie

xx

'We're going to have to keep this,' Dan said, as he slipped the letter back into the envelope and bagged it as evidence. 'So, tell me what happened when you went round there.'

'Nothing.' Timothy looked up at him through the corner of his eyes. 'I screwed the trellis back into the wall.'

'And what did Celia Aspen say to you?'

'I didn't speak to her. She didn't like me very much, so I thought it was best to keep out of her way.'

'But you saw her?'

Timothy nodded. 'I waved to her,' he said, 'through the living-room window.'

'And did she wave back?'

He nodded again. 'I didn't stick around for long. Like I say, Celia didn't like me much.'

'I believe you used to dig Celia's vegetable patch for her as well,' Lucas said, following up on the information Zoe had passed on to him.

Timothy stared at his hands, head bowed. 'I like gardening,' he said. 'She used to let me dig up her potatoes when they were ready and pull up the carrots and beetroot. Then, when everything had finished growing, I'd turn the soil over, ready for the spring planting.'

'Is it true that you went round there a few times, uninvited? That you worked in Celia's garden even though she hadn't asked you to?'

'Who told you that?' Joyce snapped.

Lucas ignored her. 'Can you answer the question please, Timothy?'

'I wanted to help. Celia was skinny and frail and although I'm not very big, I'm fit. I didn't mind doing the work, but I think she was annoyed.'

'She was worried she'd have to pay you, that's what was bothering her,' Joyce said. 'She came round here one day, knocking on the door, telling me to keep Timothy out of her garden unless she expressly requested him to do some work. I didn't need telling twice, let me tell you.'

'So you didn't go round there much after that, Timothy? You stopped doing Celia's gardening for her on a regular basis?'

He shrugged and reached for the remote.

'He only went round if Celia or Julie specifically asked him to,' said Joyce, 'and that wasn't very often. They sometimes roped him in if there was heavy-duty donkey work to be done. I'd rather he'd kept away altogether, but it was Tim's decision whether to lend a hand or not. The last time he went round there was to fix that trellis. Now, unless there's something else you want to ask, I'd appreciate you leaving us in peace. My son would like to watch his programme. *Countdown* is his favourite.'

***

'I think he's our killer,' Lucas said, as they got back into the car. 'He looks shifty. Like a guilty man.'

'I think that's just his way,' said Dan. 'I don't think he's comfortable around strangers.'

'He could have killed Celia Aspen accidentally.'

'If he did, I can guarantee he would have told his mother. If you're right, she would have helped him dispose of the body.'

'It sounds like a plausible explanation to me,' Lucas said, 'but I don't think the boss will buy it.'

Dan smiled. 'No, neither do I. Actually, she's probably right not to. I mean, what possible motive would Timothy have had for harming the victim?'

'That's the thing though, isn't it? If it was an accident, he wouldn't have needed a motive.'

Chapter 38

Amy could hear Paul in the kitchen. He was ripping out the old units, smashing them up and carrying the pieces out through the hallway to the skip that now stood on the front driveway. He had the radio on and was humming along to a Chemical Brothers song. It was giving Amy a headache and she wished he'd turn it down, but he seemed happy, so she said nothing and closed the door instead.

She was in the living room, scraping embossed Anaglypta wallpaper off the wall. It was a tough, messy job because the paper had been painted over with yellow emulsion.

She had a special steam machine that was supposed to make the removal of wallpaper an absolute doddle, but the layer of cold-custard-coloured emulsion was proving to be resilient. Amy switched off the machine and resorted to the old-fashioned method, using a wallpaper scraper and a generous application of elbow grease. It was going to be a long job.

Prising the metal scraper under the edge of the first strip of paper, she heard the satisfying sound it made as it separated from the paste. The scraper slid under a large piece of Anaglypta. Amy grabbed hold of it and pulled, cheering as it peeled away from the wall in a long, uneven strip.

Smiling, she threw the first piece of wallpaper onto the dust sheet beneath her feet. Happy to be making progress, she looked up and felt the smile slip from her face. Beneath the Anaglypta was another layer of flowery wallpaper – the kind of twee pattern popular in the Eighties. Honeysuckle intertwined with forget-me-nots and violets. Another layer to remove, requiring even more time and effort. Amy was beginning to wonder whether this property renovation was a mistake.

Gripping the scraper, she attacked the Anaglypta, working in time to the music filtering through from Paul's radio.

Chapter 39

By nine-thirty the next day Isabel and Dan were on the outskirts of Nottingham. It was a bright, shiny morning – the kind that would normally fill Isabel with optimism. Today though, her head was thick and fuggy, stuffed with thoughts of her father and what to do about him.

Now that she had sent the email to his solicitor, he could get back in touch any day. If he did write to her, she'd be forced to decide what her next step would be and she wasn't ready to do that yet. She needed more time to mull things over. She wanted to do the right thing, but wasn't sure what that was.

When they reached their destination in West Bridgford, Isabel pulled her Toyota onto the gravelled driveway of Eric Mundy's sprawling bungalow. It was at the end of a quiet cul-de-sac that had the air of somewhere sedate and expensive. The sun was catching the leaves of a large beech tree on the front lawn, turning them a rich shade of russet-brown. A purple clump of Michaelmas daisies near the front door provided a late splash of colour.

'I'm not a fan of bungalows,' Dan said, 'but I have to say this looks impressive.'

'He's obviously not short of a bob or two,' said Isabel.

'Can't be,' Dan agreed. 'Zoe reckons this is one of Nottingham's most expensive suburbs. I wonder what Eric Mundy's story is?'

'Let's go and find out.'

The doorbell was answered by a petite woman in her mid-forties, who introduced herself as Gillian Statham.

'I'm Eric Mundy's daughter,' she explained. 'Before I take you through to see my father, can I ask what you'd like to talk to him about?'

'We have some questions about someone who attended his mother's funeral,' Isabel told her.

'I see. In that case, you'd better come in.'

Remarkably, the reason for their visit didn't appear to have surprised Gillian Statham. On the contrary, she seemed singularly unperturbed by their interest in an event that had taken place more than thirty years earlier.

Such an out-of-the-blue request would normally have elicited a negative reaction of some kind. Incredulity. Bemusement. Irritation. Gillian Statham displayed none of the usual responses. *She knows something*, Isabel thought. *Something must have happened at that funeral: something momentous.*

They were taken along a hallway, through into a long and luxuriously carpeted living room that had a mini-grand piano at one end and a dining table at the other. In the centre was a grouping of large, comfortable-looking settees set around a wide fireplace.

Eric Mundy was old-school. He stood up to greet them as they approached and shook their hands as they introduced themselves.

'We're sorry to bother you, Mr Mundy, but we're hoping you might be able to help us solve a crime that has recently come to light.'

He indicated for them to sit down and made sure they were settled before he sat down himself. Eric Mundy looked considerably younger than his seventy-seven years. He had a neatly trimmed beard and, although his hair was grey and thinning on top, he was still exceedingly slim and fit. He sat back, folded his legs and beckoned his daughter to sit next to him.

'Tell me how I can help,' he said.

'We're here to ask about someone who attended your mother's funeral back in 1986,' Isabel began. 'We believe she came to the service at the crematorium.'

'There were a lot of people at my grandmother's funeral,' Gillian Statham interjected. 'She was a popular lady.'

'The person we're here to ask about was called Celia Aspen. Did you know her?'

Eric Mundy placed a hand across his mouth and then used it to rake through his beard. 'I never actually met her,' he said. 'We weren't introduced. I know she attended the funeral, but I didn't learn that until afterwards.'

'You didn't see her?'

'I'm afraid not. You know what funerals are like … it was all an emotional blur. I sat through the whole service in a trance – I was certainly in no state to notice who was there and who wasn't. I presume Celia must have sat at the back, out of the way. She didn't come to the wake.'

'How did you know she was there then?' asked Dan. 'Who told you?'

'My uncle. Jim Whetton. He was Mum's brother. He knew Celia.'

'Jim? He didn't happen to live in Canada, did he?'

'Yes, he did. He emigrated after the war, but he used to come back to visit from time to time. When he found out that Mum had cancer, he flew over to spend time with her. He stayed with her until the end.'

'Based on information we've been given by a witness, we believe your uncle … Jim … may have visited Celia Aspen's home in April of 1986,' said Isabel. 'If he did, I assume it must have been to tell her about your mother's death and the funeral arrangements.'

209

'Your assumptions are correct, Detective. My uncle told me all about his visit to Celia.'

'And did he tell you how he knew her?' Isabel asked. 'Or how Celia knew your mother?'

'Yes, he told me everything. About Celia, and about Cecil.'

Isabel and Dan exchanged a startled look. Jim had obviously known that Celia was transgender. Why had he chosen to share that knowledge with Eric Mundy, and had he divulged that information to anyone else?

'Can you tell us how Celia, Jim and your mother were connected?'

Eric looked at his daughter, who gave a shrug of resignation.

'It's all right, Dad. Go ahead. You may as well tell them.'

Eric leaned over and patted his daughter's arm before turning back to Isabel. 'I'm happy to answer your questions, Detective, but … first … can you tell me why you're here? You said you were investigating a crime. What did you mean by that?'

Isabel cleared her throat. 'Celia Aspen's remains were found last week in the garden of her house in Bainbridge. We believe she was murdered sometime during the summer of 1986.'

Eric Mundy pulled in a short, sharp breath and closed his eyes. Gillian shuffled along the sofa and put her arm around him.

'I thought she'd chosen not to come,' he said, his voice crackling with emotion. 'I assumed she didn't want to see me.'

His shoulders dropped for a moment and then, pulling himself together, he sat up and pushed his hands over his forehead and through his hair. Isabel could see there were tears in his eyes.

'Please, Mr Mundy. It's important that you tell us everything you know. Any information you can give us will help with our investigation.'

He took a couple more shuddering breaths.

'My mum, Uncle Jim and Cecil grew up together,' Eric Mundy said. 'They lived next door to each other. Jim and Cecil were best pals, and my mother, Violet, was the kid sister who used to hang

210

around with them from time to time. They lived in a fairly poverty-stricken part of Nottingham, but things were hard for everyone back then. Despite everything, I believe they had some happy times together.'

'So they were childhood friends?'

'Yes. My mother's reminiscences suggest it was a close-knit community. They didn't have much money, but they were rich in other ways. But then, of course, the war broke out.'

'We understand Cecil Aspen ended up going out to the Far East,' Dan said.

'That's right, he did, and Uncle Jim joined the Navy. But something happened before all that.'

Isabel eased forward, hoping to hear something significant. 'What was that, Mr Mundy?'

'My mother fell in love with Cecil. Uncle Jim saw it coming apparently. It seemed she'd always had a crush on him ... the boy next door. The problem was, Cecil wasn't interested.'

'Are you saying he rebuffed her?'

Eric smiled sadly. 'Let me put it this way, I don't think he did anything to encourage her, but my mother knew how to get her own way. Apparently, she was very attractive when she was a young woman and she could be exceedingly charming and persistent.'

Isabel tilted her head at Dan, prompting him to reach into an inside pocket and pull out a copy of the black-and-white photograph.

'Could you take a look at this, please?' He handed the photo to Eric. 'Is that your mother?'

Eric Mundy nodded with another sad smile. 'Yes, that's her. And I believe that's Cecil Aspen she's with. I saw an old picture of him once, and that looks very much like him.'

'Did Cecil and your mother get engaged before the war?' Dan asked.

'They did, yes. Shortly before Cecil was posted overseas.'

'So what happened?' said Isabel. 'Why didn't they get married when he got back from the war?'

'There were many reasons, the main one being that my mother had married someone else by then.'

The conversation seemed to be unsettling Eric Mundy. He shifted uncomfortably and chewed at a fingernail.

'Dad, why don't you give them the letters? It would save you having to explain it all.'

'What letters, Mr Mundy?' Isabel asked.

'Uncle Jim gave them to me after my mother died. One is a letter from Cecil to my mother, written to her in 1946. The other is the letter my mother wrote to me when she knew she was dying. They're pretty self-explanatory. They'll tell you everything you need to know.'

I doubt that, thought Isabel, as she watched Gillian get up and leave the room. *In cases like this, there are usually far more questions than answers.*

After a minute, Gillian Statham returned carrying two envelopes.

'These are part of our family history.' She clung to the letters possessively. 'You're welcome to read them and take a copy, but we'd like to hold on to them. We don't want them to get lost, do we, Dad?'

One of the envelopes was addressed in copperplate script to Violet. The other was addressed to Eric in shaky, spidery handwriting. Gillian passed them over to Dan, who removed and bagged the contents of the envelopes before pulling out his phone to photograph each of the pages.

'Can we get you both a cup of tea or coffee?' Eric Mundy offered. 'I must have read those letters a hundred times and I know from experience it will take you a while. There's a lot of information to take in.'

They agreed on tea and Gillian Statham went off – rather begrudgingly – to put the kettle on.

'We'll need to keep hold of the originals for a while,' Isabel explained. 'Don't worry though, we'll make sure they're safely returned to you.'

Eric Mundy nodded his consent, sat back and watched as she and Dan began to read. Isabel started with Cecil's letter to Violet.

Dear Violet,

Now that I am finally home, I thought I would write to you, rather than try to arrange a meeting. I hope that you are well and settled in your new life as Mrs Mundy.

I pray that you and your husband will be happy together, because no one deserves happiness more than you do. I want you to know that I hold no grudge about your choosing to marry someone else. I was gone for such a long time with no one knowing whether I was alive or dead. You must have been so worried and lonely.

I never expected you to wait for me. It wouldn't have been fair and, to be perfectly honest with you, I don't think I would have made a very good husband anyway. I won't ever get married now. Don't worry, it's not that you've broken my heart (well, maybe a little), but rather I don't believe marriage would suit me.

I did an awful lot of thinking while I was a prisoner of war – goodness knows, I had plenty of time on my hands. I can't begin to describe what it was like out there. Suffice to say, it was a living hell. The stuff of nightmares. I wasn't sure whether I would ever get back home … but I promised myself that, if I did, I would make changes to my life. Major changes.

You're better off without me, Violet. I'm different to other people, and not in a good way. I intend to make a fresh start for myself and I'll admit that I'm scared about what the future holds, but I swore that if I survived the war, I would live the life I was born to. That's what I'm determined to do. My mother and my sister won't be happy when I tell them about the choices I intend to make, of that I'm certain. The tittle-tattling gossipmongers will have a field day too, I shouldn't wonder. You may get to hear about me over the coming years. If you do, I ask only that you think kindly of me.

In case you're wondering, I did love you, in my own unique way. I know I never told you that, and I'm sorry. You were my sunshine in an otherwise cloud-filled existence. You have brought joy to me throughout my life and the memories I have of you will continue to lift me whenever my spirits are low.

Mother tells me that you and your husband have a little boy. I know that you will be a wonderful mother, and I am sure your son will bring you endless pride and pleasure.

Jim tells me he's thinking of moving to Canada, which I think will suit him well. British Columbia will be very different to our old life in Nottingham, but I'm confident your brother will enjoy the challenge and do well for himself. It's a shame there will be such a distance between you and Jim, because I know you have always been close. However, I'm sure he will keep in touch.

As for me, I won't write to you again. We have shared some happy times together, but I think it's wise for us to draw a line under our friendship. Know that I will care for you always and I will think about you often.

I wish you and your whole family all the love and happiness in the world, Violet. You were, and always will be, the sunshine that warms my heart.

With fondest love always,
Cecil

***

For the first time, Isabel felt a real connection to the victim. So far, her impression of Celia had been of someone who was frosty and aloof, but this short, poignant note from Cecil to Violet was oozing with warmth and kindness.

Violet's letter to Eric was much longer. It was dated March 1986, written only a few weeks before her death.

Dear Eric,

This isn't an easy letter to write, but when I was diagnosed with cancer, I realised it was something I couldn't put off indefinitely. As well as an explanation, this is my confession and one that is long overdue.

I should have told you everything many years ago, but I'm not a brave person. I never have been. I'm sorry that I've left it so late and I hope you won't be angry with me for not having the guts to tell you in person.

I've asked Jim to give this letter to you after I've gone. I think it provides a full and honest account of what you need to know – but if you have any questions you should talk to your Uncle Jim.

Also, there is someone else that may wish to get in touch with you after I've passed away – someone special. If they come looking for you, I hope you will be kind and welcome them into your life. They played a very important part in yours.

When I was a kid, growing up in the Twenties and Thirties, my family was poor. There were days when we didn't have enough to eat and we often went to bed hungry. We weren't the only ones, of course – most families struggled back then. There was a depression on and times were tough.

Before you start feeling too sorry for me, I should add that the Great Depression brought some of the happiest years of my life.

Your Uncle Jim and I lived on Dalton Road next door to a family called the Aspens. There was a son, Cecil, and a younger daughter, Elizabeth. Cecil and your Uncle Jim were the same age and inseparable. They were the best of mates right through school and beyond and I used to hang around with them whenever I could. I worshipped Cecil. He was my hero. I liked him because he was different. All the other boys I knew took the mickey out of me and pulled my ponytail. Cecil was kind. Sensitive. He used to tie my tatty old ribbons for me (they were always falling out).

To cut a long story short, as I grew older, I realised I was in love with him. I was pretty sure the reverse wasn't true, but I didn't care. I followed him around like an adoring puppy and told him that, when I was old enough, I was going to marry him.

Cecil used to laugh about that – not laugh at me, but laugh with me – as though it was something funny and yet inevitable.

I know I'm not much to look at these days, and I don't like blowing my own trumpet, but I did blossom into a nice-looking young woman. I could have had my pick of any of the local lads, but my heart was set on Cecil.

In 1938, when Cecil was nineteen and I was seventeen, he finally agreed to take me to the pictures. We went to see *Pygmalion* starring Leslie Howard as Henry Higgins and Wendy Hiller as Eliza Doolittle. It was about a man who makes a bet that he can teach a cockney flower girl to speak proper English so that he can pass her off as a lady in high society. I remember how much Cecil enjoyed the film. I thought it was because he was watching it with me – although, with hindsight, I realise that probably wasn't the reason at all.

As we walked back home from the pictures, I slipped my hand into his. I was looking for romance. Cecil wasn't. He let me hold his hand, but he didn't try to kiss me when we got home. I thought it was because he was worried his mother might be spying through the net curtain. That's what I told myself.

We went out like that from time to time – to the pictures,

to the local cafés, and once to a classical concert (very posh!). We never went out for a meal, but hardly anyone ate out in restaurants in those days – not unless they were rich.

People began to talk about us as though we were a couple, and Cecil didn't discourage them. He enjoyed my company, I know he did. When he got paid, he'd sometimes take me into Nottingham and treat me to something nice to wear. He liked to go round the shops with me. He had a good eye for what suited me. I always looked very sophisticated whenever I wore the clothes Cecil had chosen for me.

Everything came to a head when war broke out. Cecil and Jim didn't join up straight away, but I knew it was inevitable. Cecil was working in the sales office at the Player's factory, and Jim was making machine parts at an engineering firm. Neither of them were in protected occupations.

Jim went first. He joined the Navy. A month later, Cecil told me he'd joined the Army. I was heartsick.

I don't think Cecil had the first clue what to do to comfort me. I had to show him (if you get my drift). I think he was quite shocked. It wasn't the done thing back then for girls to take the lead. I took Cecil by surprise and, looking back, I'm not sure that he was too happy about it.

Anyway, having made love to me and being an old-fashioned chap, Cecil thought he ought to do the right thing. He presented me with a pretty little ring and asked me to marry him. We got engaged just after Christmas 1941. He had a few days before he had to report back for duty – so, on a whim, we went off to Blackpool for the weekend. A lot of seaside resorts were off limits during the war years, with piers closed down and beaches covered in barbed wire – but good old Blackpool managed to keep on going. There were lots of troops there during the war – mostly airmen – and a lot of them were billeted in local hotels. We managed to get a room in a boarding house on the sea front. It was blooming freezing, but

217

I was so happy. Of course, there were no illuminations, but most of the theatres were open and we were able to take in a couple of shows. I can't begin to tell you how wonderful it felt to finally be with Cecil.

That feeling of bliss was short-lived. Cecil was shipped to the Far East and, within a couple of months, he'd been captured by the Japanese. I was distraught. My emotions were all over the place – so much so that, when I started to feel nauseous, I put it down to my frazzled nerves. By mid-March I realised there was more to it. I was pregnant. My fiancé was halfway around the world and he was a prisoner of war. I had no way of contacting him and, quite frankly, I didn't know what to do. I had no one to talk to. My mother had died a few years earlier, and I couldn't confide in my dad – he would have thrown me out of the house. I was at my wit's end.

I kept the truth from Cecil's mother, of course. If she'd learned that I was having her son's baby, she would have taken control. She was like that. Domineering and overbearing.

Eventually, after a fraught couple of weeks, I unburdened myself on someone I knew from work. I'd been to the dance hall with her a few times, and she was very open-minded. I knew she wouldn't judge me. There was a war on, after all. A lot of girls were in the same boat as me.

When my friend asked me what I was going to do, I told her I hadn't a clue.

After a few more days of worry, she asked me to meet her after work. There was a café in the park down by the river and I arranged to see her there one weekend. When I arrived, I was surprised to find that she'd brought her brother along. I'd met him before a few times, and even danced with him on a couple of occasions at the dance hall (not because I fancied him – but because it was rude to say 'no' if a nice young man asked you to dance). My friend's brother was a couple of years older than me. He'd had an accident at work which had left him with a limp and that ruled him out for active duty.

By now, I think you will have guessed that my friend was your Aunty Doreen and her brother was William, the man you know as your dad. Except he wasn't. That's what I needed to tell you, Eric. Your real dad was Cecil and, if he hadn't have been a POW over in the Far East, I'm sure he would have done the decent thing and married me 'toot-sweet' (as we used to say)!

Anyway, that's the secret I've been carrying around all these years. It feels good to unburden myself.

Before I run out of energy or paper, I'd better try and tell you the rest and bring this letter to a conclusion.

Doreen had told William about my predicament ... she knew he was soft on me and would sympathise with my situation (which he did). He offered to marry me and bring you up as his own. So that's what we did.

I went round to see Mrs Aspen to return Cecil's engagement ring and break the news to her that I was marrying someone else. She was furious ... called me disloyal and uncaring. I legged it out of there as fast as I could, glad I wouldn't have to put up with her as a mother-in-law.

As for your Uncle Jim, I decided not to tell him that William wasn't your father. Jim was away of course, fighting in the war, and he didn't get much in the way of leave, so I didn't see him often. I'd already written to tell him that I'd got engaged to Cecil, so I had to write to him again to explain that I was marrying William Mundy instead. When he eventually came home on a few days' leave, Jim assumed that William was the father of the baby I was expecting and that we'd had to 'marry in haste'.

Your 'dad' and I moved away to a different suburb and I tried to avoid going back to my old neighbourhood. My dad used to come over and visit us instead – but a year later, he died. After that, there was no need for me to ever go back to Dalton Road.

I'm pleased to say that Cecil survived the war, but when he arrived back in Nottingham in 1946, he was (according to reports) physically and emotionally drained. His mother had already broken the news to him that I'd married someone else, and I'm sure she would have taken great pleasure in painting me as a wicked, heartless hussy.

I worried about what Cecil would think of me. I still loved him, you see. I eventually got news of him through your Uncle Jim, who arranged to meet up with his old friend a few times. Cecil wasn't very tall and he'd always been slightly built, but when Jim saw him, he said he was shocked by his appearance. Apparently, Cecil was frail and very, very thin – 'half-starved' was how Jim described him. Jim thought he'd altered in other ways too, but he couldn't quite put his finger on what had changed.

'You know how highly strung Cecil used to be,' Jim said to me. 'Now he seems calmer, quieter – a little withdrawn. He's got big plans for the rest of his life, but he won't tell me what they are – even though I've told him about my plan to move to Canada. He always asks about you, sis. He doesn't hold any grudges and he's glad to know that you're happy.'

At their last meeting, Cecil gave Jim a note to pass on to me. (I've enclosed it with this letter).

Finally, I want to tell you what I heard about what became of Cecil. In some ways, this is the hardest part to write, because I don't know what your reaction will be.

It was a couple of years later. Your Uncle Jim had gone to Vancouver and you were growing up fast. I was shopping in Nottingham one day, on my own, minding my own business, when someone tapped me on the shoulder. It was Elizabeth, Cecil's sister. She was about five years younger than him, and she must have been about twenty-five at the time.

'Hello, Elizabeth,' I said, trying to be friendly – not knowing what sort of reception I'd get. I hadn't seen her since I married William.

'Have you heard about Cecil?' she said, going straight to the point. No polite chit-chat or preamble.

Of course, my heart went in my mouth. I thought straight away that something must have happened to him … and, in a way, it had.

'What about him?' I said.

'It's all your fault,' Elizabeth replied. I could tell she was bitter and angry, but I didn't know why. 'You broke his heart. You should have done the right thing and waited for him. It's what any decent girl would have done.'

I'd never liked Cecil's mother, and Elizabeth seemed to have inherited the same spiteful streak. I started to walk away, but she caught hold of my arm.

'He's brought shame on the family,' she said. 'No doubt you'll get to hear about it sooner or later, so you may as well hear it from me. After all, you're to blame. You and the bloody war! Mother's inconsolable.'

'Has something happened to Cecil?' I shook my arm to free it from her grasp. 'Tell me.'

'He's gone off to live in Derby.' She looked around and dropped her voice. 'He's passing himself off as a woman. Wearing dresses and cosmetics. He's grown his hair long and he's calling himself Celia. To top it all, he's gone and got himself a job in the ladies' clothing floor of Bradshaw & Trent. Mother's disowned him. The whole family has.'

I thought of Cecil's letter, and of the changes he said he was going to make in his life. I have to confess, I was shocked. Appalled even. It was unheard of, back then, for someone to live their life like that, at least in our neck of the woods. And yet, I still felt a bond of loyalty to Cecil. His family may have disowned him, but I wasn't going to forsake him.

'Well, I hope he's happy,' I said. 'He must have gone through some terrible times when he was a prisoner of war. He deserves contentment and if the things that bring him joy don't meet with your approval, that's your tough luck. I doubt your concerns are for Cecil. I reckon you're more worried about what people might think of YOU if they find out what he's done.'

Elizabeth thrust her scowling face to within inches of mine. 'I might have known you'd stick up for him,' she said. 'You two always were thick as thieves. As far as mother and I are concerned, he's dead to us … died in the war. That person he's turned into is nothing to do with us. I'm only glad he had the decency to move away.'

'Wherever he is,' I said, 'I hope he's happy. I hope she's happy.'

I went home, shaking. I thought about writing to Jim, or telling William – but, in the end, I decided against it. If Cecil had chosen to move away, it was for a good reason. I realised his life wouldn't be easy, and the fewer people that knew about his background, the better.

I toyed with the idea of catching the bus over to Derby and going into Bradshaw & Trent. I had a yearning to see this Celia for myself, if only to confirm that Elizabeth had been telling the truth – but then I thought about what Cecil would want. When he'd written to me, he'd said he wouldn't contact me again. He had a new life. A different life. I didn't think he'd want me turning up, reminding him of the past, so I decided against visiting the department store. It was for the best.

I strived to get on with making my own life a happy one. I threw myself into being a good wife and mother and my efforts paid off. I came to love William – not in that crazy, passionate way you read about in romantic novels. With him, it was a slow-growing kind of love, and made all the stronger

222

*and more solid because of it. We hoped to have another child.
We tried, but it never happened. William thought the world
of you though. You were his pride and joy. His treasure.*

*Jim came back to visit in 1954 and, as soon as he clapped
eyes on you, he knew. I could see it in his face. You do look a
lot like your father, and you resembled him even more as a
child.*

*Jim cornered me about it before he went back to Canada.
I told him the truth – at least about your parentage. I didn't
tell him what had become of Cecil.*

*Time is a strange, liquid thing. It moves in one direction,
of course, but it's capricious. Sometimes it flows swiftly, other
times it can be sluggish and wearisome. When the doctor told
me I had three months to live at most, time shifted to
maximum speed, hurtling me towards my inevitable conclusion. Like I say, time is capricious and it's also contrary. Just
when I wanted it to creep slowly, it decided to go fast. As I
write this, I know that the minutes and days and weeks will
soon overtake me and leave me behind. When I get to the end
of my journey, things will stop abruptly. Completely. There
will be no going back.*

*That's why I had to write this letter. I wanted you to know
the truth, but I couldn't face telling you myself – so I've taken
the coward's way out. When it's finished ... when I've got the
words right ... I'll pass this letter to your Uncle Jim to give
to you once I've passed away. I'm looking forward to him
coming over for a visit. It will be good to see Jim one last time.*

*I'm going to talk to him ... tell him what became of Cecil
and ask him to try and track down Celia, to let her know she
is your biological father. I realise how bizarre those words
must sound to you, reading them now with all that I've told
you still fresh in your mind – but I'd like Celia to know about
you. I think it will make her happy.*

If Jim can find her, I'll ask him to pay Celia a visit – but only after I'm dead. I wouldn't want her to feel obliged to visit me (I don't think either of us would relish a melodramatic death bed reunion!). However, I will suggest that Jim asks Celia to visit you – that is if you would like to see her. I can understand if you'd rather not. It will be your choice to make. I'm sure you'll want some time to think about it. When you've come to a decision, let Jim know. Please read Cecil's letter again before you make up your mind – and remember what he said … think kindly of me.

I'm sorry to spring this on you at the end of my life. I hope it won't cause you to feel differently about me, or about William – who was, in every respect but one, your father. He loved you so much, as do I.

I'm so lucky to have had such a wonderful son. Cecil was right – you have brought me endless pride and pleasure.

Thank you for all the happiness you have given me.

With love, always and forever

Mum

xx

Chapter 40

Carefully, Isabel placed the letters on her lap and looked first at Eric Mundy, and then at Dan.

Cecil's letter had provided an insight into one of the early chapters in his life, but it was Violet's letter to Eric that told the bigger story.

Two lost voices, sounding across time, like echoes from the past.

Eric Mundy was gazing at her solemnly, gauging her reaction.

'So, that was it,' Isabel said. 'Cecil was your father.'

'Biological father,' he replied. 'I'll always think of William Mundy as my real dad.'

There was no getting away from it: this was a monumental piece of information and a strong motive for murder. Violet's confession would have caused ripples – waves even. Would the impact have been devastating enough to turn someone into a killer? Violet's death; Jim's handing over of the letters; Celia's murder. The three events had followed one after another in quick succession. Like dominoes lined up in a row, all it would have taken was one push.

'Talk me through what happened after your mother died ... when your uncle gave you the letters.'

Eric Mundy leaned forward. 'The nurse told us that Mum was close to the end, so Uncle Jim and I sat together by her bedside, holding her hand. She passed away peacefully a few minutes before midnight on 11th April. I'd known it was coming, of course, and I'd tried to prepare myself – but I wasn't ready to lose her. She was only sixty-six.

'The next day, Uncle Jim took me to one side and talked to me in private. It wasn't easy for him, but he fulfilled his promise to my mother. He told me about my real father and passed on the letters. It was hard for me to take in, especially so close on the heels of Mum's death.'

'That's understandable,' said Dan. 'It must have been quite a shock, learning that your father wasn't who you thought he was. It would certainly have knocked me for six. I take it you were upset?'

Almost imperceptibly, Eric Mundy shook his head. 'I was grieving for my mother. I didn't have any emotion to spare for anything else.'

'But you must have felt something.' Dan pressed home his point. 'Especially when you learned that your biological father was living as a woman.'

'The truth is I didn't *feel* anything very much. I was in shock. All I felt was a kind of dull numbness. I don't know if you've ever lost anyone close to you, young man, but that's what grief does to you. It puts you in limbo.'

'When did you find out that your uncle was going to see Celia and tell her about the funeral arrangements?' Isabel asked.

'He told me he planned to visit her, but I didn't know he was going to invite her to the funeral. That certainly wasn't the main purpose of his visit.'

'So, what was?'

'Uncle Jim had delivered on the first part of his promise when he told me the truth about my biological father. My mother had also asked him to try and find out where Celia lived. God knows how he managed to track her down, but he did. As you will have seen in her letter to me, my mother wanted Jim to let Celia know about me.'

'Did you consider going with him? To see Celia for yourself?'

Had she been in Eric Mundy's shoes, Isabel didn't think she could have passed up such an alluring opportunity. Then again, given the way she was dithering over whether to re-engage with her own father, perhaps that's exactly what she would have done.

Eric Mundy shook his head dismissively. 'Not at that stage, although Uncle Jim did ask whether I'd be interested in meeting her eventually ... if she was willing. I told him that if she wanted to see me, it was fine as far as I was concerned, but I needed to get the funeral out of the way first. That was all I could think about.'

'Did Jim tell you where Celia was living?' said Isabel.

'No. I did ask him to give me her address, but he refused. He said he wanted to speak to her first ... that she should be the one to decide whether to let me know where she lived. I think he was trying to protect her privacy.'

'And you say you didn't see Celia Aspen at the funeral?'

'No. I never did get to meet her.'

'What about you, Mrs Statham?' Isabel turned to Eric Mundy's daughter, who was standing behind her father's chair listening intently. 'Did you spot Celia Aspen at the funeral?'

'I'm afraid I didn't,' she said. 'I knew nothing about Celia. Besides, I was only twelve when my grandmother died, and hers was the first funeral I'd attended. I found the whole thing rather overwhelming.'

'Celia was a stranger to us, Detective,' Eric Mundy said. 'There were a lot of people at the service that we didn't know ... anonymous friends of my mother's ... all of them dressed in black.'

'So what happened after the funeral was over?'

'Uncle Jim told me that he'd given Celia my phone number

227

and address and he was hopeful she'd be in touch to arrange a visit.'

'But she didn't contact you?'

'No, and Uncle Jim wasn't happy about it. Before he left for Canada, he went round to Celia's house again to talk to her one last time. He told me he knocked but there was no answer. She must have been out, he said, or she'd seen him and had refused to come to the door.'

'Can you remember when your uncle made that last visit? What date?' said Dan.

Eric Mundy scratched his beard. 'Not precisely, but what I can tell you is that Jim stayed on for a few weeks after the funeral, to help me through my grief and give me a hand sorting through Mum's belongings. I believe he flew back towards the middle of May. The 15th, maybe. Or the 16th.'

'And he visited Celia for the second time the day before that?'

'A couple of days before, I'd say.'

'And he suspected that Celia was avoiding him?' Dan was scribbling in his notebook. 'I'd imagine your uncle would have been angry about that.'

Eric Mundy glowered. 'Not at all, and I'm sorry if I've given that impression. He certainly wasn't angry. Sad would be a better way to describe his mood. Melancholic. Uncle Jim and Cecil were boyhood friends. They shared a bond of affection and loyalty that stretched back years. They were like family, and family meant everything to Uncle Jim. I'm sure he felt let down by Celia's reluctance to visit me. He was disappointed, yes, but most definitely not angry.'

'Sometimes, if it's intense enough, a sense of disappointment can be enough to make someone lose their temper,' Dan persisted. 'Do you think that could have happened with Jim and Celia?'

Eric Mundy straightened his spine, as if to get up, but settled back down when his daughter placed a soothing hand on his shoulder.

'What you're really asking is, do I think my uncle killed Celia in a fit of rage? Am I right?'

Dan tapped his pencil against the open page of his notebook. 'Do you think he did?'

'No, Detective, my uncle wasn't like that. I don't remember him losing his temper with anyone. Ever. Even when he did feel angry about something, he never reacted physically.'

Gillian backed him up. 'Dad's right,' she said. 'Uncle Jim was a lovely man. Kind. He didn't have a violent bone in his body. He worked in a national park in British Columbia as a conservationist. His instinct was to preserve and protect life, not endanger it.'

Father and daughter's defence of their long-dead relative was commendable, but Isabel knew from experience that even the gentlest of people could sometimes be drawn unwittingly into situations that had devastating consequences.

'What about you?' Dan said, risking Eric Mundy's wrath once more. 'Did you feel let down?'

Eric Mundy uncrossed his legs and placed his feet squarely in front of him. Dan's line of questioning had clearly rattled him, but he was doing his best not to show his annoyance.

'I felt let down, yes. I did my best to give Celia the benefit of the doubt … I waited patiently … hoping she'd get in touch. I'll admit that the longer it went on, the more intrigued I became about her. She was my parent and I was disappointed, infuriated even, when I didn't hear from her. I assumed she'd decided not to get in touch, and I had no choice but to accept that decision.'

Isabel felt a rush of sympathy for Eric Mundy. She knew only too well what it was like to wait in vain for word from a missing parent.

'If it's any consolation,' she said, 'Celia may have had every intention of getting in touch with you. I suspect her death was the thing that stopped her from doing that.'

229

Eric Mundy smiled half-heartedly and a faraway look came into his eyes.

'I take it you didn't know that Celia Aspen had disappeared?' asked Dan. 'You didn't hear about it at the time?'

'No. I didn't see anything about it on television, and I've never been one for reading newspapers. Obviously if I'd heard she'd gone missing, I would have spoken to the police.'

Isabel drained the cup of tea provided by Gillian Statham. It was weak, milky and had gone cold.

'The thing is, Mr Mundy, at the time of her disappearance, it was believed that Celia Aspen had only one living relative – her niece. If the police had known you existed, they would have contacted you. As it was, the niece was the sole beneficiary in Celia Aspen's will – although she had to wait until your aunt was declared dead before she could inherit.'

'That seems rather unfair,' Gillian said. 'If Dad had known, he might have considered challenging the will.'

Eric Mundy raised his right hand to silence his daughter. 'No, Gillian, I wouldn't. I didn't know Celia Aspen. I never met her. I didn't even know where she lived. I would never have expected to inherit anything.'

'Nevertheless, you were her closest relative,' Isabel said. 'So we'll make sure we keep you informed about when the remains can be released. There will have to be a funeral.'

Gillian Statham folded her arms. 'You're surely not suggesting Dad will have to arrange and pay for a funeral service? Shouldn't the niece sort that out? Dad got nothing from Celia Aspen during her life, or after it. Why should he have to foot the bill?'

'Hush, Gillian,' Eric Mundy said. 'I may not have received anything from Celia, but Cecil Aspen gave me something very precious … he gave me life. I wouldn't be here if it wasn't for him – and neither would you. I think paying for Celia's funeral is the least I can do. It's not as if I can't afford it.'

Chapter 41

'So, are we adding them to our list of suspects?' Dan said, as they drove back to Bainbridge.

'We have a list?' Isabel lifted an eyebrow.

'Well, technically, we don't have a list right *now*, but I'm sure we can put one together when we get back to the office. I know you won't agree, but I think Timothy Littlewood's name should go at the top, along with Joyce Littlewood ... and now Eric Mundy.'

'Why not go the whole hog and add Gillian Statham's name?'

Dan smiled. 'Much as I'd like to, she was only twelve in 1986. I think we can rule her out.'

'I take it you didn't warm to her?'

He pulled a face. 'I thought she was a cold fish, and the sort of woman who looks down her nose at coppers.'

'That's harsh,' said Isabel. 'I agree she seemed out of sorts, but that may have been because we were questioning her father. He's a pensioner. She was being protective of him, that's all.'

'I'm sure Eric Mundy can look after himself. I have to confess he seemed like a decent bloke. He sounded genuinely cut up when he was talking about Celia Aspen not getting in touch. That says a lot about his character.'

'You're right, it does. It says that he's either got a big heart, or he's a good actor. The jury's out on that one, as far as I'm concerned.'

When they got to the A52, Isabel put her foot down, nudging the car to eighty-five miles an hour. She was keen to get back to the office to update the team and work out how this latest piece of information slotted into the bigger picture.

'Interesting that no one noticed Celia Aspen at the funeral,' Dan said.

'It's understandable, but Jim would have been on the lookout … seeing if she'd turned up. Mind you, she might not have been easy to spot. If there were a lot of people at the service, Celia would have blended in with the other black-clad mourners.'

'I guess so,' Dan said. 'Wouldn't be so easy nowadays. Nobody wears black for funerals anymore.'

'You're absolutely right,' Isabel said, as she overtook a tatty looking camper van that, despite its clapped-out appearance, was doing a steady seventy. 'When did all that change? At one time it was considered disrespectful if you didn't wear dark colours at a funeral. Nobody gives a damn these days. That's something else to add to the list of things that have disappeared from British society.'

'We have a list?' Dan quipped.

Isabel laughed. 'Well, *I* have a list.'

'Really? Go on then, boss. What else is on it?'

'Do you genuinely want to know, or are you just taking the piss?'

'No. Truly. I'm interested. Although maybe not the whole list …'

Isabel smiled. 'I'll give you the top three.' She pointed to the car's dashboard. 'Number one … CD players in cars.'

'Who has CDs these days? They're ancient history.'

She chortled. 'Oh, Dan. You do make me feel old. I remember having cassette tapes in my first car. People used to break into cars purely to steal the radio.'

232

'What's number two?'

'Sticking with the car theme ...' She pointed upwards. 'Sunroofs.'

'Why the hell would anyone need a sunroof? Most cars have air-conditioning, don't they?'

'Most modern cars do – but back in the day, a sunroof was considered the height of luxury. You were someone if you had a sunroof.'

'Sad times,' Dan said, scratching the side of his face and looking at her with amused eyes.

'Number three is milk deliveries,' Isabel said. 'Everybody, and I mean *everybody*, had their milk delivered to their doorstep every morning, rain or shine ... and in glass bottles. The sound of an electric milk float whirring by was like a back-up alarm clock. And that's something else for the list. Alarm clocks. Nobody uses them now.'

'Again, why would you need to when you can use your phone?'

'That's what I mean.' She lifted her left hand and waved it around to emphasise her point. 'Technology has changed so many things. Don't get me wrong, I'm the first to embrace new technology, especially if it helps us do our job, but it still fascinates me how the everyday things we once took for granted are silently disappearing ... without any fanfare or grieving.'

'Get with it, boss.' He gave a broad smile. 'You have to let them go. Move on.'

They were on the outskirts of Derby and, inevitably, the traffic was slowing as they approached the Pentagon Island and filtered through the city's bottleneck.

'You're right. Let's forget my list of disappearing things and go back to your list of suspects. Is dear old Uncle Jim on the list? Should he be? Do you think he's too good to be true?'

'No, surprisingly, I don't. Until he can be eliminated, I think it's right that we put his name on the list, but Gillian Statham did give a very convincing argument as to why he isn't our man.'

233

'I'm not so sure. I agree that Jim sounds like a great guy, but he was very close to his sister and, in his younger days, to Cecil. A close bond like that, once betrayed, can engender a lot of bitterness.'

'We'll have to agree to disagree on that,' Dan said. 'Still, like I say, we'll put him on the list.'

'There's someone else I've been wondering about.'

'Who?'

'Julie Desmond. What we've learned today gives her a very strong motive for killing her aunt. Think about it ... Celia found out she had a biological son ... what's to say she wasn't planning on changing her will in his favour? The gambling habits of Julie's stepfather had already caused her to lose out on one potential inheritance. She wouldn't have been too thrilled at the prospect of being usurped by Eric Mundy.'

'True, and I'd tend to agree with you, except for two crucial details. Firstly, we have no evidence that Julie knew anything about Eric. Secondly – and more importantly – she was in Australia when her aunt went missing. She had a watertight alibi.'

Isabel tapped the steering wheel. 'Bearing in mind what we've just learned, I think it's time to take another look at that alibi. It may not be as watertight as Julie Desmond would have us think.'

Chapter 42

'This puts a whole new spin on things,' Lucas said, when Isabel had finished briefing the DCs about what she and Dan had learned from Eric Mundy.

'It certainly gives us a couple of extra suspects,' she said. 'At least in theory.'

'Does it though?' Zoe said. 'Why would Jim want to kill Celia? You've told us he was trying to bring about a reconciliation between her and Eric.'

'Well, strictly speaking, it wouldn't have been a reconciliation,' said Isabel. 'That suggests he was trying to get them back together … like a reunion. The reality is, Celia and Eric never met.'

'OK, let's call Jim Whetton a go-between then,' Zoe persisted. 'An intermediary. It sounds like he was very fond of his sister and nephew … and, once upon a time, he'd cared about Celia too – or at least about his friend, Cecil. His aim was to bring about a meeting between Eric and his long-lost parent. Harming Celia would have put the kibosh on that.'

'What about Eric Mundy?' said Lucas 'Would he have had reason to kill Celia?'

'I don't think he's our man,' Dan replied. 'He doesn't seem like the kind of guy who could kill in cold blood. Besides, he didn't even know where Celia lived – although, admittedly, we've only got his word on that.'

'What if either Jim or Eric killed Celia accidentally?' Lucas said. 'In those circumstances they might have enlisted the other's help to dispose of the body. Two people would have made the job a lot easier and quicker.'

'You seem stuck on the idea this was accidental, Lucas,' said Dan.

'Well, that doesn't quite work for me,' said Isabel. 'At a push, I'll accept that one or other of them *might* have killed Celia in a fit of rage or even accidentally, but I don't buy the idea of them working together to dispose of the body.'

'If you ask me, the working-together scenario fits much better with Timothy and Joyce Littlewood,' Dan said.

'Again, I'm struggling to imagine either of them as the perpetrator.' Isabel cleared her throat. 'Neither has a motive for murder, at least not one that we know of. Having said that, I don't suppose we can rule out an accidental killing.'

'Of the two of them, Timothy is the most obvious suspect,' Dan said. 'If he killed Celia – accidentally or otherwise – the first person he'd have turned to would have been his mother. She'd do anything to protect her son.'

'What about Mary Summers?' Zoe asked. 'Celia refused to give her a loan to pay off the bailiffs. That's a motive.'

'Not a particularly compelling one,' Dan said. 'That all happened years before Celia's death. If Mary Summers had wanted to lash out, surely she would have done it at the time? Why wait?'

'The one person we've not considered yet is Julie Desmond,' said Isabel.

'That's because she wasn't around when Celia Aspen disappeared,' Lucas said.

'Allegedly.'

Lucas sat up and shuffled. 'What're you saying, boss?'

236

Isabel smiled. 'Sit still, Lucas. Stop waggling. You look like a cat getting ready to pounce. What I'm saying is that the facts we've discovered today give Julie Desmond one hell of a motive.'

'She's also got one hell of an alibi.'

'Yeah, I've been hearing that a lot over the last few days, but I think it's time for us to stand back and reconsider, especially in light of the latest revelations.' Isabel paused to let what she was saying sink in. 'How solid is Julie Desmond's alibi? How thoroughly was it explored?'

Zoe studied her notes. 'As you know, Julie's movements and passport were routinely checked as part of the missing person's investigation. She flew out of the country in the early hours of Sunday 11th May 1986 and returned on 13th August. She said she rang and spoke to her aunt a couple of times during the first week of her holiday, and the phone records backed that up. There were two incoming calls from Australia. The first was made on the 14th of May and the second was four days later on the 18th of May.'

'And when was Celia last seen alive?' Lucas asked.

'On May the 15th, by Timothy Littlewood.'

Isabel ran a knuckle over her chin. 'Why did Julie ring again so soon after the first phone call? She's already told us that long-distance calls were expensive … why ring her aunt twice in four days and then not bother for the rest of the trip?'

Dan took off his jacket and hung it on the back of his chair.

'She said her aunt didn't seem fussed about whether she heard from her or not. Celia wasn't interested in chatting, so Julie decided not to waste her money after the first couple of calls. Seems fair enough to me.'

Isabel made a note of the dates of the phone calls, together with the date of Timothy Littlewood's last sighting of the victim.

'The bottom line is that Julie was eliminated as a suspect based on the fact that Celia was seen alive after she left for Australia,' she said. 'But what if Timothy Littlewood was wrong? He says he saw Celia, but maybe that wasn't the case.'

'Why would he tell us he'd seen her if he hadn't?'

'I'm not sure,' Isabel said. 'Where Timothy is concerned, not everything is straightforward and logical. I think we need to talk to him again about what he saw, or *thinks* he saw.'

'There are still the phone calls,' Zoe said. 'Julie Desmond spoke to her aunt on the 18th of May. Timothy Littlewood may have been the last person to see Celia Aspen, but Julie was the last person to speak to her.'

'I keep coming back to one detail.' Isabel held her hands above her head. 'That Julie had the most to gain from Celia's death. On top of that, we now know there was a rival for her aunt's affections and money. Did Julie find out about Eric Mundy? Did Celia tell her that she planned to change her will?'

'Where are you going with this?' Dan said. 'You think Julie Desmond killed her aunt and disposed of the body *before* she left for Australia?'

'I'm simply throwing it out there, for consideration.' She stood with her hands on her hips. 'Feel free to argue against the idea.'

'It sounds as though you've already discounted Timothy's sighting of Celia,' Lucas said. 'I don't get it though. If Julie is guilty, why would she ask him to go round there, knowing her aunt was already dead?'

'That's one of the details I've yet to work out,' Isabel replied. 'I do have a theory though.'

'Go on,' said Dan.

'Julie was aware that Timothy was afraid of Celia. His autism means he isn't always comfortable making eye contact, and Julie would have known that. The letter she sent to Timothy told him not to knock on the door ... to instead give Celia a quick wave when he'd finished the job. The Timothy I knew always did exactly as he was told – so, if he *was* feeling fearful or nervous, who's to say he looked through the window at all? It's possible Julie was counting on him scurrying away without a backward glance.'

'And if he *had* bothered looking through the window?'

'He might have seen that the room was empty,' said Isabel. 'That Celia Aspen was already gone.'

'It sounds feasible, boss,' said Dan, 'but it does contradict what Timothy has already said.'

'Like I say, it's only a theory.'

'Yes, but how can we prove it?'

'I'm not sure, Dan. I could be way off beam and we'll never prove anything – but we need to check. Let's start by going to see the Littlewoods again tomorrow. We need Timothy to tell us precisely what he saw when he was round at Celia's – or, more to the point, what he *didn't* see.'

***

After she'd finished updating her team, Isabel slipped out of the office and headed towards the town's biggest supermarket to buy a healthy lunch from its extensive and expensive salad bar. As she walked down the high street, she heard the reedy, bellowing drone of a bagpipe.

On alternate Saturdays musicians, poets and mime artists were invited to perform at the bottom of Bainbridge's pedestrianised shopping street, in a paved-off section designated as the town's entertainment arena. Occasionally, and unofficially, buskers also appeared midweek, playing for a few hours until they were moved on. Today, a man in full highland dress with puffed-up cheeks was doing his best to coax a tune from a saggy-looking bagpipe.

The shrill, wailing sound always made Isabel feel nostalgic, and she threw a couple of pound coins into his collection box as she walked past. She was reminded of the song that had been released a few weeks after her father left home – 'Mull of Kintyre' by Wings. Her dad was a big Paul McCartney fan, and Isabel had bought the single to cheer herself up. To her mother's annoyance, she had played the song over and over on the portable record player in her bedroom.

With each revolution, Isabel had become increasingly fixated with the idea that the higher the song reached in the charts, the more likely it was her dad would come home. By early December, when 'Mull of Kintyre' hit the number one slot, her belief grew into something close to an obsession.

She waited, and waited, and even though her dad failed to materialise, she refused to give up her preoccupation with the song. She told herself he'd come home if it hung on to the number one position until Christmas.

Christmases in their house had always been low key. Most years, much to Isabel's disappointment, her dad had opted to work through the holidays – although now, of course, she realised he probably hadn't been working at all. She'd always longed for a normal Christmas – the kind of big family gathering everyone else seemed to have. Instead, most years, Isabel and her mother ended up sitting quietly at the dining table with only a roasted capon for company. They would pull crackers and feign bonhomie and every year Barbara would give the same, tired explanation.

'Your dad gets a generous bonus for working at Christmas. We need the money, Isabel. Cheer up. He'll be here for the new year.'

In 1978, when the new year dawned and her absent father still hadn't reappeared, the true seriousness of the situation became apparent to Isabel. And yet, while ever 'Mull of Kintyre' remained at number one, she refused to give up hope. Whenever she tuned in to watch *Top of the Pops* on Thursday evenings, she was a tender bundle of nervous energy, totally convinced that her father's return was tied in with Paul McCartney and Wings staying at the top of the charts.

She clung desperately to that belief, even after her birthday came and went with no sign of her father, not even a card.

Wings managed to fly high in the charts until the end of January 1978, when after nine weeks at number one, they were knocked off the top spot by a reggae song called 'Uptown Top Ranking' by Althea and Donna. Isabel had hated that song ever since.

***

She took her healthy lunch back to the office and ate it at her desk. By half past two, she was absorbing a two-hundred-page report on the rise of knife crime in the East Midlands. It made for thoroughly depressing reading.

Half an hour later, as she waded through several pages of statistical data, she was beginning to think she'd never reach the end of the report. The last thing she needed was a call from Nathan.

'What's up?' she said, when she answered her phone.

'We're needed up at the school.'

'Both of us? I've got an appointment with Val in an hour.'

'You need to be there, Isabel,' Nathan said. 'Ellie and her class-mates are being questioned about some kind of incident.'

Isabel's heart began to thud uncomfortably. Were Ellie and her friends being questioned as part of the investigation into Skye Hawton's complaint? What if David Allerton had been abusing other pupils? Could Ellie be one of them?

'Have you been told what it's about?' she asked, her voice hesitant. She was tempted to share what she knew about the situation, but their summons to the school might be nothing to do with David Allerton.

241

'I haven't been told anything,' Nathan said. 'All I know is, you need to be there. Ellie will want you with her.'

'I'll rearrange my meeting with Val,' she said. 'I'll see you at the school in twenty minutes.'

***

For the second time in a few days, Isabel was facing an awkward conundrum. Through her job, she was privy to confidential information regarding the nature of the allegations against David Allerton, but it was knowledge she wasn't in a position to use. She'd been asked to attend the school in her role as a parent, not in a professional capacity.

There was no opportunity to fill Nathan in on what she knew either. She met him at the school's reception desk, and they were immediately whisked off to a small meeting room next to the headteacher's office. Ellie was there ahead of them, having been taken out of class and held back after lessons finished for the day. When she saw them, her stiff, worried expression melted into one of relief.

'What's happening?' she said.

'We're not sure,' Nathan said. 'All we know is we've been asked to come in because they want to ask you some questions.'

'What about?'

Isabel put an arm around her daughter's shoulder. 'Let's wait and see, eh? I'm sure it's nothing to worry about.'

'Am I in trouble?'

'No,' Isabel said. 'Of course not.'

Within a couple of minutes they had been joined by the headteacher and the school's safeguarding officer. The meeting room felt tiny and claustrophobic, but at least it was warm and well lit.

The safeguarding officer introduced herself, and explained that she needed to ask some questions. 'We'd like to talk to you about the art class you had last Wednesday,' she began. 'Did anything happen during the lesson that you'd like to tell us about?'

Ellie looked puzzled and nervous. 'No,' she said. 'We had to draw a still life. A bowl of oranges and some other stuff.'

'And it was Mr Allerton who took the class?'

'Yes. He's my favourite teacher.'

The head and the safeguarding officer exchanged a brief glance.

'Is he your favourite teacher for any particular reason?'

'I like art,' Ellie said. 'And Mr Allerton makes the lessons interesting.'

'In what way?'

Ellie thought for a moment. 'He talks about different artists and the impact their work has had on the world. He lets you try different artistic styles and doesn't tell you off if you experiment with something that doesn't quite work.'

'Has Mr Allerton ever made you feel uncomfortable?'

'I don't know what you mean?'

'Has he ever done or said anything inappropriate?'

'No, of course not. He's nice and he encourages you, but not in a creepy way.'

'And what about your other classmates? Does he treat them in the same way?'

'As far as I know. There are a couple of people who don't like him, but only because he won't let them mess around in class.'

'Is there anyone in particular who has a problem with him?' asked the head.

Ellie turned to her mother. Isabel nodded, encouraging her daughter to speak.

'There are a couple of girls ... one of them used to be a friend of mine, but she's not anymore.'

'Have you fallen out?'

'We haven't had a big, blazing argument, if that's what you mean. It's like we don't seem to get on anymore. We're not interested in the same things and, to be honest, I don't enjoy being

243

with her these days. She can be weird. She also has a problem with Mr Allerton.'

'What kind of problem?'

'She doesn't like him. She seemed to get on OK with him at the beginning of term, but then she started being cocky and answering back whenever he asked her to put more effort into her work.'

The headteacher pressed the palms of her hands together. 'Can you tell us who this person is please, Ellie?'

Once again, Ellie hesitated. 'Skye,' she said. 'Skye Hawton. Has she said something about Mr Allerton?'

'Why do you ask that?'

'Because she was throwing paint around a couple of weeks ago and Mr Allerton shouted at her. She said she was going to get him done for it.'

'Did she say that?' Isabel asked.

'Yes. She was telling anyone who'd listen that she was going to get him in trouble.'

'Going back to last week's lesson,' the safeguarding officer said, 'you and the other pupils were working at easels, is that right?'

'Yes. We were using charcoal. The easels were in a circle around the room.'

'And did Mr Allerton take a look at your work? At what you were drawing?'

'Yeah, he went round the whole class, making suggestions on how we could improve on what we'd done.'

'And did he stand close to you when he observed your work?'

Ellie looked horrified. 'No, of course he didn't. Mr Allerton wouldn't do that. He always keeps his distance. He makes a point of it. He has a way of explaining things without getting in your face.'

'He's never done or said anything inappropriate?'

'No.'

'Have you ever seen him acting inappropriately towards anyone else?'

'No, definitely not, and if Skye Hawton says otherwise, she's a liar and I'm glad I'm not friends with her anymore.'

The headteacher asked the final question. 'Do you consider Mr Allerton to be a friend?'

'What? No way.' Ellie puckered her face. 'He's my teacher, not my friend. He's a good teacher and I kind of respect him, but he's not the sort of person I'd want to hang out with.'

Chapter 43

By the time Isabel got back to the station, she was tired and the dull pain of a stress headache was tightening around her forehead. The summons from the school had complicated an already difficult day. All she wanted to do was go home and take a long, hot bath and soak away her troubles. For now, she'd have to grit her teeth, ignore her headache, and get through her rearranged meeting with the Super.

'I hope you've got good news for me on the Celia Aspen case,' Val said, when Isabel walked into her office.

'I wouldn't say the news was good, but we are making progress.'

Isabel settled into the caress of the black leather chair, unexpectedly grateful for its soft, embracing contours. She delivered the kind of succinct briefing she knew the detective superintendent would appreciate. After summarising her conversations with Eric Mundy and Gillian Statham, she handed over copies of Cecil and Violet's letters. Next, she ran through her team's thinking behind each person of interest. Val listened attentively and without interruption until Isabel had finished.

'You now have three, possibly four people in the frame. So why the sudden interest in Julie Desmond?'

'She has the strongest motive.'

'She also has a strong alibi. You told me that yourself.'

'True, but that relies heavily on a sighting of the victim *after* Julie had gone to Australia. No one's ever questioned the reliability of that sighting. We're going to talk to the witness again tomorrow and, depending on what Timothy has to say, we may decide to investigate Julie more thoroughly.'

'As Timothy Littlewood has ASD, I assume you'll be talking to him in one of the special interview suites?'

'I did consider it,' Isabel replied, 'but even that kind of informal atmosphere might frighten him ... make him clam up. He knows me, and if DS Fairfax and I talk to him in his own home with his mother present as the appropriate adult, there's a good chance he'll open up.'

'OK, but don't be too gentle. If he *has* fabricated evidence, then he's guilty of perverting the course of justice.'

'There's no suggestion that his statement was deliberately fabricated. I don't think there was ever any intention on Timothy's part to mislead us. He may genuinely believe that he saw Celia that day. He *may* have seen her. That's what we need to clarify.'

The detective superintendent stared at Isabel with a pinched expression. 'It's a pity the niece's alibi wasn't checked more thoroughly at the time of her aunt's disappearance.'

'I agree. The missing person's investigation was handled ineffectually. If it had been dealt with more scrupulously, the victim's body might have been discovered a lot sooner ... along with her killer.'

'I suppose the discovery of a body always gives new impetus to a missing person's case.'

'If Julie Desmond is guilty, it's going to be hard to prove it more than thirty years after the event.'

'You're right,' Val said. 'I can't imagine much has survived in the way of tangible evidence.'

'No. It's bloody frustrating. So far, the only thing we've managed to prove conclusively is that the skeleton belongs to Celia Aspen. Everything else is supposition … a working hypothesis at best. As yet, there's no evidence that Julie knew about the appearance of Eric Mundy in her aunt's life, and it's pure speculation on our part that Celia was thinking of changing her will.'

'Has anyone checked with her lawyer?'

'Yes, Lucas has been in touch with the firm. Unfortunately, the solicitor who drew up Celia's will died eight years ago. The office manager was very helpful though. She checked their archives, but there was nothing on file to suggest Celia Aspen was planning to draw up a new will.'

'That's not to say she wasn't thinking about it. What about the press appeal? Any response to that?'

'A few calls,' said Isabel. 'Most of them were time-wasters. A woman who used to work at the newsagent's on Ecclesdale Drive confirmed she'd seen Celia in the shop at the end of April 1986. Other than that, no one's come forward with any new information.'

'OK. Well, tread carefully on this one, Isabel. We don't want to alert Julie Desmond that she's under suspicion.'

***

When she returned to the CID room, Isabel opened a window to allow the stuffy, end-of-day feel to escape. Lucas's desk was empty, save for three unwashed mugs. Dan had gone home after announcing that his parents were driving down from Sunderland to take him out for dinner.

Zoe was still there, leaning into her desk. An open packet of biscuits lay next to her keyboard. Isabel watched her for a moment.

'How come you're always the last to leave, Zoe?'

The DC lifted her blonde head and smiled. 'I'm doing the late shift today.'

'But you were here this morning before I set off for Nottingham.'

'Yes, well … I've been catching up on some paperwork and following up on a few things. There's a lot to do and I get restless at home if I'm working on an interesting case.'

Isabel parked her backside on the edge of Lucas's desk. 'The Celia Aspen case is certainly interesting, I'll give you that.'

'Do you think we're any closer to finding an answer?'

'Definitely, but proving how she was murdered is going to be tricky. Without some solid evidence, we're not even close to charging anyone, let alone getting a conviction.'

'What did the detective superintendent say?'

'Not a lot,' Isabel replied. 'She could see why we have concerns about Julie Desmond and she's happy for us to pursue them, but I don't think she's convinced we'd be able to make anything stick.'

Zoe glanced at the clock on the wall. It was almost six.

'Are you finishing for the day, boss?'

Isabel nodded. 'My mother's going back to Spain tomorrow, so I feel as though I should spend some time with her while she's still here. I take it you plan to stay at your desk for a while yet? Have you eaten anything, besides crisps and biscuits?'

Zoe laughed guiltily. 'You're beginning to sound like *my* mother. She tells me I'll never be slim unless I have three square meals a day.'

'I'm sure she means well,' Isabel replied. Then, realising how that sounded, added: 'Not that you're fat. You've got a nice figure.'

Zoe toyed with a biscuit that was protruding from the open packet.

'I'm not sure about that. I could do with losing a stone.'

'Have you thought about running? I go out at least twice a week and it helps keep me in shape … now that I'm getting on in years.' Isabel flashed a self-deprecating smile.

'I might come with you one day,' Zoe said.

'You're welcome to. I usually go up to the top of the hill behind my house. The going up can be tough, but it's a breeze on the way down. I tend to go out in the mornings, but sometimes I run in the evenings as well. In fact, I might go for a run when I get home tonight. It might clear my head. I've got a thumping migraine.'

***

When she was back home, Isabel presented Ellie with a menu from the local Chinese takeaway.

'Your gran's going home tomorrow,' she said. 'I thought we'd have a night off from cooking and have a treat. I think you deserve it. You answered the school's questions very eloquently, Ellie. I'm proud of you.'

Even though Ellie was thoroughly scrutinising the list of dishes, Isabel knew she'd end up ordering chicken with cashew nuts.

'You do know that you can tell me anything, don't you?' Isabel said. 'I mean, if Mr Allerton did ever say or do anything that made you feel uncomfortable ... even *slightly* uncomfortable, you would let me know?'

'I don't suppose I'd want to,' Ellie replied. 'It would be beyond embarrassing, but ... yes, of course I'd tell you. Honestly, Mum, there's nothing to worry about as far as Mr Allerton's concerned. He's a nice man. A cool dude. He's safe and just ... a teacher.'

'So you think Skye Hawton is being vindictive? Assuming she's complained about him that is.'

'Do you know something, Mum? Have you got some kind of insider knowledge?'

'If I had, you know I wouldn't be able to tell you.'

Ellie made a show of studying the menu.

'Why didn't you tell me that you and Skye had fallen out?' Isabel said.

'There wasn't much to tell. Like I said at school, we didn't have a huge bust-up or anything.'

'The two of you have been friends for years. Why the sudden decision to not hang out with her?'

Ellie twirled a strand of hair around the middle finger of her right hand. 'I prefer to spend time with Lily. She's a nicer person. Skye … well, Skye doesn't like school very much. She messes about in class, and drags me into things and gets me in trouble. She's the reason I got such a crap report this term.'

'And is she the reason you've been turning up late for school?'

Ellie tugged at the strand of hair. 'In a way,' she said. 'I decided to start walking to school to avoid seeing Skye on the bus. It was the only way I could think of to dodge her. It's a long walk though … it takes ages, and I don't always set off in time.'

'I see. Have things been better since Dad's been giving you a lift?'

'Yep.' Ellie nodded. 'Although it's not fair to expect him to do it every day … it'd be good if you could take me occasionally.'

'I'll try, Ellie. I just need to get this case out of the way first.'

'Yeah, yeah. That's what you always say.'

Unable to deny the charge, Isabel squirmed. She wasn't proud of the fact that she often had to dip out of family commitments because of work, but this was the first time Ellie had called her out on it.

'What can I say, other than sorry? It's my job, love. It's what I do.'

Ellie scrunched her nose and performed an eye-roll. 'I know it is, I'm not stupid. It's just sometimes I wish you did something else, that's all.'

'If I did, then I wouldn't be me, would I?'

Ellie responded with a slight shake of her head, an almost indiscernible acceptance of Isabel's point.

'Tell me something else,' Isabel said. 'Is Skye one of the reasons you stopped going to book club?'

'Yeah. We used to go together, but Skye never read any of the books. She used to go along to take the piss.'

'Ellie!'

'What? It's true. I used to love talking about books, but Skye spoilt it for me.'

'Do you think there's a reason for her suddenly acting up?'

'She's always been the same, Mum. I didn't mind when we were younger, but school is getting serious now. You might not believe it, but I don't want to mess up. I'd like to do well and get good grades and, if I stick with Skye, that's not going to happen.'

Isabel was reassured by her daughter's desire to make her mark academically. If Skye Hawton's accusation was false, she also felt a massive sense of relief that Ellie had chosen not to hang around with her.

'I'm glad you're working hard again. You're an amazing girl, Ellie, but even if you weren't, your dad and I would love you anyway.' Isabel pulled her in for a hug. 'Try not to turn your back on Skye completely. Something tells me she might need a friend round about now.'

Their brief moment of mother–daughter harmony was brought to an end by the arrival of Nathan and Barbara. They wandered into the kitchen together, Barbara laughing at something Nathan was telling her. It was nice to see them getting on.

'What's all this?' Nathan leaned over Ellie's shoulder and pointed to the menu. 'Are we having a takeaway? Brill. What're you having, Ellie?'

'Chicken,' she said. 'With cashew nuts.'

***

Isabel didn't usually run alone so late in the evening, especially during the short, dark days of autumn and winter – but today was an exception. After they'd eaten their Chinese meal, she'd informed Nathan, Ellie and her mother where she was going and when she would be back, and then set off.

As she ran onto the dark, bleak slopes of the hill, high above the town, she realised what a joy it was to be out on such a clear night. Up here there was no street lighting, no lamp posts, houses or pubs – just the silvery glow of an almost full moon and a skyful of stars. Thousands of winking, twinkling stars. Her eyes quickly adjusted as she pressed on to the brow of the empty hill. There was a damp, earthy smell in the air as she paused for a moment, soaking up the silence and looking east, towards the network of houses that formed the Ecclesdale estate.

She couldn't make it out, but down there – somewhere among the lamp-lit avenues and cul-de-sacs – was 23 Ecclesdale Drive. It had been there for as long as Isabel could remember, and it would still be there decades from now, long after she was gone. New people would move in, things would change, and new memories would be made. The circle of life would continue.

Tomorrow, after she'd talked to the Littlewoods, she intended questioning Julie Desmond. Since speaking to Eric Mundy, Isabel had been unable to shake off the feeling that Julie had killed Celia Aspen. She was certain of it, but how on earth was she going to prove it?

Chapter 44

The welcome they received from Joyce Littlewood the next day was lukewarm. The old woman's eyes looked tired and although she invited them in, she seemed reluctant to talk.

'Timothy isn't here,' she said. 'I did tell you he was working earlies this week. He won't be home until two.'

Isabel was irritated – more with herself than by Timothy Littlewood's absence. Joyce *had* told her he was working the early shift, but it had slipped her mind – elbowed aside by other, more pressing matters.

'We'll have to come back later then,' she said. 'We need to talk to him about the last time he saw Celia Aspen.'

'I'll tell him as soon as he gets in,' Joyce said, 'but I do hope my son isn't a suspect in her murder. You know Timothy. He hasn't got a nasty bone in his body. There's no way he would have hurt Celia. It's not possible.'

'I'll be totally honest with you, Joyce. We're keeping an open mind about who killed Celia. At the moment, we don't have enough evidence to point to any one person, which is why we're asking more questions.'

'We want to talk to Timothy about what he saw the day he mended the trellis,' Dan added.

Joyce was standing at the kitchen sink. She'd wrung out a dishcloth and had been using it to wipe the draining board. Now she threw it bad-temperedly into the washing-up bowl.

'Again? You talked to him about it the other day. How many more times? He's already told you everything.' She wiped her hands on her apron. 'My son wouldn't lie.'

'I don't think DS Fairfax is suggesting he would,' Isabel said. 'But we need to check that Timothy wasn't mistaken or confused. I know he found Celia rather daunting … I think he was afraid of her. If that is the case, wouldn't he have done everything possible to keep out of her way? Even something as simple as avoiding eye contact with her?'

Joyce untied her apron, pulled it over her neck and folded it neatly. 'Celia did make him nervous,' she said. 'It wasn't always that way, mind you. When she first moved in they were quite good pals – and making friends has never been easy for Timothy, not with his autism.'

'So when did his nervousness around Celia begin?' said Isabel.

'After the first telling off she gave him, I suppose. I can't even remember what it was about, but it scared Timothy witless.' Joyce placed a liver-spotted hand on the back of a chair and leaned against it. 'Celia was a small, scrawny woman, but she could be absolutely terrifying and very intimidating. It got to the point that if she asked him to help with something, he'd finish the job as quickly as possible and hurry home. He didn't want to spend a second more than he had to round at number 23.'

'Can't you recall anything about what caused the rift?'

'There was no one incident,' Joyce replied. 'It was the culmination of a few things – like Timothy going round to dig the garden without her permission, or hanging around in the hope that he'd run into Julie. Celia was very protective of her privacy. She wasn't happy about anyone going round there unless they were expressly invited.'

'Did you know that Celia was transgender?' Isabel asked.

'Transgender?' Joyce frowned. 'What exactly does that mean?'

'Celia was living as a woman, but she was born male. From what we can tell, she'd been transgender for most of her life. She transitioned decades before she moved next door.'

'Well, I'll be damned.' Joyce pulled out the chair she was leaning on and sat down. 'I had no idea – although, thinking back, she did have a certain look. She always dressed smartly, but there was something about her … I hesitate to say hard-faced, because that would be wrong. Her face lacked softness, that's what it was.'

'As far as we know, Celia didn't tell anyone that she was transgender,' Isabel said. 'Reading between the lines, her desire for privacy may well have been her way of safeguarding that secret.'

Joyce scratched an eyebrow. 'When you get to my age, you think you've heard it all and that nothing can surprise you – but what you've just told me has taken my breath away. As my grand-daughter would say, I'm gobsmacked.'

'There is something else we'd like to clarify,' Dan said. 'When was the last time *you* saw Celia?'

'It would have been very early in May,' Joyce said. 'I remember I was out in the front, sweeping the drive, when Celia walked by the gate. She'd obviously been shopping and I'm sure she wouldn't have bothered speaking, but I thought I'd try to make an effort … be friendly, like.'

'Can you remember what you said to her?'

Joyce thought for a moment, tapping her fingertips on the tabletop as she called to mind the conversation. 'She had a carrier bag in one hand … one of those long ones that are specially designed for rolls of wallpaper. "Been to the DIY shop, have you Celia?" I said. She told me she had, and that she was redecorating her living room because she was hoping to have visitors. She said she wanted the place to look nice for them. You know, I'd forgotten about that until just now. Celia was obviously planning to invite people round. That wasn't like her. Not at all.'

'Did she say who the visitors were?'

Joyce laughed quietly. 'Of course not. This is Celia we're talking about. She only ever told you the bare minimum. She did show me the wallpaper though. It was a pretty pattern. Flowery. Honeysuckle and violets, as I recall. I asked whether she planned on getting someone in to do the work for her, but she said she was more than capable of doing the job herself. I was relieved she didn't try to rope Timothy in to help. Wallpapering has never been his forte.'

'I wonder if she ever got around to hanging the new paper,' said Isabel.

'Oh, she did,' Joyce assured her. 'I know that for certain. A few weeks later, when I couldn't get her on the phone, I popped round and knocked on her door. There was no reply, but I had a quick look through the front window ... seeing as there was no answer. I remember seeing the wallpaper, and very nice it looked too. It was only on one wall, what they call the feature wall these days. Everything looked neat and tidy inside, but there was no one in. No sign of life. I assumed she'd gone away.'

Gone away. No sign of life. Joyce Littlewood had been absolutely right.

***

They had agreed that Joyce would call Dan as soon as Timothy got home.

'I've got to drive my mother to the airport this afternoon,' Isabel said, as they went back to the station. 'You may have to talk to Timothy without me. It's a shame, because I would have liked to have been the one asking the questions. He trusts me, and I think he'd open up to me. You, on the other hand ... I think you scare him.'

'Me?' Dan said. 'I'm a pussy cat.'

'Bollocks. I've not worked out what kind of animal you are

yet, Dan, but I do know you're no pussy cat. Actually, if I'm not back from the airport before the call comes through from Joyce, take Zoe with you when you speak to Timothy. And let her ask the questions.'

Chapter 45

In theory, the journey to East Midlands airport should have taken less than an hour, but Isabel knew from bitter experience that there were often inexplicable problems on the traffic-infested approach roads.

She'd left the office at one o'clock, stopped at home to collect Barbara, and set off to deliver her to the check-in desk in plenty of time for her four-fifteen flight to Malaga.

Barbara had said her goodbyes to Ellie and Kate the previous evening, and had waved cheerily to Nathan, who'd stood on the front step as they'd pulled away from the house. He'd offered to take Barbara to the airport himself, but Isabel wanted to do it. The trip would give her a little extra time alone with her mother. There was something important she wanted to talk to her about.

'Thanks for flying over to see me, Mum, and for telling me everything. I needed to hear the truth.'

They were on the A52, skirting around Derby. Traffic was light and they were making good progress.

'I know,' Barbara said. 'Thanks for putting up with me, and for listening. I would have stayed longer, but my neighbour's looking after the cat, and I don't like to impose on her for too long. I'll come back again in the spring, or you could bring Nathan and the girls out to see me. Bailey too, if he's back by then.'

The invitation wasn't meant as an admonishment, but Isabel knew that a family visit to Spain was long overdue. She decided they would make the effort to head over there, maybe even for Christmas.

'I promise we'll come out within the next four months,' Isabel said. 'It's not always easy for me to get time off at short notice, so we'll arrange something properly, well in advance.'

'You're welcome any time, you know that.'

'Thanks, Mum. I must admit, I could do with some Spanish sunshine.'

'Have you considered a trip to France?' Barbara smiled. 'I hear it's lovely in the spring.'

After dinner the previous evening, Isabel had finally told her mother that she'd emailed her dad's solicitor.

'It's much too early to be thinking in terms of a visit to France,' she replied. 'I'm still rather nervous about re-opening the channel of communication, but …' She paused, glancing nervously at the back seat. 'There is an update that I wanted to share with you before you head back. Dad has sent me an email.'

Barbara yanked her seatbelt and twisted around in the passenger seat. 'He has? When?'

Isabel smiled. 'It came through last night. It was after midnight and I decided to check my emails one last time before going to bed, and there it was … after all these years, an email from Donald Corrington in my inbox. I couldn't quite believe it. I was almost afraid to open it.'

'But you did?'

Isabel laughed. 'Of course I did. I thought about waking you up and telling you about it, but decided it was best to wait until the morning – and then you chose to have a lie-in.'

'You should have woken me before you went to work. What did the email say?' She slapped her knees expectantly.

'I printed it out,' Isabel said. 'There's a copy in my handbag. Take a look if you like. It's on the back seat.'

Barbara leaned through the gap behind the handbrake, hooked the long handle of Isabel's bag with her finger, and quickly pulled it through to the front of the car.

'Are you sure you want me to read it?'

'Yes, I'd like you to. I'd appreciate your opinion on what I should do next.'

Barbara retrieved the folded sheets of A4 paper. Isabel had slipped them into her bag that morning and had been carrying them around all day. She had taken them out several times to re-read, marvelling at the fact that her father had replied so quickly. So eagerly.

She noticed that her mother's hands were trembling as she unfolded and read the printed email. It was a short message, but a heartfelt one. Isabel had pretty much memorised every word.

Dear Isabel,

I can't begin to tell you how pleased I was to hear from you after all these years. When the solicitor gave me your message and the opportunity to get in touch, I was ecstatic, but also humbled. After the way I treated you and your mother, I don't deserve your forgiveness, let alone the chance to contact you again.

When I think back over the years I spent in Bainbridge – and I often do – the thing that I remember most is the joy you brought into my life. I recall how much I loved you and how happy and beautiful you were – but all of those memories are tainted by a sense of shame.

I was a selfish, thoughtless man and my actions were unbelievably stupid and cruel. I don't think your mother ever truly believed that I loved her – but I did. I was inclined to hold back my emotions, because I knew that I'd wronged her.

I should have been honest with her from the beginning.

My behaviour was appalling. The lies I told were disrespectful – not only to Barbara, but to my other family. In short, I was a complete idiot. Your mother deserved so much better.

I will always be grateful to her for not reporting me. I'm sure she felt like punishing me – God knows I deserved it! You may not believe me, but when I left you and your mother behind in 1977, I felt as though I'd been given a lifelong sentence. I've had to endure the pain of our separation every day since then. They say that time heals, but for me, the longer the separation, the more intense that pain has become.

Leaving you behind was the worst, most heart-breaking punishment I could have suffered. I longed to keep in touch with you, but it would have been too complicated and would have involved more lies or, worse, telling everyone the truth – and that would have been the ruination of the lives of all the people I loved. You probably think I sacrificed you and your mother in order to keep my family in France. In a way, that's true – but it's not because I loved you any less. It was the least messy option, the one that hurt the fewest people. I'm sorry.

It's good to know you and your mother are both well. I would love to hear from you again, Issy. I learned, many years ago, that you had joined the police force. Are you still a copper? Are you married? Do you have children? I'm desperate to find out what you've done with your life, but I accept that you might not want to tell me. You don't owe me anything, not even a reply to this letter.

My wife, Jeanne, passed away four years ago. A few months after she died, I told my two sons about you. They don't know everything (you see, I am still a coward, even now I'm an old man). They know I had a relationship with your mother and that we were together for many years, and that we had you. What I haven't told them is the way I deceived Barbara by marrying her. I will tell them, if you want me to. I will do it

*willingly if that is the price I have to pay to rebuild a
relationship with you.*

*Please tell your mother that I think of her often and that
I am so, so sorry. I told her that before I left, but she wasn't
in any state to accept my apology. I feel so guilty about what
I did, and the way I abandoned you. I walked away knowing
that you would have to go through the rest of your life without
a father, and that's not something I'm proud of. Life can be
hard enough at the best of times, but I made things so much
harder than they needed to be for you. I know your message
said that you forgive me, but I find that hard to believe. I
certainly can't forgive myself.*

*You've always been very precious to me, Isabel. You are my
little girl. I loved you so much. I still do. Not a day has gone
by when I've not thought of you. I hope you've had a happy
life. I've often wondered what you've been up to and tried to
imagine how things have turned out for you.*

*It would be wonderful to hear your voice again, and I very
much hope you will give me a call. I will understand if you
choose not to, or if you want to take some time to think about
it. All I'll say is this: I'm eighty-one. If you would like to talk
to me again, or even see me one more time, please don't leave
it too late.*

With love,
Dad
xx

***

With gentle fingers, her mother traced the words on each page.
She looked tense, her body straight and stiff as though she was
holding back an emotional tsunami.

'I see he's included his telephone number. It's a lovely letter,
Isabel. Very contrite and reconciliatory.'

'You think so?' Isabel was less captivated by the letter than her mother appeared to be. Yes, its tone was warm and appeasing, but it would take more than a few words on a page to make amends.

She focused on driving, keeping her eyes on an approaching road island. One of the lanes up ahead was coned off because of roadworks.

'He comes across as very apologetic.' Barbara was being mulishly insistent. 'Very remorseful.'

'Yes, he does. He talks a lot about his pain – but what about our pain, Mum? He shows very little understanding of what we've been through.' Isabel tried to recover her equilibrium, mentally crushing the hard lump of residual anger that was challenging her willingness to forgive.

Barbara shuffled through the pages and pointed to one of the paragraphs. 'He says here that he's not proud about walking away and leaving you without a father.'

'But he did walk away.' Isabel was having to work hard to maintain her composure. 'Even now, he hasn't told his sons that he married you. I want him to stand up and be counted.'

'Why?' Barbara frowned. 'Will it make you feel better? It certainly won't do your halfbrothers any good to find out their father's a bigamist.'

Why was her mother being like this? Isabel had expected her to be sympathetic and understanding, an ally in a shared dilemma.

'How come you're full of the milk of human kindness all of a sudden?' she asked.

Barbara turned to rebuke her, but appeared to have a change of heart. Her face softened as she spoke. 'This is all new for you, Issy. Fresh and raw. You forget I've had a long time to come to terms with the situation. This is a secret I've lived with for years.'

The roadworks ended and Isabel switched lanes, following the signs for the airport.

'I suppose you're right, but I still can't believe how reasonable you're being. Just because forty years have passed doesn't mean Dad's behaviour has become any less appalling.'

'Perhaps not,' Barbara said, 'but it does lessen its impact. I've *had* to let go of my anger, Isabel. It was the only way I could move on and enjoy life again.'

'And you're suggesting I should do the same?' She felt her forehead crumple involuntarily. 'That I need to let go of my anger?'

'That would be presumptuous of me,' Barbara said. 'I wouldn't dream of telling you what to do or how to feel, especially as I have a distinct advantage over you.'

'Advantage? What kind of advantage?'

Barbara lowered her eyes. 'With each year that's gone by, your father's betrayal has lost its ability to hurt me. It lost its potency completely a couple of decades ago. I still think of Donald occasionally, but I'm not his wife anymore – I never was. You, on the other hand, will always be his daughter. You have an unbreakable bond. For you, the hurt may never go away entirely.'

Isabel knew that her mother was right. That father–daughter bond had the power to hurt. It also offered the potential to heal, but was that what she wanted?

'In his letter, he talks of his memories being tainted by shame,' she said. 'I can't help but wonder … is it himself he's ashamed of, or me?'

'Good grief.' Barbara's voice was suddenly waspy and curt. 'I thought you'd be happy to receive a letter like this.' She held it aloft, fluttering the pages. 'Instead, you sound angry, as though you're desperate to have it out with him.'

'Maybe I am,' Isabel said, realising that was *exactly* what she wanted. 'I think I need to get all the rage out of my system before we try to move on.'

Barbara sighed. 'Just remember your dad's an old man now. Don't be too hard on him. By all means vent your spleen, but don't jeopardise the chance to reconcile with him. You'll regret it if you do.'

Isabel recalled the residents of White Laurels, the old people's home, and recognised that Barbara was talking sense.

'It's not my intention to jeopardise anything,' she replied. 'But I do feel strongly about what Dad has done. Yes, I still love him and I can forgive him, but I'm not willing to pretend that nothing happened. I need to talk to him about what he did and clear the air, otherwise there'll be another elephant in the room. A different elephant in a different room.'

'Sounds like a good title for a song.' Barbara smiled mutinously before gazing out of the passenger door window, off into the distance where the entrance to the airport awaited them. 'I understand what you're saying, Isabel, truly I do – but it worries me. You can be so impulsive. You say things in the heat of the moment … hurtful, wounding things that can be cuttingly devastating to the person on the receiving end. All I ask is that you take a few deep breaths and think before you say anything you might regret. The relationship you have with a parent – no matter how strained – is irreplaceable. That doesn't mean to say it has to be perfect. We can't change who we are, or what's happened in the past, but we can do our best to be positive and behave in a way that makes life better for everyone.'

Isabel indicated right and turned into the airport road. 'That sort of advice is all well and good in the agony aunt pages of a women's magazine, Mum. It's good advice and it makes sense, but I can't guarantee I'll take it on board. Impulsive is my middle name, you should know that.'

'I do.' Barbara smiled softly. 'I wonder where you get that from?'

266

Chapter 46

Amy had finished removing the Anaglypta the previous evening. Today, as she listened to the latest House of Commons debate on the Brexit Bill, she planned to scrape off the flowery wallpaper that lay beneath. She hoped it would be a lot easier to strip away and was crossing her fingers there wouldn't be a third layer of paper beneath it.

After spraying the wall with a fine mist of water and taking care not to scratch the plaster with the metal scraper, Amy began to attack the little sprigs of honeysuckle and violets. As she removed long strips of the paper, she was pleased to expose bare, skin-coloured plaster.

She'd started at the left-hand side of the wall and, as she began to remove the second strip of paper, she realised there was something written underneath it.

She scraped some more, frantically pulling at the wet, sticky pieces. The first thing she uncovered was a heart, drawn on the wall in pencil. Written inside the heart was the word Violet. Given the choice of wallpaper, she wondered whether violets had held some special significance for whoever had hung it.

She turned off the radio and continued to scrape, exposing

more of the pale pink plaster. Words appeared below the heart.
Names and dates.

Cecil Aspen | 1918–1947
Celia Aspen | 1947–
Violet Mundy née Whetton | 1920–1986
Eric Mundy | 1942–
Gillian Mundy | 1974–

Amy wondered what it all meant. Was it connected to the
photo and the ring she'd found upstairs? More to the point, did
it have anything to do with the murder that had taken place at
the house? She should call DS Fairfax to let him know. He'd told
her to ring him if she found anything, no matter how insignificant.

Chapter 47

Dan examined the writing on the wall and took photographs with his phone.

'The names do tie in with our investigation,' he said. 'It's a pity you didn't find these a week ago. It would have saved us a lot of work. Unfortunately, at this stage, they don't tell us anything we don't already know, although they do confirm a few things.'

'Who are these people?'

Dan wondered whether to share some basic information with Amy, but decided it wouldn't be wise.

'They all connect to the victim, but it's complicated,' he said instead. 'I'm sorry to do this to you, but I'm going to have to ask you to stop work on the wall for now, until I can get a CSI in to have a proper look. It's possible there might be more scribblings that you haven't uncovered yet. I know it's a pain when you're trying to crack on, but look at it this way – it means someone else will be removing the wallpaper for you. I can't say fairer than that, can I?'

Amy laughed. 'Don't worry,' she said, 'there are plenty of other jobs for me to be getting on with.'

Dan had received Amy's call at 1.30 p.m. He'd considered

sending someone else to take a look at the latest piece of evidence the house had relinquished, but then he remembered that Timothy Littlewood was due home at 2 p.m. He decided to call in on Amy and then follow up next door with the Littlewoods. The trouble was, he was on his own. He'd left Zoe in the office, dealing with another call. He'd have to go ahead and question Timothy without her. The DI wouldn't be happy, but that's the way it was.

'Where's your brother today?' Dan said, as he and Amy strolled back into the empty kitchen. The units had been removed and the breakfast bar dismantled. 'I thought he'd be outside, working on the foundations now that the crime scene has been handed back.'

'He's got a boiler to fix today,' Amy said. 'Paul's a plumber by trade and he doesn't like to let his customers down. It's one of the busiest times of year for him. Everybody switches their central heating back on when the cold weather kicks in, and that's when the old, cranky boilers tend to give up the ghost. For Paul, it's like ker-ching! He loves the autumn.'

Dan laughed. 'I take it he'll be doing the renovation work here, at the house?'

'Most of it. He'll bring in help with bricklaying, electrics and plastering when the time comes, but he can turn his hand to pretty much everything else. My part of the deal is to manage the project ... pay the bills, keep an eye on the budget and make sure everything stays on schedule.'

'So your brother's the beef and you're the brains.'

Amy smiled up at him. 'Something like that. I'm also responsible for interior design, which is a fancy way of saying that I get to choose the colour scheme.'

'Whatever you go for, I'm sure it will be class.' Dan smiled back and then glanced at his watch. It was quarter to three. 'I'd better get off. Thanks again for calling me. I'll get someone over to check out the rest of the wall.'

'Are you sure I can't offer you a tea or a coffee?' Amy said. She pointed to a tea trolley set up in the corner of the empty kitchen. It housed a kettle, teapot, cups and other mashing tackle, as well as a packet of chocolate digestives.

'It's tempting,' Dan said, 'but I've got to go. I'm glad you're starting to make progress on the house again.'

'It should be pretty nifty when it's finished.' Amy seemed reluctant to let him go. 'We aim to have it on the market by the spring, if you're interested.'

Dan pulled a doubtful face. 'I don't think so,' he said. 'This is more of a family home, and I'm a single man.'

'I see.' A dimple appeared in Amy's left cheek.

'Mind you, I'm thirty-four at my next birthday,' Dan added. 'I'm at the age where I should be settling down – but there's a big part of me that still feels like a student. I'm just a big kid at heart, I don't think I'll ever grow up completely.'

She laughed. 'Hey, where's the fun in growing up? Stay young, that's what I say … do you live in Bainbridge?'

'No, I'm renting a flat over in Duffield for now.'

'Duffield, eh? Very posh.'

'Is it?' Dan said, liking the fact that Amy was teasing him. 'I wouldn't know. I'm not familiar with the area yet. I'm from the north east originally, and I only moved down here a few months ago when I joined Bainbridge CID.'

'Well, I was born and bred here,' Amy said. 'So if you need someone to take you on a guided tour, just say the word. I have a lot of local knowledge.'

'When this case is over and you're no longer a witness in an ongoing investigation I might take you up on that offer.'

Amy gave him a dazzling smile. 'OK,' she said. 'I'll hold you to that.'

***

271

It was ten to three by the time Dan knocked at the Littlewoods' door. Timothy would be back from work, *Countdown* would be almost over, and hopefully he'd be receptive to questions.

Joyce Littlewood held a tea towel in her hand as she answered the door. She looked flustered.

'You've just missed him,' she said. 'He's gone out.'

Dan let out a long, irritated breath. 'Out? Didn't you tell him we wanted to speak to him? The questions we have are important to our investigation, Mrs Littlewood. We could have picked Timothy up and brought him down to our interview suite, but we thought he'd be happier talking here, in his own home – with you around. I thought you understood that.'

'I told him you needed to talk to him, but he wouldn't listen. He's been invited out somewhere by a friend.' She placed her left knuckle on her hip. It was a stance that was both peevish and uncompromising. 'It's very rare for my son to get an invitation to any sort of social event,' she said. 'He's a lonely lad, and if he gets the chance to meet some friends, I'm hardly going to stand in his way – whether you want to speak to him or not.'

She arranged the tea towel over her arm and took a deep, calming breath. 'Timothy will be back this evening,' she said. 'He'll be gone a couple of hours at the most. You're welcome to drop by later.'

Chapter 48

Isabel felt unexpectedly emotional when she dropped her mother at the airport. As she hugged her goodbye, she realised that things had changed between them. They were more relaxed in each other's company and less critical of one another. How long this new, tolerant regime would last was anyone's guess, but it was certainly a breakthrough and very welcome as far as Isabel was concerned.

It was late afternoon by the time she'd driven back to Bainbridge, and it didn't seem worth going back to the office. Instead, she texted Dan and asked him to call over to her house to update her on his way home.

When she got back home, she was greeted by Ellie, who was clapping her hands feverishly, the way she always did when she was excited.

'Dad says we can get a puppy,' she said, before Isabel had even taken off her coat.

'*What?* I don't think so, Ellie. Owning a dog is a big commitment – and not one to be taken lightly. That kind of decision has to be discussed properly and considered very carefully.'

Ellie's hands stilled and tears of disappointment pooled in her eyes. Her sulky expression suggested she was both upset and petulant, and Isabel cursed Nathan for putting her in this position.

'Where's your dad?'

'In his studio. He *said* I could have a dog.'

'And I'm saying that it's not a done deal.'

'Why do you always have to be so mean, Mum? I was really excited and now you've ruined everything.'

Ellie retreated upstairs – no doubt to throw herself across her bed and cry. Isabel pulled off her jacket, hung it in the hallway and weaved through to the back of the house and into the studio.

'Why did you tell Ellie she could have a puppy?'

Nathan was sitting at his Mac, working on a colourful illustration of a blue butterfly and a large purple iris.

'I thought it was a good idea,' he said, without looking up. 'An incentive for her to keep working hard. Besides, I'd like a dog. I'm here at home most days. It's not as if it would be left on its own.'

'Dogs need to be taken for regular walks. I can't see Ellie doing that, can you?'

'I don't mind going out with it. It'd do me good to get more exercise and fresh air.'

'And what about me? Do I get a say?'

He put down his digital pen. 'Isabel, when have I ever stopped you having your ten penn'orth?'

His words took the wind out of her sails, calming her down.

'Why do we need to give Ellie something to motivate her?' she said, changing tack. 'Wouldn't it be better to let her have a dog if and when she *achieves* something?'

Nathan turned his chair around to face her. 'I thought she was very brave yesterday,' he said. 'I was proud of the way she spoke up at the school.'

'So you're rewarding her for telling the truth?'

Nathan spun back to his desk. 'I've told her she can have a dog, Isabel. I'm not going back on my word. You won't have to

274

worry about a thing. I'll do the walks and take responsibility for everything else. It'll be my dog more than Ellie's.'

'Nathan, I know you mean well, but please don't present me with a fait accompli. Let me at least feel as if I have some say in this.'

'OK. Take some time to think about it. We'll talk again in a couple of days.'

Isabel hadn't realised it, but she'd been holding her breath. She exhaled, hoping Nathan wouldn't interpret it as a sigh.

'So you'll talk to Ellie?' she said. 'Let her know the idea's on hold?'

He turned back to face her again. 'If that's what you want. It won't go down well though. You're not going to be popular.'

'So what's new?' Isabel smiled defeatedly.

Shaking his head, Nathan stood up and cautiously pulled her into his arms.

'How's the case going?' he asked, moving the conversation to a less inflammatory topic.

'Slowly,' she replied. 'Nothing's cut and dried, but I think we're getting there. I bloody well hope so. I've asked Dan to call in on his way home. He should be here any minute.'

'I'll stay here and finish this off.' He pointed to the illustration. 'I'll leave you and Dan to talk police business.'

Chapter 49

Dan decided to leave his car at the station and make the ten-minute walk to the DI's on foot. It was easier than trying to find somewhere to park on her busy road.

As he dashed up the high street, the teeth of a north wind bit into his thin cotton jacket. He veered off to the right, along Queen Street and down towards his boss's house.

This would be the first time he'd been inside her home and, as he banged the brass knocker, he felt awkward.

'Thanks for dropping by, Dan,' she said, when she answered the door.

'You're sure I'm not intruding?'

'Of course not. I wouldn't have asked you to come round if you were.'

She led him into a small hallway and then turned right, through into a living room that opened into a dining kitchen. There was another room at the back, but the DI invited him to sit down at the kitchen table.

'Would you like a drink?' she asked. 'Beer? Wine? You're off duty, right?'

He smiled. 'I might go back to the office, actually. Besides, I wouldn't mind a hot drink. It's freezing out there.'

'Coffee? White, one sugar?'

He nodded, watching as she reached up into an eye-level cupboard and pulled out a cafetière.

Looking around to assess his surroundings, he realised the DI's place wasn't what he'd been expecting. Although it was a period property, it had a sleek, modern kitchen. Clean lines had been integrated with a touch of homeliness. There were pots of herbs on the kitchen windowsill and a chalkboard next to the fridge. Someone had written *Buy bog roll!* on it and added a cartoon drawing of a roll of toilet paper. Isabel caught him smiling at the illustration.

'That's my daughter's handiwork,' she said. 'It's hard to tell from that, but she's becoming a very talented artist.'

'Your husband … Nathan isn't it? You said he's an illustrator and designer. Do you think she'll follow in his footsteps?'

'I have no idea, and I hardly dare suggest it as a career path. She's at an age where, whatever I say, she does the opposite.'

'I was like that with my parents. They wanted me to become a doctor.'

Isabel looked at him questioningly. 'Is that the family trade then? Do you come from a long line of medics?'

Dan threw his head back and laughed. 'Are you kidding me? Dad works in a car factory and Mum's got a part-time job in a school kitchen. I've no idea why they thought I should be a doctor. It was never going to happen. I always wanted to be a copper. It was my dream job.'

The rich smell of ground coffee filled the kitchen as Isabel dropped three scoops into the cafetière 'Well, at least you followed your heart. Were your parents disappointed?'

'I think my dad was. Mum goes along with anything as long as she knows I'm happy.'

'She sounds like a wise woman.'

'She is, although she does worry about me. She's under the misapprehension that I'm in mortal danger every second of every day of my working life. She doesn't seem to realise that most of my time is spent stuck in front of a computer screen.'

'Or asking questions in a sweaty interview room.'

'Yeah.' He grinned. 'That as well.'

'Talking of asking questions, how did it go with Timothy?' She pressed the plunger on the cafetière and poured the coffee.

'Ah, I was about to tell you about that,' he said, reaching for one of the mugs. 'I didn't manage to catch him. I got there at ten to three, but he'd gone out.'

'What? Didn't his mother tell him you were coming?'

'She did, but he took no notice. He's gone out with a friend, and apparently that's a rare occurrence. Far more preferable than talking to me, it would seem. He'll be back home in about an hour. I'll call in on my way home.'

He took a sip of coffee and told the DI about his latest visit to see Amy Whitworth. He showed her the photo he'd taken of the writing on the wall.

'How odd,' she said.

'Yeah, it seemed weirdly futile to me. I mean, why write something on a wall and then paper over it?'

'It could be that Celia wanted to record the information … but somewhere no one would see it. If you've held on to a secret for a long time, there's something cathartic about writing things down, even if you do cover them up again. Celia may have found it comforting, knowing that someone would eventually find those marks. It was a record of her connection to her family.'

'Zoe wasn't with me when I went round to the Littlewoods,' Dan confessed. 'She was on the phone when I left. Turns out it was an update about the situation up at the school.'

'Has something happened?'

'The complaint has been dropped.'

For Isabel, the news was a shot in the arm, bringing a welcome surge of relief. 'What's the story?' she asked.

'The school is satisfied that Skye's complaint was malicious,

278

with intent to deceive. David Allerton said that she sent him a friend request on Facebook, and when he declined it, she took umbrage. Skye began to play up in class, and he told her off. The complaint was her way of getting back at him.'

'Sounds like a drastic form of revenge for something that was rather innocuous,' Isabel said. 'Is the school absolutely certain there's no truth in what she said?'

'The complaint's been thoroughly investigated and the LADO and the school are satisfied there's nothing to back up Skye's claim. On the contrary, the statements made by other pupils, including your daughter, completely absolve the teacher of any wrongdoing. The head and the safeguarding officer spoke to Skye again this morning and she broke down and admitted she'd lied in order to cause trouble for Mr Allerton.'

Isabel banged her forehead with the heel of her hand. 'Stupid, stupid girl. What the hell was she thinking? She could have ruined the man's reputation.'

'It sounds like it was all a big game to her.'

'The world's gone mad, Dan.'

'When you're that age, I don't suppose you realise how devastating that kind of false accusation can be.'

'People's jobs are on the line,' Isabel said. 'Their marriages too … their whole lives.'

'The headteacher has asked if a detective or a uniformed officer can have a word with Skye and give her an informal verbal warning. That's what Zoe was trying to arrange this afternoon.'

'Hopefully Skye will think twice about making false accusations in the future. God! When did the world become such a scary place? The minute you have kids you start to worry about them … you wonder what they're up to and what's being done to them. They bring a huge amount of joy, but also a whole load of lost sleep.'

'As I don't have kids, it's not something I need worry about,' Dan said. 'I haven't even got a twinkle in my eye.'

Isabel smiled. 'You might have kids one day and, if you do, you'll remember this conversation.'

'At least the school managed to nip the whole thing in the bud,' Dan said. 'From what I hear, that was largely thanks to the information your daughter and her friends provided when the school questioned them. If she decides against a career in the arts, Ellie could always join the force.'

'Heaven help us!' Isabel rolled her eyes. 'Mind you, stranger things have happened, so watch this space.'

'I thought she might be here actually … that I'd get chance to meet her.'

Isabel pointed to the ceiling. 'She's up in her room, sulking. Nathan told her we could get a puppy, and I've put the brakes on the idea. She's not happy with me.'

'You don't fancy getting a sweet little pup then, boss?' He laughed.

'It's tempting, but aside from the cuteness factor, I don't think there's too much in it for me. I don't want to come home to find that an animal has peed on the floor or chewed my favourite shoes.'

'They soon grow out of that,' Dan said. 'My parents have always had a dog. They've got a couple at the moment, a Westie and a border terrier. They're good company. Dogs are loyal. They don't mind if you're in a bad mood or you don't feel like talking. They'll sit with you regardless. They give their affection freely and ask for nothing in return.'

'Has Nathan paid you to say all this?'

'Just telling it like it is.' He held up his hands in mock surrender. 'Dogs are amazing. I'd have one myself if I wasn't out at work all hours.'

Isabel was sceptical. 'I'll think about it.'

'If you don't fancy a puppy, you could always go to the rescue centre and pick up an adult dog that needs a good home.'

Isabel nodded. 'I could warm to that idea. It sounds more

appealing than taking on a mischievous pup. I'll have a look online, see what's available. Don't let on to Nathan or Ellie that I'm weakening though. I don't want them to think I'm a pushover.'

'I'm sure the thought never entered their heads, boss.'

Laughing, Isabel stood up and carried the empty mugs to the sink.

'Why don't you give Joyce Littlewood a call ... see if Timothy's back yet. If he is, I'll come with you to question him.'

Dan pulled out his phone and made the call.

'Well?' Isabel said, when the conversation with Joyce Littlewood had concluded.

Dan looked annoyed. 'He's not back yet. Looks like we might have to leave it until tomorrow.'

'Hmm,' Isabel said. 'If I didn't know better, I'd say Timothy Littlewood is trying to avoid us.'

Chapter 50

When she woke the next morning, Isabel's muscles ached through sleeping too tensely. She'd lain awake until after two, a pain of worry nagging at her like a toothache. She realised it was fear that was niggling at her – fear that, by contacting her father's solicitor, she'd made the wrong choice.

Although her message hadn't specifically asked for him to get back in touch, her father's swift reply meant that the hot potato had now landed back in her lap. She was obliged to make a decision and respond to his email.

A bouncy, chiming noise sounded from Nathan's phone, bursting into the silent room like an unwelcome visitor. Nathan stirred. Silencing the blaring alarm, he rolled over in bed to face her.

'I had a dream that your dad paid us a visit,' he said. 'We had a big row. I didn't like him and he didn't like me.'

Isabel winced. 'Who knows, it might be a premonition. There's no guarantee you'll hit it off.'

He pulled her close. 'You do realise you're talking as if you've made up your mind about meeting him.'

'Am I? In that case, it's a Freudian slip. I still haven't decided whether to call him, never mind arrange a visit.'

'What's holding you back?'

'I suppose I'm scared. Sometimes it's easier to hold on to hope and do nothing.'

'What is it you're afraid of?'

She pulled the duvet tight across her shoulder and suppressed a shudder. 'That I'll ring him, arrange to meet, and we'll be unable to reconnect. The worst-case scenario is that I won't be able to let go of the anger I've been holding on to. What if we meet and I spend the whole time ranting and raving at him?'

'You won't do that.'

'I'm more than capable,' Isabel said. 'I excel at ranting and raving.'

Nathan laughed. 'I know you do. I've been on the receiving end enough times – but I don't think you'll let rip if you see your dad.'

He pushed her fringe away from her eyes. 'All the time I've known you, Isabel, there's been a yearning inside you … a hidden space that no one can find and nothing can fill. You've spent the last forty-odd years wanting to see your father, and now your wish has come true. I can't understand why you haven't jumped at the chance. What have you got to lose?'

'The good memories I've held on to, I suppose … the image I've created in my mind of a wonderful, loving parent. What if I meet him and find out he isn't how I remember him? I might be disappointed. What if I don't like him? The *real* him?'

'Then all the sadness you've carried around for the whole of your adult life will have been for nothing,' Nathan said. 'Perhaps *that's* what you're afraid of.'

***

At eight o'clock, when she got to work, Isabel picked up the phone and rang Joyce Littlewood to arrange a time to go and see Timothy.

'He's not here,' Joyce said, her voice shrill with panic. 'He's not come home.'

'You mean he stayed out all night?'

'Yes,' said Joyce.

'Has he done that before?'

'No. Never. I'm really worried about him, Isabel.'

'Have you tried calling the person he was supposed to be with? Maybe he's found himself a girlfriend.'

'I doubt it. I don't know who he was going to meet. He didn't tell me. I made some calls last night … rang round a few of the people he works with, but none of them had been out with him and they didn't know where he might be.'

'But Tim does sometimes go out with work friends?' Isabel felt a creeping sense of unease.

'Occasionally, but he only ever stays out for a couple of hours. He doesn't drink, you see. Never has. It's a good job really because he's on medication.'

'When he went out, did he say anything to suggest he might be doing something different? Something other than the usual afterwork get-together?'

'No, he didn't say very much at all, and it's not like him to be secretive. He did have his best jacket on though, and he was wearing some of the aftershave his sister bought him last Christmas.'

'Aftershave? That does sound like he was meeting a girl. Are you sure there's no one special in his life? Someone he works with or who he might have met elsewhere?'

'No.' Joyce sighed heavily. 'It'd be hard for him to keep something like that under wraps. He would have said something. Timothy's a loving son and also a very trusting person. I know I can be a fusspot, but I'm ever so worried. He's the sort of lad that can easily be taken advantage of.'

'I think you should report him missing. Officially,' Isabel said.

'Can I do that? Don't I have to wait until he's been gone for more than twenty-four hours?'

'Not if it's out of character for him to stay away from home without letting you know where he is. Timothy's ASD makes him vulnerable. We need to report this, Joyce.'

'OK. You know best. Let's do it.'

'I realise it won't be easy, but try not to worry,' Isabel said. 'We'll see if we can track him down. I'm going to contact the local force control room to give them Timothy's details so that they can create an incident report. Let us know if Timothy turns up, and of course we'll do the same for you if we find him.'

***

'So where do you think he is?' Dan said, when Isabel told him about her conversation with Mrs L.

'I don't know. He could be at a friend's house, but Joyce reckons it's out of character. I don't think he'd stay out all night without letting his mother know where he was. I didn't say this to her, obviously, but I am concerned for his safety.'

'What's the thinking then, boss? That Timothy's our killer and he's done something out of remorse? Run away somewhere? Or suicide?'

'It's possible. Whatever's happened to him, I think it's connected to something that stretches a long way into the past.'

'To Celia Aspen's murder?'

'Precisely. It's got to be more than a coincidence that Timothy has disappeared just when we want to speak to him about his last sighting of Celia.' She sat down sideways on the edge of Dan's desk. 'If we'd questioned him yesterday when we planned to, we might have been able to blow a great big hole through Julie Desmond's alibi. What if she knows that?'

'What are you suggesting? That she's abducted him?'

'It sounds extremely melodramatic when you put it like that,'

285

Isabel said. 'But she could have lured him somewhere. Timothy always had a soft spot for Julie. Maybe she got in touch with him and invited him out for a drink.'

'What … and then back to her place?' Dan sounded extremely dubious. 'I don't think so.'

'All right, he might not merit an invite to Chez Julie, but think about it. Joyce says that Timothy doesn't drink. He's on medication. If Julie plied him with a few beers or shorts, she could easily persuade him to go with her somewhere … anywhere.'

'If you're serious, then there's a possibility Timothy is being held against his will. Shouldn't we at least check out Julie's house?'

'We could be overreacting,' Isabel said. 'But let's not risk it. Come on. Let's go and talk to her.'

***

'There's no answer at the back either, boss.'

Dan had driven them over to Julie Desmond's home just outside Melbourne. It was a detached, brickbuilt property standing in an elevated position at the end of a driveway that curved off the main road out of town. The view from the parking area was of misty meadows, ploughed fields and distant copses. The setting was considerably more impressive than the house itself, which – apart from an ostentatious front door – was plain and squat, with narrow windows.

'Are there any outhouses at the back?'

'There's a small summerhouse. I've checked and it's empty. There's no sign of Timothy and Julie doesn't appear to be here either.'

Isabel leaned against the bonnet of the car and looked up at the house.

'Ring the Melbourne salon,' she said. 'Speak to the girl with the eyelashes. Daisy, wasn't it? She liked you. She might be able to tell you where Julie is, or where she's supposed to be.'

286

As Dan called Daisy, Isabel rang Lucas and asked him to send someone over to Mary Summers' flat to check whether Julie was there, or had been there.

'Julie had a nine o'clock appointment lined up for this morning,' Dan said, when Isabel had finished her call. 'She hasn't shown up. Daisy's rung her mobile, but it's going straight to voicemail.'

'Shit.' Anxiety gnawed at her insides. It was possible she was letting her imagination run riot, but if Timothy Littlewood was with Julie and she *had* killed her aunt, Isabel had grave concerns for his safety.

'I take it Timothy has a mobile phone?' Dan said.

'Joyce has been trying it since last night. It's switched off.'

'So what do we do now?'

'What we do, Dan, is the thing I always warn against. We make assumptions. Assumption one is a big one.'

'Go on.'

'First of all we'll assume that – for whatever reason – Julie Desmond killed her aunt. Assumption two is that Julie is with Timothy.'

'And assumption three?'

'That Timothy could be her next victim.'

'*What?* Why? Even if assumptions one and two are correct, why would she risk everything by harming Timothy?'

'Because, I think he knows something that will destroy Julie's alibi.'

The sky had darkened and it began to rain as they got back inside the car.

'What if Julie has decided to silence Timothy and make it look as though he killed Celia.'

'Frame him?' Dan said. 'How?'

'By faking his suicide. Julie doesn't know we're on to her yet, so if we can find Timothy quickly, we stand a chance of keeping him safe and proving our theory.'

287

Dan looked worried. 'What if we're already too late?'

'Then Joyce Littlewood will never forgive us.'

Dan flinched. 'She'll be gutted if anything's happened to her lad.'

'I know. Let's not even think about it.'

She leaned back, pressing her neck against the headrest and listening as heavy raindrops smacked against the car roof.

'Where do you think they are?' Dan said. 'Celia's old house?'

'That would be a good place for her to go to try and frame him … the scene of Timothy's alleged crime, but I doubt Julie would run the risk of Joyce Littlewood spotting their arrival. Besides, how would they get in?'

'Julie used to have a key to the house.'

'That was a long time ago. Surely the doors or locks have been changed at least once since 1986. No, I don't buy it. If we're right, Julie's got to be somewhere else, biding her time.'

'Yeah, but where?'

Isabel pressed an index finger to her left temple. 'It would need to be a place that she controls. One of her salons?'

Dan shook his head. 'They're too busy. Staff and clients are coming and going all the time. Hiding Timothy wouldn't be easy. Someone's bound to see or hear him, especially if he's being held against his will.'

Isabel was running several possibilities through her mind. 'Julie could have told him he's there for his own good, or spun some story about how he's protecting his mother. If she told him to be quiet, I'm sure he'd follow her instructions.'

'Keeping him at one of the salons would still be too big a risk,' Dan insisted. 'It's got to be some other place. Somewhere outdoors or somewhere that's empty.'

'You do realise that if Julie has taken him somewhere remote, or even to an empty building, she could have killed him already.'

Dan snapped his fingers. 'You've reminded me of something.

Remember what she said the other day, when you asked her how many salons she had?'

'She said six,' said Isabel, 'soon to be seven. What? You think she's acquired new premises?'

'That's how I interpreted it at the time. If she has the keys to an empty building, it'd be an ideal place to keep someone.'

'You might be on to something, Dan. Get Zoe to check it out.'

He pulled out his phone. 'If Julie Desmond has recently bought or leased new shop premises, Zoe'll soon find out where it is.'

***

She rang through with an answer five minutes later.

'It's in Wirksworth,' Dan said, when he'd ended the call from Zoe. 'St John Street.'

'What are we waiting for?' Isabel said. 'Let's get going.'

Dan turned the car around and they sped out of the driveway, onto the main road, back along the Swarkestone Bridge and on through a curtain of miserable grey rain towards Derby.

Isabel gripped the edge of the front passenger seat, wondering what they would find when they got to their destination. Would Timothy be there? Would Julie be with him? Her biggest fear was that they were already too late.

Chapter 51

The property was a three-storey Georgian terrace in a quiet stretch of Wirksworth's main street. The road directly in front of the building was marked with double yellow lines, but Dan slowed the car to a stop and parked there anyway. The shop premises had a wide glass double frontage that was grubby and dark. The flaking window frames hadn't yet been painted the *Jules* shade of grey.

Dan stood in front of one of the windows and put a hand to his forehead to shade his eyes. It looked as though the building had previously been a clothes shop. Along one wall he could make out a series of metal racks with empty wooden hangers and there was a pile of junk mail on the other side of the door. Other than that, the building was empty and there was no sign of any refurbishment work.

'See anything?' said the DI.

'Nothing,' Dan replied. 'Just an empty shop. Do you think there's a back entrance?'

'There's got to be. There are three floors to the building. There's bound to be a storage area upstairs, or even a separate flat. Let's see if we can find an alleyway. We might be able to access the back of the building from there.'

They moved uphill along the terrace. Three doors along, they found an entryway. Dan went ahead, turning left at the end along a back alley that ran alongside a long wall dotted with gates. When he reached the rear entrance to Julie Desmond's premises, he twisted the handle and pushed. The gate was locked. Cursing silently, he stood back, looked up at the wall, and then shimmied over the top of it. He landed in a yard littered with old wooden pallets and a motley collection of terracotta pots containing dead and dying plants.

He unbolted the gate from the inside to let the DI in and she followed him to the solid, wooden back door of the premises. Dan banged on it with his fist, not expecting an answer. A metal shutter covered the larger of the two ground-floor back windows, but there was a higher, narrow window on the other side of the door. He grabbed the pallets, dragged them across to the area beneath the window, and climbed on top of them.

'Careful, Dan. That wood looks rotten to me.'

'Don't worry, I'm as sure-footed as an old goat.'

He leaned in and peered through the window into the room beyond.

'It's a right mess,' he said. 'Looks like some sort of storage area.'

'Is there anything in there? Anyone?'

'I'm not sure ... hang on.'

He eased himself up, pulling closer to the window and stretching higher to get a better view of what lay inside.

'There's someone in there, at the back, lying on the floor. I can't see who it is, and they're not moving. Whoever it is, they're either, drunk, unconscious or dead.'

'If there's a life at risk, we're going to have to force entry,' Isabel said. 'Do it, Dan. I'll call for back-up and an ambulance.'

Chapter 52

Lying on his side, pale faced and with a pool of vomit drying nearby, Timothy Littlewood was unconscious at the back of the storeroom. Isabel kneeled down and put him into the recovery position, checking for a pulse and praying she'd find one.

Dan left her to it, rushing off to explore the other rooms.

'The rest of the building's clear,' he said, as he strode back into the storeroom and came to stand next to Isabel, who was leaning over Timothy Littlewood's unconscious form.

'He doesn't look too good, boss,' he said, folding his arms and glancing at her questioningly.

'His pulse is weak but at least he's alive,' she told him. 'I can smell alcohol and he appears to have taken some pills.'

She pointed to an empty plastic pill bottle that had rolled over to the far wall. Dan bent down to retrieve it and bagged it for evidence.

'Do you think this *is* a suicide attempt?' Dan asked.

Hesitantly, Isabel shook her head. Mingled in with the smell of brandy, she could detect citrusy traces of the aftershave Joyce Littlewood had told her about. Timothy was wearing a smart green jacket and a purple shirt which, although crumpled and vomit-stained now, would no doubt have been pristine when he put it on.

'No, I don't think he tried to kill himself,' she said, her voice growing increasingly confident. 'He's dressed up for a night out.'

'Or maybe he wanted to look his best when he popped his clogs.'

Isabel wasn't convinced. 'But why here? Why come to Julie's newly acquired salon? How did he even know it existed unless she told him about it?'

'You're certain she's involved, aren't you?'

She stood up. 'I am. Trouble is, there's no evidence to back me up.'

'I'll get Forensics over here,' Dan said. 'They might be able to find something.'

'And we need to locate Julie Desmond and get her down to the station to answer some questions.'

'I'll get Lucas onto it. By the way, he rang while I was upstairs. There's no sign of Julie at Mary Summers' flat. Where else could she be?'

'My best guess is that, by now, she's heading over to the Melbourne salon. If she *has* gone there, Daisy will tell her we're looking for her, so she'll be on her guard.'

'Are we going to arrest her?'

The DI rubbed a hand over her face. 'Not yet. We don't have reasonable grounds. For now, it's going to have to be a voluntary interview.'

'Do you think she'll agree to that?'

'You know what, Dan? I have absolutely no idea.'

Chapter 53

'Is he going to be all right?' Isabel asked, as the stretcher carrying Timothy Littlewood was lifted into the ambulance.

'It's touch and go,' the paramedic said. 'He's obviously been lying here for a while. He must have the constitution of an ox to still be hanging in there.'

Dan came over and together they watched the ambulance pull away with its blue lights flashing and sirens wailing.

'I've had word from Lucas. Julie has been located at her home in Melbourne. She reckons she's been there all night.'

'Well, we know that's not true. She wasn't there earlier when we went knocking.'

'Maybe she was there but chose not to answer the door.'

Isabel frowned. 'Did she give a reason for not attending her nine o'clock meeting?'

'Reckons she's been in bed … not feeling well. Says she's eaten something that's upset her. You know, dodgy tummy.'

'I agree there's something dodgy about her, but I don't think there's anything wrong with her stomach. Tell Lucas to get her down to the station for an interview under caution.'

'OK, will do. Are we heading back to the station now then?'

'Yep, come on. Let's go and find out what Ms Desmond has to say for herself.'

***

There were three interview rooms at the station, all of them situated on the ground floor. Julie was waiting in interview room two, sitting on an orange plastic chair, looking annoyed and defiant. Her long legs were folded one behind the other, and her stocky forearms were placed flat on the table in front of her.

Isabel and Dan sat down on the other side of the table.

'Sorry to keep you waiting, Julie.' Isabel smiled. 'And thanks for agreeing to come in to answer some questions.'

'I didn't feel as though I had much choice.'

'Well, as DC Killingworth has already explained, you do have a choice. We've asked you here to help with our investigation, but this is a voluntary interview.' Isabel kept her tone low and calm and ostensibly neutral. 'You don't have to answer my questions or say anything at all, and you have the right to free and independent legal advice if you want it. You're not under arrest and you're free to leave at any time.'

She watched Julie eye the door desirously and dither over whether to get up and walk away.

'Although you're not under arrest, this interview is being recorded and I'm going to caution you,' Isabel continued. 'You do not have to say anything, but it may harm your defence if you do not mention when questioned something you may later rely on in court. Anything you do say may be given in evidence.'

Isabel paused to let the caution sink in.

'This interview is your opportunity to account for yourself, Julie. You don't have to talk to us, but be aware that if you do, this interview can be used as evidence in court. Do you understand?'

'Do I need a lawyer?'

'That has to be your decision,' Isabel said. 'You have the right to legal advice if you want it. Would you like us to delay the interview until you've spoken to a solicitor?'

Julie glared, first at Isabel and then at Dan, and then waved for them to proceed.

'I've got nothing to hide,' she said. 'Please carry on. I don't know what it is you want from me, but I can assure you I've done nothing wrong.'

'If that's the case, I'm sure we'll soon be able to clear up a few anomalies.'

Isabel sat back and turned to Dan, nodding for him to take over the questioning.

'We'd like to ask you about Timothy Littlewood,' he said.

'Timothy?' Julie lifted her left arm and rested her chin on the knuckle. 'What about him?'

'So you don't deny knowing him?'

'Of course not, why would I? He lived next to my aunt on Ecclesdale Drive.'

'And when was the last time you saw Timothy?'

Julie hesitated, pondering momentarily before answering.

'As it happens, I saw him last night. We met up for a quick drink at the Talkative Parrot.'

Isabel knew the pub. Contrary to its name, it was a quiet place on the outskirts of Bainbridge – an old coaching inn that was much too far out of town for people to walk to. Customers invariably arrived by car and, consequently, the landlord relied heavily on the sale of meals in the restaurant, rather than beer in the bar. It was popular on Friday and Saturday evenings, but a lot less busy midweek. The ideal place to rendezvous with someone on the quiet.

'What time did you see him?' Isabel asked.

'I arranged to meet him there at four-thirty, but he was a few minutes late because he'd struggled to find a taxi. We stayed until about six-thirty. I wasn't feeling too good and I needed to get home.'

'Prior to yesterday, when did you last see Timothy?' said Dan.

'Years ago.' Julie shrugged her left shoulder. 'I don't remember exactly.'

'Was it before your aunt went missing?'

'Round about that time. I can't recall precisely.'

'So, why the sudden urge to meet up with him again after all these years?'

'There was no sudden urge. He got in touch recently, when he heard that my aunt's body had been found. He wanted to say how sorry he was.'

'So he rang you?' Dan said.

'Yes.'

'If he offered his condolences over the telephone, why the need to meet you at the Talkative Parrot?'

'We got chatting and decided it would be nice to meet up … for old times' sake.'

Isabel huffed, unable to keep quiet. 'I happen to know that Timothy is very shy,' she said. 'I find it hard to imagine him ringing up and asking to meet you for a drink. Would it be more accurate to say that it was you who suggested the meeting?'

'I can't remember exactly how the conversation went.' Julie scratched her forehead. 'Does it matter?'

Isabel ignored the question. 'So, to clarify, you and Timothy went your separate ways around six-thirty? Is that right?'

Julie nodded. 'Yes, like I say, I wasn't feeling well. Besides, Timothy isn't the best conversationalist in the world. A couple of hours with him is about an hour and fifty-five minutes too long.'

'You said that Timothy arrived by taxi,' Dan said, picking up the questioning. 'Did he leave the same way or did you give him a lift?'

Julie sighed. 'I dropped him in town.'

'Bainbridge?'

'Yes.'

'During the two hours you spent together, did you talk to Timothy about your salons?'

'Briefly.'

'He knew of them?'

'Not really, although it turns out his sister uses the one in Bainbridge.'

'And did you tell him about your plans for a new salon?' he said. 'The one in Wirksworth?'

Again, Julie hesitated, giving Dan a long, stony look before answering.

'I may have mentioned it.'

'May have? Did you or didn't you?'

'Yes. I did. Why do you ask? What is all this?'

Isabel wove her fingers together and placed her hands on the desk. 'We visited your Wirksworth premises a short while ago,' she said. 'We found Timothy Littlewood in the building. Can you explain how he came to be there?'

A vertical furrow appeared between Julie's eyebrows. 'I have absolutely no idea.'

'You didn't take him there yourself then?'

'No. I most certainly did not.'

'So how do you think he got inside? There was no sign of forced entry when we arrived.'

Julie considered the question for a second or two.

'There's a window at the back,' she said. 'A tall, narrow one. It's possible I may have left it open the last time I was up there. I can't be sure. The premises are empty at the moment, so security isn't really a concern. There's nothing for anyone to steal.'

'Do you have any idea what Timothy might have been doing there?' Dan asked.

'None whatsoever.' Julie leaned back and folded her arms. 'Timothy has always been … different. There's no way of knowing what might be going through his mind. He did seem a little out of sorts last night though, especially when we talked about my aunt. It disturbed him when I mentioned her murder.'

'Why do you think that was?' said Isabel.

'How would I know?' She scowled. 'It's hardly my place to speculate on what was bothering him.'

'I'm asking you to. In your opinion, why do you think he felt uncomfortable discussing your aunt's death?'

Julie unfolded her arms and stared down at her immaculately polished nails, which were painted bubble-gum pink. 'I don't know. I did wonder whether he might have been responsible for her death – or at least know something about it. The subject seemed to depress him. When I mentioned it, it was as though someone had thrown a wet towel over him. It made him shiver.'

'What frame of mind was Timothy in when you left him?' Dan asked.

'Why? Has something happened to him?'

'You tell us, Julie.'

She pushed her chair back from the table and sat up straight. 'Look,' she said. 'I agreed to answer your questions voluntarily, but I don't like your attitude. I've told you all I know about Timothy Littlewood. I think I'd like to go now.'

'The trouble is, we've still got a few more questions for you,' Dan said. 'We need answers, Julie. I'm sure you understand.'

'How about we take a break?' Isabel suggested. 'You can seek legal advice and bring a solicitor in with you to answer the rest of our questions. Can I request we reconvene at four o'clock this afternoon?'

'I'll see if that's convenient for my lawyer,' Julie replied.

Isabel smiled. 'Oh, I'm sure there'll be someone available to advise you. If not, we can ask the duty solicitor to attend. Either way, I'll see you again at four o'clock.'

***

'It's a pity we had to let her go,' said Dan, as Julie marched out of the interview room.

'We didn't have a choice. She wasn't under arrest. She didn't have to talk to us.'

'She was willing enough to start with. I notice she got cold feet as soon as the questions started to get tricky.'

'What she doesn't know is what kind of state Timothy Littlewood is in. She'll be hoping and expecting him to be dead, but she can hardly ask us that, can she?'

'It would give the game away, wouldn't it?' Dan said. 'To tell you the truth, I'm staggered that Timothy's still in the land of the living. Most people wouldn't be, given the quantity of tablets and alcohol he appears to have consumed. He's a small bloke, but he obviously has a strong constitution – not as easy to dispose of as Celia Aspen. Julie will be shit scared when she finds out Timothy has survived.'

'Let's hope he's still hanging in there,' Isabel said. 'Come on, let's go back to the office and find out if there's any word on his condition.'

***

As they walked back upstairs, Isabel chided herself for not getting to the truth sooner. She was sure now that Julie Desmond was a killer. She had murdered Celia Aspen in cold blood. Her guilt had been there all along – lurking beneath her swagger and over-confident smiles.

'Have you arrested her?' asked Lucas, as she and Dan re-entered the stuffy CID room.

Someone had plugged an extra heater into the wall and it was throwing out warm wafts of dry heat.

'For God's sake,' said Isabel. 'It's bloody sweltering in here. Who plugged that in?' She pointed to the electric heater.

'I did.' Lucas looked sheepish. 'I got wet and cold when I went out earlier.'

'You should buy yourself a decent raincoat, Lucas, then we wouldn't all have to suffer a dry, suffocating atmosphere. I can feel my contact lenses drying out already.'

Lucas threw her a petulant look before getting up and unplugging the heater.

'In answer to your question, Lucas … no, Julie Desmond hasn't been arrested, but she has gone off to get herself a brief. We're going to talk to her again later.'

'Any news on Timothy Littlewood?' Dan asked.

Zoe smiled. 'We got word a couple of minutes ago. He's regained consciousness.'

'He has?' Isabel felt herself relax. 'Well, that is good news. I'll head over to the hospital and see what he can tell us. While I'm out, I need one of you to get hold of the manager of the Talkative Parrot. Find out who was working behind the bar yesterday evening and check whether they've got CCTV.'

301

Chapter 54

Timothy was in a room of his own off Ward 10. When Isabel approached his bed, she could see he was on an intravenous drip. His skin was ashen and sallow and he appeared to be sleeping. Joyce Littlewood was sitting at his side, holding his hand. She looked up and, after patting Timothy's arm, pushed herself out of the visitor's chair and crossed the room.

'Can I have a word with you?' she said. 'Outside.'

'How is he?' Isabel asked, as they stood in the corridor. 'Is he going to pull through?'

'They say so. He's sleeping at the moment and he's on a drip, but they think he's going to be OK.'

'I'm so glad, Joyce.'

'Yes, I know you are. As am I. What bothers me is that they've offered him counselling. They're treating this whole thing as though it were a suicide attempt.'

'But you don't think it was?'

Joyce bristled. 'I *know* it wasn't. Timothy would never do that. He enjoys life too much. Anyway, even if he did decide to do himself in, he wouldn't choose alcohol and drugs. Timothy doesn't drink. He never touches the stuff.'

'Is there any chance he'd resort to alcohol if he was desperate, or very depressed?' Isabel said.

'No.' Joyce gave a firm shake of the head. 'Absolutely not.'

Isabel nodded, unsurprised. 'Do you think it's possible that someone else was involved?' she asked, her voice gentle but insistent. 'Someone who wanted Timothy out of the way?'

Joyce looked shaken and frail. 'That's exactly what I think,' she said, leaning against the wall to steady herself. 'But who would do such a thing? And why?'

'That's what I intend to find out,' Isabel said. 'I know Tim's asleep, but I need to talk to him. The doctors have said I can have a few minutes. Is that all right with you?'

Joyce nodded and led the way back into the hospital room.

Timothy was already stirring, his eyes flickering open. His mother returned to the visitor's chair to resume her vigil, while Isabel stood at the other side of the bed.

'I'm glad to see you looking better, Timothy.' She spoke softly, reassuringly. 'I've been worried about you.'

He managed a weak grin. 'I'm all right, Isabel. I've got a headache though.'

'I'm not surprised.' She smiled. 'Can you tell me what happened last night?'

Timothy closed his eyes for a moment. When he opened them again, he looked hurt and frightened, as if the memories he was recalling were dark and painful.

'I met Julie for a drink,' he said. 'Julie Desmond. She asked me out.'

Isabel nodded. 'I gather you met at the Talkative Parrot at four-thirty.'

'That's right,' he said. 'Although I was late. We ordered some food. Tapas. Julie said it was Spanish. I'd never had it before.'

'Did you enjoy it, duck?' Joyce asked.

'It was OK,' he replied. 'The portions were a bit small. I don't think I'd have it again.'

'What did you have to drink, Timothy?' said Isabel. 'Did you have some wine? Some beer?'

'No.' He frowned. 'I don't drink. Julie bought a bottle of red wine and she poured some for me, but I didn't have it. I think she was annoyed, but I don't like it. I tried it once at my sister's wedding and it made me feel sad.'

'Wine can do that sometimes.'

'Mum said I'm better off not drinking alcohol.'

'You should always listen to your mother. So what did you have instead?'

'I had a Coke. A pint.'

'Just the one drink?'

'No,' Timothy said. 'I had three. The second two were diet tonic waters because I'm not supposed to have too much sugar. Julie bought them for me. She went up to the bar and fetched them.'

She could have slipped a double vodka and something else into any one of those drinks, Isabel thought. *Some GHB or a roofie in the last drink, and then all she had to do was take Timothy to her car on the pretext of giving him a lift. Except, instead of taking him home, she'd taken him to her new salon in Wirksworth and forced drugs and alcohol into his system.*

'Can you remember what happened when you left the pub?'

Timothy looked confused. He lifted his right hand and rubbed it feebly across his eyes.

'I felt hazy and strange,' he said. 'I remember being in the car park and Julie offering me a lift home. I got in the car and didn't understand why she turned left out of the car park, instead of right towards Bainbridge. I think I must have fallen asleep after that. I don't remember anything else – not until I woke up here.'

'I need to ask you something else, Timothy.' Isabel paused. 'Think carefully, because the answer you give me is important. Did you take any tablets or drink any alcohol at all last night?'

'No.' He started to move his head to shake off the accusation,

304

but it must have been painful, because he winced. 'I don't drink. I told you.'

'That's all right. Don't get upset. I believe you.'

'I think you should let him rest now,' Joyce said.

'I will,' Isabel replied. 'But there's one more thing I need to ask, and it's the most important question of all. Do you feel up to telling me one last thing, Timothy?'

'Yes, I'm OK. What do you need to know?'

'That day, back in 1986 when you went round to fix Celia Aspen's trellis – are you absolutely certain you saw Celia? It's imperative that you tell me the truth, Timothy. You're not in trouble, but we need to know exactly what you saw that day.'

He wriggled uncomfortably and turned to his mother.

'It's all right, Timothy.' Joyce squeezed his hand. 'Isabel's an old friend. Tell her what she needs to know.'

He turned back towards Isabel, but couldn't quite meet her eye.

'I was frightened of Celia. I used to think she was my friend, but then she stopped liking me. She got mad at me a couple of times, and it scared me.'

'I can see why that would put you off going round there. I don't suppose you were very keen to do odd jobs for her after that?'

'No.' His pale blue eyes met Isabel's. 'I only went round that day because Julie asked me to. She sent a letter and some money and I didn't want to let her down. She'd gone to Australia and she was relying on me.'

'So you went to the house and fixed the trellis. You didn't go inside the house?'

'No.'

'Did you knock on the door?'

'No, Julie told me not to … in her letter.'

'So you sorted out the trellis … and then what did you do?'

'I gave Celia a quick wave to let her know I'd finished the job.'

'So she was inside the living room, looking out at you?'

'I don't know. I think so. Julie said she was expecting me, so I knew she'd be watching, checking up on me. She was like that, wasn't she, Mum?'

Joyce gave his hand a reassuring shake. 'Yes, my duck, she was. She liked everything to be done properly, did Celia.'

'The other day, when DS Fairfax asked you whether Celia had waved back, you said she had. Is that true?'

Distress pulled at Timothy's face. His skin was the colour of putty, and his breathing was fast and shallow. Isabel knew she should let him rest, but she desperately needed an answer. She *had* to know whether he'd seen Celia. A lot depended on it.

'I ... I'm not sure. I think she was there, but I didn't actually see her. When I'm scared, I'm not good at talking with people ... and looking at them. Sometimes it takes all my strength not to run away when I'm feeling nervous.'

'I promise I'll let you rest in a minute, Timothy, but to recap ... you're saying you assumed Celia was there, but you didn't look through the window when you waved to her? You didn't see her inside? Is that right?'

'Yes. No, I didn't see her,' he said, 'but she must have been there. Julie said she was. Besides, while I was fastening up the trellis I heard the phone and it stopped after three rings, so she must have answered it.'

'That doesn't mean that Celia was there, me duck,' said Joyce. 'It was probably her answering machine kicking in.'

Isabel had begun to pull on her coat. She paused, one arm in the air. 'She had an answering machine? Are you sure about that?'

Joyce nodded emphatically. 'Yes. I mentioned it to the other detectives. I rang her a couple of times to have a go at her about asking Timothy to fix the trellis, but all I got was the machine. Celia had this message, recorded in her poshest voice. *This is the Aspen residence. I'm unable to come to the telephone, so please leave a message after the beep.* Something like that, anyway. I didn't leave a message.'

'And when she didn't answer your phone call, Joyce, is that when you decided to go round and speak to her in person?' Isabel said. 'That was when you looked through the window and saw the wallpaper?'

'Yes, it was. Like I told you before, I knocked, but there was no answer and no sign of her in the garden. It was as though she'd disappeared into thin air.'

'One more thing, Timothy. When Julie got back from Australia, did she talk to you?'

'Yes,' he replied. 'I saw her when she came round to the house next door, looking for her aunty.'

'And what did she say to you?'

'She asked whether I'd seen anything of Celia. When I told her I hadn't set eyes on her for months, she wanted to know when I saw her last. She said it was important. I couldn't remember, but then Julie reminded me I'd been round to fix the trellis. She said that Celia had been there that day, and I must have seen her then.'

'And you wanted to please Julie, so you told her you had?'

Timothy looked embarrassed. 'Yes. She said I'd have to tell the police what I'd seen and that I'd be an important witness. She said it would help the investigation. She said she was relying on me.'

***

Isabel drove back from the hospital along roads littered with fallen leaves. Every so often, a gust of cold wind swirled them around, lifting them into the air and onto the windscreen. The weather was turning decidedly wintery.

As she drove down into Bainbridge, she passed a young mother, kneeling down to pull a pair of mittens onto her child's hands. The scene took her back instantly to a scene from her own childhood. When she was six years old, her father had given her a gift of a pair of pink fluffy mittens. They'd been attached to either end of a yard of ribbon so that they could be threaded through the sleeves of Isabel's coat to make sure she didn't lose them.

'These mittens are like us, Issy,' he had said. 'A pair: always connected. They'll never get lost or separated. They'll always be together.'

Isabel had been young and naïve. She had believed him.

***

Back in the office, someone had plugged the extra heater in again but, for once, Isabel was grateful for the warmth that was billowing from it.

'Lucas, Dan, when you spoke to Joyce Littlewood on Monday, did she mention an answering machine?'

'Yeah,' Lucas replied. 'She said she rang Celia to have it out with her about the letter Julie had sent, but ended up getting through to the answering machine.'

'Answering machines ...' Dan smiled. 'The 1980s must-have that's now obsolete, thanks to voicemail and the 1571 service. Another item for your list of disappearing things, boss.'

'And talking of disappearing, why isn't there any mention of an answering machine in the missing person's file?' Isabel thought she could hear a crack forming in Julie Desmond's alibi.

Zoe flipped through the file to double-check the inventory. 'You're right. There was no record of an answering machine at the house when Celia disappeared. In fact, someone has noted specifically that there was no computer or answering machine found at the property.'

'Julie had access to the house,' Dan said. 'She could easily have removed the answering machine before she reported her aunt's disappearance.'

Lucas looked puzzled. 'Why bother?' he said.

'Because, Lucas, it was part of her alibi,' Isabel said. 'I think

Julie killed her aunt before she went to Australia. Then, when she got to Sydney, she rang Celia's number, knowing full well she'd reach the answering machine. All she had to do was leave a couple of short messages. The phone records would show that a call had taken place and its duration, but there would be no way of telling whether a person had answered or a machine.'

'So when Julie got back from her trip, she let herself into the house and removed the answering machine before reporting her aunt missing?' Lucas said.

'Exactly. Timothy has now admitted he didn't actually see Celia Aspen when he went round there on the 15th of May. Julie Desmond knew he was afraid of her aunt. She took advantage of that … led him to believe that Celia was in the house, hoping he'd tell people that he'd seen her. The phone calls to the answering machine were her back-up plan.'

Zoe brandished a piece of paper she had extracted from the file. 'I didn't pick up on this before but, back in 1986, when the police contacted the dental surgery to get hold of Celia Aspen's records, the receptionist said that Celia had missed an appointment for a check-up. Her patient notes showed that on 2nd June they left a message on her answering machine asking her to rearrange the appointment.'

'Have we got enough to make an arrest?' Dan asked.

'Julie and her brief are due back here at four o'clock,' Isabel said. 'I think we can arrest her in connection with the attempt on Timothy Littlewood's life. As for Celia Aspen's murder, as yet we have nothing concrete to tie Julie to the crime. However, Timothy's revised statement and the reports of Celia having an answering machine suggest that Julie may have provided us with a false alibi. Once she's been arrested we can search her home and work premises. Meanwhile, I'm going to go and update the detective superintendent. Wish me luck, guys.'

Chapter 55

Julie Desmond arrived promptly at four o'clock and was immediately arrested on suspicion of the attempted murder of Timothy Littlewood. She had been accompanied to the station by her solicitor – a slim, smartly dressed woman of about forty. Following the arrest, the solicitor asked for information about the case and time to consult privately with her client.

An hour later, when Isabel and Dan entered the interview room to question Julie under caution, she had adopted a steely, narroweyed pose that suggested she wasn't going to cooperate.

'You've told us that you met Timothy Littlewood yesterday evening,' Isabel began. 'Do you want to know what I think happened then?'

'Not especially.'

'I believe you drugged his drink and took him in your car to your empty business premises in Wirksworth, where you forced him to consume a combination of alcohol and drugs, with the intention of causing him to overdose. You then left him there, not expecting him to regain consciousness. Is that what happened?'

Julie rolled her shoulders, as if to work out a knot of tension.

'Absolutely not,' she said, her features impassive. 'I did meet

Timothy for a drink, he's an old friend. We spent a couple of hours together and then I gave him a lift back to Bainbridge. I dropped him off in the centre of town just before seven o'clock and then I went home. I know nothing about him taking any drugs.'

'Where did you drop him?'

'Near the marketplace, by the Co-op.'

'Just before seven, you say? Well, that's good to know. We can check the CCTV cameras around there. They should be able to back up your story, if what you're saying is true.'

Julie sat back and folded her arms.

'Timothy says that you bought him three drinks and, after he'd finished the last one, you took him to your car. After that, he remembers nothing until he came round in hospital.'

Julie looked startled and a red flush began to work its way up her neck.

'That's right, Julie. Timothy has regained consciousness and he's going to be OK. It was touch and go for a while though. The doctor said that if we hadn't found him when we did, Timothy would have died.'

Julie stayed silent, staring first at Isabel and then at Dan.

'The thing is, Timothy doesn't remember drinking any alcohol or taking any tablets.'

'He may not remember, but that doesn't mean he didn't take them,' Julie said.

'But why would he go to your new salon in Wirksworth?' asked Dan.

Julie scowled. 'You tell me.'

'OK, I will,' said Isabel. 'He was there because you took him there yourself. You're out of touch, Julie. I don't think you realise how many CCTV cameras are around these days, even in a small town like Bainbridge ... and in Wirksworth too. We're still checking the footage, but your car has already been spotted on camera driving through the top end of Wirksworth.'

Isabel pushed a screenshot across the desk. It showed Julie's car pulling out of a junction.

'Why did you force Timothy to swallow a combination of drugs and alcohol, Julie? Were you trying to make it look as though he'd taken his own life? Were you hoping we'd interpret his suicide as an admission of guilt for the murder of your aunt?'

'No comment.'

'What was your plan? Were you going to go back when it got dark and move Timothy's body somewhere else? Somewhere well away from your salon and any connection to you?'

The solicitor placed a quieting hand on Julie's forearm. 'You're not obliged to respond, and I'd advise you not to,' the solicitor said. 'There is no proof, not even circumstantial evidence. This is pure conjecture based on the statement of a less than credible witness.'

Isabel tapped the CCTV evidence. 'You're forgetting this.'

The solicitor pointed to the screenshot. 'This footage shows my client's car, certainly, but the image isn't clear. There's no way of telling who is behind the wheel, or indeed whether there's anyone in the passenger seat.'

'Officers are in the process of checking footage from other cameras.' Isabel smiled. 'We're also carrying out a search of your client's home, car and business premises. Who knows what we'll find?'

Isabel hoped she had managed to burst the solicitor's confidence bubble.

'I'd now like to take you back to 1986,' Isabel said. 'Tell me, Julie, where were you at the time of Celia Aspen's death?'

'I was in Australia,' she replied, before her solicitor had chance to once again place a cautionary hand on her arm.

'Can you remember when you left for Australia?' Dan said.

'Again, my client doesn't have to answer your questions,' the solicitor interjected. 'I believe she gave a full statement at the time of reporting her aunt missing.'

312

'It's all right,' Julie said. 'I've got nothing to hide. I flew out from Heathrow to Sydney on 11th May 1986. My passport was checked and stamped.'

'You seem very sure about the date,' said Dan.

'Obviously I wouldn't usually remember the details of something that happened so long ago, but my aunt's disappearance wasn't a normal occurrence. I had to account for my whereabouts with the police when I reported Aunt Celia missing. Those dates have stuck in my memory.'

'There is no clear evidence of when Celia Aspen was murdered,' Isabel said. 'How can you be so sure she was killed while you were in Australia?'

'Because that's when she disappeared.' Julie released an exasperated sigh. 'I rang and spoke to her during my first week in Sydney. Plus, someone saw her after I left. Timothy Littlewood, as I'm sure you know.'

'Ah, yes, that's right. Timothy Littlewood.' Isabel smiled at the solicitor. 'What was it you called him a minute ago? A less than credible witness?'

'Timothy went round to my aunt's house while I was away,' Julie said, her voice carrying with it a hint of desperation. 'He *saw* her there.'

'Timothy did go to Celia's house,' Dan said, 'but only because you asked him to. We have the letter that you posted to him.'

'I spoke to Timothy an hour or so ago,' said Isabel. 'I asked him to describe exactly what he saw the day he went to fix the trellis. He's admitted that he didn't actually see your aunt that day. He was scared of Celia and, as I'm sure you're aware, Timothy isn't good at making eye contact with people who make him nervous. He did the work and kept his head down. He believed he'd seen Celia that day because you planted that idea in his mind. When you got back to Bainbridge, you spoke to Timothy and made it clear you were relying on him to tell the police what he'd seen. I believe you called him an important witness.'

313

'Timothy *did* see her. He told me so himself. If he's saying something different now, it's because he's scared of you ... of the police. Timothy has issues. He doesn't always say what he means.'

'Are you suggesting he's unreliable?'

The solicitor turned to Julie and shook her head.

'No comment,' Julie said.

'Either Timothy is reliable or he's not,' said Isabel. 'You can't say he's reliable only if his witness statement backs up your alibi.'

'Forget Timothy.' Julie drummed her fingers on the tabletop. 'I telephoned my aunt while I was away.'

'You called her,' Dan said. 'But did you speak to her in person?'

'Of course I did.'

'We think you spoke to her answering machine,' Dan said. 'On both occasions.'

'What answering machine? She didn't have one.'

'We know she did,' said Dan. 'We have witnesses who confirmed that they rang Celia Aspen in the weeks following your departure to Australia. All they got was a recorded message.'

'Well, if she had an answering machine, I didn't know about it.'

'I think you did,' Isabel said. 'I think you removed it from the house when you returned from Australia – before you reported your aunt missing.'

'I would have no reason to do that,' Julie replied.

'I think you had a very good reason,' said Isabel. 'I believe you killed your aunt before you left for Australia, and the telephone calls were one of the things you were relying on to prove she was alive after you'd left the country. You knew the phone records would show you'd called. You disposed of the answering machine to conceal the fact that your conversation was with a tape recorder, and not with your aunt.'

'No comment,' Julie said.

'The phone calls were your back-up plan, but Timothy was your ace card. You planted a seed in his head knowing he'd tell

314

people, including the police, that he'd seen Celia days after you left for Australia.'

'You're talking rubbish,' Julie said. 'You have no proof of any of this, and you won't find any, because it isn't true. I've done nothing wrong. I wasn't involved in my aunt's death.'

'I think my client has answered more than enough of your questions, despite most of them not being relevant to why she's under arrest,' the solicitor intervened. 'As she says, you have no proof of any wrongdoing on her part, and without it, you're in no position to charge her. If you have nothing else to put to my client, I suggest you release her immediately.'

Isabel spoke directly to Julie. 'We aren't going to charge you yet,' she said. 'But we can hold you for up to twenty-four hours. We're confident that the searches our officers are carrying out will uncover incriminating evidence. That's when we'll charge you.'

***

Julie Desmond's solicitor was absolutely right. As yet, they had no solid evidence of her alleged crimes and, despite the bravado Isabel had displayed during the interview with Julie, she knew there was no guarantee her officers would find any. Unless they could come up with something tangible within twenty-four hours, they would have no choice but to release Julie without charge.

She and Dan had gone back to the CID office, where Zoe was chewing her nails while checking the CCTV footage from the Wirksworth cameras. Lucas was out with a team searching Julie's home and car. They also had a warrant to search the Melbourne salon.

'Zoe, please give me some good news,' Isabel said.

'Lucas just called,' she replied. 'They've found a small quantity of what they believe is Rohypnol in a desk drawer in the back office of the Melbourne salon. Apart from that, they've found no

315

other incriminating evidence – although Lucas is bringing back a couple of laptop computers to give to Digital Forensics.'

'Julie Desmond could claim that someone else put the roofies in the drawer,' Dan said. 'Or she'll maintain she took them off a client in order to prevent them being used illegally.'

'She can say whatever she likes, but it doesn't alter the fact that she had access to a date rape drug that she could have slipped into Timothy's drink at the Talkative Parrot.

'Unfortunately there's no CCTV at the pub,' Zoe said, 'but we have a witness statement from the landlord confirming that he saw Julie and Timothy together. I've also checked the CCTV from Bainbridge marketplace. There's no sign of Julie's car in the time-frame she claims she dropped Timothy off.'

'But we do have Julie's car on CCTV in Wirksworth and the fact that Timothy ended up overdosing in her Wirksworth premises,' Isabel said. 'All in all, the situation isn't looking too clever for Ms Desmond.'

Dan didn't look convinced. 'Seriously?' he said. 'Based on the evidence we've got so far, I'm not sure it'll even get to trial, never mind convince a jury.'

Isabel tapped the side of her nose. 'Oh ye of little faith, Danny boy,' she said. 'This is no time to give up hope.'

Chapter 56

Lucas returned to the CID room an hour later.

'Digital Forensics are examining the computers,' he said. 'I'm not sure what they're likely to find though. Considering most people didn't own a computer in 1986, what are the chances of there being anything to tie Julie Desmond to Celia Aspen's murder?'

'Non-existent to zero, I would say,' Dan said. 'Despite what the DI thinks.'

'Has she gone home?' Lucas asked.

'Yes,' Dan replied. 'Julie Desmond is under arrest, but we can only hold her until four o'clock tomorrow. We need the digital guys to work fast.'

Zoe rubbed her eyes. 'I think I've found something else on CCTV. Take a look.'

Dan and Lucas gathered around the computer screen as Zoe played a short section of remarkably clear colour footage from a camera on Wirksworth's main shopping street. They watched as Julie's metallic-blue BMW moved towards the camera, heading into Wirksworth along the Cromford Road.

Zoe paused the film and zoomed in. The woman behind the wheel was clearly Julie Desmond. There was someone in the passenger seat, but it wasn't possible to see their face because they were leaning back, head lolling against the headrest.

What was clear though was what the passenger was wearing: a green jacket and a purple shirt.

Chapter 57

'Zoe's found CCTV footage of Julie Desmond in Wirksworth,' Lucas said, when Isabel walked into the office at eight o'clock the following morning. 'Digital Forensics have also come up trumps.'

Isabel smiled. 'Lucas, is that the same shirt you were wearing yesterday? You've not been here all night, have you?'

'No chance. I did get home pretty late last night though.' He grinned. 'No time to iron a clean shirt for today, I'm afraid.' He lifted his right arm and sniffed. 'Don't worry, this one's not too bad.'

Isabel laughed. 'Show me the CCTV footage.'

Lucas played the relevant segment.

'It's definitely them,' she said. 'It's a good, clear image of Julie, but not so good of Timothy. His sartorial faux pas of a green jacket with a purple shirt are pretty unmistakable though. Is there any other footage? Is there anything closer to Julie's business premises?'

'This is the best we've got. Her place is out of the range of the cameras.'

'Not to worry,' Isabel said. 'Julie has strongly denied, under caution, being anywhere near Wirksworth the night before last. This is pretty damning.'

'Yep,' said Lucas. 'She's going to have a hard time talking her way out of this.'

'So what have Digital Forensics turned up?'

'They recovered some old documents that had been deleted from a cloud storage system accessed from Julie's computer. One of the documents is Celia Aspen's last will and testament.'

Isabel was unimpressed. 'Zoe's already got us a copy of that.'

'Yes, but something else has been saved in the same folder – a letter, scanned in and saved as a PDF.'

'And who was the letter from?'

'Celia Aspen.'

'To?'

'Eric Mundy.'

'And? Come on, Lucas. This is like pulling teeth.'

He grinned and reached across his desk. 'It'd be quicker for you to read the letter, boss. Here, I printed it out.'

Isabel took the wodge of papers Lucas held out to her. Sitting in Dan's chair, she spread the pages across his empty desk, and saw immediately that it was written in the same handwriting as Cecil Aspen's letter to Violet. This one was dated 7th May 1986. Isabel picked up the first page and began to read.

23 Ecclesdale Drive
Bainbridge
Derbyshire
7th May 1986

Dear Eric,

When your Uncle Jim visited me last month and told me about you, I was amazed and delighted. I know you have been told about my circumstances, so you will understand that I never dreamed I would be a parent. Knowing that I have a son is exciting, but also a responsibility I feel I have failed to meet. I only wish I'd learned of your existence before now, but I understand and respect your mother's reasons for choosing not to tell me.

I am so sorry for your loss. Your mother was more than special to me. She was, truly, the only person who ever saw inside my soul. She understood me – not as a man or a woman, but as a human being. She made me laugh and there were times when she made my heart sing. She also made me cry.

Finding out that she had married William Mundy brought an end to my play-acting. Up to that point, I'd spent my whole life pretending to be something I wasn't. Your mother was so lovely and so beautiful, and because of that I tried to be the man she longed for – even though it wasn't what I wanted to be.

When I knew she'd married William, I was glad, because it released me from my obligation and made me resolute. The war had taught me many things – most of them were hard, bitter lessons that I would rather not have learned. There were several times during my imprisonment when I thought I was dying. During those terrible moments, the thing I regretted more than anything was that I'd never had the chance to live my life as the woman I felt I was inside.

I came back from the war with the intention of doing something about that. Only one thing held me back ... and that was the promise I'd made to Violet. I found the prospect of letting her down abhorrent. So, when I found out that she'd passed me over for another man, rather than feeling heart-broken, I was relieved – set free. If I'd known about you then, perhaps I would have felt differently. We will never know now.

My life since the war hasn't been easy. Society can be cruel and judgemental. When I told my family what I intended to do, they rejected me – banished me from their lives. My mother was always small-minded, so that was no great loss. I suspect my sister was very much like her.

I began a new life in Derby, where no one had known

Cecil. To my neighbours and the people I worked with, I was Celia. I'm sure they all thought – think – that I am stuck up and aloof and cold, although I'm none of those things. I never have been. Unfortunately though, my secret has meant that I've never been able to let anyone get close to me. To do so would have been dangerous.

In 1978, I read a death notice for my sister which also included details of her funeral. I went along, although I'm not sure why. Curiosity perhaps, or a sense of family duty. While I was there, I met my niece. Her name is Julie Desmond and she is now twenty-two years old. I'd like to say that the two of us get along like a house on fire, but I'd be lying if I did. Like everyone in my life, I've kept her at bay. She doesn't know my secret and, until recently, I had no intention of telling her. She visits me regularly and we muddle along together quite well, but I don't think she has any real affection for me.

My hope is that one day (I realise it may not be in my lifetime) people like me will be accepted and respected. I have lived most of my life as a woman, and that has made me happy – but that happiness has never been truly complete because I've had to hide my secret. In covering up my past, I also find that I am forced to live a life in which my true personality must remain hidden. Inside, I am a warm, loving woman. On the outside, I am seen as a frosty, fussy old biddy who provokes fear or dislike in those I wish to befriend. It makes me sad, because my dream was always to match the way I look on the outside with the person I am on the inside. I have the heart and soul of a lady and I look and dress like a woman – but despite everything I've been through, there are times when I am still two different people.

I'm not telling you all this to provoke pity – on the contrary, that is the last thing I would want from you. The reason I am baring my soul to you is to help you understand. I have spent so many years hiding my past and it goes against the grain to break that silence. I prefer to tell you all this in a letter, rather than talking about it face-to-face, which I would find difficult.

That is enough about me. I hope that you will agree to meet me and we will have many opportunities to get to know one another. It would be wonderful to establish a friendship with you and your family. Jim tells me I have a granddaughter. I wonder if you have told her about me yet? I would like to see her, and see you. It is the thing I want most in the world.

The truth is, I have been lonely: never feeling as though I belong anywhere or to anyone. Now that I know about you, Eric, I feel content. Even if you choose not to see me, I will be happy simply knowing that you exist.

Jim has asked me to go out and visit him in Canada. I'm not sure yet whether I'll take up his invitation, but I'll think about it.

My niece, Julie, is going off shortly to spend three months in Australia. Before she goes, I have decided to tell her everything about my life ... and about you. I will also let her know that I am going to change my will. Until the visit from Jim, I thought Julie was my only relative and I had named her as my sole beneficiary. Since learning about you and knowing that I have a growing granddaughter, I have decided to change my will in your favour. I tell you this not to influence your thoughts on whether to meet me. I will stand by my decision regardless, and I hope it will be a few more decades before you come into your inheritance.

I will still leave a small legacy for Julie. She is my sister's grandchild after all, and she means well, even if she can be a little brusque. She and I have never enjoyed a close relationship, but she has visited me regularly and she shows concern for my wellbeing. I'm under no illusion that her motives are selfless, and it will be interesting to see whether she continues

323

to visit me once I have informed her of my intentions regarding my will.

I hope you have had a happy life. Jim tells me that William was a good father to you and, for that, I am grateful.

I look forward to getting to know you. Jim has given me your telephone number and address. I will be in touch by phone a few days after you have received this letter. You can let me know if

Frustratingly, the letter ended mid-sentence. Isabel laid the last sheet of paper on the desk and cogitated on why Celia Aspen hadn't finished it. It seemed likely that she had been interrupted. Had Julie turned up as Celia was writing the letter? Had the contents enraged her enough to make her lash out at her aunt?

'It's pretty incriminating, isn't it?' Lucas said. 'What on earth was Julie thinking, hanging on to it for so long? She must have been crazy.'

'Maybe she got rid of the original letter and didn't realise the digital copy could be recovered, even after it had been deleted. She may have held on to it because it was a reminder of why she killed her aunt. It's possible she viewed the contents of this letter as her justification for murder and she kept it to ease her guilt … maybe it was something she could turn to whenever her conscience pricked her.'

Lucas stood up. 'Let's go and ask her, shall we?'

Chapter 58

'We have several more questions for you, Julie. First of all, can you tell us why you had a quantity of Rohypnol in your desk drawer at the Melbourne salon?'

They were back in interview room 2. Julie was clutching a paper cup of water as though her life depended on it. After being kept in a cell overnight, she looked washedout and worried. Her mascara had smudged, her hair was sticking out on one side, and her self-confidence had evaporated.

In stark contrast, the solicitor was fresh-faced and alert. She looked at her client and gave a slight shake of her head.

'No comment,' Julie said.

'Aren't you going to explain it away?' said Lucas. 'Say that you confiscated it from a wayward customer?'

'No comment.'

'Or did you buy it for the sole purpose of drugging Timothy Littlewood in order to stage his supposed suicide?'

'No comment.'

'The thing about roofies is that traces are usually eliminated from the body fairly quickly,' Isabel said. 'The drug's metabolite, on the other hand, can be detected for several days if the right techniques are used. Timothy's blood and urine are being tested as we speak.'

Isabel turned to Lucas, who pushed a folder sideways across the desk.

'We've also found more CCTV footage, showing your car in Wirksworth the evening before last. I think you'll agree that's you driving the car?' Isabel pointed to the still CCTV image she was handing to Julie. 'It's remarkably clear footage. That's Timothy Littlewood in the passenger seat, isn't it?'

Julie stared at the image, but said nothing.

'You have to admit, Julie, this contradicts your own account of where you were on the evening in question.'

Again, Julie said nothing.

'We found something else that we'd like you to explain,' Isabel continued. 'It's an unfinished letter from Celia Aspen to her son, telling him that she planned to change her will. It was recovered from your cloud storage account.'

Isabel extracted a copy of the letter and slid it across the desk to Julie, whose face flushed hot and crimson. She looked down at the handwritten pages, rubbed her nose, and then sat back, pinning her arms against her stomach.

The solicitor glanced down at the pages before turning a questioning gaze on Julie. 'If you don't mind, I'd like some time alone to consult with my client.'

'No problem.' Isabel suspended the interview. 'Let's reconvene in an hour.'

The solicitor nodded as Lucas switched off the recording devices and followed Isabel out of the interview room.

Chapter 59

Traffic noise penetrated the double-glazed window in Isabel's office. She went over and looked out of it, down towards the high street where rain was spattering across the road, and the green and red colours of traffic lights were reflecting off the puddles.

Dan knocked on her door and entered.

'Lucas tells me that Julie Desmond is consulting with her brief.'

'Yes. I hope to God she won't be advised to make no comment.'

'The letter on her computer is pretty incriminating. It's going to be hard for her to explain it away.'

'The fact that it was in her possession proves that she's been lying to us all along,' Isabel said. 'She knew Celia was transgender and she knew about Eric Mundy. More to the point, the contents of the letter suggest that Celia may have told Julie she was changing her will. The letter was dated 7th May, which means Julie had plenty of time to kill her aunt and dispose of her body before jetting off to Australia.'

'Do you think she planned it? Or was it a spur of the moment thing?'

'I don't know, Dan. Either way, the end result was the same.'

They were interrupted by an urgent knock. Lucas poked his

head around the door. His hair was sticking up and he looked both pleased with himself and rather startled.

'You'd better get back to the interview room quick,' he said. 'The solicitor has just informed me that Julie wishes to make a statement. She's confessing.'

'Confessing to what? Drugging Timothy? Or murdering Celia Aspen?'

'Everything,' Lucas said. 'The whole shooting match.'

***

Julie Desmond appeared to have aged ten years. It may have been the lack of make-up, or the paleness of her complexion that was to blame. *Or guilt*, Isabel thought. *After years of getting away with murder, she's finally been found out.*

After reminding Julie that she was still under caution and reading the full caution to her once again, Isabel and Dan sat down and listened to Julie's confession. Even her voice had aged. Gone was the confident, slightly dismissive tone of a few days earlier. Now, her speech was low, monotonous and completely devoid of timbre.

'If my aunt had been a more generous woman, I probably wouldn't have done what I did,' she said. 'When I talked to her about my plans to travel to Australia, she said that she'd help me … financially.'

'And did she?'

'Phh! She gave me fifty quid. Made a real thing of it too, as if she was giving me the crown jewels. I mean, £50. That wasn't going to get me very far, was it? I ended up having to sell my car to raise the money for my air ticket and accommodation costs.'

'So you were angry with your aunt?'

'Yes, I was angry, but I was used to her stinginess, so it didn't come as a total surprise. It was when she told me about her son that I lost it.'

'When did she tell you?'

'She invited me round a few days before I was due to leave for Australia. She said she had something important to tell me … that she wanted to be honest with me. When I got there she told me about her son.'

Julie examined a chip on her nail varnish before continuing.

'When she explained it to me, I assumed she'd had a child out of wedlock during the war and had him adopted. She said she'd found out where he was living and she was hoping to go and see him. She also told me she was going to change her will.'

'And how did that make you feel?' Isabel asked.

'I couldn't believe it.' Julie leaned back. 'I felt totally betrayed. I'd been visiting her for years, and there she was, telling me she was going to leave the house and most of her money to a complete stranger.'

'That stranger happened to be her biological son,' said Dan, who was summarising the key points of Julie's confession in his notebook.

'Celia didn't tell you she was transgender?' Isabel asked.

'No.' Julie shook her head. 'I think she would have done, but I didn't give her the chance. I found out later, when I came across the letter she'd been writing to her son. It came as a complete shock. I had no idea.'

'Can you tell us how you killed her?'

'I smothered her. I told her I'd go out to get a bottle of Australian chardonnay to celebrate my trip. I'd cadged some sleeping tablets from my mother to help me get through the flight to Australia. They were in my handbag. I crushed a couple of them and mixed them into the two glasses of wine I poured for her. The combination of the wine and the sleeping tablets soon had her snoozing on the sofa. I suffocated her with a cushion.'

Julie shuddered. 'It was horrible,' she said. 'For saying she was once a man, there was nothing strong about Celia. She was weak and frail. It didn't take long for her to stop breathing.'

'What did you do then?'

'I waited until well after midnight before going out to the garden to dig a grave. I knew that the Littlewoods always went to bed early. I chose the old vegetable patch because it was hidden away behind the garage and it had always been well tended, which made it easier to dig. No one could see me, which is a good job because it took a while to dig a hole deep enough.

'My aunt had abandoned the veggie patch the previous year because she was getting arthritic and she was too proud to ask Timothy Littlewood to help her with it. She'd had a falling out with the Littlewoods and she didn't like to involve Timothy in anything unless it was a real emergency.

'After I'd buried her, I went back inside and emptied the fridge. Thankfully my aunt was too tight to have a newspaper delivered and she didn't have a milkman. Cancelling milk or papers would have been a problem. Someone might have remembered it ... and, of course, bottles of milk lined up on the front step would have alerted the neighbours that something was wrong. So you see, on that occasion, I benefited from my aunt's tightfistedness.

'I searched through her address book and correspondence, but there was nothing linking her with her son. She'd told me his name – Eric Mundy – so I knew she hadn't written his address in her book. Then I came across the letter. It had been shoved into the drawer of a dresser. I think she may have been working on it when I arrived. I don't imagine a letter like that would have been an easy thing to write – which, again, was to my advantage. If she'd finished it sooner and posted it, the game would have been up for me. As it was, I got away with murder for over thirty years. You must admit, that's not bad going.'

'You really shouldn't have kept the letter, Julie,' said Dan. 'It wasn't a wise move.'

She rubbed her forehead. 'No, I realise that. It's been my undoing, hasn't it?'

'What made you hold on to it?'

Julie sighed. 'After what I've just told you, I'm sure you won't have a very high opinion of me – but, believe it or not, I felt terrible remorse about what I'd done. There's not a day that's gone by when I haven't regretted it. Even when I eventually inherited Aunt Celia's house, I couldn't convince myself it had been worth it. I tried to push the whole thing to the back of my mind … pretend it never happened. It helped that I was away in Australia for three months immediately afterwards. That gave me time to calm my nerves, get my head together and plan what I'd do when I got back. I took Celia's unfinished letter with me to Sydney, as a reminder. Much as I wanted to forget what had happened, I couldn't quite allow myself that luxury. I destroyed the original letter ages ago, but I scanned a copy and stored it online. Whenever my feelings of guilt threatened to drag me down, I'd read it again to rationalise what I'd done.'

'When did you delete the scanned copy?' Isabel said.

'As soon as I heard you'd found my aunt's body. I didn't realise you'd be able to recover the document from my storage account.'

'Did you ring your aunt's number from Australia and leave a message on her answering machine?' Dan asked.

'Yes, you were right about that. When I got back to the UK, I let myself into the house and removed the machine. I didn't think anyone else would remember it.

'Then, after a couple of weeks had gone by, I reported my aunt missing. I was terrified the police would suspect me, but I knew Timothy would tell them he'd seen Celia after I'd gone to Australia. I wrote to him, asking him to fix the trellis, and I posted the letter second class just before I left for the airport. I flew out on a Sunday, so I knew Timothy wouldn't get the letter until a few days later – by which time I'd be safely in Sydney. I knew he was scared of Aunt Celia, so I led him to believe she'd be watching him from inside the house when he went round there. After I got back and talked to him about it, it was easy to plant the idea

331

in his mind that he'd seen her and waved to her. Timothy liked me. I suppose he thought he was helping me.'

'He was,' Dan said. 'Telling the police he'd seen your aunt while you were in Australia put you in the clear. You should have gone on to show him more gratitude, Julie.'

Julie shrugged defiantly.

'When I reported my aunt missing, no one seemed particularly interested in her whereabouts,' she continued. 'After a few months, when the investigation began to peter out, I went back to Australia. I'd met someone out there – Jed. He and I ended up living together and then we got married. I stayed out in Sydney until we broke up in 1999.'

'And then you came back to the UK and set up your first salon?'

'That's right. Jed and I divorced and I reverted to my maiden name. I'd trained as a hairdresser and beauty therapist while I was out in Australia and I wanted to set up my own business.'

'I assume you used the money you'd inherited from your aunt to buy the salon?'

'I did, yes. I'd had to wait until she'd been missing for seven years, so it was a long time before I got my hands on my inheritance. Of course, Jed was exceptionally keen to help me spend it, but I wasn't having any of that. It was mine. I forfeited a clear conscience to make sure that money came my way.'

'You also sacrificed your aunt's life,' Dan said. 'Was it worth it, Julie?'

'I told myself it was and, gradually, I came to believe it. I was OK, providing I thought only of the money. If I allowed myself to remember how I'd come by it, I struggled.'

'But you never felt guilty enough to confess?' Isabel asked. 'Not even when your aunt's body was discovered?'

Julie looked at her solicitor before replying. 'I considered it … but I had too much to lose by then. Even though I used my inheritance to fund the first salon, I set up the other branches through sheer graft. It turns out I have a talent for business. I'd worked hard and I didn't want to lose everything I'd strived for. I panicked. I told myself I had a rock-solid alibi, but I also knew that Timothy might prove to be a massive chink in my armour. I could tell by the way you were questioning me that it was only a matter of time before you re-examined everything. I knew you'd look again at Tim's statement and get to the bottom of what he really saw that day.'

'So you decided to silence him.'

'It's not a decision I took lightly,' Julie said. 'I liked Timothy. He was sweet. But all of my focus was on self-preservation. I thought if I made his death look like suicide, the police would assume he'd murdered Celia and chosen to take his own life out of remorse.'

Isabel smiled feebly. 'As DS Fairfax will tell you, I'm not big on making assumptions. Even if you *had* managed to stage Tim's death to make it look like suicide, we would still have investigated.'

'Can you tell us about Timothy?' Dan said. 'Talk us through what happened the other night.'

'It was almost exactly as you thought. I slipped a vodka into the last tonic water and spiked his drink with a roofie, and then I offered him a lift and drove him to Wirksworth. He was still just about able to walk when we got there. I helped him in through the front door of the shop and into the back room. He said he felt weird and I offered him some tablets ... told him they'd make him feel better. He believed me ... trusted me, I even gave him a glass of water to wash them all down. Then I offered him some brandy. He didn't want it ... said he didn't drink, but I told him it was purely for medicinal purposes. I promised him it would make him feel better.'

'And then?'

'I gave him more pills and more booze and waited with him while they took effect. My plan was to move his body later on,

333

but it took ages for him to even lose consciousness. In the end, I decided to leave him there and let nature take its course.'

'There's nothing natural about an overdose and half a bottle of brandy,' Isabel said.

'Whatever. I left him there anyway. My plan was to go back last night when it got dark again. By then, I thought the overdose would have taken effect.'

'You mean you intended going back when he was dead?'

'Yes, I expect that is what I mean – but you found him, didn't you? I'm not sure how, but you did.'

'We're detectives,' Dan said, flipping his notebook closed. 'It's what we're trained to do.'

Chapter 60

'So, that's it then,' said Lucas. 'Case closed.'

'I think you're forgetting all the paperwork, Lucas,' Isabel said.

He pulled a horrified face. 'The Super will be pleased,' he said. 'Do we get brownie points?'

'You do from me,' Isabel replied. 'I'm not sure Detective Superintendent Tibbet hands out brownie points when a suspect confesses.'

'We did OK though, didn't we, boss?'

'You did more than OK, Lucas. We all did. Every one of us played our part.'

'Does that mean you're going to take us to the pub later for a celebratory drink?' Dan said.

'Why not?' she replied. 'I'll only be able to stay for one, but I'll put some money behind the bar for you lot. I've got to get back. Unlike you singletons, I have a family waiting for me at home.'

She retreated into her office, sank down into her chair and leaned her elbows on her desk. The sense of closure she'd felt as she'd listened to Julie Desmond admit to her crimes had been gratifying and exhilarating, and yet things still seemed somehow incomplete. An element of dissatisfaction lingered. Glancing

335

down, she realised what was causing that sense of unfinished business.

A copy of Celia's letter to Eric Mundy was tucked into a file on her desk. She pulled it out and re-read it, reflecting on the way missed opportunities could send cracks through time.

Eric Mundy had longed to hear from his biological father, and for more than thirty years he'd been under the misapprehension that Celia Aspen had chosen to have nothing to do with him. How must that have made him feel? What conversations would he have had with Celia if her life hadn't been cut short? How much more fulfilled would Celia have felt if she'd had the time to develop an enriching relationship with her son?

Celia and Eric had lost their chance to get to know one another – but for a short while, hope had burned brightly for the two of them. Until Julie Desmond snuffed it out.

Life is too short to pass up important opportunities, Isabel thought. *Fate sometimes throws up a chance to discover something you didn't know existed, or rediscover something that has been lost. Only a fool would overlook those kinds of possibilities.*

She picked up the letter, stood up and marched through to the main office.

'I'm going out,' she said. 'I'll be back in a couple of hours.'

***

When she rang the doorbell at Eric Mundy's bungalow, he answered the door himself. There was no sign of Gillian Statham. Classical music floated from somewhere inside the house and the aroma of a freshly baked cake drifted from the kitchen on the left.

'Mr Mundy,' Isabel said. 'I'm sorry to bother you, but I'm here to give you an update. I thought it was best to talk to you in person, rather than speak to you over the phone.'

336

'Come inside.' He stepped back. 'If you have news, then I'm glad you came.'

Isabel sat in the seat she had occupied on her previous visit. Eric Mundy listened intently as she informed him of Julie Desmond's confession. When she'd finished, he nodded.

'Thank you, detective. For pursuing the case, and letting me know the outcome.'

'There is something else … after Julie killed her aunt, she found an unfinished letter that Celia had been writing.'

Isabel stood up and handed the letter to him. 'Unfortunately, the original has been destroyed, but I wanted to make sure you got a copy. I think it will mean a lot to you. I won't stand over you while you read it. I'll get off. No need to show me out.'

Isabel walked towards the hallway. Turning at the door, she stood for a moment and looked back at Celia Aspen's son, watching as he began to read the letter he'd waited thirty-three years to receive.

Chapter 61

At sixty-thirty that evening, Isabel emerged from the warmth of the pub into weather that seemed to have skipped forward towards winter. The sky was dark and cloudless, pricked with stars that shone out a warning of an overnight freeze.

She'd left her team in the bar, huddled around a table near the fire, consuming a fresh bottle of red wine and exchanging increasingly raucous stories from their university days. Something told her it would be a long evening, but at least they'd promised to go home by taxi.

By the time Isabel arrived home, the temperature had dropped to below zero and the rose bushes in the front garden were developing a glistening coat of frost.

Ellie was waiting for her in the kitchen. She was sitting at the table with a textbook open, ostensibly reading. A notebook lay at her elbow, but Isabel could see that its pages were blank.

'Hi, Mum,' she said. 'Have you had a good day?'

Isabel leaned in from behind and kissed the top of her daughter's head.

'I've had an excellent day,' she said. 'You know about the bones we found last week?'

Ellie spun round and nodded. 'Have you caught the killer?'

'We have. Or, rather, she's confessed.'

'Could she have gotten away with murder if she hadn't admitted what she'd done?'

'It's possible,' Isabel said. 'We had some evidence, but not necessarily enough to prove beyond reasonable doubt that she committed the crime.'

'So why did she confess?'

'I'm not sure,' Isabel said. 'I have to say, it's unusual. Perhaps she wanted to unburden herself. They say that confession is good for the soul. More likely she's confessed because her solicitor told her she'll receive a reduced sentence for pleading guilty.'

'So what will happen now?'

'Well, she's been charged and next she'll go to court. Providing she sticks to a guilty plea she'll be sentenced by the judge at a hearing.'

'Is that what they call a result?'

Isabel laughed. 'Yes, love. I reckon it is.'

Ellie turned back and flipped the pages of her book with false casualness.

'Have you thought any more about getting a puppy, Mum?' There was anxiety in her tone.

'I have been thinking about it, yes.' Isabel pulled out a chair and sat at the table. 'And I don't think we should.'

Ellie's face fell. 'But, Mum—'

'Hang on, let me finish,' she said. 'I don't think a puppy is a good idea. They pee everywhere and chew things. All of your best shoes and trainers are likely to be destroyed.'

'I don't care.'

'Instead of a puppy, I was thinking we could get a fully grown dog. I'm sure there are lots of gorgeous animals down at the rescue centre who are desperate for a second chance. What do you say?'

Ellie considered the possibility. 'Could we get a terrier? A cute, scruffy one?'

'You mean a mutt?' Isabel laughed. 'That sounds fine to me.'

'When can we go to the rescue centre?'

'At the weekend. We'll take a look at what they've got and, if there isn't one that meets with your approval, we can always wait a few weeks.'

'I'm sure we'll find one I like,' Ellie said. 'Can I choose a name?'

'Most of the dogs at the centre will already have a name they've grown used to. It might be confusing if you changed it to something else.'

'OK. I can tell my friends that we're getting a dog though, right? You're not going to change your mind, are you Mum?'

'No, I promise,' said Isabel. 'I know I let you down sometimes, Ellie, but I never commit to a promise unless I'm sure I can keep it.'

Ellie jumped up from the table, grabbed her books and headed for the door.

'Where are you going?'

'To tell Dad,' she said. 'He's going to be *so* excited. I think he wants a dog even more than I do.'

'Thanks for giving in,' Nathan said later, when Ellie had gone to bed.

'It's not a case of giving in,' she said. 'Owning a dog is a big commitment. I wanted to think it through carefully, that's all. It was the thought of having to train a puppy that I wasn't keen on. It will be a lot easier if we adopt an older dog.'

'You won't be able to teach it any new tricks. You know that, don't you?'

She knocked his arm playfully. 'I taught you a few, didn't I?'

'You certainly did.' Nathan laughed. 'Even if I'm not always as obedient as you'd like.'

***

At eleven o'clock, Nathan put down the newspaper he was reading and stretched.

'I'm going to bed,' he said. 'Coming?'

'Not yet,' Isabel said. 'I'm not sleepy.'

After he'd gone, she turned on the television and channel-hopped, jumping between a latenight chat show, a celebrity cooking contest and the sports channel. Nothing held her interest, so she switched off.

Reaching for the paperback novel she was reading, she stretched out on the sofa and read the opening paragraph of a new chapter three times. The words wouldn't sink in. She was restless. Unable to focus. Thoughts of her father were breaking into her head like a burglar, stealing away her concentration.

She decided to open her mind for a minute and invite in the past. She thought about her dad's voice and remembered his smile. Memories from long ago materialised for a while and then slowly evaporated, as if they had never existed in the first place.

She didn't want to have to rely on the past – on worn, faded memories. She wanted to know what her dad sounded like now. *Today*. This very moment.

Pushing the book behind a cushion, she reached for her phone and dialled the number she had stored away, just in case.

It rang five times. Isabel held her breath. On the sixth ring, he answered. He spoke in French, but his voice was exactly as she remembered it.

'Hello, Dad,' she said. 'It's Isabel.'

Acknowledgements

First and foremost, I'd like to thank the judges of the Gransnet and HQ writing competition for believing in my novel and choosing it as the winner. Special thanks to Cari Rosen, Editor of Gransnet, for championing the cause of older female characters in fiction.

It's been an absolute pleasure working with the HQ team, especially Belinda Toor, whose intelligent editorial insights have been a great help to me as a debut novelist.

I'd also like to thank author Sarah Ward, whose crime fiction course set me on the right path for writing *In Cold Blood*. As well as being a brilliant novelist, Sarah is a wonderful and generous teacher. Attending her course in Bakewell led to the formation of a writing group that has continued to meet ever since. Thank you, Ann, Frank, Georgina, Helen, Loreen and Stephen for your continued friendship and encouragement. I'm looking forward to seeing you all again soon.

I feel lucky to live in an area that is hugely supportive of writers. Derby offers regular writing events, festivals, workshops and courses, many of which are held at The Quad – which is a fantastic venue and the city's cultural hub. Over the last few years, it's also been my pleasure to be a volunteer with the Derby Book

Festival. The passion, creativity, enthusiasm and hard work of the Festival team is exceptional. Listening to some of the fabulous authors they have brought to Derby has been a real inspiration to me.

Although I've been writing short fiction for many years, it has taken me a long time to knuckle down and write a novel. I've always enjoyed reading crime fiction, and so it was inevitable that my debut would be in that genre. Having spent most of my career in marketing and communications, I had no experience of police procedures when I started to write this book. Thankfully, I was able to refer to two guides that are essential reading for any crime writer – *The Crime Writer's Casebook* and *Being a Detective* by Stephen Wade and Stuart Gibbon. For the trickier nuances of procedure within my plot, I contacted the GIB Consultancy for advice. Thank you, Stuart, for answering my questions so comprehensively. If there are errors in this book, they are my own. I am aware that real murder investigations involve many, many people, but grappling with a cast of hundreds isn't practical in a work of fiction. For that reason, responsibility for investigating and solving the crime in this novel rests with a handful of people. I hope my readers will prefer this approach and enjoy getting to know DI Isabel Blood, DS Dan Fairfax, and DCs Lucas Killingworth and Zoe Piper.

Sending love and thanks to my family, especially my mum, Eileen, and my sister, Dawn, who are always eager to read anything that I've written. I hope you both enjoy *In Cold Blood*.

Finally, I'd like to thank my husband, Howard, who has always been a great supporter of my writing. His faith in me has been unwavering, and his words of encouragement have helped to keep me focused. I'm also grateful for the delicious flagons of coffee he makes every morning. Those cups of Maragogype certainly helped to bolster me through the first draft! Thanks for all the love, Howard, and for the wonderful things you do for me each and every day.

Dear Reader,

We hope you enjoyed reading this book. If you did, we'd be so appreciative if you left a review. It really helps us and the author to bring more books like this to you.

Here at HQ Digital we are dedicated to publishing fiction that will keep you turning the pages into the early hours. Don't want to miss a thing? To find out more about our books, promotions, discover exclusive content and enter competitions you can keep in touch in the following ways:

JOIN OUR COMMUNITY:
Sign up to our new email newsletter: hyperurl.co/hqnewsletter
Read our new blog www.hqstories.co.uk
🐦 : https://twitter.com/HQStories
📘 : www.facebook.com/HQStories

BUDDING WRITER?
We're also looking for authors to join the HQ Digital family!
Find out more here:
https://www.hqstories.co.uk/want-to-write-for-us/
Thanks for reading, from the HQ Digital team

ONE PLACE. MANY STORIES

HQ

If you enjoyed *In Cold Blood*, then why not try another gripping crime mystery from HQ Digital?

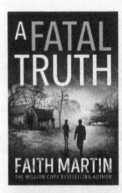

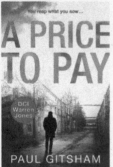